OF WOLVES AND WILDFLOWERS

JULIE MCCULLOUGH

Of Wolves and Wildflowers
© Julie McCullough

National Library of Australia Cataloguing-in-Publication entry
Author: McCullough, Julie, author.

Title: Of Wolves and Wildflowers / Julie McCullough.

ISBN: 9780992358808 (paperback)

Dewey Number: A823.4

Published with the assistance of www.loveofbooks.com.au

DEDICATION

'I would like to thank my very patient husband, Richard and two children, Dylan and Ayla, for putting up with me spending so much time on the computer instead of in the kitchen and also their support and enthusiasm while I chased my dream.

Also thanks to Christine for pointing me in the right direction, Tracey for helping me with computer "stuff" and also to Gina for her computer skills in setting up my website and a BIG thanks to Ocean at *Love Of Books (www.loveofbooks.com.au)* for making this all happen.'

PROLOGUE

The man stared at the photo he held firmly in his hands, like it was precious gold. His heart thumped in his chest as his eyes lingered on the eyes smiling back at him. With one finger, he traced the outline of the face - the beautiful face, the face that he desperately longed to hold tenderly in his hands, before kissing those warm, soft lips. "We WILL be together," he whispered. His plans were coming together nicely. He had decided that enough was enough. The time was now! No more being brushed aside, waiting in the wings. He deserved to be happy too. Life was short. Go after what you want and be happy! Everyone else will get used to it even if some people are shocked and hurt.

"No!" he spat angrily, as he ripped the photo clean down the middle, removing the second person in it. Carefully, he kissed the other half before putting it in his pocket and picked up a box of matches. With hatred in his eyes and heart, he took out a match, lit it and held the burning end downwards for a second or two to get it going. When the flame was hungry and strong, he slowly moved the picture into it. Within seconds coloured flames shot up the sides of the photo. The face in it began to distort and melt. He smiled at the sight but refused to let it go, even when the flames licked at his finger and thumb. When there was nothing but charred ash in his burnt finger tips he dropped it. Little pieces of ash drifted downwards to settle near his feet. Grounding them into nothing with his shoe, he then took the picture out of his pocket and sucked in his breath. "I know one thing for sure," he declared, staring at the person looking directly at him. "If I can't have you, NO-ONE else will either."

CHAPTER ONE

Recorded rock and roll pumped from the massive speakers each side of the stage, as the road crews scurried about setting up the expensive musical, lighting and audio equipment. "Stonefish", one of Australia's most successful rock bands, was playing a sell-out gig tonight, as part of their national and world tour. The doors would open at seven-thirty and the support band was due on stage at eight. Stonefish would appear around nine-thirty.

Just as Jo Slater arrived behind the bar in "The Playroom", the entertainment section of Blazes Hotel on The Sunshine Coast, a burly, bearded man seemingly appeared from nowhere and asked for a jug of iced water and four glasses. The harder stuff would come later when the stage gear was dismantled and packed back on the truck ready to haul to the next stop on the tour. Roadies worked long, late hours but few would trade their jobs.

Jo handed the jug of water to the man and turned to take the glasses out of the fridge. Suddenly, something over to one side of the large, empty room caught her eye. She hesitated for a moment, then quickly grabbed the glasses and handed them to the thirsty man before returning her gaze across the room. Although the area was dimly lit, she recognised the man sitting alone at a small table strumming an acoustic guitar, his right foot resting casually on his left knee. Jo held her breath and stared. It was Luke Summers, one of the guitarists of Stonefish. His brown, wavy, collar length hair, tanned skin and brown eyes shadowed by long, thick eyelashes had caught her attention from the very first time she had seen a picture of the band in a magazine. Jo then noticed the empty glass on the table beside him and her heart skipped a beat.

Oh well, she smiled to herself, plucking up courage and becoming excited at this rare opportunity, *it IS my job to supply drinks.*

She took a deep breath and walked over to where Luke sat, wiping her sweaty palms on the sides of her skirt as she went. As she got closer to his table she recognised that he was strumming one of the bands early ballads. He didn't seem to notice she was there.

'E-excuse me,' she stammered quite loudly over the music and almost adding "Luke" but then realised that would be too casual. "Are you right for another drink?" Jo wished she had rephrased that question and felt like a shy sixteen year old rather than twenty-six. Luke stopped strumming his guitar and looked up, a surprised expression on his face. Their eyes locked. He wasn't wearing the sunnies he normally wore on stage. Jo felt her hands and legs shaking while her mouth suddenly became very dry.

"Um......yeah, I'll just have an orange juice, thanks," he answered after several seconds. "I can come over and get it."

"It's okay," smiled Jo, regaining her composure. She picked up the empty glass and walked back to the bar, turning to look at him once again as she went. He was wearing white runners, faded blue jeans and a black, V-neck tee shirt.

"Wow, he's even more gorgeous in real life," she sighed to herself after only ever seeing him on television or in magazines. The last time Stonefish had toured Queensland she had been incapacitated with a broken leg following a minor car accident. What a huge let down that had been for her.

Luke watched her go and smiled when she had turned back to look at him. In his lifestyle he had seen and met many beautiful women – and some not-so-beautiful ones – but there was something about this one he had never seen before. It wasn't just her stunning, natural beauty. He noticed she had a soft, happy look about her and, even in the dim light, he couldn't help noticing how her eyes sparkled. He also admired the way she had her blonde hair pulled back in a French Plait. She returned with his drink and he only took his eyes off her face long enough to glance at the fingers on her left hand and was surprised, but glad, to see they were bare.

"Thanks," Luke smiled as Jo set the glass of juice on the table before him.

"You're welcome", she replied then suddenly felt lost for words again. Looking toward the bar Jo saw another of the road crew approaching it. "I'd better go and serve this guy," she said hurriedly, spinning on her heels and walking quickly back to the bar feeling both frustrated and relieved at the interruption. She had thought she had more self-confidence, but at that moment she felt like a blithering fool.

After serving the man she began to stock the fridges with several varieties of canned beer and UDL's brought out from the large cold room. Due to crowd numbers and reckless behaviour, alcohol is served only in non-breakable containers at rock concerts. She also replaced glasses with the hard plastic variety for the post mixes and other drinks that would normally be served in a glass. Jo couldn't take her mind off Luke sitting across the room and every now and then glanced over in his direction. After filling the last fridge she once again looked over and her heart sank when she noticed he was gone. The table was bare as if he had never been sitting there in the first place.

Then she saw him coming from the direction of the stage straight to the bar, the half drank orange juice in his hand. Jo mentally scolded herself as she grew nervous again, but was able to smile when he placed the drink on the bar.

"I've been watching you and to be very sexist, isn't that a man's job you are doing there?" Luke asked.

"Well usually a man DOES do it.......... are you offering?" Jo replied cheekily, now feeling more relaxed and confident. She wasn't normally shy, working in bars among all types of people had put an end to her childhood shyness, but coming face to face with one of her idols seemed to bring some of it back.

Luke laughed. "I would if I could, but I have to go and get ready. So," he smiled persistently, "How come you are doing a man's job?"

Jo sensed a come-on here and was flattered of course, but at the same time she knew this scene probably would have been played out many times before and, as much as she was attracted to Luke, she wasn't prepared to become another conquest of this charming rock star.

"Because," she stated firmly, "the guy that was here setting up ready for the thirsty crowd, cut his hand pretty bad this afternoon and the boss asked me to fill in for him."

"Oh!" was all Luke could answer, taken aback by her sudden change in attitude. He felt a little dejected as he had a strong yearning to get to know her after being enthralled by her beauty. Even the scent of her exotic perfume aroused his senses.

Jo looked him straight in the eye and scanned his face. He had perfect white teeth and dimples in his cheeks when he smiled. Suddenly a lightning bolt of desire swept through her from head to toe.

"Have a good gig........Luke", she said to him quietly, showing a smile tinged with a little regret. She sighed heavily, knowing anything with him was just a pipe dream.

"Thanks, umm.......what's your name?" He leaned over the bar toward her.

"Jo," she replied, still looking him in the eyes. The invisible magnetic pull she felt made it impossible to avert hers.

"Thanks Jo," he smiled, straightening up and beginning to turn, then stopped and hesitated a second before facing back to her. "By the way, I think you are a very beautiful lady. See you later." He gave her a wink and one last smile before turning and walking toward the stage. Jo stood entrenched to the spot as she watched him disappear behind a black curtain at the side of the stage. Suddenly, she was jolted back to reality by a tap on the shoulder. She spun around to find Graham, her boss, standing there, slightly shaking his head. He was tall, solid man in his late forties and enjoyed a good rapport with his staff.

"Graham!" she gasped. "Don't do that. You scared the shh....daylights out of me."

"Well, if you weren't so smitten by Mr Charm there, you would have heard me come in," he said with his ginger eyebrows raised. "I've been watching you for the last few minutes and I could see what was happening."

"Nothing happened. I just met Luke Summers, one of the guys in Stonefish," shrugged Jo, hoping Graham couldn't see the redness from the heat she felt rushing to her face.

"Just be careful Jo," Graham warned in a big-brotherly way. "I've been in this game for a long time and I have seen a lot of bands come and go. They've all got their share of good looking dudes. Trouble is - they're only after one thing and then move on to the next town and willing girl......or girls."

Jo expelled a deep sigh and lowered her eyes forlornly. She knew Graham was right, but she just didn't want to hear it, when only a short time ago she was on such a high.

"Yeah, well don't worry, Graham," she assured him, "I am not about to turn into a groupie for Luke Summers or anyone else for that matter." Jo looked back at the curtain he had disappeared behind, bit her bottom lip and pondered...........

"Smart girl," said Graham, placing his hand protectively on her shoulder without seeing her face. "Now, do you want to go and have a break? Not long until we open these doors. I'll finish things off here."

"Yeah, okay," enthused Jo. "See you at seven-thirty, ready for the onslaught!" She walked out, her mind in turmoil, not sure whether to laugh or cry.

Later, just as Jo anticipated, the place was packed for the concert. Around two thousand fans were jammed in The Playroom, soaking up the electric atmosphere. Stonefish certainly didn't disappoint them either, belting out all their well-known hits and some previously unheard of new songs. Jo worked at fever pitch, serving drink after drink, occasionally wiping the sweat from her brow, but couldn't help looking over at Luke on stage whenever she got the chance. Although it was difficult to tell with his sunnies on, she was sure he was occasionally watching her while he played. She hoped he was because, despite Grahams warning, the excitement in her stomach still had not gone away.

Just as she passed one man his change she frowned with confusion when he thrust a piece of paper into her hand.

"JO, CAN YOU PLEASE MEET ME AFTER THE SHOW. LUKE" *WOW!* She was ecstatic! She looked up to the stranger who had given it to her but he had disappeared. Although she had immense respect for Graham, at this point in time all she wanted was to spend time with Luke. She looked over to him while placing the note securely in her hip pocket and, without knowing if he was actually looking at her, gave one definite nod of her head and continued serving customers. The knot in her stomach suddenly grew bigger and she felt like jumping up and shouting her excitement to the world. Not long to go now.

Jo finished her shift at eleven-thirty, grabbed a can of ice-cold beer as her knock-off drink, went into the office to sign off and collect her bag before entering The Playroom to catch the last of Stonefish's set. She had requested the whole night off to attend the concert, but all staff were needed. She did, however, feel compensated at being able to begin her shift in the afternoon, therefore finishing up early. Her feet craved a warm foot spa and she was tired, but the discomfort seemed totally irrelevant compared to meeting Luke. Most of the people in the room were quite drunk by now and, although Jo enjoyed a few drinks now and then and, at times had certainly been in the same situation as these fans, she couldn't help shaking her head and smiling as how silly she thought some of them looked. Sometimes she hated finishing her shift late, tired and footsore, to see everyone in the place already in the swing of things. Friends would ask her to stay and have a drink with them. Occasionally, she would refuse politely and go home to bed, other times, if she was in a party mood, she would skoll a few drinks to catch up. Jo momentarily toyed with that idea to help calm her nerves but then decided she'd rather keep her wits about her when she sees Luke. As exciting as the prospect was, she was not about to let herself be used. She'd had a boyfriend, Jeff, for three years who was on security at another night club, but things started to go wrong months earlier and they had broken up, on Jo's initiative.

However, Jeff couldn't accept this and continuously called her and they reconciled. It didn't last long and they were soon arguing again. Jo firmly announced once more that it was over for good this time but Jeff told her that it would NEVER be over. It had been a week since then and she had not heard from him so she hoped this was a reassuring sign that he had finally accepted the break-up. It wasn't because there was someone else, she still cared for Jeff, but occasionally he had the tendency to become moody and possessive and she was beginning to feel smothered by him.

She sipped her beer and stood over to one side of the dance floor and let her body go with the beat of the music as much as it was possible in the packed room. Her ears were beginning to ring from the loudness. A lot of the dancers were moving with reckless abandon, oblivious to anyone and everyone around them. Occasionally one would lose their balance and fall down but several hands would soon appear to help them back on to their feet where they would continue dancing as if nothing had happened. A lot of fans, especially females, were crammed up against the stage to be as close to their idols as possible. Jo couldn't help noticing there seemed to be more in front of Luke than any of the other band members. She certainly understood why. There were dancers arms flailing about and a few drinks getting spilt but everyone was in high spirits, all there for one reason – to rage to some good Aussie Rock N Roll!

At the end of the set Stonefish did their planned encore but were not let off that lightly. After they'd said their "Thankyous" and "Goodbyes" the crowd refused to budge. They began chanting, clapping and whistling for MORE. Several minutes later, with the roar of the elated crowd hitting the high decibels, Stonefish reappeared and burst into two more high energy numbers, sending the fans into a frenzy. After that they left the stage and the exhausted but satiated crowd began to disperse, some with sweat literally running off them.

Jo looked about her, unsure of what to do. Did he want her to go backstage or was he going to come back out to see her? This was a totally new experience for her and she began to feel a little anxious. She had no idea if Luke had seen her in the crowd. What if he saw someone he liked better? What if the note was a fake, written by someone else? But why would anyone else write it? Her mind was in a flurry. There was nobody left on the dance floor and she didn't want to look like a groupie so she walked over further to one side of the room and sat at a now empty, but dirty table, littered with cans and plastic glasses. There were still some people about, finishing off drinks and chatting. She sat, facing the stage and fidgeted with her bag strap. Looking at her watch, Jo decided that if nothing happened in ten minutes she would leave, but even as she was thinking those words, she know deep down that she would wait forever if she had to.

Within a few minutes a man approached her table. He was not the one who had given her the note. As he grew nearer her heart began racing. *The note MUST be for real!*

"Are you Jo?" he asked gruffly, without a hint of a smile.

"Yes, I am," she nodded nervously.

"Follow me. Luke's waiting for you out the back," he ordered and began walking back toward the stage. Jo frowned at his attitude but quickly got up and followed him backstage. She wasn't game to look back to see if Graham was anywhere in the room and could see her. She followed the man through several doors backstage until they came to the backstage entrance/exit. It was relief to hit the cool, fresh night air. A group of people were standing about outside the door, some drinking and smoking cigarettes. Jo recognised the band's lead singer and suddenly saw Luke walking toward her with a huge smile on his handsome face. Her face involuntarily lit up too. At that point she realised she had no control over this anymore, it was in fate's hands now.

"Hi Jo," he smiled. "I'm glad you came."

"I got your note. Who was that bloke that gave it to me?"

"That was Nev, one of the crew. Do you want to go somewhere quiet?" he asked, gazing intensely into her blue eyes.

"Mmm, that'd be nice," Jo answered rather shyly, the butterflies still doing backflips in her stomach. "What do you have in mind?" She already knew the answer to that!

"Well, we could go back to my resort room," he suggested casually.

"You certainly don't believe in beating around the bush do you? I'm not really into the groupie scene."

"No, I didn't mean........I just meant it's somewhere private where no-one will hassle us. If you have a better idea I'm all ears."

Jo smiled at him. He seemed genuinely concerned that he had offended her. "No, that's a good idea, but just remember what I said," she replied. "Do you want to go in my car?"

"Only if it's safe," he joked, as she began to lead them in the direction of her car. "Hang on a sec Jo, I'll just tell the others I'm going."

He spun around and jogged back to the group.

Jo stood and watched as he spoke to two other members of the band and then pointed in her direction. The other two laughed and one gave Luke a friendly punch in the shoulder. She felt a little indignant as she could guess what sort of comments they were making. Luke walked quickly back to her, shaking his head and laughing to himself.

"What was all that about?" Jo asked, a little embarrassed, when Luke caught up with her.

"Oh nothing," he grinned at her. "Those guys are crazy. They're just jealous. C'mon, let's go."

"Where exactly are we going?" she asked, turning back in the direction of her car.

Before Luke could answer he heard his name being called out and turned to see a group of young women in the car park calling out and running toward him.

"Quick Jo, get to the car!" He grabbed her hand and began to run. "Which one is it?" he asked, frantically. The women were getting closer, squealing out his name and what they would like to do with him.

"The little blue Fiesta, over here!" she tugged him in the right direction before letting go of his hand to search her bag for the keys. As usual, the keys were the last thing she found but after some frenzied searching she heard the familiar jingle.

"Hurry Jo!" Luke panicked. The women had almost reached them, but luckily their intoxicated state had slowed them down a little. They were determined though and had only one goal – to get their hands on Luke Summers. Jo pressed the button to unlock the doors and Luke swiftly jumped in, locking his door. Jo was in her seat in a flash and locked her door as well. One of the women grabbed Luke's door handle and tried to open it. Another tried a back door while others began banging on the roof and bonnet, pleading with him to get out of the car and go with them.

"GO!" Luke shouted above the commotion. "Let's get the hell out of here."

"WHERE?" cried Jo, bewildered by the scene and the loud pounding.

"Just DRIVE!" ordered Luke as one woman pressed her face to his window and began hungrily licking the glass. Jo started the car, put it into reverse and pressed the accelerator hard. The car jerked into action. The one who had been licking the window now had her top raised and was pressing her bare breasts against Luke's window. As the car lurched backward she was thrown off balance and staggered back a little. Jo put the car into first gear and took off, as Luke looked back at the over-zealous fans. Two of the women were running after the car and waving their arms around. He couldn't hear what they were saying, nor did he care. The others were standing nearby while the half-naked one was putting her top back into place.

"Phew," he whistled, shaking his head, "that was close."

"A bit too close for my comfort," agreed Jo. "They probably would have ripped my head off if they'd got their hands on me." She shuddered at the thought.

"Do you know where Twin Waters resort is?" Luke asked. "That's where we are staying"

"Yep, sure do," smiled Jo. "Ahh, the perils and pitfalls of being a gorgeous rock star - half naked women throwing themselves at you and lusting after your body. It must be terrible."

"Yes," he sighed in mock seriousness. "It's a tough life all right, but somebody has to do it."

They looked at each other and simultaneously burst out in incontrollable laughter. All the nervousness, tension and confused feelings Jo experienced earlier had all but disappeared. She now felt completely relaxed and at ease with Luke. She loved to laugh and had a good sense of humour and couldn't help feeling that Luke did too.

As she drove, she glanced over at him, still totally in awe of his presence. Closing her eyes for a split second, she shook her head before reopening them. It definitely was NOT a dream! She was actually driving her car with Luke Summers sitting beside her.

"What's wrong, Jo?'' he asked.

"Oh, nothing," she smiled at him. "I was just making sure I'm not dreaming."

"No," he laughed, not being able to resist taking hold of her left hand. "You're not dreaming."

They drove on until they reached the resort, chatting along the way about the concert and the band's tour in general. Luke also wanted to know more about Jo and she talked about how she'd lived on the Sunshine Coast all her life and enjoyed her job at Blazes. She mentioned that Stonefish had always been one of her favourite bands and the disappointment she felt at not being able to enjoy the whole concert. He couldn't refrain from enquiring about a man in her life. She told him she had recently broke it off with someone and left it at that.

Luke smiled and nodded to himself with that reply.

They reached the car park of the resort, set in manicured lawns and landscaped gardens. Jo had felt relaxed and happy during the drive, but a few butterflies were creeping back now. Luke got out of the car as Jo opened her door, but she hesitated a little before stepping out. Luke sensed her trepidation and walked around to her side of the car.

"It's a nice night. Do you want to go for a walk over to the beach?" he suggested. He certainly didn't want to scare her off.

"Okay," agreed Jo, realising that Luke must have sensed her uneasiness, "that sounds good."

There was some moonlight as they made their way along the sandy walkway to the beach. Luke took hold of Jo's hand as they walked. It seemed like the natural thing to do and she didn't resist. The moonlight sparkled on the water as the tiny, whispering waves gently kissed the shore. Apart from them, the beach was deserted.

"I could go a swim right now!" declared Luke, inhaling the fresh, salty, sea air deeply.

"Are you crazy?" laughed Jo.

"Yep!" nodded Luke. "It helps to be in this world."

"Well, you wouldn't get me going in there at night. You never know what is lurking about in the water."

Luke turned to her and smiled. "Shall we go for a walk or sit on the sand for a while?"

"Hmmm, sitting sounds soooo good right now," replied Jo. "I have been running around on my feet all night."

As they sat down on the sand, Jo began to laugh.

"What's tickling you?" grinned Luke.

She shook her head. "I was just thinking about before, back at the car park and those girls going crazy over you."

"I'm just glad we beat them to the car. Hey, imagine if you had lost your keys," shuddered Luke. "Like in one of those nightmares."

"Well, I'm just glad one of them didn't pull a lasso out of her bag and rope you with it", Jo stated, feigning seriousness.

"Even if she did have one she would have been too pissed to get it over my head." They cracked up laughing again.

"I bet that is pretty mild though, compared with some of the situations you would have been in, Luke," said Jo, a little more serious.

"You know a bit about me now so how about telling me a bit of your life story?"

"Um…okay……it's not that earth shattering though," he began.

"I bet!" laughed Jo.

"Well, I was born and bred in Perth. I'm twenty-nine years old, the youngest in the band and apart from playing music I love surfing and riding my Harley".

"Hmmm, a Harley. I'm impressed!" stated Jo, eyebrows raised.

"Looks like I have finally put a glint in your eye," said Luke, leaning over and putting his arm around her shoulders.

"You put a glint in my eyes a long time ago, Luke Summers," Jo smiled, turning to face him.

"And they're beautiful blue eyes too. I noticed that when I first saw you this afternoon. You were pretty nervous then weren't you?" he teased, enjoying her reciprocated smile and nod.

Luke gently cupped her jaw in his hands and then began stroking the sides of her face. Jo's heart was racing and those old familiar butterflies came dancing back, but she wasn't going to fight it. Slowly, he leaned in closer as her breathing deepened. Her right hand rested on his thigh and she raised her left hand slowly to his back. Their eyes locked intensely before closing , as his lips tenderly touched hers. Jo's body tingled all over as she responded passionately to his feathery touch. He drew back a little and softly touched her lips with his thumb.

"You've got the lips to match the eyes," he whispered.

"And you've certainly got the charm…..and the right words." Suddenly, Graham's warning came back to haunt her and she pulled away slightly from Luke.

"What's wrong?"

"Luke, I am going to ask you something straight out. Will you be honest with me?"

"Promise!" he vowed.

"Did you only want me for sex tonight and do you do this after every concert?"

"Whoa, hold on Jo!" He leaned back, placing both hands in the air in a truce mode. "To answer your second question – no, I don't do this after EVERY concert. I only broke up with my lady just before we went on this tour. She wanted to go and work overseas and be her own person, so off she went. We had been together for three years and I was faithful to her. I might have played around a bit when I was younger but these days you can't be too careful."

"That's true," she agreed. "Wow, you don't seem to fit the typical rockstar persona then, do you?"

He laughed. "Now, to your first question, no I didn't only want you for your body. Of course I want to make love to you. Any man would, but I can see where you are coming from and I respect that," he reassured her. "I like you a lot. I'm just disappointed we live on opposite sides of the continent or you never know what may have eventuated. I don't know about being a typical 'rock star', I'm just me."

"I'd like to see more of YOU. When do you move on?" Jo enquired.

"The day after tomorrow. We have a few more shows up the coast and then that's it."

"You sound like you will be glad when it is over."

"I will!" he stated firmly. "It's been a long one and we've been through a few countries. Oh, it's been fun though, but I will be glad to get home for some R and R. Jo, I've got a great idea," he suddenly added, as excited as a schoolboy. "Come back to Perth with me. You'll love it!"

He embraced and kissed her passionately. At first she was too shocked at his request to respond to his eager lips but soon returned the kiss, placing her hands around the back of his neck. He pulled back, cupping the sides of her face in his hands with the biggest smile she had ever seen emanate from him. With eyes dancing over her face, he was obviously searching for some positive response.

"Well!" he urged. "What do you reckon? I've got a great house right on the beach," then added seriously, "I'll look after you, Jo."

She stared at him, speechless, for several seconds. "Well......um.....I'll have to think about it for a bit. You've certainly caught me off guard. I really was NOT expecting THIS!" she exclaimed. "But......tell me more about Perth."

Luke told Jo about his beloved home city, his life there and his family which included an older brother and younger sister. Jo was definitely growing more and more interested. They discussed the implications of her leaving her job and family, and what their reaction would be on her moving thousands of kilometres away with a man she barely knew and a rock star at that!!! No, her parents would not be too impressed! Her friends would certainly be envious, but Mum and Dad were a different kettle of fish. She had been living away from home for 5 years now in a shared flat, but she still shared a close relationship with her parents and 2 younger brothers. It was an exciting and extremely tempting prospect, one that made her heart surge and skip a few beats.

They sat on the lonely beach, Luke with his arms enveloped affectionately around Jo, their hands and fingers entwined, so deep in conversation that they hadn't noticed the time passing. Luke let go of Jo's hands and looked at his watch, using the inbuilt light.

"Do you know what time it is already?"

"No, what?" Jo shrugged, not really caring.

"It's nearly four AM. The birds will be up soon. Let's go to my room," Luke suggested, standing up and helping her up by the hand. "To SLEEP," he added reassuringly.

"I'll only stay a little while. I've promised my flat-mate I'd help her to shop for an outfit tomorrow to wear to her boss's wedding," Jo said, brushing the sand from her clothes.

"When do you have to work again?" Luke asked, embracing her shoulders and holding her close to him.

"Not 'til Sunday, thankfully. I don't think I could handle a shift there tomorrow," she yawned, returning his embrace.

"You mean TODAY," he reminded her.

They gently kissed once more and walked, holding hands, back along the track to the resort and Luke's room, as the moon was sinking low. The room was large and airy with an inviting Queen sized bed. Jo looked out the window and down on to the water that partially surrounds the resort then closed the curtains. Luke removed his shoes and socks and began unbuttoning his white shirt. Jo watched him from the opposite side of the room as she took her shoes off. He hung his shirt over a chair and, leaving his jeans on, lay on the bed.

"It's okay Jo, really," Luke said, beckoning her to lay down beside him. Slowly she walked to the bed and sat on the edge for a moment, still fully clothed, before moving into his arms. Luke was lying on his side and slid one arm under Jo's neck. He put the other arm around her, snuggled her closer to him and softly kissed her on the forehead. She put one arm around him, holding the other one close to her body and lifted her head a little to kiss him on the lips.

"If you start that I will have to go and have a cold shower," he murmured into her ear.

"Oops, sorry," she laughed. "Goodnight Luke."

He reached over and switched the lamp off, kissed her once more on the forehead and closed his eyes. As sleep beckoned, he silently prayed that she would come home with him.

Lying in Luke's arms, Jo's mind was crammed with images, possibilities and questions, but she soon drifted off into a deep sleep, as the eastern sky began to lighten and welcome the new day.

CHAPTER TWO

"Hey Frank, what say we get a cup of coffee up here?" suggested the tall, young policeman to his older, larger colleague as they walked along a Kings Cross street in the heart of Sydney. The beckoning rich aromas from the nearby coffee shops were teasing his nostrils and taste buds.

"Good idea," yawned Frank. "These graveyard shifts are getting harder to finish the older I get."

"Oh, come on Frank," laughed the younger one, John, "you're not that old and decrepit yet."

They continued walking along the footpath as dawn was breaking and Sydney began awakening to the hustle and bustle of yet another day. John and Frank had worked from midnight and would finish at eight that morning. Most of the time they had been on foot patrol around Kings Cross, the notorious hub of Sydney's nightlife. There had been a few scuffles, drunks loitering about and streetwalkers plying their wares, but overall it had been a surprisingly quiet night for a Friday. Suddenly, as they passed an entrance to one of the back alleys, a barking dog caught their attention. They stopped to look in its direction.

"Ah, just some mangy mutt," said Frank, starting to walk on. "It's probably found a dead cat or something."

"Hang on, Frank!" replied John, walking into the alley. Frank stopped and watched John walk over to the barking dog. There were several rubbish bins and cardboard boxes strewn about and rubbish scattered over the ground, but that was not an uncommon sight in these alleys, especially early in the mornings.

"Oh shit!" exclaimed John. "Come here, Frank!" he shouted, then yelled at the scruffy dog to get away.

"What's there?" sighed Frank, shaking his head and quickly walking over to John and looking down. "What a bloody mess!"

On the ground before them, amidst the putrid rubbish, was a battered and bloodied body of a young man, his clothes dirty and worn. He was lying on his side with both arms out in front of him. His face and short, spikey hair were covered in blood. One eye was badly swollen while his mouth was slightly ajar, still dribbling blood and saliva. Several flies buzzed about his face and a bloodstained fence paling lay on the ground beside him.

"I'll check if he's alive," said John, bending down and taking hold of the man's wrist, not being prepared to risk feeling his neck and coming into contact with his blood.

"Just," he nodded, as Frank rang for an ambulance. "Somebody certainly has a grudge against him."

"Hmph! He's probably just some low-life drug addict who can't pay his pusher," grunted Frank, after finishing the call and returning his phone to its place on his belt.

"Oh, come on Frank," John frowned. "Whatever he is, don't forget he's still somebody's son or brother.....or father even."

"Well, where was his so-called supportive family when he was getting himself into this mess?" asked Frank, angrily shaking his head. "I've got no sympathy for these street punks when they get themselves into trouble. If you ask me they deserve all they get!"

"I didn't know you were so cynical, Frank," remarked John, disappointment in his voice.

"Listen Mate," Frank shook his finger at John, "you're only young yet. A greenhorn. When you have been around as long as I have and seen the things I have, you'll take off those rose-coloured glasses."

A low moan escaped the man's bloody lips. John crouched down near his head but he was then silent.

"Hey!" declared John, forgetting Frank's sudden outburst. "I think I know this bloke!"

"How the hell do YOU know him?"

"From that Drop-In centre over in Riley Street. You know, the one that George Simpson and his wife run."

"Yeah, I know the one," nodded Frank, frowning, "but..."

"I've seen him there a couple of times," continued John, "when I've had to go over and find or question someone. Occasionally, I just drop in to see how they're going. I think it is great what they do. I'm positive it's him. I think his name might be Pete." He searched his victim's pockets for a wallet but found nothing.

At that moment, an ambulance screamed to a halt at the entrance to the alley, followed by a police car. Two paramedics got out of their vehicle and took a roller stretcher from the back and quickly carried it over to the scene. Wearing protective gloves, they swiftly checked his vital signs, then gently lifted him onto the stretcher, secured him, dropped the wheels and pushed it back to the waiting ambulance. Frank and John followed to the ambulance while the two policemen who'd just arrived, surveyed the scene for clues and placed the bloodied board in a plastic bag for evidence.

"How bad is he?" John asked one of the paramedics.

"It's a bit hard to tell until he has been checked out at the hospital, but I think he'll live," he replied, closing the back door of the ambulance after his counterpart had climbed in. "We'll leave you guys to it." He got into the driver's seat, started the engine, turned on the lights and siren and sped off in the direction of St Vincent's hospital.

"Listen Frank, when we're finished here, and the paper work is all taken care of at the station, I might go over and talk to George Simpson. He might be able to go to the hospital and identify the bloke since he didn't appear to have any ID on him," said John as they walked back to the scene of the crime.

"Yeah, good idea," agreed Frank.

When John had finished his shift, he headed over to the Drop-In centre. It was owned and run by George and Vera Simpson, a middle aged couple, plus several younger volunteers. They received a small government subsidy but most of their costs were met by donations and fund-raising efforts by the volunteers. The Centre was a huge, converted house where the homeless could go for a meal, bed, counselling or just for some company. People of all ages dropped by, some stayed a week or two, some just one night and some were regulars that stayed several days a week.

John parked his car and walked along the footpath to the wrought iron gate at the front of the house yard. The house was a large, high set style with an open veranda across the front. He never ceased to admire the huge, immaculate gardens and shady trees here. It was obvious to him that there was pride in the place. He walked across the wide veranda and, even though the door was open, rang the doorbell. An old man sat on a cane chair up one end of the veranda looking sad and lonely. He looked up at John with a faraway look in his eyes for several seconds before looking back down at the coffee cup he held in his gnarled, shaky hands. John felt sorry for him and smiled and waved but the old man didn't respond.

Suddenly, a short be-spectacled woman appeared at the door. "Can I help you?" she asked pleasantly.

"Mrs Simpson?" John enquired.

"Yes," she replied. "How may I help you?

John had changed out of his police uniform before he left the station and was wearing a white tee shirt, jeans and joggers. He was tired from working the night shift but felt a responsibility to help the man found in the alley.

"I'm Constable John Pryor. I know your husband, George, and I've been here a few times talking to different people."

"Oh Yes! I know you," she smiled. "George is out in the main kitchen." The Simpsons lived in a small flat attached to the back of the house. Anyone who stayed at the centre shared the main kitchen, lounge, small library and two bathrooms.

She led him along a freshly painted hallway past several rooms, some with doors closed while others were open. He glanced through one doorway as he walked and saw double wooden bunks against the far wall. A longhaired, teenaged girl was asleep in the bottom one. John couldn't help wondering to himself if she had run away from home and why.

"George, you remember Constable John Pryor?" she announced as they entered the large kitchen. "He's been here a few times."

"Yeah, sure! How are you John?" He walked over from the stove and shook John's hand. He was a tall, slim man with short, greying hair, bushy eyebrows, rosy cheeks and a big smile. "Haven't seen you in a while. Want a cuppa.......some toast?"

"No thanks," answered John, shaking his head. "I can't stay long. I've just finished night shift and want to get home to bed."

"What's up?" asked George, as he placed some bread in the toaster, then began making a large pot of tea while Vera set the table. They prepared most of the meals in the centre.

"You know that young bloke, Pete, that stays here sometimes with the short, gingery coloured hair? I think it might be dyed," John said, sitting in a chair Vera had beckoned him to.

"Pete! Yes, what about him?" asked Vera, concerned.

"Yeah, Pete," nodded George.

"When is the last time you saw him?" asked John, sensing by the tone of their voices, that the couple thought a lot of Pete. Though he was sure they would treat everyone that came here like family.

"Yesterday morning," answered Vera. "He had some breakfast and left. What's wrong?"

"Yeah, that's right." added George. "He said he probably wouldn't be back for a couple of days. He just comes and goes as he pleases. Has he done something wrong?"

"I don't know, I hope not anyway," replied John. He told them about the man in the alley and how he felt it was Pete. George and Vera were worried and George agreed to go to the hospital after breakfast and see if the victim was, in fact, Pete.

"Thanks very much for taking the time to come and tell us John," said Vera as John was getting up to leave.

"Yeah, thanks John." George shook his hand gratefully. "I just hope it isn't Pete. He gets himself into some scrapes sometimes but he has never ended up in hospital before....... that WE know of anyway."

"Well," smiled John, "I just hope it isn't him – for your sake. But if it is," he added seriously, "and he wants to press charges or if..........he doesn't make it, we'll be back to ask you some questions."   Vera gasped and let out a sob.

"Questions?" frowned George.

"We'll have to find out who he spent time with and what sort of things he did in his spare time. The standard questions," John reassured them.

"He never really tells us much," sighed Vera.

"Don't worry, Love," George said, placing an arm around his wife. "First things first. It might not even be him. I'll go in soon and find out."

"I'll be off then," waved John. "I'll be in touch." He walked down the hallway and heard George knock on a bedroom door, then inform the occupants that breakfast was ready.

Arriving at the hospital at around ten AM that morning, George gave as many details as he could to the lady in reception and was advised as to which ward to go to and how to get there. On arrival, he spoke briefly to the ward nurse who took him to the bed of the man brought in early that morning. The battered and bruised patient just lay there with his eyes closed. A bandage was wrapped around his forehead and right eye. His lips were puffy and cut in several places, his nose misshapen and his left eye darkening. Awakened by the voices of George and the nurse, he slowly opened his eye.

"George," he whispered in a raspy voice. "What are you doin' here?"

"I could ask you the same question, Pete," said George, shaking his head in hopelessness. He had expected the man to be Pete. The nurse left them alone.

"How did you know?" asked Pete.

"One of the policemen who found you thought he recognised you from the Centre and came and told us. What happened?" he frowned, sitting on a chair next to Pete's bed.

Pete remained silent for a few moments, trying to piece everything together. "I don't know," he eventually answered. "I can't remember."

"You must be able to remember something," urged George, suspecting that Pete was holding something back from him, but Pete just shook his head. "Vera's worried about you. Just how bad are your injuries?"

Pete coughed, closed his exposed eye and moaned before he spoke. "Not that bad," he mumbled, trying to reassure George.

Just then, an elderly, greying Doctor with horn rimmed glasses came over to Pete's bed.

"How are you feeling now?" he asked. "You look a bit more lively than you did a while ago."

"Mmm," Pete opened his eye and nodded weakly to the Doctor, certainly not feeling very lively.

"What's the extent of his injuries, Doc?" queried George, standing up.

The Doctor looked at Pete, who'd closed his eye again and then looked at George. "Are you a relative?"

"No," answered George. "My wife and I run a drop-in centre and Pete stays there pretty often. He's never mentioned anything about his family, but I don't think they live in Sydney." Pete remained silent with his eye closed.

"Well," the Doctor began, "he's got 3 cracked ribs and a broken nose. No other broken bones, amazingly! There were no internal injuries but he's got some nasty cuts around his right eye. So apart from a few other cuts and bruises, concussion and a few loose teeth, he's in top shape!" Pete let out a low moan.

"How long will he have to stay here?" George asked.

"Oh, a few days at least," smiled the Doctor. "I will leave you two to it." He walked over to a patient on the opposite side of the ward.

"Well, Pete," said George, sitting back down on the chair, "have you remembered anything yet?"

Pete opened his eye and gazed at George. "Tell Vera I'm sorry for worryin' her. It'll never happen again!" he stated, avoiding the question.

"She'll be glad to know you're all right," George nodded. "That reminds me, I'd better ring her and let her know what is going on. I'll be back soon, so don't go away." He laughed to Pete and walked into the corridor to use his phone.

"Don't worry, Georgie," he sighed to himself. "I ain't going nowhere. At least not yet!"

A few minutes later he was back at Pete's bedside.

"She's not too upset is she?" asked Pete, concerned.

"Well, she was at first, then calmed down when I told her you would be okay."

"Thanks, George.........for everything," said Pete. "I'd really be up the creek without you and Vera."   George's eyes widened then he frowned, smiled and shook his head, taken aback by Pete's sudden sentimentality. He'd never seen that in him before. "And," continued Pete, "yous don't need a no-hoper like me hanging around stressing yous out."

"We like having you around, Pete," George responded, choking back a tear. "You make us laugh, and the others too."

"Well, I don't think I will be up to cracking too many jokes for a while," declared Pete.

"You'll be back to normal in no time," George assured him, patting his forearm, which was adorned with several badly done tattoos.

Pete was twenty-nine years old but looked older. He was slightly built with pale skin and hazel eyes. He'd come to Sydney several years earlier and bummed around doing odd jobs, living on the streets or in shelters like George and Vera's. Unfortunately, he had also gotten himself mixed up in the seedy world of drugs, alcohol and, at times, crime. Even though he tried to stay on the straight and narrow, he often found himself in situations he had no control over – like the one last night. He remembered bits and pieces and tried to put it all together since regaining consciousness in the hospital bed, but most of it was a blur because he had been too out of it at the time. He vaguely remembered somebody demanding money from him, threatening to kill him and the word, "faggot" being used. The memory made him shudder. It was the worst beating he'd ever had!

"I've been thinking, George," Pete mused.

"What about?" urged George, hopeful he was going to open up.

"I haven't been home in years and I think it is about time I went back to see me family and catch up with some old mates," pondered Pete.

"Probably not a bad idea," affirmed George, sensing more to the decision but not pushing the issue. "I don't think you ever told us where they are. Where DO you come from, Pete?"

"Perth,'' Pete replied.

CHAPTER THREE

"Oh, no!" gasped Jo, when she awoke wrapped in Luke's warm arms and noticed the time on his watch. She threw back the sheet, jumped up and rushed into the bathroom.

Luke opened his eyes groggily and sat up.

"What's wrong, Jo?" he yawned, rubbing his eyes.

"Do you know what time it is?" she yelled frantically from the bathroom then came out wiping her face on a large white towel.

"Midday!" announced Luke, glancing at his watch. "Oh, that's right, you had to go shopping with your friend." He got up and went to the bathroom while Jo put her shoes on.

"Shit! She won't be happy," panicked Jo. "We were supposed to go this morning and then have lunch together." Quickly, she found her phone in her bag and turned it on. "Flat!" she groaned and threw it back into the bag.

Luke walked from the bathroom, over to Jo and put his arms around her as she stood up.

"Luke, I really have to go. As much as I'd love to stay longer I don't want to let her down." Jo was practically begging, but could feel her defences dropping.

"You're already late, five more minutes are not going to make any difference," Luke smiled and kissed her softly, but passionately on the lips. "Will you be back later?"

Jo didn't resist and returned the passion. "Sure will," she smiled. "This afternoon!"

"With an answer about coming to Perth with me?" Luke asked hopefully, eyebrows raised.

"I won't be thinking of anything else all day, I promise," she answered, kissing him quickly one more time before hurrying out the door.

Luke took a deep breath, removed his jeans, fell back on to the bed and into dreamland.

Jo drove as quickly as she legally could back to her flat in Maroochydore, hoping all the way that her friend, Meg, would not be too upset with her. She anticipated that Meg would forgive her once she learned where she had been all night. Well and truly on a natural high, Jo couldn't wipe the smile from her face. It all seemed like a dream, the chance meeting with Luke, driving him in her car after the concert, the beach and sleeping in his arms.

Pulling into the driveway of the low-set brick unit, she noticed the front door shut and Meg's car missing from the open carport and realised she would have gone. Meg was usually very easy going but this shopping trip was important to her. After parking the car and walking in to find, as expected, an empty flat she headed to her bedroom. A note on the table bearing her name caught her attention.

"JO, COULDN'T WAIT ANY LONGER. TRIED TO CALL YOU, PHONE OFF. HAVE GONE TO PLAZA IF YOU STILL WANT TO COME. MEG. PS. JEFF CAME TO SEE YOU THIS MORNING. "

Jeff was definitely the last person Jo wanted to see right now. She threw the note into the bin beside the fridge, put her phone on the charger and went for a shower. It was a relief to get out of her regulation uniform of a tight fitting, calf length black skirt and turquoise blouse. Meg's note didn't indicate if she was cranky or not, and this concerned Jo a little, but not enough to prevent her singing in the shower.

After showering and blow drying her hair, Jo walked to her bedroom wrapped only in a towel and put on white, loose cotton shorts and a pink tank top. She sung a Stonefish song to herself as she returned the towel to the bathroom and headed to the kitchen for some food, her mind still in turmoil over Luke's request. Suddenly she stopped and gasped in fright, looking toward the lounge chair. Jeff was sitting there, his arms folded and a serious look on his face.

"Jeff! What are YOU doing?" She hadn't heard him come in and with her state of euphoria she had forgotten to lock the front door while she showered.

"I came 'round this morning to see you," he stated sternly, "but Meg said you hadn't come home last night." He stood up, placing his hands on his hips menacingly. "Where have you been all night, Jo?"

Jo was taken aback by his anger. "I just stayed at a friend's place," she shrugged, but becoming annoyed by his attitude. There was no way she was telling him where she spent the night. As far as she was concerned, they were history and it was none of his damn business. She poured herself a glass of apple juice from the fridge, took out the bread and butter and put some bread in the toaster while trying to ignore Jeff, hoping he would just go away, but he was persistent.

"Megan was worried about you. She said you two were going shopping this morning. You could have at least called her," nagged Jeff.

Jo took the hot toast out of the toaster when it popped up, rolled her eyes and began buttering it hard and fast. She knew Jeff wasn't concerned about Meg's feelings. He was only thinking of himself and that he hated the thought of her having her own life.

"I couldn't call!" She spun around to face him. "I didn't mean to be late, but I just could NOT help it, okay."

"So.....where were you?" Jeff insisted, walking closer to her.

"Jeff, it's really NONE of your business!" Jo stated, suddenly losing her appetite and throwing the uneaten piece of toast into the bin. "Have you forgotten? We are NOT going out together anymore."

"Yeah, well, that wasn't my idea. I still love you, Jo and I didn't want us to break up," he said in a less harsh tone.

Jo wondered if it was a tear she saw in his eye. No! She wasn't about to let him get to her this way again. He'd begged her for a reconciliation in the past and she'd relented only to regret it, but NOT this time!

"Look Jeff," she sighed, "I've told you over and over and I hate hurting you, but I don't love you anymore. I'm really sorry." She WAS genuinely sorry. They had known each other since high school and she hated hurting ANYBODY, but it was over and she had to make him accept that once and for all.

Jeff turned his back to her, clasped his hands behind his head, took in and expelled several deep breaths. Jo was sometimes unsure of his behaviour and didn't know what to expect from him next. Lately, she had wondered how she had loved him so much for so long. He was twenty-seven years old, tall and muscular with short blond hair and a goatee beard. She had always thought of him as good looking but he lacked the handsomeness and charm of Luke.

Suddenly, he turned to her. "Who is he?" he demanded, his green eyes glaring savagely.

"Who?" frowned Jo, taking several quick steps backwards. They'd shared some blazing arguments in the past but he had never hit her. While she was sure he wouldn't, she saw the sinister look in his eyes that she had never seen before. Her stomach began to churn as her heart raced.

"You know damn well who I am talking about!" Jeff shouted. "The bloke you spent the night with." Jo knew it was pointless trying to deny it. She could try until she was blue in the face and he still wouldn't believe her.

"It's someone I met just recently," she answered calmly, hoping he would follow suit and mellow down. No such luck.

"WHO THE FUCK IS HE?" Jeff roared, taking hold of her arms above the elbows and shaking her.

"Let go of me, Jeff!" cried Jo, trying to pull away from him. She was really frightened now.

"Not until you tell me who the slimy bastard is," he demanded, with his reddening face so close to Jo's that his spit flew into her face.

She was terrified, angry and disgusted with his outburst. "It's none of your frigging business," she screamed back at him. "Now let me go!"

"No-one else is going to have you!" he declared, pulling her closer, holding her tightly about the shoulders and attempting to kiss her roughly on the lips. Suddenly thinking of Luke's gentle, passionate kisses, Jo felt repulsed and struggled to get out of his tight grip. Even though she was tall and fit, he was much too strong and overpowered her. He slobbered over her lips and forced his tongue into her mouth, jarring her neck as she quickly jerked her head back to get away from it.

Jo despised that. For a split second she was tempted to bite it but thought better and swiftly brought her knee up hard and drove it into his groin.

"You fucking bitch!" he screamed in pain, doubling over and holding his crotch. "I'll get you for that!"

Jo ran to the front door. The main door was open but the screen was closed. She frantically tried to open it but it was locked with a key and it was nowhere to be seen. Terrified, she realised he must have locked it when he snuck in. Sobbing, she quickly scanned the room for the keys, noticing Jeff slowly straightening up, over near the table. He started toward her, fury in his eyes, knocking a chair over as he came.

"No Jeff, leave me alone!" she screamed and went to run toward the back door in the laundry, hoping she could get it unlocked and be outside before he could reach her.

"I'll teach you to go screwing around on me, you slut," he threatened as he quickly grabbed her arm hard and dragged her back over to the large lounge chair. She kicked and struggled but to no avail. He held his hand tightly over her mouth then threw her down on the lounge. "How many were there?" he demanded, leaning over her.

"I haven't screwed anybody!" she spat back at him.

"LYING BITCH" he exploded, hitting her hard across the cheek with the back of his hand.

Jo brought her hands to her face to protect it and lifted her foot up hoping for another direct hit. She kicked out blindly with all her strength. He gasped loudly and she uncovered her face to see him fall to the floor but she had only got him in the stomach this time and as she got up to run Jeff sprang forward, grabbing her ankle with his large, strong hand. She crashed heavily to the floor. He was on her in no time, turning her onto her back and straddling her stomach. Jo punched wildly at him with her fists but he soon pinned them down. She tasted the salty blood in the corner of her mouth as the tears trickled down to her ears. Who was this monster?

"You think you're so smart giving your pretty little body to someone else, don't you?" he snarled, "Well, let's see what he thinks of this."

He leaned down and began biting her hard on the neck, obviously to Jo, with intent to bruise. That was another thing she hated. Struggling in vain, she screamed for him to stop, hoping a neighbour might hear her and ring the police.

His mouth moved down toward her chest and he let go of one of her hands long enough to pull her top up and roughly lift her bra off her breasts. She grabbed his hair with her free hand and pulled hard. Jeff yelped as strands of it came out in her hands. Shaking his head, he hit her in the face again before pinning her arm back down. He stared in her eyes for several seconds, drooling at the mouth, before leaning down and savagely biting her breast. Jo whimpered from pain and fear.

"I'm going to have you now, Baby. Right here on the floor!" he stated smugly. "And I promise you, you're going to really know what pain feels like." His mouth honed in on her exposed nipple. Jo prayed for unconsciousness.

Suddenly, the screen door opened and Meg walked inside, laden with bags of shopping. She was a tall, fair skinned, curvaceous lady with long dark hair.

"What's going on?" Meg frowned, noticing the upturned chair before looking at Jo and Jeff on the floor. Jeff pulled Jo's top down, casually got off her and stood up.

"We were just mucking around," shrugged Jeff, smiling. "I'd better go, Jo. I'll be back though."

Even Meg detected a slight threat in those last words as he walked out.

After Jeff had gotten off her, Jo rolled to her side, facing away from Meg and sobbed, her body shaking violently. Meg dropped the bags she was carrying and ran over to Jo, kneeling down and gently turning Jo toward her. She gasped in horror at the sight of Jo's bloody lip, darkening eye and the red abrasions and bruises on her neck.

"What the hell happened?"

Jo could only shake her head and wipe her tears away as she struggled to calm down enough to speak. Meg raced to the bathroom, wet a facecloth and grabbed some tissues, before running back to Jo, who was now sitting up on the lounge chair, her sobbing slowly subsiding.

"Did Jeff do this to you?" she demanded, sitting down next to Jo and wiping her face with the cloth.

"Yes," sobbed Jo quietly, taking a tissue and blowing her nose. "I'm sorry I didn't get home to go shopping with you, Meg."

"Hell, don't worry about THAT!" Meg reassured her. "Did he hurt you anywhere else?"

"No," replied Jo, shaking her head. "But I hate to think what would have happened if you hadn't come in when you did. He just went crazy. I have never seen him like that before."

Meg got an icepack from the freezer and gave it to Jo for her eye, which was puffing up. "He was pretty irate this morning when he found out you hadn't come home," Meg said, sitting back down beside Jo. "I didn't mean to tell him. He kept at me and wouldn't leave. He was really making me nervous, but I never dreamed he would hurt you like this." She put her arm around Jo for several minutes before Jo got up and said she wanted a shower. Her skin crawled from his touch. Meg put the shopping away, wracked by niggling feelings of guilt and put the kettle on.

When Jo came out of the shower she felt a little better and welcomed the extra strong cup of tea Meg had made for her as well as one for herself.

"Times like this I wished I smoked," joked Jo. "I could really use a cigarette right now." She sat at the table, sipping her tea and staring at the floor.

"Do you want to tell me what happened last night?" Meg asked, after several minutes of silence.

"I met the most incredible, gorgeous man," said Jo slowly, with a distant look in her eyes and just a slight smile. "We sat on the beach until dawn, then we fell asleep in each other's arms."

"Go on....." urged Meg, smiling. "Who is he?"

"You wouldn't believe me if I told you," Jo smiled dreamily.

"Try me," insisted Meg.

Suddenly, the realisation of the immediate situation came back to hit Jo. "No, I can't Meg! Not yet anyway." She jumped up, put the mug on the sink, grabbed her phone from the charger, her bag from her bedroom and headed for the door.

"Where are you going, Jo?" frowned Meg.

"I have to see him," stated Jo, then turned and rushed back to her bedroom.

Meg wondered if she meant Jeff or the mystery man. Surely she meant the mystery man.

Jo came out a few minutes later with her overnight bag. "I'll be back in the morning," she told Meg as she walked to the door, her bruised face throbbing. "If Jeff comes back, tell him I am at my parents place. He wouldn't be game to show his demented face there. Dad would kill him."

"Be careful and stay safe," advised Meg and waved her out the door. Shaking her head, she sat at the table stunned by everything that had just happened. She hoped Jo knew what she was doing and that she would be okay.

Jo drove straight to Twin Waters resort, clutching the steering wheel tightly and trying to work out what she was going to say to Luke. She shuddered and sobbed several times as the scene with Jeff played over and over in her head. Going to the police entered her mind briefly, but quickly dismissed it as it would only be his word against hers and she certainly didn't want to drag Luke or Meg into it. Right now she despised Jeff with every ounce of her being and never wanted to set eyes on him again.

She parked her car, locked it and hurried toward the wing containing Luke's room. Just as she was entering the building a man's voice called to her. She spun around.

"You can't go in there!" he declared sternly.

"But Luke is expecting me," Jo answered. She didn't need this. She desperately needed Luke to hold her in his arms and comfort her.

"What's your name?" the uniformed man asked her calmly, sensing her distress. He'd sent a number of disappointed fans away so far that day.

"Jo Slater," she replied, suddenly feeling very vulnerable and alone. She prayed that Luke had been sincere. A high necked shirt hid her bruises and she had her sunnies on to hide her darkened eye.

"Wait here!" ordered the security guard and disappeared inside the building. Jo took several deep breaths hoping to calm her nerves. Her tongue kept subconsciously darting to the small cut on her lip which had swelled a little by now.

Luke probably wasn't expecting her back so soon. She frantically hoped that he hadn't gone out anywhere. There was no way she could face going back to her flat today and didn't feel like facing her parents either, like this. Silently, she cursed Jeff, as she stared at the door the guard had gone through.

The man came back. "You can go in now," he said, looking her up and down.

Jo noticed and screwed up her face in disgust as she walked past him. She could feel his eyes on her as she walked along the corridor. With the mood she was in, it was very tempting to turn around and give him the finger, but then she realised that having him perve on her was the least of her worries.

Luke opened the door just as she raised her hand to knock. At first he just stared, not sure for a second or two if it really was Jo. She looked different with her hair out and sunnies on, but then he realised it was her. He saw her bottom lip begin to quiver and sensed something was very wrong, then noticed how swollen her lip was.

"Jo!" he exclaimed. "What happened? Did you have a car accident?"

Jo threw herself into his arms and sobbed heavily. Luke held her tightly until her crying eased and she pulled back, facing him but remaining silent, unsure of how to tell him, afraid he may not want the emotional baggage.

"Babe, what happened?" he repeated, removing Jo's sunglasses and gasping at what he saw under them. "What the......?"

"Do you still want me to come to Perth with you, Luke?" she asked, her voice quavering.

"Of course I do," replied Luke, frowning and anxious for her to tell him how she got her injuries.

"Then it's YES! Definitely YES! I'd love to come and live in Perth with you."

CHAPTER FOUR

Luke hugged Jo again before taking her by the hand and sitting on the bed. "Sit down and tell me what happened. It wasn't a car accident was it?" he said. It was more of a statement than a question.

"No," murmured Jo, shaking her head and wiping her eyes. Luke stroked her face lovingly as she took a deep breath and evaded his eyes, then eventually she spoke. "Remember I told you that I had recently broken up with someone?" she asked, now able to look him in the eye.

"Yes," replied Luke, becoming agitated as he began to get the picture.

"Well, he came to my place, just after I got home."

"Did HE do this to you?" Luke demanded angrily.

"He just can't accept it is over and when he found out that I didn't come home last night he went crazy with jealousy," Jo blurted out then poured her heart out to Luke, telling him in detail what had happened at her flat.

Luke's face grew red hot with fury and he sucked in his breath through clenched teeth. She was crying again by the time she had told him everything and he comforted her in his arms. He wanted to kill Jeff for hurting Jo. His beautiful Jo.

She leaned back a little and searched his face for a dreaded sign that he may have changed his mind about taking her home with him.

The collar of her shirt had dropped a little and Luke noticed the ugly marks on her neck. He was visibly shocked. Slowly, he raised his hand and lowered the collar some more. Jo sat dead still and held her breath, watching his face. He shook his head and tears welled in his eyes when he realised that the bruises continued down to her chest. Looking into her teary eyes, he questioned her silently. When she gave no response, he tenderly undid several of her shirt buttons and slowly moved the material aside to expose her bra and more bruises. He was speechless. The bruises were large and dark, obviously causing a lot of pain as they were inflicted. Shaking his head slowly, he did the buttons back up and returned his shocked gaze to her eyes.

"Did he........rape you?" whispered Luke, hating to ask and dreading the answer.

"No," Jo shook her head. "I've never been so terrified in my life. He just went crazy. He's never done anything like this before."

"The bastard certainly won't ever be doing it again either!" declared Luke, taking hold of both her hands. "You're coming with me for the rest of the tour. It's only a week, but I am not letting you out of my sight."

Jo managed a big smile of relief. He still wanted her. "I'd love that, Luke," she beamed and hugged him again. Suddenly she realised what his words really meant and sat back. "But, that's tomorrow! There's so much I will have to do. Tell my family, Meg and my boss!" Graham! She had forgotten about him! She dreaded the thought of facing him with these bruises, imagining that he would assume Luke did it. Even if she explained the Jeff did, she believed Graham would still say that Luke was indirectly to blame. After his stern warning, which she blatantly ignored, how would he react to her news about going to Perth with him? As much as she respected Graham, she knew he would be disappointed, not to mention let down at her sudden resignation, BUT she had to follow her heart AND get away from Jeff.

"Well, let's go and do it then," enthused Luke, standing up and pulling Jo up by the hands.

"Are you coming with me?" she smiled, feeling much better.

"Sure am, Kiddo," he grinned. "From now on we are in this together." Then added more seriously, "it's my fault this happened to you so the least I can do is make sure nothing else happens."

"No, it's not!" Jo declared angrily. "You can't help it if he is fucked in the head!"

Luke's eyes widened at her choice of words but, under the circumstances, said nothing.

Jo went into the bathroom to wash her face before they left the room to tackle the unpleasant tasks that lay ahead.

"Where do you want to start?" asked Luke when they got to Jo's car.

"At work I suppose," sighed Jo, dreading it. "Luke, are you absolutely certain that this is what you want and you won't regret it?"

"Absolutely! Definitely! Unquestionably! Unconditionally! Want me to go on?"

"No," she laughed. "But then again......" They laughed together for the first time all afternoon as she started the car and drove off. She knew in her heart that this was the right thing to do and confident she and Luke would have a long and happy life together.

Pulling up outside Blazes Hotel, Luke could see that Jo was extremely nervous and took hold of her hand, which was sweating profusely.

"I'll come in with you," he consoled her.

"Thanks, but you had better not," she said. "It's better if I do this alone. Graham's a top bloke, but I'm afraid he thinks that all rock stars are root rats that prey on every female that comes within twenty metres of them."

"All the more reason for me to come in with you," Luke urged, "then he can see that we are not all like that."

"You're a Honey," she smiled affectionately and leaned over to kiss him. "But, I'll be right.......really."

Jo made sure her buttons were done right up and kept her sunglasses on before entering the hotel. She was sure he would be on duty. There weren't many days Graham wasn't at work, such was his love of the job. She and all the staff enjoyed a harmonious working releationship with their forty-five year old, ginger haired boss. Jo searched around several areas before she spotted him going toward the office. Hopefully, she would not run into any of her colleagues. Talking to Graham would be hard enough without having to explain things to others as well. Her stomach fluttered as she walked to the open door and knocked lightly. Graham was sitting at the desk writing and looked at her immediately.

"Jo! What are you doing here today?"

"H-Have you got a minute?" she stammered. "I need to talk to you."

"Yeah, sure Love, sit down," he said, beckoning her to another chair and sensing something was wrong. "What's up?" he frowned, then looked at her more intensely. He treated her like his own daughter.

"What's happened to you, Jo?" he asked, worriedly. He had never seen her in this state before. She was generally so bubbly and happy. Reaching toward her he gently took her sunglasses off. His eyes widened and his jaw dropped in shock. Jo looked downward, obvious to Graham, to avoid his eyes and fiddled with her bag. "Who did this to you, Jo?" he pushed. Then he noticed her swollen lip and the bruise on her neck, just above her collar. "It was that bloke from the band, wasn't it?" He was furious! "You went with him last night, didn't you?"

"No! I..... Jeff did it!" she declared, angry at Graham for thinking that Luke would have done such a thing. She decided to keep Luke's name right out of it, if possible.

"JEFF?" fumed Graham, standing up and running his thumb and forefinger down each side of his thick moustache – something he had a habit of doing when he was angry. He'd known Jeff for a few years and always found him to be polite and likable and couldn't imagine him hurting Jo this way. It had been obvious to him that Jeff worshipped the ground she walked on.

Jo poured out the whole story about their recent break-up and what had happened earlier that day at her place. Graham shook his head in clear shock and disbelief. Jo felt that it would be best not to tell him that she spent the night and morning with Luke and that he was sitting out in her car.

She decided that she would come back to see him in a week when the band's tour was over and drop the next bombshell on him. Not telling him about Luke at all, briefly entered her mind, but she knew he would be bitterly disappointed if he heard it from someone else, which he would......... eventually.

"Where are you going to go?" asked Graham. "You can't run away from him forever. You SHOULD go to the police!"

"No!" Jo said, adamantly. "I don't ever want to see him again. Ever! I just want to go away for a week and see how things are then. I can't work anyway, looking like this."

"No, I guess not," he agreed. "The bastard sure made a mess of you. He'll be sorry if he shows his face around me again. He shouldn't get away with this."

"Graham, I would really appreciate it if you kept this between you and me and I'm sorry to mess up the rosters at such short notice," Jo said.

"Oh, don't worry about that," shrugged Graham. "You just have a rest and get yourself better. If you're not ready to come back to work in a week, just ring and let me know. You're one of the best Jo, we don't want to lose you."

She looked away from him and felt a lump rise in her throat. Deceiving him like this made her feel bad, but she felt she had no choice. "Graham," she said awkwardly, "it's possible I might resign and leave the Coast for good. I'm thinking very seriously about it."

"I sure hope not Jo," he stated. "But don't make any hasty decisions yet. Take a week to think hard about it and then we will talk some more."

"Thanks Graham, I really appreciate it," she said sincerely, getting up and placing her sunnies back on.

"No worries, Love. You just look after yourself," he insisted. "See you in a week."

"Bye. And.......thanks again," she smiled and turned out of the office. Letting out an immense sigh of relief as she headed for the outside door, she was thankful she didn't have to explain the situation with Luke and also that she had a week's grace. At least, she shuddered at the thought, if things didn't work out with Luke in that time, she still had a job to come back to. She rushed back to her car.

"Well?" Luke asked anxiously, once she was in her seat beside him.

Jo told him the details of her talk with Graham, but he wasn't real pleased that she had left him out completely and didn't actually resign yet. "I thought that was the whole purpose of coming to see him," he said.

"It was," Jo insisted, "but I was too nervous to tell him everything. I'm still shaking. I think I need a drink!"

"I reckon you deserve one after everything you have been through today," nodded Luke, leaning over and kissing her on the cheek. "I'm sorry about getting a bit upset before. I guess I'm a bit worried that you will change your mind about coming home with me."

"Not a chance," she reassured him, gently stroking his cheek with the back of her fingers. "It's okay. What time does the plane go tomorrow?" she enquired, before starting the car. "Will I get a seat?"

"I'll make sure you do!" Luke declared. "It goes just before lunch, why?"

"Because I can't face any more people this afternoon," she sighed. "Can we just go back to your room? I'll pack my stuff early in the morning and ring my family then. I'd rather they didn't see me like this. Mum would freak!"

They drove back to the resort just as the sun was setting and went straight to Luke's room.

"So, Beautiful Lady," stated Luke, opening the bar fridge. "What would you like to drink?"

"Have you got any bourbon?" asked Jo, sinking gratefully back into one of the two luxury lounge chairs in the room.

"My favourite," said Luke, smiling. "How do you like it?"

"Strong....with Dry," she answered, resting her head on the back of the chair and taking a deep breath. What a day. She had never experienced a day so full of highs and lows before. Luke brought the drinks over and handed Jo's to her before sitting in the other single chair beside hers. He raised his glass as Jo followed suit.

"Cheers," he smiled, as their glasses clinked together. "May the rest of our days be NOTHING like this one!"

"I'll drink to that," agreed Jo, taking a mouthful. "Mmm, that's good." They sat quietly for a minute or two, sipping their drinks.

"Luke, do you mind if I stay here tonight?"

"Of course you can," Luke answered, frowning. "I thought that was understood. I am not letting you out of my sight!"

"Do you mind if we don't........," she hesitated.

"What? Make love? It's up to you, Jo," Luke reassured her.

"I'm sorry. I do want to, but not with all these horrible marks on my body," she said, subconsciously pulling her collar up higher.

"It's okay Babe, really," Luke said, tenderly. "I don't want to do anything to hurt you or make you feel uncomfortable. You've had a rough time today and we've got forever."

"Thanks," Jo smiled, reaching out for his hand. "You're pretty special you know. There wouldn't be too many blokes around like you."

"Well, don't tell anyone," he winked, "it might ruin my reputation." He was pleased that that made Jo laugh. "Hungry?" Luke put his glass down on the table.

"Starved!" stated Jo, realising that she hadn't eaten anything all day. "But I don't want to go down to the restaurant, if you don't mind."

"I don't either," he shook his head. "I'll ring and get them to bring something up. What's your favourite?"

"Seafood," replied Jo, without hesitating.

Luke rang and ordered a hot and cold seafood platter as well as salad and fruit then poured them another drink. While he was doing that, Jo rang Meg to let her know all was okay. The food arrived in thirty minutes and it was enormous. Jo wondered how the two of them would get through it, but knew she would make a fair impression. After dinner, they had a couple more drinks, chatted a while then decided that sleep was needed. Jo changed into a long, baggy tee shirt she had brought. Not that flattering, she knew, but she'd packed her bag in a hurry.

Luke slept in a pair of board shorts. He held Jo tenderly in his arms, wanting to caress her body, but he exercised restraint. Jo was so physically and emotionally exhausted she soon fell into a deep sleep, feeling secure in Luke's strong arms. But it was a fitful sleep, wracked with images of Jeff attacking her.

The following morning, Jo awoke and rang her Mum first thing. She didn't tell her about the attack or that she was actually going away with Luke. Cheerfully, she explained that she was going up north with a friend for a holiday and that she would send a postcard.

Her mother was a bit surprised by the suddenness of the trip but accepted it and urged them to be careful, in a typical motherly way.

After eating some of the leftovers for breakfast, Jo informed Luke she was going home to pack.

"I'll come with you," he said, "in case What's-His-Face turns up." Luke still had not heard his actual name.

"No!" stated Jo. "That's exactly why I don't want you to come. He might kill you. After yesterday, who knows what's going through his warped mind."

"I'm not giving the mongrel a chance to touch you again!" declared Luke. "I'm coming with you."

Luke showered then they drove to her flat. Jo hoped Meg wouldn't be home and her wish was granted. She pulled up in the carport and quickly looked around for any sign of Jeff lurking. Thankfully, she saw nothing. As quickly as she could, she showered then packed a large suitcase with plenty of summer gear for the North Queensland climate. Luke looked about her flat, adorned with many pictures, posters and ornaments depicting an ocean theme.

Jo decided a note for Meg would be better than calling her, in case she accidently blurted something out about Luke. She told Meg the same story she told her mother. As much as she would have loved to tell Meg about Luke, and she would in time, she just could not risk putting her in an awkward and frightening position like the previous day. No, she decided that it would be best for everyone if they only learned about Luke at the last minute. The thought of Jeff finding out was too much for her to cope with, as she had no idea what he would be capable of now.

Once they drove away from the flat in a taxi, leaving Jo's car there, locked, she was finally able to relax a little and actually began to get excited about what adventures and excitement lay ahead for her.......and for THEM! They returned to the resort where Luke introduced her to the other members of Stonefish and their immediate crew. He then made the necessary arrangement to have her included on the flight and in his room. By eleven o'clock that morning everyone was ready to go. Two limousines arrived at the resort to take them to the airport. Jo's excitement grew and it helped erase the painful memories of yesterday. She noticed some of the others looking strangely at her, but she did her best to pretend nothing was wrong.

At eleven-thirty they were seated comfortably on the privately chartered plane, bound for the next city on the itinerary. The semi-trailer loaded with their equipment would already be there and the roadies would soon be setting up for the show that night. Luke winked and smiled at Jo, taking hold of her hand as the plane glided effortlessly into the air. She smiled back, so grateful to be escaping the chilling memories and threats of Jeff and so eager to create new, wonderful memories with this incredibly gorgeous man.

CHAPTER FIVE

"Well, Pete," smiled the elderly doctor, standing beside Pete's hospital bed, "today's the big day, I think you can go home this morning."

Pete smiled at the sound of those words. It had been four days since he had been found beat up in the alley and admitted to hospital. His injuries were healing well, although his cracked ribs were still a bit tender and his face still bruised and sore. He couldn't wait to get out. Either George or Vera had visited him daily but he'd had no other visitors. Pete didn't actually have any close friends, usually just preferring his own company and he'd asked George and Vera to keep it to themselves anyway. The police asked him if he wanted to press charges, but he declined, as he didn't really know who attacked him and just shrugged it off as yet another chapter in his mixed-up life. He felt he was partly to blame for the situation, even without recalling what happened.

He ate a little of the breakfast brought to him on a tray, but he had never been a big eater, especially at breakfast time. Just as he swallowed the last of the orange juice, George came into the ward and spoke to the doctor, who was tending to another patient, before coming over to Pete.

"How are you going today, Pete?" George grinned, patting him on the sheet covered leg. "Ready to come home?"

"G'day George," Pete replied cheerfully. "You bet!"

"I brought you some clothes to wear home," George said, placing a plastic bag on the bed beside Pete. "Didn't think you would want to wear Pj's home."

Pete laughed and shook his head. "That's nice of you George. I really appreciate all you and Vera have done for me and I don't just mean washing me clothes either."

George pulled the curtains closed around Pete's bed so he could get changed and waited for him. Several minutes later he emerged from behind the curtain dressed in the faded jeans and black tee shirt that George had brought in. He had the plastic bag containing his other items tucked under his arm.

"Now Pete," instructed the doctor. "You take it easy for a while and don't get into any mischief!"

Pete liked the doctor's warm, friendly manner and thanked him, shaking his hand. He also thanked the nurses and took one last look around the ward at the other patients in their beds and was relieved to be leaving. Not having spoken to the others much while he was in there, he didn't see the need to say goodbye to them. He wasn't interested in their problems and was sure they wouldn't be interested in his.

"I'm ready!" he announced to George. "Are you ready?"

"Let's go," nodded George and they walked out of the ward together.

Pete was silent during the drive home and was more determined than ever to head back to Perth. He just couldn't work out how he was going to get there. His bank account was practically nil, and his job prospects were limited, besides, he didn't want to wait months to save up the cash, he wanted to go NOW! Vera gave Pete a loving hug when he and George arrived back at the Drop-In centre. Pete wasn't used to so much personal attention and was quite embarrassed by all the fuss.

"I've just made a fresh pot of tea," said Vera, leading them in the back door to the kitchen.

Pete went into the bedroom he normally stayed in and put his bag on the lower bunk. Most of the rooms contained one or two sets of double bunks to save room.

"Have I still got the same bed?" he asked, coming back into the kitchen and sitting at the table just as another young man walked in. Pete had never seen him before and wondered who he was.

"Yes," confirmed Vera, "it's been waiting for you. Oh, Mark, do you want a cup of tea or coffee?"

"Yeah......okay, coffee would be good, thanks. Black, two sugars," shrugged the young man as he sat down at the table. He was in his late teens, tall and thin with long, straight, black hair.

Quietly spoken, Vera had sensed he was quite shy. "Pete, this is Mark," introduced Vera as she placed the steaming mugs on the table. "He came in yesterday. Mark, this is Pete. He's been here a while."

Mark mumbled hello to Pete and sipped his coffee. Pete just nodded in return, taking a sip from his cup. He didn't trust many people anymore and felt a little suspicious of Mark.

"Pete," Vera said, sitting down opposite him at the table, "George told me you want to go home to Perth?"

"That's right," replied Pete, glancing over at Mark. He appeared, to Pete, to be in his own little world, which made him feel more comfortable talking to Vera about his plans.

"Have you thought about how you are going to get there yet, Mate?" asked George, sitting down beside Vera and placing a plate of biscuits in the middle of the table. Pete and Mark both ignored the offering.

"Oh yeah, I've thought about it, but I haven't come up with anything yet," Pete said with a hint of frustration in his voice. "I suppose I'll have to hitch."

"I wish we could help you," Vera sighed, "but our finances are not that good lately, after just paying the insurances on the car and this place."

"I don't expect yous to help me," Pete frowned. "I'll work something out," he mused, then sipped his tea while staring blankly at nothing.

"Well, you will have to wait until your injuries are better anyway, before you go traipsing off across the country," George said.

"I just wish there was a better way of getting to Perth," said Vera, shaking her head. "Hitching is so dangerous."

"Did you say Perth?" asked Mark from the end of the table.

Pete frowned at him. He had been sure Mark was off in his own little world and not paying any attention to what he, George and Vera were discussing.

"Yes, that's right," nodded George, also surprised by Mark's intervention. "You wouldn't happen to know anyone driving over there soon would you?" He was sure Mark wouldn't, but wanted to make him feel more comfortable by including him in the conversation.

"I might, actually!" Mark stated, suddenly perking up and smiling.

"Who?" asked Pete, sceptically.

"A girl I know," answered Mark indignantly, sensing Pete's cynicism.

"Do you want to tell us about her?" asked Vera, pleased to see Mark finally interested in something. He'd arrived there the day before saying he had nowhere else to go and hadn't spoken much. They decided it was best to let him settle in at his own pace.

Mark eyed Pete, who was still looking suspicious. This made Mark a little reluctant to help him. "I suppose," nodded Mark, "but only if he stops looking at me like that!" He pointed at Pete accusingly which made George and Vera both shoot Pete a look of disapproval.

"Sorry!" declared Pete, shaking his head and widening his eyes. "I'm listening."

"Go on, Mark," urged Vera, softly.

Mark looked at Pete again, before he spoke and was pleased to see he no longer held a frown on his face. "She's a friend of my brother," began Mark slowly, staring into his coffee cup. "I don't know her very well, but I heard her telling him last week that she is heading to the West Coast soon for a wedding."

"How soon? What's she like?" asked Pete, his eyes lighting up, but still feeling a little doubtful of Mark.

"She's all right. A bit crazy. Nothing much bothers her," he said grinning and shaking his head, obviously thinking about her. "She'd probably love the company."

"So, what's her name?" enquired Pete, liking the sound of her.

"Mo," replied Mark. "It's short for something, don't know what."

"Do you know how to contact her, Mark?" asked George.

"No," he shook his head, "but my brother would know."

"Well, can you ring him and find out?" urged Pete, finally beginning to feel optimistic. "Do you have a phone?"

"Nah, lost it," shrugged Mark, "it was stuffed anyway."

"Use ours," smiled George, taking it off his belt and handing it to Mark. "Do you know the number?"

"Not sure I can remember it," he said, which made Pete's heart sink. Mark thought for a moment before dialing a number. After several seconds he spoke. The conversation was brief and abrupt. There was no brotherly affection in his voice.

Pete began to feel bad about his earlier contempt toward Mark. Even he could tell that it wasn't easy for Mark to ask this request of his brother. Mark hand signalled writing something to Vera and she quickly jumped up and grabbed a pen and piece of paper from the top of the fridge. Mark scribbled down a number on the paper, thanked his brother politely, but coldly, said goodbye and handed the phone back to George.

"Here's her number," stated Mark, throwing the piece of paper toward Pete.

"I hate to ask," said Pete hopefully, "but do you think you could call her and tell her what it's about and then I will talk to her?" He expected a refusal from Mark.

"All right!" snapped Mark. "But that's all I'm doing then. I've got enough problems of my own without trying to sort someone else's out." He took the phone that George had passed to him again and dialled the number on the paper. After speaking very briefly, he hung up. "She's not answering," he informed Pete. "She's probably at work so I left a message and asked her to call back to this phone tonight. Satisfied?" Mark grumbled inaudibly to himself as he got up, pushed his chair back and walked out the door, shoulders slumped.

"Thanks Mark," Pete called after him. "Now!" he stated, turning back to Vera and George, "We've just gotta wait 'til tonight. But I have a good feeling about this."

"What are you going to do for the rest of the day, Pete?" George asked out of curiosity.

"Dunno," Pete shrugged. "I might go for a bit of a walk now." He got up and put his empty mug on the sink. "I'll be back later."

Pete walked out the front gate and dawdled along the footpath. He had absolutely no idea where he was going, but knew one thing for sure – he was hanging out for a drink or something stronger, but he had no money. What little he did have was stolen in the alley and he was days away from his next dole payment. Kicking an empty soft drink can with his bare foot, he cursed silently to himself. He knew very well what he could do to get himself some cash and as he walked along, the temptation grew stronger. Part of him was trying to say no, but that part was weak and gutless.

He walked several blocks before stopping in front of a large, old set of units, badly needing a paint job.

"One last time," he promised himself with a sigh, before walking to the second door and knocking. A balding, middle aged, pudgy man opened the door, greeted him and beckoned him inside.

Thirty minutes later, Pete emerged from the flat, stuffing thirty dollars into his hip pocket and walked to the nearest bar that would accept him barefooted. The beer went down well, but he needed something stronger. He ordered a double straight scotch, downed it in one gulp, then bought two UDL cans of scotch and coke and left the bar. Soon he found himself in a nearby park, sitting against a tree. He opened one can, took several mouthfuls and leaned back against the tree trunk, feeling disgusted with himself but powerless to do anything about it.

Pete arrived back at the Drop-In centre late in the afternoon. He'd had a sleep in the park and had sobered up a little. Now he was anxious for a call from Mo so he quickly went straight to the bathroom for a shower, hoping Vera and George wouldn't be able to tell he had been drinking. They were perceptive and Pete knew he probably would not be able to hide it from them. They dealt with so many different people, that he was sure they could even read minds! It wasn't them knowing he'd been drinking that worried him so much, but they would ask how he afforded to pay for it. That was something he would NEVER disclose to them. Just after he'd finished his shower and was in his room there was a loud knock on his door that made him jump.

"Pete!" George called. "Phone call for you." Pete quickly opened the door and took the phone from George, thanking him as he did so and sat on his bed.

"Hello," he said keenly, "is that Mo?"

"Yeah, Man! Who's askin'?" replied a loud voice on the other end.

Pete suddenly felt awkward talking to her, but managed to tell her who he was, how he got her number and what he wanted. He then crossed his fingers – hard.

"You're in luck, Dude!" Mo stated. "I'm headin' west in a couple of weeks. Just need to get a bit more bread together and a few things done to my wheels and we're off."

"Sounds good to me," said Pete, although he was a bit disappointed that it couldn't be a bit sooner. However, he wasn't going to pass up this opportunity. He just hoped he would be able to stay alive until then. "I don't suppose you could come around here, so we could meet and make some plans for the trip? I'm at the Drop-In centre in Riley Street. You know where that is?"

"I do," Mo answered. "And listen, Mate, I don't plan things. They happen as they happen, but I will come round and see you. Will tomorrow morning be all right. I work pretty close to there and I can call in on my way to work. "

"Yeah, that sounds good," said Pete, not really sure what to think of Mo, but he gave her the exact address and hung up. Pete took the phone into George and Vera who were preparing that night's meal and told them she would be around early in the morning. "She's a bit weird, though," said Pete, screwing up his face a little.

Vera shook her head and laughed a little at the irony of Pete's words. She knew that plenty of people would think that Pete was a little weird too.

"As long as she gets you to Perth safely, Pete," said George, "that's all that matters."

They ate their tea along with Mark and three other occupants of the centre. Meals were a relatively quiet affair with George and Vera doing most of the talking, trying to encourage others into the conversation. The people that came here all had problems weighing heavily on their minds. From battered wives to teenage victims of sexual abuse, to pensioners evicted from their homes and unwanted by their families, all were welcome. Nobody ever felt jovial enough to talk a lot and joke in a relaxed, casual way, but George and Vera persisted. Pete often provided some light relief, but since his beating, he wasn't feeling like telling too many jokes. After tea, the washing up was shared, which was one of the rules of the house, Pete watched some TV before heading to bed. He slept badly, his mind buzzing with images and bad dreams. Dreams of the beating, the man he'd visited in the flat that day and most vividly, dreams of his father beating him up and throwing him out of the house.

Finally it was morning and Pete was glad to be out of bed and away from the nightmares. It was still very early, so he made himself a cup of coffee and sat out on the veranda to await Mo's arrival. He didn't have to wait long when an old, bright pink, Holden HK station wagon pulled up in front of the house. He guessed immediately it was Mo – the car and the voice on the phone matched perfectly! Grinning, he shook his head, thinking to himself that he was in for some adventure. He couldn't see her properly for the low hanging trees in the front yard until she arrived at the steps and then he stood up so she could see him.

"You Pete?" she asked loudly, walking up the steps.

"Uh…that's me," he answered, too stunned by her appearance to say anything else. Pete thought she looked about in her mid- twenties and, although not tall, a little taller than him. Her bright orange hair was pulled up on top of her head, tied together in a black scrunchie and sticking straight up and out several centimetres. Her face was rounded and full, with dark eyes and a pointy, little nose. She'd used the make-up heavily, especially the extra dark red lipstick, black mascara and eye liner. Countless gold and silver earrings adorned each ear from the lobes to the top and gold stud sat on the left side of her nose. A black and red choker made from large beads hung around her neck, and her wrists held several colourful bracelets. Each finger on both hands bore a ring on it and her finger nails were painted the colours of the rainbow. She wore a bright, multi-coloured tank top, which barely concealed her ample breasts, dark green baggy trousers and black hiking boots.

"So, what are you starin' at?" she demanded, when Pete remained speechless, mouth agape.

"N-nothing ....I.......do you want a coffee?" he offered, feeling foolish. "Sit down, Mo."

"No thanks," replied Mo, plonking onto a chair beside Pete, "that shit rotts ya brain. I can't stay long anyhow."

"Yeah, I know," agreed Pete, "but what doesn't these days?" He rolled a cigarette from some tobacco he'd almost forgotten was in one of his drawers.

"So! You wanna go to Perth?" she stated, more so than asked.

"Yeah," nodded Pete. "It's where I'm from and I haven't been back for a few years. Are you from there too?"

"Nah.......well, sort of," shrugged Mo. "When I was little, but I've still got some rellies over there and my cousin is gettin' married soon. That's why I'm goin', but I might decide to stay awhile."

"I'll give you some cash for the fuel," assured Pete, hoping he would have enough by then but wasn't all that optimistic. He suddenly pictured her turfing him out in the middle of the Nullabor Plain and throwing his meagre possessions out after him. Banishing the unpleasant thought quickly from his mind, he vowed he would get the money together no matter what!

"Well, I hope so!" declared Mo. "Petrol ain't cheap, but if worst comes to worst we might be able to pick up some work along the way or hustle a bit of pool. What are you like with a cue?"

"Not too bad," nodded Pete, wondering what he was getting himself in for. "So, where do you work, Mo?"

"The Frog's Leaf Café, over in Oxford Street. It's not that exciting but it's bread in the pocket each week."

Just then George walked out on to the veranda. "I thought I heard voices out…." He stopped suddenly when he laid eyes on Mo. "Hello, you must be Mo," he smiled, composing himself. "I'm George. My wife and I run this place." He extended his hand which she immediately shook without standing up.

"Hi there, George!" she responded loudly, which Pete was beginning to realise was her usual way of speaking.

"We'll be off in a few weeks," Pete told George, who nodded in return.

"So, Mark's here, is he?" questioned Mo.

"Yes," replied George reluctantly. "He doesn't want to see anyone yet, though."

"No worries. I'll keep it to myself," Mo said. "I really couldn't give a shit. It's nothin' to do with me."

"I'll leave you two to it and go and start breakfast," said George, turning to leave. Suddenly he stopped and turned back. "Do you want to stay for breakfast Mo?" he offered, "or a cuppa?"

"No thanks George, I have to get to work," she smiled back. "He's not a bad old dude," she said after he had gone inside.

"Him and Vera are tops!" declared Pete. "I'd probably be dead by now if it wasn't for them."

"Speaking of dead,'" she leaned closer to him. "Who jumped on your face in size twelve footy boots?"

Pete smiled at her choice of words. He admired her brashness and honesty and decided that they would get along fine. "Got beat up in an alley," he shrugged and laughed, then grimaced when his ribs hurt.

"Yeah sure, that's what they all say around here," laughed Mo, causing Pete to attempt a painful giggle.

They chatted several more minutes before Mo looked at her watch among the bracelets, jumped up and said she had to get to work. She hurried off, saying she'd come back to see him before it was time to leave. It was a very long trip to Perth and she was glad she would have someone to share it with.

Pete was pleased with he and Mo's meeting and no longer had any reservations about her. He was looking forward to the trip and decided there and then that he wouldn't let his family know beforehand that he was coming, rather waiting to see their reaction when he arrived. His only sister, Debbie, had written him an occasional letter but he rarely made the effort to reply so, consequently, her letters became fewer and further between.

Debbie was four years older than him and there were no other siblings. He hoped she would forgive him for being so slack. Seeing his mum again, was something he was really looking forward to but his father was a different story………

CHAPTER SIX

"Passengers, please fasten your seatbelts. We are now beginning our descent into Maroochydore airport. We will be landing in approximately twenty minutes," announced the flight attendant over the Public Address System of the plane on which Luke and Jo were returning to the Sunshine Coast.

"Nervous?" asked Luke, after he'd clipped up his belt and taken hold of Jo's hand.

"A bit, no actually a lot," replied Jo, turning to look out the window. She was as nervous as hell!

"You're not going to change your mind on me now, are you?" he frowned.

She turned back to him. "No, of course not," she said, affectionately squeezing his hand. "There is nothing I want more than to be with you." The bruises on her face, neck and chest were almost gone. It had been eight days since they left the Coast to complete the Queensland leg of Stonefish's tour. The last few shows had been very successful and Jo had soaked up the excitement of it all.

She and Luke had grown closer in that time, although they still only shared a platonic relationship. Jo knew that would soon change, though. The sexual chemistry was extremely strong and growing stronger. She appreciated Luke's patience in waiting for her bruises to heal, knowing it has not been easy. It was difficult enough trying to erase the memory of Jeff's vicious attack and certainly did not want to be reminded of him when she and Luke finally made love. That was going to be extra special and nothing would spoil it.

"I still think it would be best if you stayed at a motel and not my place," said Jo, worriedly. "He might kill you if he turns up and finds you there."

"I'm not scared of him, Jo," Luke asserted.

"Well maybe you SHOULD be!" she said. "He's a maniac. He's just as likely to turn up in the middle of the night and set fire to the place or something, if he knows I am there with someone."

Luke could see her concern and didn't want to add to her worries. "Okay," he nodded, "if it worries you THAT much I will book back into Twin Waters, BUT........only if you will stay with me."

"It's a deal," smiled Jo, relieved. At least that was one weight off her mind. Now all she had to do was tell her family, boss and flat mate that she was leaving to live in Perth with Luke. She knew it wasn't going to be easy and prayed that they could leave the Sunshine Coast without Jeff knowing. He couldn't do any harm to her once she was on the other side of the continent, she assured herself.

The plane touched down smoothly and they collected their bags from the carousel. Luke wore a floppy, black hat and sunnies, hoping not to be recognised. Several people, women especially, took a second glance, but it was not uncommon to spot celebrities at this airport. Noosa is a popular playground for the rich and famous.

Luke called the resort on his mobile and booked a room for him and Jo. They avoided the shuttle bus and grabbed a waiting taxi to take them straight to Twin Waters, not far from the airport.

The room was smaller than the one Luke had previously been in. They put their bags on the bed and Jo had a shower while Luke ordered a lunch of cold seafood and salad. She didn't have much of an appetite, her nerves saw to that, but it was delicious and she was able to force some down.

"Feel any better?" Luke asked, once they had finished eating.

"A little," answered Jo, unconvincingly.

"I wish I could do something to take your mind off it, Babe," Luke said softly, taking her in his arms and holding her close.

"You are," she sighed, resting her head on his shoulder.

"So," Luke spoke after a while, "who do you want to see first?"

"Graham again, I think. For some reason I am more nervous about telling him than anyone else. We'll go to my place and get my car."

Luke showered and changed while Jo called for a taxi to take them to Jo's flat. As she expected, Meg, who was a hairdresser, was at work, so the flat was empty. She'd rung Meg several times while she was away and had told her she would be back today. Jo had also asked about Jeff, and much to her relief, Meg had not seen or heard from him. She still had not told Meg who she was with yet. While at her place she rang Blazes Hotel and spoke briefly to Graham, telling him she was back and would be in shortly to see him. Jo couldn't help sensing that he knew what she was going to tell him.

After parking in the hotel car park, Jo and Luke walked hand in hand inside. She wasn't going to hide him anymore. Seeing a female bar attendant that she didn't recognise, Jo asked where Graham was and was told he was in the office. Jo took a deep breath and led Luke in that direction, hoping he would not be too upset with her or hostile toward Luke.

She knocked on the office door and Graham looked up from the desk. "Jo! Come in," he smiled, pleased to see her.

Jo walked into the office, closely followed by Luke, who was just a little bit nervous by now too as he was expecting a tongue lashing from Graham.

"Graham, this is Luke," Jo said apprehensively. "Luke, this is Graham, my boss." The two men shook hands and acknowledged each other politely.

"Graham, Luke is from Stonefish. I've been with him all week. I'm really sorry that I lied to you last week and ignored what you said to me the night of the concert, but you're wrong. Luke's NOT like that!" The words were coming out faster and faster. "Everything is true that I told you about Jeff, though. He DID do what I said he did! Luke's been fantastic and hasn't taken advantage of me. Hell, we haven't even had sex yet! I love him with all my heart and he's asked me to go and live in Perth with him and I said yes. I'm really sorry to be doing this to you, but we leave in a few days."

Luke felt proud of her, getting it all out in one go, but he had grimaced when she mentioned sex, or the lack of it. That was private.

Jo drew a deep breath and waited for Graham's response.

"I love Jo too, Graham and I WILL look after her," Luke stated, squeezing Jo's hand. They were still standing. Luke felt like he was asking a father's permission to marry his daughter. In a way he was, as Graham obviously thought so much of Jo.

"So, you've definitely made up your mind?" asked Graham, looking from one to the other. He knew this wasn't easy for Jo, but he could see the determination and, especially, the love in her eyes.

"Yes," answered Jo and Luke simultaneously. Jo was expecting a lecture. She nervously held her breath.

Graham smiled and shook his head a little. "Jo, I knew you went up north with Luke."

"You knew?" she frowned, stunned. "How?"

"I saw you go backstage after the concert," he answered, "and I must admit, I was NOT very happy, but I know how strong willed you can be and I felt the vibes earlier between the two of you, so it didn't surprise me. When you came in the next day to tell me you were going up north, it didn't take a genius to work it out."

Jo looked at Luke and back to Graham, shaking her head in amazement. All this time he knew!

"Jo was expecting you to get pretty angry, Graham," said Luke, sceptically. "So, how come you're not.......at me especially?"

"Because I was expecting it, although I was hoping it wouldn't come to this," replied Graham. "Jo's a level headed girl. I figured after a week she'd know what she wanted to do."

"I do," nodded Jo, firmly.

"I can see that," said Graham. "I hate the thought of losing my best worker and I am going to miss you, Jo. When are you leaving?"

Jo and Luke looked at each other. "In a couple of days," answered Luke. "I'm pretty anxious to get home after the tour and Jo wants to leave before her ex gets wind of it."

"Well, I suppose that's a good idea," agreed Graham. "Your bruises are nearly gone, Jo. I haven't seen his face around here. I'd better not either, or he'll be wearing it on the other side of his boof head!"

"Even that would be too good for him!" spat Luke.

"I don't want to think about him," said Jo, shaking her head. "We'd better go, Graham. There's still more people to see yet."

"Ok, well your pay was put in the other day and I will do up a reference for you. I am going to miss you, Girl," he said, standing up and giving Jo a hug. "Call in and say hooray before you leave, if you have time." He let go of her and stood back. "You'd better look after her, Luke," he advised. "You're getting a very special lady here. She's one in a million."

"Don't worry, I know how special she is," Luke replied, placing his left arm affectionately around Jo's waist and shaking Graham's hand with his right.

"I'll come in tomorrow or the next day and pick up the reference," said Jo as she and Luke walked out the door. She would have loved to find some of her work mates and tell them, but most of them knew Jeff and she just couldn't risk it.

They walked back to her car, laughing. Jo couldn't believe Graham took it so calmly. She felt as though a huge weight had just been lifted from her shoulders.

"Where to now?" asked Luke, as they got into Jo's car.

"Well, it's still a while until Meg gets home, so what would you say to a guided tour of the Sunshine Coast, Mr Summers?" suggested Jo.

"A splendid idea, Miss Slater," declared Luke, in an upper crust English accent.

They laughed as Jo started the car and drove out of the car park. The next couple of hours were spent driving around the area. Jo showed him her favourite beaches, night-clubs and her old schools and kept him amused with anecdotes from each. She decided to put off the visit to her family for a day or two, but she would ring them later to inform them she was home safe.

Late in the afternoon, they arrived back at Jo's flat, where she had decided to cook a special meal for Meg, Luke and herself. She'd stopped at a shop on the way to get the necessary ingredients. Meg wasn't home yet so Jo began preparing the dinner, with some help from Luke.

The apricot chicken was simmering deliciously in the pot, the home made garlic bread was heating in the oven and Jo was just putting the rice on to cook when she heard Meg's car drive in.

"Quick Luke, she's here! Go into my bedroom until I break it gently to her. If she walks in and sees Luke Summers standing in her kitchen she might keel over," ushered Jo, laughing and playfully pushing Luke toward her bedroom.

"Whatever you say," laughed Luke, shaking his head. "I might start howling or crowing like a rooster or something."

"Don't you dare," grinned Jo. She walked out of her room just as Meg walked in the front door.

"Jo! So good to see you back. I got such a nice surprise when I saw your car in a different spot, as I drove in."

"Hi Meg." The two friends embraced.

"Your face is nearly better," said Meg, stepping back and looking at Jo. "How do you feel?"

"I feel absolutely wonderful!" declared Jo. "Better than words can describe. Woops! The rice!" She raced to the stove and lifted the saucepan up as it began to boil over and turned the burner down to a low simmer. "I'm cooking tea - Apricot Chicken."

"Oh yum," said Meg. "I'm starved!" She went to her room and took her shoes off. "So, how was the holiday?" she asked Jo as she walked back to the kitchen.

"Sit down Meg, I have something to tell you," Jo said excitedly, as she poured a glass of wine each for Meg and herself.

Meg frowned and sat down. She noticed that Jo seemed to be bursting with excitement, especially when she kept pacing the kitchen floor.

"Remember I told you that I'd met a really gorgeous man?" Jo asked.

"Yes, I sure do. I've been wondering about that ever since," replied Meg. "You've been with him the past week haven't you?" Meg could see Jo's eyes sparkling with enthusiasm. Something good had happened for her and this made Meg happy.

Jo smiled and nodded. "I'm so sorry I couldn't tell you before I left. I didn't tell a single soul. I just couldn't risk Jeff finding out."

"So THAT'S the pricks name," thought Luke to himself, standing just inside Jo's door and listening to every word they were saying.

"Don't blame you," nodded Meg. "I understand. So where is this mystery man now? WHO is he?"

"Take a mouthful of your wine and brace yourself, Meg." Jo walked to her bedroom, took hold of Luke's hand and led him to the kitchen. "Meg, this is Luke Summers. He's the guit……"

"I know who Luke Summers is!" shrieked Meg. She jumped up and shook his hand. "Wow! It really IS you!"

"Yep. It really is me. Pleased to meet you, Meg," smiled Luke. "Jo has told me a lot about you."

Meg was stunned and couldn't do much more than laugh and shake her head. She was a huge fan of Stonefish too, but had missed the concert due to her boyfriend's birthday party. He was not such a great fan.

Jo turned the stove off under the rice and poured Luke a glass of wine. They sat around the table talking and laughing. Jo told Meg all about meeting Luke, the week up north and their plans to live together in Perth. Meg was sad to learn of her best friend leaving, especially going so far away, but she was excited for her and just a little bit envious.

They ate their dinner and washed the dishes. By this time Jo was tired so she and Luke decided to head back to the resort.

"You're not sleeping here?" Meg asked, disappointed.

"No, sorry" replied Jo. "I'm too scared of Jeff coming around and doing something crazy."

"I haven't seen hide nor hair of him since that horrible day," said Meg, shaking her head. "Hopefully you won't see him again."

"Yeah, hopefully," agreed Jo.

"When are you going to start packing?" enquired Meg.

"Maybe tomorrow," replied Jo. "You're welcome to keep my share of the household stuff and I might have to leave a bit of stuff at Mums and send for it later. I haven't told Mum and Dad yet." She screwed up her face in trepidation. "That's on the agenda for tomorrow."

"Good luck," Meg smiled and hugged Jo. "Will I see you tomorrow?"

"Yeah, we'll probably be here when you get home," said Jo. "See you then." Jo and Luke waved to Meg before getting into the car and heading back to Twin Waters resort.

It had been a long day and both were exhausted- flying back from Cairns in the morning, driving about that afternoon and chatting to Meg until quite late had tired them out. The rest of the band had stayed on in North Queensland to visit some of the Great Barrier Reef islands and unwind after the hectic tour. The luxurious bed welcomed them. Luke held her close, as he did every night. Even though he promised to wait until she was ready to make love, it was getting more difficult every night to hold and feel her body next to his. He wanted her so much. Jo sensed this and the feeling was definitely mutual.

"Tomorrow night," she whispered sleepily and kissed him lightly on the bare, tanned chest before falling asleep. Luke smiled and kissed her tenderly on the forehead.

The following morning Jo rang her parents and told them she would be down shortly to see them and would have a friend with her – a male friend.

They had known she'd broken up with Jeff, but hadn't expected her to find someone else so soon.

After breakfast and showers Jo and Luke drove to her parent's house at Moolooaba. She'd put a little make-up on what was left of the bruises. They were almost completely gone but she didn't want to risk her parents knowing about Jeff's attack. It would only worry them and her father had already had one mild heart attack.

She was nervous as they drove into the driveway as she was certain they would not be happy about her news. Her mother came out to greet her as soon as they pulled up. She was a tall, slim woman in her late forties with long, blonde hair tied back in a pony tail. It was slightly greying at the sides, and she had a tanned, lined face and blue eyes like Jo. It was clear they were mother and daughter.

"Jo, welcome home," she beamed happily and hugged her daughter warmly. "You look marvellous."

"Thanks Mum, you look pretty good yourself," smiled Jo. "Mum, this is Luke."

"Pleased to meet you Mrs Slater," Luke smiled and walked closer to shake her hand.

"Same!" greeted Jo's mother. "Please," she grimaced, "call me Liz. I feel too old otherwise."

They walked into the lowset brick veneer home, surrounded by well kept lawns and flower beds.

"Jo!" called her father happily, as he walked in the back door.

"Hi Dad," smiled Jo and gave him a big hug. He was also tall and slim with short brown hair and a greying moustache.

Luke sensed that the Slaters must spend a lot of time outdoors, especially when he noticed a large boat in the back yard.

"This is Luke, Dad," Jo said, placing her hand affectionately on Luke's back.

"Tom Slater!" stated Jo's father, extending his hand to Luke's. "How do you do, Luke?"

"Good..........thanks Tom," relied Luke, a little nervous as he shook Tom's hand. Suddenly it dawned on him that this time he really was seeking a father's approval. It was very important to him that Jo's parents accepted him and their decision to live together in Perth.

Luke was anxious to marry Jo, even though he had not spoken to her about it yet. He wanted the time and place to be absolutely perfect when he proposed.

Liz put the kettle on and cut some pieces of cake she had not long taken out of the oven.

Jo's mind was in turmoil. How was she going to break the news to them? Luckily, they didn't know that Luke was a member of one of the most famous rock bands in the country and in some other countries as well! She decided that the only thing to do was tell them everything from the beginning, including Jeff's attack. Well, maybe she might scale that down a bit. They had the right to know everything. She had always been close to her parents and had never held anything back form them before so why start now? They liked Jeff and to learn about what he did would shock and anger them, but she realised it would be worse if they found out later from someone else.

"Jo, what's wrong? You seem troubled, Sweetie," frowned her mother as the four of them sat down at the table.

"There's something I need to talk to you both about," said Jo, uneasily, as she poured herself a cup of tea from the freshly made pot before handing it to Luke.

"What's up, Love?" asked her father, concerned.

Jo took a deep breath, looked at Luke, back to her parents and began the story. She told them how she met Luke and who he actually was. They had heard of the band of course. Jo went on to tell them about their night on the beach and what happened at the flat the next day with Jeff. This appalled them, as she knew it would, so she didn't let on just how bad her injuries were. Continuing, Jo confessed that the trip up north was with Luke and not a work mate, as she had led them to believe. She apologised for lying but they understood once she explained that she could not risk Jeff finding out anything at all.

While Jo was telling her unsettling story, it was clear to Tom and Liz the amount of love and affection between Jo and Luke. The looks and touches, together with the words of encouragement and support showed a strong bond between them, like soul mates.

Then came the bombshell! Jo told them she was going to Perth with Luke to live. Trying to soften the blow, Luke quickly added that they would be getting married. The room remained silent for several moments while everything sunk in for Jo's parents.

"Well," said Tom, finally, "that's a pretty big decision you've made in a short amount of time. Are you absolutely sure it's what you really want? Perth is a long way from home."

"I know Dad and I am positive it's what I want. What WE want!" she added, taking hold of Luke's hand.

Luke assured them of his intentions to keep her happy and told them about his home at the beach.

Naturally, being a concerned mother, Liz had plenty of questions for Luke. Being a rock star, she was worried about the type of lifestyle he led and, more importantly, other women.

Luke was a bit embarrassed by some of the questions but handled it all well. Jo made sure to emphasise that they had not yet been intimate and Luke wasn't pushing her. That seemed to make Tom and Liz a little more relaxed.

They sat talking about the plans and Luke telling them about his family and childhood, for so long that it was lunch time before anyone had realised. No-one had touched the cake, either from nerves on Jo and Luke's part or shock on her parents. Gradually they were all able to relax more and laugh a lot while they chatted. Tom and Liz liked Luke and it became more obvious to them, as the morning wore on, that he adored their only daughter.

A lunch of chicken and salad sandwiches was enjoyed by all before Jo announced her and Luke were going for a swim. It was a glorious, sunny, spring day and she felt elated that all was going so well. Most importantly, she sensed that Luke had had enough of being under the spotlight and wanted to get him out of there. She knew he was too polite to instigate them leaving. They said goodbye to her parents, saying that they would be back tomorrow with some of her stuff from the flat. Liz suggested that they have a family barbecue the same night, to which Jo and Luke happily agreed and drove off.

"I think they like you," smiled Jo, as they drove toward North Shore beach, close to Twin Waters.

"Hope so," sighed Luke. "I wasn't too sure there for a while, though. Your mother certainly didn't leave too many stones unturned."

"Don't worry, she is only being a mother," reassured Jo, rubbing his thigh. "Imagine if your only daughter came and hit you with that news."

"I suppose it would be a bit of a spin out," grinned Luke, nodding.

"Do you mind if I just call into my place and pick up a few things?" she asked Luke.

"No," Luke shook his head. "Of course I don't mind."

Jo drove into her driveway and stopped the car. "I won't be long!" she stated, jumping out of the car and quickly walking inside. She was glad he waited in the car, as she had some surprises in store for him later. Coming back with an overnight bag, she started the car and drove off, relieved he didn't ask what was in the bag.

Arriving back at the resort, they changed into swimmers, grabbed towels, hats and sunscreen before heading over to the beach. Luke wore board shorts while Jo wore a pair of floral bikinis that he had not seen before. She'd worn several different pairs while up north but these stunned him. Luke thought she looked breathtaking in them and could hardly take his eyes off her as they walked along the track to the beach. There were about twenty or so other beach lovers about and they were pleased and surprised that there weren't more. They spread their towels alongside each other on the sand and rubbed lotion onto each other's backs.

"So, is there anyone else you have to see before we leave for Perth?" Luke asked casually as he rubbed the cream into Jo's shoulders.

"No," answered Jo, enjoying his touch. "Oh, there are a few friends I want to tell, but I'll catch up with them online once we get there and I'm settled in. The less that know, before we leave, the better."

"Do you still want to go back to your flat later, when Meg gets home?" enquired Luke.

"No, I've changed my mind, I left Meg a note telling her we'll see her tomorrow. Why?"

"Well, what do you say to a game of golf this afternoon, after our swim?" he suggested.

Jo laughed and turned to face him. "I can't play golf. I've never played in my life."

"Well, I'm no White Shark, but I can teach you. That is.......if you're game," challenged Luke.

"I'll try anything once," she shrugged, smiling. This was a perfect day and it would get even better. She was on top of the world. "Race you to the water, Luke!" Jo sprinted to the water with Luke in hot pursuit.

Luke tackled her in the waves and playfully dunked her. They laughed, splashed and frolicked in the water, occasionally embracing and kissing passionately. Other swimmers couldn't help noticing the young couple so obviously in love. Eventually, they left the water and walked hand in hand back to the towels, where they sat down and let the sun dry them naturally.

"Happy?" asked Luke, leaning over and kissing Jo on the cheek.

"Ecstatic," smiled Jo and kissed him on the lips.

Once they were dry, they decided to hit the golf course. It was a huge, attractive course, and was situated about half a kilometre away from the resort. After Jo had put on shorts and a shirt over her swimmers and some shoes, they drove to the clubhouse. Luke had kept his boardies on and just added a tee shirt and shoes.

They hired clubs, balls and tees then set off for the first hole. Just as Jo promised, she was hopeless. Even with Luke showing her how to hold the club and swing, she took countless swings to hit a ball and when she eventually would hit it, it usually went off in the wrong direction. She even managed to hit a kangaroo resting in the shade over near the side of the course!   A lot of laughs were enjoyed and they finally made it to the fourth hole as the sun was setting.

"I've had enough," groaned Jo, as yet another of her balls went haywire. "Golf is definitely NOT for me!"

"Fair enough," smiled Luke. He'd enjoyed the afternoon but was looking forward to the night even more.

The weary golfers packed and returned the gear that they had rented and drove back to the resort. Jo took her time showering and washing her hair. Luke ordered a special meal to be delivered to the room at a set time, complete with candles and wine.

Jo emerged from the bathroom in a low-cut, black, sleeveless dress. It hugged her tightly to the waist and dropped to a calf-length skirt. Her hair fell freely past her shoulders and she wore just a hint of make-up.

"Wow!" Luke sucked in his breath. "You look.......stunning." He walked toward her and was just about to put his arms around her waist when she pushed him away.

"Nuh, uh," she teased, shaking her head. "Not until you've had a shower."

He didn't need to be told twice! Grabbing some clothes from his suitcase, he sprinted to the shower.

Jo laughed as she watched him go. The love she felt for him was so powerful it almost frightened her. Never has she experienced such strong, intense emotions before. She mixed them both a drink of bourbon and dry, being careful not to make hers too strong as she didn't want any of her senses dulled tonight.

In less than ten minutes Luke was back out, wearing faded jeans and a white, knitted V-neck shirt. His hair was still damp and uncombed. Now it was her turn. She gave him a wolf whistle.

"You look stunning," she mimicked, handing him his drink. "Remember the last time we were here having a drink?"

"Yep" replied Luke. "You were pretty down then. Today's certainly a bit different."

"Mmm," agreed Jo. "I'll drink to that and lots more good days to come." They touched glasses and sipped their drinks.

"I've ordered our tea," said Luke. "It will be here in about half an hour."

"What is it?"

"Roast pork, crackle, apple sauce and roast vegies," answered Luke. "I remember you saying one day you loved it. I hope that's okay."

"Sounds perfect," replied Jo. "It's been a long time since lunch."

They chatted while enjoying their drinks. The knowing looks, without using the actual words made it clear this was going to be their night.

The dinner arrived and Jo was pleasantly surprised by the candles and wine. It was superb but Jo only ate and drank a little. Those old butterflies were back, but it wasn't nerves this time, just excitement building. After dinner and dessert of fresh strawberries and cream, Jo turned on the radio. Chris Isaak's "Wicked Game" was just beginning. She loved that song. It is very sensual with almost hypnotic guitar sounds. Jo reached out to Luke and he stood up placing his arms around her.

Slowly, they moved to the music, their two bodies becoming as one. With white-hot desire, Luke's eyes penetrated Jo's, stirring the very depths of her soul. He drank in her soft beauty for several seconds before slowly placing his lips on hers.

Her mouth opened slightly, welcoming him as she kissed his lips passionately. Jo's body tingled as all the nerve endings seemed to come alive at once and her breathing became louder as desire grew stronger. There was no stopping this now.

"I love you, Jo," Luke murmured between heavy breaths as he slowly and tenderly kissed her chin before moving down her neck.

"I love you too, Luke," she moaned softly into his hair.

Suddenly he picked her up, one arm under her shoulders, the other behind her knees and carried her to the bed. She placed her hands behind his neck and kissed him hungrily as he walked. He lowered her gently onto the bed and lay beside her, staring into her face. How he adored her. She was the most stunning woman he had ever known. Jo caressed his cheek and neck before reaching down to slowly lift his shirt over his shoulders and head. The candles on the table were the only light in the room and another slow song had begun. Once his shirt was off, Luke kissed her softly again and smiled reassuringly into her eyes. She smiled back as he began caressing her chest above the dress. "Hop up," he whispered tenderly, as he stood up beside the bed. She stood and faced him, trembling. Slowly, with his eyes never leaving hers, he reached around her back and undid the zip on her dress. Immediately, it fell to the floor. She stood before him in a white, lacy, strapless bra and high cut, white knickers. Against her tanned, taut body, Luke gasped at the breathtaking sight.

Jo reached for his jeans and slowly undid the button and zip, then slid them down to the floor so Luke could step out of them, leaving him in only a pair of brief, black jocks. Jo's eyes widened. Luke picked her up while kissing her deeply, and lay her back onto the bed. Jo rolled over, pushed him down and sat astride his waist. He leaned around and expertly undid her bra then dropped it down beside the bed. Her firm breasts became free and the nipples were already erect and hard, yearning for the impending touch. Luke cupped them in his hands as Jo leaned forward and kissed him voraciously. She kissed his neck, then down to his chest, sliding her body down his as she did so. Very soon she encountered his hardness with the very centre of her being, bringing the tingling to an intense throbbing as her heart rate skyrocketed. All this time spent so close together had brought the sexual tension to its peak. "I need you NOW, Luke!" she gasped, tearing his briefs down his legs and off his feet. She kissed him fervently on the mouth while he removed her lace pants.

He'd rather have taken more time with foreplay, but there'd be plenty of time for that later and he wanted her badly.

Jo straddled his hips and let out a low moan as he entered her. She was soaking wet and his hardness was no problem. Luke moved his hands from her hips to her back, bringing her down to him so their lips could meet briefly, but intensely, before she sat back up. His hands moved to her breasts as her head fell backwards allowing her blonde hair to cascade down her back. Moving up and down in perfect rhythm with his thrusts, she moaned louder as their movements became faster.

Two fingers of her right hand quickly honed in to where their bodies met, rubbing in small, hard circular motions. As her breaths became shorter, Jo suddenly pushed down extra hard on Luke, held her breath for several seconds then let out a loud moan of ecstasy as the air gushed from her lungs. She was on fire, full of exploding fireworks as the powerful orgasm washed over her in waves, shaking her body. Luke immediately followed suit, groaning as he reached his own powerful climax. Jo collapsed on his chest while she slowly regained her breathing. It was several minutes before either of them could speak.

"Wow," smiled Luke, as Jo slowly sat up. "That was incredible! Not that I was expecting anything less."

"Mmmmm, sure was," she replied dreamily, getting off his body and lying beside him. "My legs have gone to jelly."

He held her to his chest as she tenderly caressed his muscular stomach with her fingertips. Gradually her hand moved lower. He was stirring again, but this time HE would be in control. Kissing her, he rolled her over on to her back.

"You are so beautiful," he whispered, shaking his head before leaning down to her nipples. Taking one gently between his lips, he kissed it tenderly before slowly encircling it with his warm tongue. Jo's mews became moans as his teeth gently nibbled her engorged nipples. He moved further down her body, darting his tongue into her navel, which made her giggle and arch her back.

They made love well into the night before finally falling into an exhausted sleep entwined in each other's arms. Jo had never felt so loved and contented before. She had the most restful night's sleep she'd had in weeks.

Waking late the following morning, they made slow, passionate love again before showering and ordering brunch.

"Owwww," Jo groaned as she was getting dressed. "Why am I sooooo sore?"

"Well, we did have a pretty good work out last night," laughed Luke.

"Yeah, but it is mainly my right side, oh, hang on, I know - swinging that bloody golf club yesterday. Never again," she laughed.

After eating, they reluctantly left the room to return to Jo's flat for the dreaded job of packing. She rang her father to ask for some cardboard boxes she knew he kept stored in his shed.

Never know when they'll come in handy, he would say. He and Liz brought them around straight away and helped her pack.

Jo felt mixed emotions as she packed. She'd been happy here, but she certainly had no second thoughts regarding Luke, especially after last night. As the four of them worked she and Luke stole tender looks, winks and touches from each other, all the while Jo felt like she was walking on air.

After two hours all was done. She kept aside what she would take on the plane, packed securely in solid boxes what she wanted sent over, had a garbage bag full for the Op shop and left a few things for Meg. Jo would really miss Meg. They'd been friends since school and had co-shared for five years. She would make sure that Meg would come over to visit her and Luke. Jo left a note for Meg asking her to come to her parents place that night for a barbie. Her and Luke decided they would leave the next day.

After everything was put into cars, Jo's parents returned home while Jo and Luke dropped the large bag of clothes into a charity bin, then went to Blazes so she could collect the reference and say goodbye to Graham. She hated goodbyes and was secretly hoping, just for ONCE, Graham wasn't there. To her relief, he was off that day and the assistant manager gave her the envelope. Jo planned to e-mail Graham once she was settled and let him know how she was doing. Luke had told her she wouldn't need to work, but she wanted a reference just in case.

They drove past a travel agent so decided to stop and pick up plane tickets, rather than going online. There was no problem with getting two for the following day, but there was a quick touch down in Sydney and a half hour stop in Adelaide.

This pleased Luke as his sister, Casey, lived in Adelaide. He rang her immediately to tell her what time the plane was landing and asked if she would be able to meet them. Disappointingly, he only got her answering service, so he just had to hope she could make it, or maybe ring him back in the meantime. He knew she had a demanding job as a nurse and occasionally worked double shifts.

By late afternoon they arrived at Jo's parent's house for the farewell barbeque. Luke wrote his address on the boxes to be sent over to Perth. Jo's brother's soon turned up followed by Meg and her boyfriend, Darcy. Jo was pleased when Meg told her he would be moving into the flat with Meg, as she had felt bad about leaving so suddenly. Chris and Jon, Jo's brothers, were suitably impressed meeting Luke. Chris was a budding guitarist and both were fans of Stonefish so they had lots to chat to him about.

Unfortunately, due to work and other commitments, nobody could see them off at the airport the next day. Jo's mother offered to cancel her medical appointment but Jo insisted she didn't. She much preferred not to have anyone there anyway, as she would only cry. With just Luke by her side, she only had to see and think about her wonderful future, not be sad for what and who she was leaving behind.

It was getting late and the plane was leaving at 8.30 the next morning, so Jo said a teary farewell to her beloved family and best friend. Luke got plenty of stern, but friendly, warnings about looking after Jo. She left her car there for her mother to drive and they called a taxi back to the resort.

Once inside their room, the realisation of everything suddenly hit her and she burst into tears.

"Hey Jo, what's wrong?" Luke asked, comforting her in his arms.

"Oh, nothing," replied Jo, wiping her eyes and feeling silly. "I guess I'm just a bit overwhelmed by it all." Suddenly she brightened up. "Let's have a shower together," she suggested with a smile and led him toward the bathroom.

The shower was a long one and so was their love making session when they finally did make it to the bed. They just could not get enough of each other.

The next morning, they awoke at dawn. Jo wanted one last swim in the Pacific Ocean before they left the east coast. Just as they were about to open the door to go out, Luke noticed an envelope with Jo's name on it had been slid under the door. He picked it up and handed it to her.

"What is it?" she asked with a frown. Luke shrugged. Quickly, Jo tore it open.

"YOU CAN'T RUN AWAY FROM ME" Jo turned white and handed it to Luke.

"The bastard!" he fumed. "Why the hell can't he leave you alone?"

"I don't think we should go over to the beach," said Jo, nervously. "Let's just stay here until it's time to go."

They arrived at the airport at 7.45 AM. Jo anxiously looked about as they unloaded the suitcases and bags from the taxi boot. Even though she could not see him, she felt sure Jeff was watching her. Her stomach churned with fear and confusion. How did he find them? What was he planning? At worst, would he get on the same plane as them?

After checking in at the desk and labelling their luggage they went into the passenger lounge to await their boarding call.

"Do you want something to eat or drink?" Luke asked, standing up.

"No thanks," stated Jo, shaking her head. Food was definitely the last thing on her mind.

Luke walked over to the cafeteria to get himself a drink.

Suddenly, Jo saw him, watching her through the glass walls from outside the building. He was wearing a suit. He NEVER wore a suit! What was happening? She gasped in fear and looked over at Luke. He was standing in the queue at the food counter. Slowly, Jeff walked toward the entrance of the terminal, still watching Jo through the glass. He had sunglasses on but she could feel his cold, calculating eyes cutting into her. She glanced back toward Luke, her fear rising, and took a deep breath. *There are plenty of people around*, she consoled herself, *he won't try anything.* Jeff came through the glass doors. Jo began to panic and looked for Luke. He was just ordering a bottle of juice. Jeff walked directly toward the passenger lounge and Jo. She stood up and screamed as two security guards rushed over.

Luke heard the scream and turned. He saw how frightened Jo was, dropped the bottle of juice and frantically pushed his way through the other waiting customers before sprinting over. Slowly, Jeff took out a pistol from his coat pocket. Luke reached Jo and tackled her to the floor as other passengers screamed and panicked. A single shot echoed through the building just as the two guards reached Jeff. Luke's body covered Jo's as chaos reigned around them. Men were shouting, women and children were crying and scrambling to take over.

Jo was frozen to the spot from fear and the weight of Luke on her. She dared not breathe in case Jeff saw her move, but very soon all was quiet except for some frightened whimpering coming from people trying to hide or lying low about them and sirens wailing in the distance.

"Luke," she sobbed quietly. "Please be okay." His body was still.

"IT'S OK EVERYONE" a man's voice shouted. "The danger is over. You can stand up and sit back in your seats."

Slowly, much to Jo's relief, Luke moved, got off her and held her in his arms as they both sobbed.

"I thought he shot you," she cried, the tears now more from relief than fear.

"I think he shot himself!" gasped Luke, his heart beating rapidly. Shuddering at the thought of Jo being shot he hugged her tightly to him.

Jo looked over to where Jeff had been standing and saw him lying on the floor, his chest soaked with blood. He wasn't moving and Jo sensed he was dead. Another security guard rushed over with a blanket and covered the body, then ordered everyone to remain calm and stating that it was over. Luke helped Jo to a chair and held her while she sobbed, her body trembling with shock. How had he found them, she wondered. Why did he do this? The police turned up and began asking questions. Fortunately, it wasn't blatantly obvious that he had singled out Jo. There were dozens of people in the lounge, many more wondering around the little shops and eateries in the airport and he had not uttered a single word. The boarding call came over the speakers and Jo stood up to leave.

"Just a moment, Miss," said a policeman to Jo, as she was about to head toward the gate. "Did you know this man?"

Jo looked about the room and noticed several police officers asking the same question to other people. "No," she answered quietly, looking down. Her knees were shaking and nearly buckling beneath her. "I've never seen him before in my life."

Taking hold of Luke's hand, together they walked across the tarmac to their waiting plane. She never looked back.

CHAPTER SEVEN

Jo was silent through the planes take off. She had the window seat and sat, in a daze, staring out the window. After some time, she finally spoke.

Luke was relieved to hear her voice as he had been worried sick as to what the previous events' impact would be on her.

"I just wish I knew how he found us and how he knew what time the plane was leaving," said Jo, shaking her head. "Meg and my family were the only ones who knew and they wouldn't have told him." Suddenly she turned to Luke in fear. "What if he threatened Meg to make her tell him, or what if he did hurt her? I wouldn't put it past him." She was frantic. "I'll ring Meg!" She found her mobile in her bag and punched Meg's number on the speed dial. "Oh NO!" she cried angrily. "No reception up here. Shit!" Angrily, she threw the phone back into her bag. "As soon as I get off this plane I am going to ring her and Mum and make sure they're all right."

"That's a good idea," agreed Luke, "but I'm sure they will be." He wasn't so sure though. He was as stunned by all this as Jo was.

"HOW did he get to our room?" she frowned. "Who did he really plan to shoot? Where did he get the gun? I never knew him to own one." She shuddered, remembering the airport scene. "Luke, do you think I broke the law by saying I didn't know him? Surely the police will find out."

"I don't know.......probably," sighed Luke. "But it doesn't make any difference now. He's dead and nobody else got hurt, that's the main thing. When I heard you scream and realised it must have been him coming in I just freaked. I just had to get to you as fast as I could. If he would have hurt you Jo, I would have killed him there and then." He put his arm around her protectively and brought her closer to him.

"When I heard the gun go off as you fell on me, I thought....." she began to sob. "I would hate it if anything ever happened to you, Luke."

"Well, nothing's ever going to happen to me," he smiled reassuringly, kissing her on the cheek. "You're stuck with me now, whether you like it or not."

"Oh, I like it." She smiled for the first time since boarding the plane.

Luke tried to get Jo's mind off Jeff by talking about their future together in Perth, telling her about the places he would take her and how beautiful the beaches are. He talked about his family's holiday home several hundred kilometres down the coast at Margaret River and how good the surf was there. He promised to take her down there soon and while they were there, let her sample the abundant seafood and wines from the area. She started to cheer up a little. He also promised to take her shopping in the city the next day. Anything her heart desired, she could have. Luke could certainly afford it and he loved to see her smile. She NEEDED to smile!

In no time the plane was touching down in Sydney. Jo couldn't believe how fast that time went. They had to change planes and as soon as she was in the terminal she tried Meg again on her work number. This time she got through and was glad it was Meg who answered.

"Meg, it's me, Jo!" she said quickly.

"Jo! Where are you?" Meg asked, surprised.

"At Sydney airport. I haven't got long. Have you seen or heard anything of Jeff since last night?"

"No, nothing," Meg answered. "Why?"

"Just wondering....... I have to go. I'll call you tomorrow sometime. Bye!" Jo ran to Luke waiting at the door leading them to the next plane. They were the last ones to board.

"Well?" asked Luke anxiously, once they'd reached their seats. "What did Meg say?"

"She hasn't seen him," frowned Jo, puzzled. "I'll ring Mum when we get to Adelaide. But I'm sure that if he hadn't hassled Meg then he wouldn't go near Mum and Dad. Then again........"

The plane took off down the runway and soon they were leaving Sydney far behind. Jo was still in a state of shock. She was desperate to contact her mother and constantly checked her watch. This leg of the journey was slightly longer than the previous one to Sydney. Answers were desperately needed, but she dreaded what they might be.

Jeff was dead! Shaking her head to herself, she tried to make it sink in. So far it just all seemed like a bad dream. Sure, she loved him once, but any positive feeling she had left for him were destroyed the day he assaulted her at the flat. She remembered the vicious look in his eyes that day, the force with which he hit her and the threats he made against her. It made her feel sick in the stomach. Then she relived the airport scene. Watching him coming toward her, hearing the gun shot and seeing him lying, bloodied, on the floor. It all became too much for Jo. She grabbed the vomit bag and threw up violently into it, her body wracked by convulsions. Tears streamed down her face as she continued dry retching into the bag. She vaguely heard Luke ask the attendant to bring Jo a glass of water and felt his arm go around her shoulders as she leaned forward.

The attendant returned with the water and took the bag away. Jo sipped the water and, feeling embarrassed, excused herself before heading to the toilet to wash her face. She looked in the mirror and didn't like what she saw. Her eyes were red and her face pale, almost white. She slumped down onto the toilet seat and took several deep breaths. Just as she was beginning to feel a little better, the plane suddenly began shaking. A cold shiver of fear ran up her spine and spread out to her extremities. She felt like fainting but stood up, turned around and dry retched into the toilet bowl. Dizziness took over as her head began to throb. "Oh, God," she moaned to herself and leaned against the wall as the shaking subsided. Her mouth tasted dry and bitter while her heart continued racing from the fear caused by the turbulence.

After several minutes her breathing became calmer and her heart slowed a little. She was washing her face one more time when there was a knock at the door.

"Jo, are you okay?" Luke called softly through the closed door, his voice tinged with worry.

"Yeah," answered Jo after looking at her pallid face in the mirror. "I'll be out soon."

Jo took several deep breaths and slowly opened the door to see Luke standing right there. She practically fell into his arms. All her strength seemed to disappear as Luke helped her back to their seats.

"I'm sorry, Luke," said Jo once they were seated. "You must think I'm a bit of a woose." She attempted a slight smile.

"Of course I don't," consoled Luke. "Considering what you've been through, I actually think you're pretty TOUGH." The way he emphasised the word "tough" at the end of the sentence made Jo smile again. "Now THAT'S what I like to see," smiled Luke as he hugged her close to him. "We're nearly to Adelaide. I can't wait for you to meet Casey. I just hope she's there when we get off the plane. You'll like her Jo."

"Well, if she's anything like her brother I will," nodded Jo. "What did you say she did?"

"She's a nurse, so she works some odd hours," replied Luke.

"You're a fine one to talk about odd hours," teased Jo. She was beginning to feel much better now. The sick feeling had eased considerably and she was managing to take her mind of Jeff a little. "When was the last time you worked nine to five?"

"Oh, a few years ago now," mused Luke. "Back when I was a sparky."

"A WHAT?" frowned Jo, laughing.

"A sparky.......an electrician," replied Luke.

"Oh yeah, I know," smiled Jo. "You never told me that before."

"Well, it was a while ago," said Luke, "but I had to do something to pay the bills while we plodded along playing in the smoky bars waiting for our break to come."

"So, how did Stonefish get their big break?" enquired Jo. "Come to think of it, how did Stonefish get their name?"

"About ten years ago we decided to try our luck on the East Coast," began Luke, pleased to see Jo keen to talk and think about something else, "and we were invited to play at a big outdoor festival near Sydney. A producer happened to be on a talent scout and got talking to our manager. Before we knew what hit us, we were in a studio recording our first album. Tell you what Jo, when our manager gave us the news we were rapt!"

"Do you still get as excited by it all now?" Jo asked, even though she could see by the way his eyes lit up that Luke enjoyed talking about his music.

"Sure do! It's a lot of fun, but the tours can get a bit tiring. I'm always glad to be home after a long one. Recording can be a bit boring at times, though," said Luke.

"Oh," replied Jo, surprised. "Why's that?"

"Sometimes you have to go over and over the same song for hours, or even days before it's just right."

"But I thought with all the modern technology and wizardry it would be pretty much cut and dry," frowned Jo.

"There is some amazing gear in a recording studio. You'll see it all when we record again. One day I might get into that side of the business, but in the end it's up to the musicians to get it right," said Luke. "Now, back to your first question about our name. If you promise not to laugh, Jo, I'll tell you what we were originally called when we started out in the pubs in Perth."

"What?" enthused Jo.

"Promise you won't laugh," ordered Luke.

"Scouts honour!" declared Jo, holding her fingers up, although she had a feeling she would.

"Ollie Prattle and the Farouts," whispered Luke in her ear.

Jo threw her head back and laughed loudly. "What!" she giggled. "Are you dinky-di?" She felt truly happy for the first time that day.

"Yep," laughed Luke. "Fair dinkum."

"How on earth did you.....?" Jo shook her head.

"What? Get that name?" He continued when he saw Jo nod and smile. "Well our first drummer was called Oliver Pratt and he was always saying 'Far out, man', so I guess that made us the Farouts," grinned Luke at the memory. "He was one of as kind, Old Ollie. The name just stuck with us, but when he left we had to change it of course. Around that time I was stung by a stonefish and the guys gave me heaps so that name just sort of stuck with us too."

Jo sucked in her breath. "I bet that hurt," she grimaced.

"Mmm," nodded Luke, rolling his eyes at the memory. "Speaking of names, what's Jo short for? Jodie? Joanne?"

"Actually, if you really must know, it's Josephine," said Jo, holding her breath while waiting for Luke's reaction.

"So, what's wrong with that?" teased Luke, sensing Jo's dislike for her full name. "Did I tell you my second name is Napoleon?" He kept a straight face.

Jo laughed and playfully attempted to strangle him. This naturally lead to a kiss which became more passionate.

"Excuse me," said a female voice. Jo and Luke let go of each other and looked up. It was the female flight attendant who'd taken the bag from Jo earlier. Jo felt her face blush red and looked down. Luke just smiled. "I take it you're feeling better now?"

Jo looked back up at her. "Yes thanks, much better."

"Can I get you anything before we descend into Adelaide airport?" she enquired with a smile and a wink.

Jo wasn't sure who the wink was directed at. "I think I could handle some juice right now," replied Jo.

"Me too," added Luke. "Thanks."

They both watched her walk along the aisle to get their drinks off the trolley still a few rows back.

"I saw her wink at you," teased Jo, digging him softly in the ribs.

"Actually, I think she has her eye on you," responded Luke in a whisper. "Here she comes."

The attendant handed them their drinks just as the announcement was made to buckle up for the descent into Adelaide airport.

They had half an hour to kill at the airport before reboarding for the final leg of the journey to Perth. Once inside the terminal, Luke immediately looked about for Casey, but was very disappointed when he couldn't see her anywhere.

"Oh well," consoled Jo, placing her arm about his waist, "I'm sure she would have been here if she could."

"Yeah," sighed Luke. "I suppose so." He didn't even notice people, especially women, pointing at him and whispering. Several came up to him and asked for autographs and photos with them. He half-heartedly obliged them, but really didn't feel up to it. After the small crowd dispersed he suggested to Jo they go for a walk around outside the terminal. Suddenly, two hands were covering his eyes.

"Guess who?" beamed an excited female voice.

Luke spun around to find Casey standing there with a smile from ear to ear.

"Case!" he exclaimed, swooping her into his arms and swinging her around.

It was obvious to Jo they were very close. He always spoke of her with a lot of affection.

"I thought you weren't coming! We looked everywhere!" said Luke, excitedly, when he let her go. "Casey, this is Jo. She's coming home with me." Luke placed his arm affectionately around Jo's waist. "Jo, this is Casey."

The two girls exchanged a greeting. Jo liked Casey immediately. She was very similar to Luke in looks – tall, brown wavy hair, brown eyes and very pretty.

"Mum told me you'd rung her from North Queensland and said you'd met someone special," said Casey. "I'm really happy for both of you."

The three of them found a relatively quiet spot to sit and chat. Luke and Casey had a chance to catch up and the girls got to know each other a little. In no time, they heard their boarding call so the siblings hugged goodbye.

"Give Mum and Dad and Kelly a hug for me," smiled Casey, "and give David a punch in the arm."

"I will," laughed Luke, giving her one last quick hug. He hadn't realised how much he missed his family.

Casey gave Jo a quick hug before she turned to leave.

"Hey Case!" said Luke, "you'll be coming home for a wedding soon."

She smiled and gave him the thumbs up signal before walking out the terminal. Jo and Luke quickly boarded their plane.

"How come we're always the last ones on?" frowned Luke.

Jo laughed and shrugged as they sat in their seats. Suddenly, the colour drained from her face and she looked at Luke in horror. "I forgot to ring Mum!" she gasped, placing her hand over her mouth. She had put Jeff completely out of her mind for the past hour or so. "I can't believe I forgot, Luke! You did such a good job keeping my mind off things then we looked for Casey….." She was almost frantic with worry as the plane began to roll down the runway.

"I'm sorry Jo, I was so wrapped up seeing Casey that I completely forgot about it too," consoled Luke, taking hold of her hand. "I'm sure your Mum and Dad are okay."

"I hope so," sighed Jo, staring out the window.

The three hour flight between Adelaide and Perth seemed to take forever for Jo. She was anxious to speak to her mother and, as much as Luke tried, he couldn't even raise a smile from her. He comforted her as best he could, feeling a little guilty that he had forgot about the situation for a while. Jo refused food that was brought around and, fortunately, she didn't get sick again.

Finally the plane touched down in Perth and Jo couldn't get off quickly enough. She raced into the terminal and called her mother. It rang several times before Liz answered.

"Mum! It's me," cried Jo into the phone, so relieved to finally hear her mother's voice.

"Jo!" exclaimed her mother. "Are you in Perth?   WHAT'S WRONG? You sound upset."

The nervous tension and anxiety had built up so much on the trip that Jo couldn't keep her emotions in any longer. She burst into tears.

"Jo Honey, what's wrong?" her mother shouted frantically into the phone.

Jo's crying had eased to sobs just as Luke caught up with her. He had seen her crying and assumed the worst. Finally Jo was able to continue speaking to her mother.

"Have you seen or heard from Jeff since last night?" asked Jo, pulling herself together.

"No," replied Liz. "Why? Sweetie, you're thousands of miles away from him now. Please, just try to forget about him. He can't hurt you over there."

Jo sensed her mother did not know about the shooting so told her everything as it happened, beginning with finding the note under their door and ending with her telling the police she did not know him. Her mother had not heard any news so far that day and was shocked, but glad that she and Luke were okay. She couldn't understand how Jeff could have found them either. They came to the conclusion together that he must have hired a private detective to follow and spy on them. Liz told Jo she would try and find out as much about it as possible, reassuring her that she would keep her name out of it.

"Thanks Mum," sighed Jo. "I'll ring you tomorrow. I love you."

"Love you too, Honey," replied her mother affectionately. "Take care. Bye."

Jo slowly hung up her phone and turned to Luke. "She didn't know anything about it and didn't think Dad or the boys did either, but she's going to try and find out what she can and I'll call her tomorrow."

"Good idea," nodded Luke. "Let's get our gear and go home." He took hold of Jo's hand and led her toward the luggage carousel. They picked up their bags and were just about to walk out the door to find a waiting taxi when Luke heard a familiar voice call his name. He turned in the direction of the voice and saw his mother coming toward them.

"Mum!" he exclaimed, dropping his suitcases. "This is a surprise. How did you know what time the plane was getting in?"

"Casey rang me last night," answered his mother, giving her son a big hug.

"Mum, this is Jo," said Luke proudly, placing his hand on Jo's back.

"Hello Jo," smiled his mother warmly, shaking Jo's hand. "Luke's told me a lot about you. I feel like I know you already. You're every bit as pretty as he said."

"Pleased to meet you, Mrs Summers," said Jo blushing.

Luke looked at Jo, rolled his eyes and smiled. He loved his mother dearly, but she could embarrass him at times.

Despite feeling just a little uncomfortable, Jo couldn't help liking Luke's Mum. Being not a real tall woman, only coming up to Luke's chin. She was slim with short, wavy, greying hair and a friendly, soft face, she was smartly dressed in a floral skirt, white dressy top, high heels and just a little make-up. She carried the two smaller bags while Luke and Jo carried the larger ones out to her car. It was a rather warm day for October and the different type of heat hit Jo as soon as she walked out into the open air. It was a drier heat, not the sticky, humid type she was used to in Queensland.

As they drove through Perth, in the general direction of Luke's house, Rose wanted to know all about the tour, but Luke was more interested in showing off landmarks to Jo as they passed them. His mother was persistent, so finally he decided to tell her all she wanted to know, realising there would be plenty of time to show Jo around later.

Jo was impressed with the Swan River and the City, but she was really looking forward to seeing the beaches after Luke telling her countless times how beautiful they were. Finally they arrived at the coast and headed northwards through Scarborough, Trigg and Sorrento Beaches.

"Wow!" gasped Jo, as she saw the pristine aqua water and the glistening white sand. "It certainly IS beautiful!"

"Thought you might like it," grinned Luke, turning to her from the front seat.

Jo couldn't take her eyes off the beaches as they drove on for almost an hour. The car then stopped behind a high, white stone fence and large wooden gate. It was on a slight rise, overlooking the Indian Ocean. Opposite, there was nothing but sand dunes and vegetation between the road and the beach. Luke opened the gate with the remote control he carried on his key ring.

His house was large, highset and almost Spanish style, with red and black trimmings against a white background. The yard was huge, containing several shady trees and it didn't surprise Jo to see it devoid of garden beds. She couldn't picture Luke spending time growing flowers. Both top and bottom floors had verandas right around them. To the left of the house was a tennis court and to the right was the entertainment area with barbecue and pool.

"What do you think?" asked Luke, after he had unloaded the car while his mother unlocked the front door. She had a key to come over and check on things while he was away. Unbeknown to Luke, she'd spent the morning doing some spring cleaning and shopping to stock up his fridge.

"I love it," gushed Jo, as she walked up to Luke, hugged and kissed him. "And I love you!"

"Let's go inside," smiled Luke eagerly, picking up two suitcases and heading for the large, carved front door.

As Jo walked through the main entrance she was taken aback. To her left was a door leading into the two car garage, which also contained Luke's home gym, and in front of her was a polished pine staircase. A wide hallway led past the staircase and out into, what she assumed was, the laundry and back door. On her right was a large arched doorway that led into a spacious entertainment room. Jo put her bags down and looked in. A pool table stood up the end of the room closest to her, a dartboard on one wall, a well- equipped and well stocked bar took up most of the far end of the room with several smaller tables and chairs in the area between the pool table and bar. Numerous gold and platinum albums and awards adorned the walls as well as framed photos of the band live on stage. What really took Jo's breath away was a large black and white print, mounted on wood, of Luke on his Harley Davidson. Leathers, sunnies, boots and no helmet, it sent her heart into a flutter.

The entry area where Jo stood was decorated with Asian and South Pacific wall hangings and artefacts. A huge, healthy fern hung on either side of the main door. Luke had taken the suitcases upstairs and was now back by Jo's side.

"This is great!" enthused Jo. "I love that picture." She pointed to the one of him on the bike. "When was it taken?"

"About two years ago," replied Luke. "My brother, David, is an amateur photographer. He took some of these other pictures too. You'll meet him soon."

Just then Luke's mother came back downstairs. "I'll be off now and let you two settle in. Your father is looking forward to seeing you Luke, and to meeting you Jo, so don't leave it too long before you come over."

"No Mum," replied Luke, feeling like a little boy again. He smiled and winked at Jo. "We'll come over tomorrow."

"Ok Love, see you both then," smiled his Mum, kissing the two of them before walking out the door to her car.

"Thanks for driving us home," Luke called after her. She nodded and waved as she started her car.

"I thought she'd NEVER leave!" laughed Luke, before he beckoned Jo up the steps before him as he carried up the last of their luggage.

Jo was just as impressed with the upstairs as she was with the bottom floor. Firstly there was a huge lounge with a cosy fireplace in one corner, a roomy kitchen and dining area with solid pine table, chairs, cupboards and bench tops. Exposed pine beams were along the whole ceiling, while numerous pictures of waves, oceans, dolphins and whales adorned the walls. There were four large bedrooms with the main one containing a spa in the ensuite. Several large pot plants were dotted about the large, airy house. Lots of windows and several sliding, glass doors leading out onto the verandas, both up and down stairs were conducive to the views and ocean breezes.

Luke opened the fridge searching for some cold water. "Wow, come here Jo," he called. Jo ran from the bathroom to where Luke was standing in front of the open fridge. She looked in and stared in amazement at all the food, including fresh fruit and vegetables. There was even some beer. "Isn't she a gem?" smiled Luke, shaking his head. "I didn't know she had done this. I knew she would have come over and vacuumed and stuff, even though I told her not to. Usually, when I get home from a tour she cooks a meal and brings it over. I think she really likes you. Hungry?"

"Actually," replied Jo, "I'm starved!" She remembered that she'd brought up her breakfast on the plane and hadn't been able to eat anything since. It was now afternoon.

They made delicious ham and salad sandwiches to eat out on the veranda.

"That's David and Kelly's house," said Luke between mouthfuls, pointing to a large house on the block next door. It wasn't quite as elaborate as Luke's, being a more modest, single storey brick veneer. "His wine cellar, down below, is nearly half the size of the house! I don't think he is into it as much these days though, seems to just prefer a beer or three now."

"When you said that your brother and his girlfriend lived next door, I didn't realise you literally meant 'next door'," said Jo. "You must be close."

"Well……yeah, we get on all right….. now. We haven't always though," replied Luke.

Jo looked puzzled, which encouraged Luke to continue. "When we were younger, we had a few run-ins. It even came to blows sometimes."

"Why?" asked Jo, shaking her head. It was hard for her to imagine Luke fighting with anyone, let alone his own brother.

"I don't know. He used to seem jealous or something, especially when we got our first recording contract. He played in another band but they broke up. He never really did tell me why he would get so pissed off, but he sure can be moody at times," said Luke, frowning at the memories, then his face lit up. "But he seems to be over it now. Whatever the problem was, the last five years or so we've gotten along okay."

"Well, that's good," smiled Jo. "You know, I'd really love a shower after this."

"Mmm, me too," nodded Luke with a twinkle in his eye.

They finished off their food, put the plates in the sink and had a glass of juice each from the fridge before heading to the ensuite shower. His mother had put out fresh towels and clean sheets on the bed.

Slowly, they undressed each other of their jeans, shirt and underwear. Their hands explored each other's bodies as they stepped into the shower. Luke turned the water on warm before he gently placed his hands on the back of Jo's neck and kissed her passionately as the water cascaded down over them. Jo's hands moved up and down his smooth back before coming to rest on his firm buttocks. She pulled him closer until their bodies touched. Luke rose proud and firm to the occasion. He reached for the soap and began to lather Jo's body, paying extra attention to her breasts. She moaned as his fingers lightly brushed her nipples. Her hand moved around to grip his hardness and she began to move her hands up and down in a rhythmic motion.

The tingling in her loins was getting stronger as Luke's hand moved down over her stomach and through her silky hair. His tongue danced lightly over one nipple and she cried out when his fingers found their yearning target. She groaned and squeezed him tighter as his fingers knew exactly how and where to touch her. Suddenly, she let him go and grabbed his moving hand, pushing it harder to her as her back arched and a loud moan escaped her lips. She shuddered and slumped against him for several seconds before her hands moved up around his neck. He lifted her up slightly, spreading her thighs. She knew what was coming and eagerly wrapped her shaky legs around his hips as she slid onto him with a contented sigh. Their lips met hungrily as their bodies thrust together. Luke's breathing became harder and faster until suddenly, he held her onto him as hard as he could and expelled a loud moan. His knees almost collapsed under him, forcing him to lean back against the cubicle wall for support.

They remained like that for a minute or so until their breathing returned to normal. Each with their face buried in the other's shoulder. Slowly, Jo dropped her legs and stood up.

"That was incredible....as usual," sighed Jo, kissing him lightly on the lips and chest.

"YOU'RE incredible," smiled Luke, touching her breasts again. "Let's get out and move to the bed. I'm not through with your gorgeous body yet."

Jo smiled, knowing what was in store for her. Luke had an extremely talented tongue and he loved to explore every part of her body with it. They quickly dried off before he carried her to the bad and gently placed her down on her back.

"Welcome home, Jo," he whispered tenderly, before kissing her softly on the lips and moving slowly down her body. They never moved off the bed for the next two hours.

As they lay there basking in the afterglow of the sensual love making and chatting idly, the doorbell rang.

"Probably David and Kelly," stated Luke, knowing nobody else except family could get into the yard. He jumped up, put on a pair of boardies and headed out of the bedroom to answer the door.

Jo watched his tall, fit and tanned body disappear out of the room and wondered how she ever got so lucky. She got up and dressed in a colourful sarong. By the time she walked out of the bedroom, Luke was already back upstairs.

"Jo, this is David and Kelly," said Luke as he handed them both a stubby of beer. "Guys, this is Jo."

"It's really good to meet you both," smiled Jo, shaking both their hands in turn. She couldn't help noticing that David seemed to grip hers harder and longer than necessary and he gazed at her intensely. Although he was taller and bigger than Luke they were very similar in looks – tall, dark and good looking. His hair was shorter than Luke's and he had a more serious, reserved look about him. Jo decided that the three must take after their father as there wasn't much resemblance to their mother.

Kelly was about Jo's height, quite slim with long, straight, dark hair. She wore large beaded earrings, beads and shells around her neck and with her floral, cheesecloth dress and sandals she looked like a sixties flower child. Her skin was very fair and her lips were full. Jo could sense she had a happy nature.

"Do you want a beer, Darl?" Luke asked, standing by the open fridge.

"Yes please," nodded Jo enthusiastically.

Luke got two more beers out of the fridge for him and Jo.

"Geez mate, you've been busy already," announced David, having a look in the well stocked fridge.

"Mum did that," stated Luke. "I didn't ask or expect her to."

"She looks after you well, doesn't she?" said David.

Jo wondered if she could detect a hint of sarcasm in his voice, but dismissed the idea.

"Yeah," laughed Luke, shrugging it off. "Let's go out on the veranda."

The four of them walked out and sat at the same table Jo and Luke had eaten at earlier. It was late afternoon as they sat and chatted over the cold beers. Kelly wanted to know about the tour and how they had met. David seemed only interested in the latter subject.

Suddenly, Luke stood up. "Come with me, Jo. I want to show you something that you've never seen before." He took her hand and led her through the house to the opposite side veranda. "Your very first sunset over the ocean."

Jo gasped as she looked out over the ocean. The sun was almost on the horizon and its rays glistened on the water like flecks of gold. The sky was totally cloudless and several boats were silhouetted against the gold. It was a truly breath taking sight that left her speechless for a moment.

"And this is a plain one," explained Luke. "Wait 'til there are some clouds around. The colours are spectacular."

"Wow!" Jo shook her head slowly, in awe of the sight. "I can't wait to see the better ones."

Luke stood behind her with his arms around her waist as they watched the sun disappear completely over the horizon. Once it was gone, they walked inside and Luke grabbed four more beers from the fridge on their way back out to Kelly and David.

"Gorgeous, isn't it?" enthused Kelly. "You'll soon get used to seeing that sight every afternoon."

"Sure is," agreed Jo. "And I can't wait to see lots more. So, how did you two come to be neighbours?"

"Our Grandfather owned about fifty acres here for years and when he died he left it to Dad," replied David, not taking his eyes off Jo.

"Yeah," continued Luke, "Dad was an only child so he got the lot. He cut an acre each off for the three of us. That block on the other side of this one is Casey's, but she hasn't decided what to do with it yet."

"Dad sold the rest and retired," said David. "He worked hard all his life as a builder. He deserved it."

"Mmm," nodded Luke in agreement. "And the best part, the people who bought the 47 acres wanted it just left as a nature reserve, so we have no neighbours."

"So, we're all stuck her together whether we like it or not," laughed David.

"Oh, it's not that bad living next door to your big brother. Cheers, big ears!" said Luke, holding his beer up to David's in a toast. The four touched their stubbies together, laughed and had a drink.

They sat chatting on the veranda an hour or so longer, until Jo yawned and Luke announced he was getting hungry. Jo offered to make toasted sandwiches for everyone. The two girls went into the kitchen to prepare the food, with Kelly politely refusing any meat on hers, stating she was a vegetarian. They chatted like old friends, with Kelly talking about her food choices and her job as a natropath, specialising in alternative medicine. Jo was fascinated and wanted to know more. She was sure her and Kelly would become good friends.

"So, what do you think of Jo?" Luke asked David, as soon as he heard the girls making a noise in the kitchen. "Not bad, hey?"

"Not bad?" David asked incredulously. "That's a bit of an understatement. She's a knockout! Then again, you do always seem to find the best looking girls around though, Luke."

Luke wasn't sure how to take that statement and even less sure how to answer it. Luckily, he didn't have to as Kelly brought out two freshly cooked ham and cheese sandwiches and placed them down in front of Luke and David. The beers made them more hungry than usual so the first one hardly touched the sides.

It was quite late when David and Kelly left, and Luke was slightly drunk, but he was a happy drunk. He made Jo laugh with his one liners and quick wit. It made her love him even more, if that was possible. They cleaned off the table and headed for the bedroom, with Luke barely able to keep his hands off Jo on the way. Suddenly he picked her up, put her over his shoulder and entered the bedroom. She screamed and laughed. They made love in their own distinct way with Luke bringing Jo to soaring heights she'd never known before meeting him. Sometimes it was so overwhelming she almost cried.

Afterwards, Luke told her what he had planned for them the next day. He would take her for a tour on his Harley, to the beaches and along the freeways. They would go shopping in the city, sailing on the river and surfing up and down the coast.

Jo laughed. "We can't do all that in one day!"

"We're going to do it every day," Luke said, snuggling her closer to him and kissing her forehead.

"We have to see your parents tomorrow, so I can meet your Dad," Jo said, "and I have to ring Mum to find out what happened about Jeff."

"Jeff! Who's Jeff?" mumbled Luke, half asleep. "Forget about him, he can't hurt you anymore."

Jo hoped he was right as she snuggled in closer to his warm body and closed her tired eyes. What a day it had been. She was exhausted. It was only that morning that they had left The Sunshine Coast, but now it seemed like days. She looked at Luke's clock radio – almost one AM. No wonder she was so tired. With the two hour time difference her body felt it was much later. She drifted off into a deep sleep thinking about all the things Luke had planned for her……. For THEM!

CHAPTER EIGHT

"PETE!" called Vera as she walked up the hallway toward the front door. "There's a call for you."

Pete was sitting out on the veranda, reading the newspaper, drinking coffee and smoking a roll-your-own. Vera came out and handed him the phone.

"Who is it?" he asked with a frown. He wasn't anticipating anyone to call him.

"I don't know, but it's female," Vera whispered.

Pete frowned even harder and accepted the phone from her. He wasn't expecting to hear from Mo for another week or so.

"Hello, Pete speaking," he answered into the phone as Vera turned back inside.

"Hey Dude. How's it hangin'?"

Pete recognised immediately that it was Mo. He'd spoken to her once since they'd met, days ago, at the very same spot he was now sitting and knew that shrill, brash voice.

"Mo," he chuckled. "I thought it was you. How's things?"

"Great!" she replied. "Listen Man, I hope you got some bread together 'cos we're leavin' sooner than expected." She let out a loud YAHOOOOO into the phone. Pete cringed and held the phone away from his ear for several seconds.

"How much sooner?" panicked Pete. He had hardly any money even though the thought of leaving earlier appealed to him.

"How does the day after tomorrow grab ya?" enthused Mo.

Shit, thought Pete to himself. "Why the change?" he asked, trying to think of a quick way to get his hands on some cash and plenty of it.

"I just decided to go sooner. I think I've got enough bread and work was givin' me the shits so I quit today."

"Did they give you your pay?" asked Pete, concerned she may have done herself out of some money and therefore made their trip harder.

"Oh shit yeah!" declared Mo. "Every last cent! The slimy old prick didn't want to, but he was always puttin' the hard word on me and tryin' to feel me up, so I threatened to report him if he didn't give me all he owed me."

"Way to go, Mo," cheered Pete.

"So!" demanded Mo. "Are ya comin' or not? Day after tomorrow."

Pete's mind was racing. He knew it would be useless trying to get Mo to change her mind. As little as he knew her, there was one thing he did know for sure – she was very strong minded. "What? Oh yeah, of course I am! Can you pick me up from here?"

"Sure thing, Bud!" she shrieked into the phone. "I sure as hell can't wait to hit the road."

"Me too," mused Pete. "So around what time?"

"Early!" ordered Mo. "How much gear ya got?"

"Not much, I always travel light."

"Good. See ya then." She hung up without giving Pete a chance to say goodbye. Not that he cared with his mind overtaken with the urgent need to get money, or miss out on this opportunity to get to Perth. There was no way he was missing out!

After several minutes, his mind still devoid of ideas, he got up and took the phone back inside, dawdling heavy heartedly up the hallway.

"What's up Pete?" asked Vera, when he walked into the kitchen. "Bad news?"

"Huh? Oh no," replied Pete. He didn't want to whinge about lack of money to Vera and George. He knew very well that when he did have money, he blew it straight away on things they certainly would not approve of. "That was Mo. She wants to leave the day after tomorrow." He handed the phone to George who had just walked in the back door.

"So soon?" frowned Vera. "I didn't think you were leaving for another week or two."

"Neither did I," sighed Pete, "but she has decided to go sooner and that's that."

"Are you ready to go so soon?" enquired George, beginning to peel some potatoes for that night's meal.

Pete hesitated for a moment. "Yeah, that's no worries," he replied, trying to sound confident but underneath he was frantic. There was no way he had enough cash to pay for his half of the fuel out of New South Wales, let alone all the way to Perth. "I'm just goin' to my room."

"We'll call you when tea is ready," said Vera. She noted that his mind was elsewhere and guessed that it may have had something to do with them leaving earlier, but she didn't want to embarrass him by asking him about his money situation.

Pete lay on his bed, hands beneath his head and stared up at the bottom of the bunk above him. *At least I've still got thirty-six hours to come up with something*, he consoled himself. There were alternatives of course, but the thought sickened him to the core. All he could think about, though, was Perth – HOME – and getting there. Besides, Mo was counting on him now, to share the trip and he didn't want to let her down.

A little while later George knocked on the door, saying that tea was ready. Pete went out and ate a big meal, just in case they couldn't afford much food on the trip. He was silent through the meal and went to bed early to mull over the possibilities.

After a restless night he rose early and went for a walk before breakfast. Short of stealing or selling himself, he couldn't think of any other way to raise some money. Hell, he didn't even have anything of value to pawn. In disgust and frustration he walked back to the Drop-In Centre for some breakfast.

As George poured out mugs of steaming coffee for Pete and several other occupants, he couldn't help noticing that Pete was extra quiet.

"You were up early this morning, Pete!" stated George, sitting on an empty chair beside him. "Anything wrong?"

"Nah…….. well nothing that about five hundred dollars wouldn't fix anyway."

"A bit short for the trip, eh?" enquired George.

"Just a bit," answered Pete, feeling uncomfortable talking about it in front of the others sitting at the table. "I've got a mate I can ask for a loan. I'll go and see him soon."

"Why don't you go and see Centrelink and ask if you can get an advance on your next payment?" suggested George.

"Hey," smiled Pete, brightening up. "That's a good idea. I'll do that after breakfast."

He finished eating his breakfast quickly and headed off to the nearest Centrelink office which was a brisk forty minute walk from the Drop-In Centre. All the way he hoped and, shocking himself, even prayed that they could help him. After waiting in line for thirty minutes and talking to one of the assistants, he came away with a smile. An advance for part of his next payment would be in his bank within a few days. Luckily, he had received new cards since losing his wallet to his assailants, so had some identification. However, he realised that this advance was still not enough to get him over to Perth.

When he told George that he had a mate he could ask for a loan, it was not entirely true. He only told him that to cover his tracks if he had to end up resorting to unfavourable means to acquire the money. Suddenly though, as he was wandering along, he did think of someone who may be able to help him out. The man was not exactly a mate, as Pete didn't have any close friends, more like an acquaintance, but they did get on okay and Pete WAS desperate.

He turned at the next corner and walked several more blocks before coming to a little old fibro house. The lawn in the small front yard needed mowing badly and what were once flower beds on either side of the old, cracked, concrete path way were now full of weeds. This, along with the house in need of a paint job, made it seem as if no-one lived there, but Pete was sure he would find who he was looking for. He knocked loudly on the old wooden door and waited anxiously. Out of the corner of his eye he noticed the faded and tattered curtain in the window to his right move slightly, then the door opened.

"Pete," the man frowned, rubbing his eyes. "What are you doing here?"

"G'day, Skunk. How's things?" Pete greeted. "Sorry to wake you up. I just came around to ask you a favour."

The man groaned and sighed then beckoned Pete inside. Skunk was in his late forties, not much taller than Pete with greying, black hair to his shoulders and a thick moustache. He had hairy shoulders and chest, visible around his faded blue singlet, a large belly and was heavily tattooed. Pete followed him into the kitchen at the far end of the house. Dirty dishes were strewn about on the small table and sink. Pete screwed up his nose at the mess and the smell in the house. Skunk certainly didn't enjoy housework. Worn clothes were lying about the floor and backs of chairs, obviously dropped where they'd been taken off.

Noisily pushing some dishes aside in the sink, Skunk filled the old, stained kettle with water and put it on the dirty electric stove then turned it on. Several large cockroaches scurried off the top of the stove and down the side. A large German Shepherd lay scratching itself by the stove, it's coat matted and dirty.

"So what can I do for you Pete? Or need I ask?" enquired Skunk, lighting up a cigarette before offering one to Pete, who accepted gratefully. "Haven't seen you in a while."

"Yeah," said Pete, blowing smoke high into the air. "I got a hiding a little while back and I've been laid up for a while."

Skunk rolled his eyes, shook his head and smiled. "Trust YOU! Do you know who it was?"

"Nah, not really," replied Pete, screwing up his face and shaking his head. "I was pretty out of it."

Just then the kettle started to whistle, faintly as first but quickly ascended to a high pitched scream. Skunk turned the stove off before rinsing out two dirty, chipped mugs that had been sitting on the sink and made two cups of black coffee, handing one to Pete. "Sorry, no milk."

He passed a half empty, paper sugar bag and teaspoon to Pete before sitting down at the table opposite him.

"I need a loan," said Pete after several sips of the coffee. "Badly."

"What for?" asked Skunk casually.

"I'm going to Perth. That's where I'm from and I want to go back for a while. I'll pay you back as soon as I get a job over there. I don't need that much."

"How much?" frowned Skunk, picturing his roll of notes growing wings and flying off into the sunset, never to be seen again.

"Five hundred," stated Pete, hopefully.

"Sorry Mate, no can do," replied Skunk, shaking his head slowly. Pete's shoulders slumped noticeably. "I just haven't got it," continued Skunk. "I haven't been doing much business lately. Someone tipped off the cops that I was dealing and they've been around hassling me a few times. Luckily, I'd got rid of the stash and they found nothing, but they drive past a bit so nobody's game to come here."

"That's a bummer," sighed Pete, referring more to the refusal of the loan than Skunk's woes.

"I'm not that upset about it. I've been wanting to get out of the business for a while now. I'm getting too old for this shit. I've been inside once and that was enough. Just got the news I'm going to be a grandfather soon so I want to be around."

"That's nice," uttered Pete, realising he was back to square one again.

"Yeah, so I've decided I'd fix this old place up a bit before the baby is born so they can come and visit," smiled Skunk, happy at that thought. "None of my family has been here for ages."

I'm not surprised, thought Pete to himself, looking around at the mouldy, paint chipped walls.

They chatted a bit longer with Pete telling Skunk about his plans for going to Perth and about Mo. Skunk apologised again for not being able to help him. The truth was, he did have enough money but he knew that he would never get it back and he really did want to do up the place. As

Pete was getting up to leave, Skunk suddenly felt a pang of pity for him. He could sense how badly Pete wanted to return to Perth, so went into the bedroom and came back out with a fifty dollar note which he handed to Pete.

"Here you go, Mate. This might help you a bit."

Pete was taken aback. "Oh gee. Thanks Mate." He gratefully took the note from Skunk's hand. "I'll send it back as soon as I can."

"No, no, don't worry about it," said Skunk, raising his hands and shaking his head. "Take it as a farewell present."

Pete thanked him again and shook his hand as he said goodbye. Skunk closed the door and Pete walked out on to the footpath. He was glad to get out of there. Skunk wasn't a bad bloke but he certainly earned his nickname!

Walking along the street, Pete looked at the note still in his hand. While he was very grateful for it, he still needed more and time was running out.

On his way home he couldn't resist calling into the old familiar block of flats. He went up to number two and knocked on the door. Soon it was opened by a tall, thin, middle-aged man he didn't recognise. Within seconds a familiar face appeared at the door also and beckoned him inside. "This will DEFINITELY be the last time!" he declared to himself, lifting his tee shirt off over his head.

An hour later he came out with over one hundred dollars in his hand. He was pleased about the money but felt like being sick. There were four men in there and he'd serviced the lot of them. Suddenly his stomach heaved and he threw up on the edge of the footpath. Wiping his mouth and watery eyes, he hurried back to the Drop-In Centre for a shower.

After his shower, Pete lay on his bed. It had been a profitable day but he still needed more. He dozed for a while, planning to go out again that night for one last attempt to raise some more travelling cash.

Realising he hadn't eaten since breakfast, he ate a hearty tea, told Vera and George he was going for a walk and headed out the front door.

He walked to the nearest bus stop and caught the next bus going toward The Cross. Soon he found himself wondering past the bars, cafés and adult shops of Kings Cross. He felt comfortable here. After entering one of the bars, he bought a scotch and coke and sat at a small, balcony table facing the street and rolled a cigarette.

He sat there, deep in thought, staring blankly ahead for several minutes, sipping his drink and drawing on his smoke. There was only about twelve hours left to come up with some more cash.

Soon, his attention was diverted to two young men arguing on the street only metres away to his right. Initially, he wasn't interested but when he had a better look he noticed something vaguely familiar about the taller one of the two. He frowned and thought hard, watching them intensely. Where had he seen that man before? The other one was not familiar at all. Then the tall one raised his voice louder and shouted at the other one. Suddenly it hit Pete! He was one of the men who beat him up and left him for dead in the alley. Pete watched them, while cursing him silently. What could he do? The man was much bigger than him but the bastard stole his money and he needed it back!

The two men soon stopped shouting and walked off together along the footpath. Pete downed the last of his drink and followed them, staying far enough behind so as not to arouse suspicion. He had no idea what he was going to do, but he knew he had to try and get his money. He wished Skunk could have been with him right then for support.

Pete followed the two men along as they came to a little side street and turned into it. He watched them enter a flat at the end of the street. It was the first one on the ground floor of a three storey block. The area was not well lit up, which pleased Pete.

Crouching down behind a car parked across the street, he waited. For what? He hadn't a clue! He knew he couldn't fight one of them, let alone two. If only he had some sort of weapon. Looking around him, it was too dark to see far. He tried the car door handles, not expecting any result. To his surprise, one of the back doors was unlocked. Looking around briefly to ensure no-one was nearby, he quickly crawled in the back door and reached down beside the driver's seat for the lever to open the boot. Pete breathed a heavy sigh of relief as the boot rose up. So far, so good!

He quickly got out of the car, locking the back door that he'd opened. Glancing around again, he was pleased there was still nobody about. He looked in the boot, expecting to find it empty, but it was filled with boxes and bags of stuff. *Oh shit!* As quickly as he could, he rummaged around underneath everything for the spare tyre. Suddenly, he noticed a couple walking along the footpath toward him. His heart skipped a beat as he frantically hoped they were not the owners of the car. As they strolled past he casually began lifting some of the gear out of the boot.

Another heavy sigh of relief. His eyes darted about again. No-one in sight. He lifted up the mat and found the wheel spanner beside the spare tyre, quickly took it out and threw the bags back into the boot. Closing the boot as quietly as he could, he heard voices coming from the entrance of the house nearest the car. He ran across the street and hid behind another car that was parked near the flat that the two men had entered. Clutching the wheel spanner tightly, he watched a young couple get into the car and drive off. Silently, he apologised to them for stealing their spanner.

He sprinted a little way along the street and hid down behind some rubbish bins. Luckily, he didn't have long to wait. Soon he heard footsteps and looked through a small gap between two of the bins to see the tall man walking along in his direction. Here was his chance to get revenge! He'd never ambushed anyone before or attacked them by surprise, but reminded himself that the scum was only going to get what he deserved. The man came closer, whistling to himself. Pete's sweaty palms gripped the wheel spanner securely as his heart thumped loudly in his chest.

Just as the man was almost up to him, Pete forcefully kicked one of the wheelie bins causing it to fall in front of him. The man was caught completely off guard and tripped over the bin, falling against it before landing on the concrete path. Before he could get up, Pete lunged forward and hit the back of his head hard, with the wheel spanner. The man let out a grunt and slumped down flat on the ground, like a cane toad that had just been clubbed. Pete was shaking and, although he despised this bloke for beating him up and taking his money, he didn't want to kill him.

He dropped the wheel spanner and rolled him onto his back then felt his pulse, relieved to find the man still alive. A car drove down the street toward them. Pete froze and held his breath, keeping his back to the car. Fortunately for him, it kept on going.

Knowing there was no time to waste, Pete crouched down and quickly searched the man's pockets. He tried the jeans first but they were empty. Next he tried the shirt pockets. Nothing! Pete couldn't believe it. He was sure he would have had something on him, especially if he was a pusher, which Pete was sure he was. Then he tried the man's jacket, found a packet of cigarettes and put them in his own pocket. Angry and frustrated he rolled the man back on to his stomach and punched him in the back, which made Pete frown and sit upright. He was sure his hand had hit something. He felt around on the man's back and could feel a bulge under his jacket, then became excited so reached and felt around under the jacket. Nothing! It must be in the lining of the jacket.

It was a well padded jacket and there would be enough room in the lining to hide something, Pete realised. He reached under each of the man's shoulders and pulled with all of his might. The man's arms were forced up and back at an awkward angle as the jacket slid off his arms and into Pete's hands. Just as he started to run off with the jacket something else dawned on him, so he spun around, ran back and pulled off one of the man's shoes, then the other one. A small, flat roll of money fell on to the ground. Pete eagerly scooped it up, kissed it then placed it in his pocket.

"Oldest trick in the book, Mate," he laughed as he ran off in the opposite direction.

He soon found a vacant taxi and jumped in, ordering the driver to a spot not far from the Drop-In Centre. Pete paid the driver with his own money and got out. He was close enough to a street light to see what he was doing. Finding the opening in the jacket lining he tore it further open before reaching in and scooping out the contents. It contained two small plastic bags of marijuana and a smaller bag of around twenty white pills. He whistled in delight! Looking around, he then searched through the rest of the jacket until he was satisfied there was nothing else and threw it in a nearby bin. Pete then walked back to the Drop-In Centre with his spirits considerably lifted.

Several people were in the lounge room watching TV so he went straight to his room. Thankfully, he didn't see George or Vera anywhere and he was also glad that no-one else was currently sharing the room he slept in. Shutting his door, he couldn't help giggling as he pulled the roll of notes out of his pocket. Eager to find out just how much he'd scored, he counted it slowly to ensure he made no mistakes. Four hundred dollars. Pete was ecstatic! It was beyond his wildest dreams as he had only been expecting much less.

He fell back on to his bed, laughing and crying at the same time. At last, he had enough money to get to Perth and had got his revenge for the beating. Bonus! Putting the cash and drugs safely beneath his mattress, he went to bed.

Sleep evaded him. Images of the man kept flooding his brain and the excitement of the trip kept him awake as well. After several hours of tossing and turning he got up and rolled himself a joint from one of the bags of marijuana, using two of his rollie papers. As he walked outside, he noticed that everyone else had gone to bed.

A stray cat ran out in front of him as he walked across the yard and he hoped it wasn't a black one. Although with the mood he was in, nothing could upset him now.

Pete sat under a small tree in the corner of the front yard, well away from George and Vera's flat and lit his joint. He inhaled the acrid smoke deeply into his lungs and held it several seconds before exhaling.

Instantly he felt his body and mind relax. Chuckling continuously to himself, he kept thinking about how he'd got the better of the man who'd beat him. Before long he had finished the joint but was too relaxed to move. He crawled several metres out from under the tree and gazed up at the stars. His mother's face appeared in them. "I'll be home soon Mum," he whispered skywards. Eventually he got up and went back to bed where he finally fell into a deep sleep.

A loud, sharp knock on his bedroom door awoke him with a jolt the next morning.

"PETE!" George called. "Are you awake? Mo's here!"

"Shit!" exclaimed Pete when George's words sank in after several seconds. He didn't mean to sleep this late. "Coming," he yelled, jumping out of bed and pulling some jeans on. Racing into the kitchen he found Mo sitting at the table, dressed as outlandishly as the first day he'd met her.

"You call this early?" she shrieked at him, although she wasn't really upset. She hadn't slept well either and had been up since before dawn making sure everything was ready. Suddenly, she began to giggle at him.

"Sorry, Mo, I didn't sleep very well last night," he mumbled, wondering to himself how he hadn't been woken up by her loud voice when she walked in.

Pete went to the bathroom to wash his face. When he looked in the mirror he understood why Mo laughed at him. His hair was sticking out in all directions, his eyes were bloodshot and almost hanging out of his head from lack of sleep. Screwing up his face at his reflection, he stripped off and had a quick shower. When he returned from the bathroom he looked up at the clock on the kitchen wall.

"What are you talking about, Mo?" he frowned. "It's not even seven o'clock!"

Mo laughed and sipped the tea that George had made for her. "No great rush," she said, "s'long's we're on the road by eight."

Pete rushed to his room to pack his one bag, being careful to hide the previous night's loot securely at the bottom of it. He looked about the room before walking out of it for the last time. Satisfied that he had everything, he went into the kitchen for some breakfast. Mo was chatting away to George and Vera as they prepared the food. She accepted their offer of some toast and Vera placed a large plate loaded with bacon, eggs, grilled tomato, baked beans and toast down on the table in front of Pete. With mouth agape, he stared at it for several seconds.

"That's your special farewell feast," smiled Vera, with a hint of sadness.

"Geez Vera, I don't think I can eat all this," he stated, shaking his head.

"Well, you bloody well better try!" said George in mock seriousness.

Surprising himself, Pete ate most of the meal and just as he placed his cutlery down, Vera handed Mo a large ice-cream container.

"Here's some sandwiches to take," she said. "It'll save you having to stop to buy lunch." She suspected that Pete wouldn't have much money.

They finished their breakfast and Pete said a sad goodbye to Vera and George, thanking them for everything they had done for him and promising to stay in touch. Vera wiped the tears from her eyes as he and Mo walked to the pink Holden. As they drove off, Pete leaned out of the window and waved to the two people he cared about most in the world, apart from family. He choked back a tear, as he would miss them immensely. They WERE family to him. The family, more precisely the FATHER, he wished he'd had.

"At last!" shouted Mo. "Perth, here we come!" She punched Pete playfully in the arm, sensing his sadness. "Ready?" she laughed.

"Ready!" affirmed Pete, smiling at the long road ahead of them and wondering what was over the horizon.

CHAPTER NINE

The first week after Jo's arrival in Perth was crammed with non-stop excitement. Luke took her shopping, wining and dining, partying in the night clubs, sailing on the Swan River, exploring Rottnest Island and cruising on his Harley. She could surf a little, so he bought her a new surfboard and coached her as they surfed some of Perth's top beaches together. They spent late afternoons walking along the beach at sunset and made love on the beach in the moonlight.

One particular day they cruised away from suburbia and headed northwards. Luke wanted to show Jo the huge, beautiful array of wildflowers that grew so abundantly in Western Australia during spring and summer. They rode north to Yanchep National Park. Jo was astounded! Never in her life had she seen such a variety of coloured wildflowers. There were Kangaroo Paw, Banksias, Verticordias, Everlastings and Wreath flowers, just to name a few. Some flowers were black and some were different shades of blue. The scenery took Jo's breath away as they set up for a picnic under a shady tree.

"This is incredible!" beamed Jo, as she ate a sandwich and surveyed the colourful carpet surrounding them and stretching on for kilometres. "These flowers are so gorgeous."

"They sure are," agreed Luke. "Like you. You're my wildflower." He leaned toward her and kissed her softly on the lips, then got up and walked several steps to pick a bright yellow Everlasting to gently place behind her ear. Luke took out his camera and took several photos of Jo sitting among large clusters of flowers of different types and colours, after he'd placed several more in her hair and shirt button holes.

"I can imagine Kelly sitting here like this," remarked Jo.

"Yeah," smiled Luke. "She's a seventies flower child, that's for sure. You two seem to be getting on pretty good."

"Mmm," nodded Jo. "Even though I've only talked to her a few times in the last week, I feel like I've known her for ages. Her and David seem a bit like chalk and cheese though, don't you think?"

"Yeah, sometimes they do," agreed Luke. "What do you think of David?"

In the week that they had been home, Jo and Luke had only seen a little of David and Kelly. The four had gone out for tea together one night and Kelly had come over one afternoon after Jo and Luke had been shopping so Jo had shown her what she'd bought. They'd chatted and laughed for an hour or more over the bags and parcels while Luke had mowed the lawn and cleaned the pool.

"Well......," pondered Jo. "To be totally honest Luke, I am not sure what to think of David yet. He's nice..... and charming..... and good looking."

"Hey, hold on there!" Luke cut in.

Jo laughed and caressed his face. "Don't worry, he's not a patch on you."

Luke smiled a big sigh of relief and they both laughed.

"But seriously," continued Jo, "there's something about David. I don't know..... I can't really put my finger on it."

"What do you mean?" frowned Luke.

"Like I said, I don't know," shrugged Jo. "Just some things he says to you sometimes. I don't know whether he's being sarcastic or just joking. He seems to look at me in strange ways at times. I don't know." She shrugged again. "Maybe it's just my imagination."

"I think it might be," reassured Luke. "We've always mucked around like that and I know he thinks you're pretty. He's a good bloke. Just wait 'til you get to know him better. Him and Kelly have been happy for years. I can't imagine them ever breaking up, even if they are like chalk and cheese."

Jo smiled and kissed him, feeling more relaxed about David. After all, if anyone knew him well it was Luke and Kelly certainly seemed happy.

They packed up the picnic gear and headed back home. As they rode along Jo began thinking about her friend, Meg. She had rung her the second day they were in Perth to tell her about Jeff, but Meg had already seen it on the news. Meg and Jo's mother had also spoken to each other about the incident, but each of them was as shocked and confused about the whole thing as the other. Jo had also told Meg all about Luke's house and how much she thought she would love living here, although she did miss her family and friends.

Just after they arrived home, Jo's phone rang while she was unpacking the picnic bag.

"Jo Honey, it's Mum," Liz replied to Jo's greeting.

"Hi Mum! This is a surprise! You sound upset…….." Jo's voice trailed off, expecting some bad news.

"Jo, I've got some bad news about what happened at the airport."

Jo felt the blood drain from her face. "What?" she asked nervously.

"The police were here earlier. They know about you being his girlfriend and that you had not long broken up with him."

"H-How did they find out?" Jo stammered softly. She had to sit down before her weakened knees gave way from under her.

"It seems that his family told them. It gets worse Jo, I'm sorry . By the way the police were talking, his family made you out to be a cold hearted………bitch and that it was all your fault." Liz almost choked the words out.

Jo began to cry, just as Luke walked up from downstairs.

"Who is……JO! What's wrong?" he frowned, rushing to her side. "Who's on the phone?"

"Mum" she mouthed silently to him, before continuing the conversation with her mother. "I can't believe they'd do that. We always got along so well. They obviously have no idea what he did to me!" she said angrily.

"Is Luke with you?" asked her Mother.

"Yes, he's right here," replied Jo, taking hold of his hand for comfort.

"Oh good. Is everything else okay there?"

"Everything's great Mum, but I can tell by the tone of your voice there's more....isn't there? What else has happened? Is someone coming after me?"

Liz hesitated for several seconds before speaking. "The police want to talk to you, Jo."

Jo gasped and began feeling a little faint.

"Don't worry Sweetie, they assured me you weren't in any kind of trouble. They just want your version of what happened," continued her Mother, trying hard to keep it together for the sake of her beloved daughter.

"Do I have to go back there?" Jo asked fearfully.

"No, they said the Perth police would come and speak to you. They asked me for your address so I had to give it to them. I hope Luke isn't angry. They'll probably be there tomorrow. "

"Thanks for warning me, Mum."

"I'm really sorry, Honey."

"It's not YOUR fault," Jo assured Liz, "and I'm sorry too that all this had to happen. I thought when there had been nothing more on the news that it would all blow over and the Jeff's family can grieve and I can get on with my life. How's Dad and the Boys?"

"They're good but they miss you already. We all do."

"Well, you'll have to come for a visit," stated Jo, trying to cheer her Mum up as much as herself. "Maybe you could come for Christmas. That's not too far away."

"Good idea," agreed her mother. "We'll talk about it. I'd better go now. I love you! Take care and keep your chin up. You've done NOTHING wrong."

"I will and you too! Love you, Mum. Bye." Jo ended the call and took a long deep breath.

"JO!" Luke demanded. "Tell me what's happened."

Jo told him everything her mother had said.

"I can't believe this," he said angrily, walking to the door that leads from the kitchen to the veranda and placing his hands on his hips.

Suddenly he spun around. "He's STILL getting at you! Even from the grave the bastard is still hurting you." He was livid!

Jo had never seen him so angry. "The police only want to know my version," she said, hoping he would calm down.

"Well, when they get here I'm going to back up everything you say. I'll tell them about the bruises he left on you." He was starting to calm down a little. "Did they talk to Meg? She'd be able to tell them what he did."

"I don't think so," sighed Jo. "I'm sure she would have told me if they had. Maybe I should ring her and ask her if she can go and give a statement. It could help."

"Yeah, good idea," nodded Luke.

Jo rang Meg and told her everything she could about the situation and asked her if she would mind going to the police with her account of what happened at the flat. Meg happily agreed to. She was stunned by Jeff's family's allegations and said she would go in the next day. Anything to put this nightmare to rest, she assured Jo.

Luke prepared a light tea of grilled fish and salad, although neither of them was very hungry.

"I'm so glad your family doesn't know anything about this, Luke," Jo said as they sat down to eat.

"Well, there is no need for them to know," shrugged Luke. "Once the police know all the facts that will be the end of it, once and for all."

Suddenly Jo dropped her fork. "Oh no!" she said, her face whitening. "I just thought of something."

"What?" frowned Luke.

"What if the media get a whiff of your involvement? They'll have a field day," Jo panicked.

Luke screwed up his nose. "Nah, they won't find out." He wasn't so convinced though, only wanting to ease Jo's worry and he knew very well how the media loved to dig up the dirt on anyone in the public eye.

"Some of the magazines write such crap," said Jo. "I can just see the headlines now,   DASHING STONEFISH GUITARIST IN BIZARRE SUICIDE TRIANGLE."

LUKE couldn't help laughing. "That makes me sound like the dead one."

"It's not funny, Luke!" Jo scolded. "This could cause a lot of hassles for you. What would the others in the band say?"

"They wouldn't take any notice," he assured her. "Steve was supposed to be marrying Jennifer Hawkins a few years ago. He'd only met her once."

Jo shook her head, but was still worried. "What if someone in his family wanted to sell their exaggerated story?"

"Do you think he would have actually known who I was and if he did, would he have told anyone?" asked Luke.

"God knows," sighed Jo, shaking her head. "Absolutely NOTHING would surprise me anymore when it comes to him."

"If anything like that DOES happen then we'd counteract it with our version – the TRUTH," Luke shrugged, smiling. "Don't worry, Babe," he urged, leaning over and kissing her on the forehead. "We'll handle anything they try to throw at us…..won't we?"

Jo nodded her head and smiled. She was amazed how he could always make light of a bad situation and how he always found the right words to soothe and reassure her when she was upset or worried. She wondered if he ever let anything upset or worry him for more than a minute or two.

They finished their meal, washed up, showered and went to bed. Jo's mind was still preoccupied with the police coming the next day so didn't feel like making love. However, Luke had other ideas, convincing her that an orgasm was the best antidote for stress. As soon as his lips and hands starting moving over her body she could no longer resist, and she didn't regret it either. Afterwards she felt much more relaxed and drifted off to sleep, snuggled in his loving arms.

She tossed and turned later throughout the night. Jagged dreams of Jeff tormented her, but by early morning she was sleeping soundly.

Just as Luke was about to go for a morning jog along the beach, the electronic buzzer on the front gate sounded. Jo was still sleeping as he looked out from upstairs and saw the police car parked at his gate. He was surprised and annoyed that they would come so early.

Reluctantly, dressed in shorts, singlet and runners, he walked to the front gate. Normally, he would just open it from the switch inside or by remote, but he hoped he could persuade them to return later when Jo had had enough sleep. He was worried about her being so restless through the night and knew the situation weighed heavily on her mind. With that in HIS mind, he was hoping he could just tell them what they wanted to know without bothering Jo at all.

Two policemen were standing outside the gate when he opened it.

"Are you Luke Summers?" enquired the older one of the two. He was around fifty, tall and slim with a small moustache and a stern look in his eyes.

"Yes," replied Luke. "How can I help you?" He decided it might be better not to let on that they'd been forewarned about this visit.

"I'm Senior Constable Davis and this is Constable Anderson."

Luke shook hands with each of them and couldn't help noticing that the younger Anderson seemed a lot friendlier than Davis. He was tall as well, with jet black hair, boyish face and a less intimidating look. He shook hands eagerly with Luke, a big smile on his face. Luke could sense he wanted to say something beyond business but wasn't sure if he should.

"We're looking for Jo Slater," stated Constable Anderson. "We believe she's here."

"She is!" stated Luke, "but she's still asleep. She's not feeling very well at the moment."

"We need to speak to her regarding a death in Queensland last week. We believe she had been well acquainted with the deceased in the past," Davis continued.

"Look, would you mind coming back a bit later, she's...."

"LUKE!" Jo called from the veranda. "It's all right. Tell them to come in." She knew he would have been trying to protect her as much as possible.

Luke opened the gate, allowing the policeman to drive up closer to the house. Jo was waiting nervously at the top of the stairs when they walked up. Her mind was abuzz but her body was still half asleep. She introduced herself to the policemen as she wanted to get this over and done with as quickly as possible. Inviting them to sit down at the table, her and Luke then sat on the opposite side as she yawned and rubbed her eyes.

Constable Anderson turned on a small recorder he'd placed on the table.

"We have to ask you some questions about Jeffrey Bowen, Miss Slater," began Constable Davis. "Do you mind?"

"No," replied Jo. "I'll tell you everything you want to know."

"Firstly, are you aware that he carried a firearm into Maroochydore airport last week and, after terrorising everyone there, shot himself dead?"

"Yes, I know that," sighed Jo, grimacing at the memory.

"Can you tell us about your relationship with him?" urged Anderson, in a softer tone.

Jo went back to when her and Jeff met in school and then to when they began dating. She mentioned how he was moody at times and how their last few months together were quite tumultuous, with him continuously refusing to accept her wish to end the relationship. Finally, she told them about the day at her flat, ensuring they heard every painful detail of what he put her through. The memory became too much and she began to shake and sob. She appreciated the glass of water Luke got for her.

"It's all true!" Luke stated angrily. "I saw Jo that afternoon and she was a total mess, physically and emotionally. It took ages for the scars to fade, and I'm not just talking about the visible ones. You can see how it still upsets her."

Both policemen had sympathetic looks on their faces.

"Check with the Maroochydore Police," continued Luke. "Jo's flatmate is giving them a statement. She walked in while he had Jo down on the floor. God only knows what would have happened to Jo if she didn't come in when she did." He choked back a tear that had started to form.

Jo had calmed down a little and told them about the chilling note they found under their door the morning they were due to leave and how she'd seen him stalking her at the airport. She had to take several sips of water and some deep breaths before she could continue with the details. Luke cut in several times to support her.

"Miss Slater," enquired Davis, in a friendlier tone than before, "weren't you asked at the airport if you knew the deceased?"

"Yes," whispered Jo, looking down at her hands fidgeting in her lap.

"And did you reply that you did NOT know him?"

"Jo's not on trial here!" frowned Luke. "She's done nothing wrong." He was becoming agitated at the mode of questioning.

"It's okay, Honey," she smiled, patting his thigh. "Yes, I said that I didn't know him."

"Why?" asked Constable Anderson simply and shaking his head in puzzlement.

Jo hesitated for a few moments, deep in thought. "Well, I didn't really know the man he'd become. He was crazy!" She shuddered. "And...... I guess I was too stunned by it all, too shocked. I just wanted to get as far away from him and the whole scene, as I could."

"You couldn't have gone much further!" the younger policeman grinned. Luke shot him a dagger look that quickly wiped the smile from his face.

"We couldn't see any point in staying there," said Luke, irritated. "The bloke obviously meant to shoot Jo, or me or even the two of us, but he decided to shoot himself at the last second. He wasn't after anyone else."

"I didn't think it would have come to this," said Jo, shaking her head. "I thought it would have been treated as a suicide and kept out of the limelight."

"If it had happened in private, yes, but it happened very publicly and a lot of innocent people were frightened and traumatised by it," stated Constable Davis. "The family of the deceased is very upset by it all too, as you can appreciate. They want answers. Obviously, this was totally out of character for their son and brother."

"And I suppose they're blaming Jo?" demanded Luke. "Isn't it obvious she has been traumatised by it all too. Part of the reason she agreed to come over here with me was to get away from him because she was terrified!"

"Calm down Mr Summers," insisted Constable Davis. "Of course we can see that Jo is upset by it all and I'm sorry that all the sordid details have to be rehashed, but there may well be an inquest into the death and everything will have to come out in the open then. I think that will be enough for now. Can you come into the station in the city later to sign this statement and we'll send it over to Queensland straight away?"

Jo nodded.

"We'll be there," assured Luke. He walked them down to the front door and used the remote to open the front gate, waited until they'd driven out and locked it again. He sprinted back up the steps, to find Jo lying on their bed.

Noticing that she had been crying, he removed his shoes and socks then lay down to comfort her.

"I've decided what I think is the best thing to do," stated Jo.

"What's that?" asked Luke.

"I'm going to write a long letter to Jeff's Mum, telling her everything, but not harshly. I don't want to shock her too much, she's a nice lady. I can understand her being angry and upset, especially at me, but I want to try and make her understand how much he frightened me. She might not believe me, but it's worth a try don't you think?"

"Mmm, yeah, may as well. I can't say for sure because I don't know her, but whatever makes you feel better, Babe." He kissed her tenderly on the lips. "All I know is that I love you!" He winked and smiled.

It gave Jo goose bumps when he winked and smiled at her. His cute dimples stood out and his eyes sparkled. "And I love you too........ twice as much!" She hugged him tightly to her for a moment before pushing him gently away. He looked disappointed. "I'm sorry, Honey," she smiled regretfully. "I'll make it up to you later...... promise. I just want to write this letter now while it's all fresh in my mind, or I might not be able to say everything I want to, the way I want to."

Grudgingly, he got off the bed. "Well, I might go for my run now. I'll hold you to that promise." He blew her a kiss, picked up his shoes and socks before walking out of the bedroom.

While he was away, Jo composed the letter to Mrs Bowen. By the time she was satisfied she was surrounded by a dozen crumpled pieces of paper. It had to be worded exactly right. She didn't want to sound like she was glad he was dead, although part of her was. On the other hand, she didn't feel that she should take the blame for his actions, as his family seemed to think she should. She expressed her feelings as best she could and her sympathy to the family. Luke came in from his run just as she was signing off. He went straight to his gym for a short workout before showering and coming upstairs.

Jo showed him the letter and he agreed it sounded appropriate to send to the Bowen family, under the circumstances. Sealing it in an addressed envelope, she then went into the kitchen to make them some breakfast. Actually, it was more like lunch. With everything that had happened, the time had slipped by and neither of them had thought of food.

They ate quietly, with Jo still obviously worried about the situation. Luke wanted to take her mind off it.

"We'll have to invite Mum and Dad over for tea one night soon......
Jo, did you hear me?"

"What? Oh yeah, that's a good idea," nodded Jo. "I haven't really
had a chance to get to know them properly yet. We haven't spent much
time with them since we've been back ."

"Well, how about tomorrow night then?" Luke suggested.

"Sounds good," mumbled Jo, playing with her half-eaten omelette.

"Might invite my ex-girlfriend too," said Luke.

"Mmm, whatever."

"Snap out of it Jo!" Luke ordered, clicking his fingers in front of her
eyes. "Everything is going to be all right," he smiled, placing his hand
on her shoulder.

She looked at him and smiled. "I'm sorry. You want your parents to
come over tomorrow night? Who else did you say was coming?"

"We'll ask Kelly and David," replied Luke, not bothering to repeat
the earlier statement.

"Hey!" Jo said, suddenly brightening up. "Let's have a barbie by the
pool!"

"Top idea!" announced Luke. "I'll ring Mum now."

He rang his parents and invited them over the following afternoon,
then left a message on David and Kelly's answering service at home. He
didn't want to bother them while they were working. It would have been
easy to call or go see them after work, but he had some very memorable
plans for him and Jo for that night. They finished their lunch, swam and
played in the pool for a while then drove into the police station in his
black four wheel drive, to sign the statement.

"I've got something special planned for tonight, Jo," Luke said,
totally out of the blue, while driving back home.

"What?" enthused Jo, raising her eyebrows.

"You'll see," he said with a smile and a wink. "It's a surprise, but I
will tell you this much, we are going over to the beach and tea is
organised."

Jo smiled then frowned. They'd gone to the beach several times at night and had sometimes eaten there, but he'd never been this secretive before. It made her excited to wonder what he could be cooking up, plus got her mind off her current worries.

"So, what dress standard is required?" she asked, pushing for a hint.

"Very little," answered Luke simply, smiling to himself, knowing Jo was fishing.

Jo was very curious, but she realised she would just have to wait and she knew she would love the surprise, whatever it was.

Not long after they'd arrived home, Luke's phone rang. It was Steve, the lead singer of Stonefish, ringing to let Luke know that everyone was back home after their extended stay on the Great Barrier Reef and suggested they all get together to talk about the tour and generally celebrate its success. Luke thought it was a great idea so invited the band members, the crew, their manager and their partners around to his place for the barbie the following afternoon. His plans were coming together even better than he'd anticipated. He sang to himself as he checked the pantry, fridge and freezer. They were looking a bit bare so he decided a shopping trip was on the cards for tomorrow. This was going to be some party tomorrow night! While Jo was in another room he made a few quick calls to confirm his plans for that night. Everything was under control.

Just before sunset they walked across the road and along a fifty metre track through the dunes to the beach. There was a small private cove, seldom visited by anyone else, right in front of Luke's house. Luke, dressed only in boardies, carried his guitar and a torch while Jo, wearing only a pale blue sarong, brought a blanket.

As they arrived at the beach, Jo's mouth dropped open in surprise. On the sand in front of them was a small fire, with a supply of wood not too far away. On a brightly coloured tablecloth next to the fire sat a huge tray laden with a large variety of fresh, cold seafood, sitting on ice. Another tray beside it contained grapes, strawberries and freshly cut mango and watermelon pieces. A small dish of water and some serviettes were beside the trays. Also, on the cloth was an esky that Jo recognised as Luke's.

"What...... When.....?" she shook her head, speechless.

"Well, I collected the wood and brought the esky down this morning when I came for a jog. I didn't actually do much jogging," he laughed. "Then I made a few phone calls throughout the day while you were preoccupied. Do you like it?"

"LIKE it?" Jo beamed. "I LOVE it!" She hugged him with all her strength.

"I hope you're hungry," Luke said, taking her hand and leading her over to the setting. He took the blanket from her and spread it on the sand next to the cloth then put his guitar down on it before they sat down. Luke reached over to the esky, opened it and took out a bottle of champagne and two crystal glasses. Jo recognised these as well.

"You HAVE been busy," she grinned, "AND sneaky."

Luke popped the champagne cork and poured them each a glass.

"What shall we drink to?" asked Jo, holding her glass up.

"How about forgetting about the past and looking forward to the future," he suggested.

"Sounds good," nodded Jo. "Not very original but it sure sounds good."

They touched glasses with a "clink", kissed softly and sipped their champagne. Jo sat between Luke's legs, leaning back against his chest, as they watched the golden sun turn to a pink then disappear over the Indian Ocean. Between sips of champagne they nibbled on the food.

"Happy?" Luke asked, nuzzling the side of Jo's neck.

"Ecstatic!" exclaimed Jo. "I've never been happier." She turned to face him, running her hands slowly over his bare, smooth chest. Then, cupping his cheeks in her hands, she leant forward to kiss him. Their breathing became deeper as their kisses intensified, but Luke pulled back. "What's wrong?" Jo frowned, sitting back.

"I've got another surprise for you," he smiled, taking his guitar out of its case.

Jo sat back opposite him, cross legged. He began to strum softly. It was a tune she'd never heard him play before. Soon he began to sing, his eyes never leaving hers. She had never heard these words before, but suddenly realised he was singing about her. The sound of his voice and the soft strumming totally mesmerised her. She watched him sitting there in the firelight as the daylight faded, with his tanned body and strumming his guitar. In her mind he was the most attractive, wonderful man she had ever known. Her heart literally swelled with love and pride as her emotions overwhelmed her causing tears to well in her eyes.

When he had finished the song, Jo just sat, spellbound. The tears rolled freely down her cheeks and she was speechless.

Luke just sat there smiling at her. It made him happy to see so much emotion aroused in her from his lyrics.

"When did you write it?" she asked eventually, in total amazement.

"I've been working on it over the past week. In my head mainly. It's very hard trying to do anything behind your back."

"Has it got a name yet?" Jo asked.

"Yep! It's just called 'Wildflower'," answered Luke. "We might even record it one day. Would you mind, Jo?"

"Not at all," she whispered seductively, crawling on her hands and knees toward him. Putting the guitar down, he encircled her in his arms. She pushed him gently back on his back and lay on top of him. He tickled her playfully on the ribs which made her giggle. Suddenly she stopped laughing. "I love you so much, Luke." She gazed intently into his eyes.

"I love you too, Jo."

She lowered her head to kiss him on the lips before kissing her way down his neck to his chest, while she could feel his hardness through his shorts. Luke sat back up, taking her with him. Jo let out a sigh of frustration. "What now?"

Luke laughed. He loved teasing her and would see that she was definitely well taken care of later, but first he reached inside his guitar case and took out a little black box. Jo's frown completely disappeared when she obviously got the picture. Luke opened the box to reveal a sparkling, diamond ring. Jo gasped as he held it closer for her to see. It was only a small diamond, but it sparkled brilliantly in the firelight and he knew she didn't like big, bulky jewellery.

"Will you marry me, Jo?" Luke asked, his eyes locked with hers. Never in his life had he felt such intense emotion. Tears formed in his eyes as he noticed the same in Jo's.

Her mouth opened to speak but no sound came out. Then her bottom lip began to tremble and she suddenly felt light headed, but not just from the champagne. Slowly and shakily, Jo raised her right hand to his face and lightly caressed his cheek. The tears were still running down her face as she leant forward and placed a feathery, lingering kiss on his lips. Sucking in her breath, she sat back a little, only inches from his face. "Yes," she whispered. "I will marry you."

Luke placed the ring on her left hand and suddenly let out a loud, shrill whistle, almost piercing Jo's ear drums. Within seconds fireworks were exploding overhead, filling the night sky with a blaze of colour. Jo sat back stunned. She shook her head and laughed. Was there no end to this man's surprises?

"Has there been someone sitting up in the bushes this whole time?" she shouted above the noise of the fireworks.

Luke looked at his watch. "No, probably only for about twenty minutes or so."

Soon the fireworks died down, but not before a huge climax of cascading brilliant colours. Within minutes Jo heard a car start up, up on the road and drive away.

"You're amazing," she laughed, still shaking her head. "Can you play Wildflower again for me please?"

Luke was happy to oblige then placed the guitar back into its case before putting some more wood on the fire. Then, without speaking a word, he took her in his arms and lay her down gently on her back on the blanket.

"Luke, I….."

"Ssh." He gently placed his finger on her lips for a second before replacing it with his own lips.

A night bird called out from the trees in the dunes and the gentle waves rolled up the beach as Luke lovingly kissed and nibbled her neck and chest. He untied the knot in the front of her sarong and she lifted her body for him to unwrap it from around her. She had nothing on underneath and shivered from delight as Luke ran his hand tenderly down over her stomach and thighs. Jo stroked his chest before reaching down and removing his shorts.

He leant over to the fruit tray and picked up a piece of mango, bringing it over and above her stomach. She smiled in anticipation as Luke slowly squeezed the mango, dribbling juice on her breasts, stomach and abdomen. She sucked in her breath sharply as the cool juice hit her warm skin. Dropping the squeezed piece of mango back on the tray, he proceeded to lick and suck every drop of juice off Jo's torso while she licked the juice from his hand. He didn't stop once that juice was gone. Picking up another piece and smiling wickedly at Jo, he slowly moved down between her parted legs. Squeezing it, he directed the sweet nectar over her silk covered mound and let it run down over her lips and into every little crevice. The sensation was breathtaking and her pelvis arched involuntarily. Luke leaned down to drink the juices of the mango and Jo's own. His tongue darted firmly over and around her throbbing pearl while he held her open to him and before long she was gasping for breath as her stomach twitched and danced.

Suddenly the waves seemed to crash louder and harder on the shore, the stars seemed brighter and the fire hotter. Jo's head was spinning as her body ignited with passion. She began to tremble and shake. Then fireworks, ten times brighter and hotter than she'd witnessed earlier, exploded with intense ferocity in her loins and throughout her body. She cried out long and hard, expelling all the built up air in her lungs, as her back suddenly arched off the blanket. Vivid, intense colours flashed through her brain as she held Luke's head tightly in her hands and pressed him harder to her.

After several seconds she pushed him away, not being able to bear being touched there for a little while after an orgasm. He kissed his way back up her stomach and chest to her mouth. Jo could taste a hint of mango on his lips as well as her own flavour. Such was the intensity of her massive orgasm, it took longer than usual for her heartbeat and breathing to return to normal.

"Your turn!" she asserted, finally sitting up and gently pushing him down on his back.

"Was it worth the wait?" he asked cheekily.

"Definitely," she breathed heavily, before kissing him hungrily on the mouth.

Jo reached for a piece of watermelon, breaking a large piece of flesh away before dropping the skin back on the tray. She smiled as she squeezed the melon juice over his torso. Licking and sucking her way over his chest, she drew little patterns with her tongue, paying extra attention to his nipples. She heard Luke moan with pleasure. Jo filled his belly button with juice then sucked and licked it up. As she slowly moved down over his abdomen she was fully aware of a huge presence, pulsating strong and hard, only centimetres from her face.

She squeezed more watermelon juice over its head, which made Luke jump slightly. After she watched the juice slide down the shaft she threw the pulp onto the sand and gently started to lick up the juice. When her lips reached the top she encircled him fully and took him deep into her mouth. She released him a little, keeping just the head between her lips as her tongue danced lightly over the sensitive tip. Luke groaned louder as his hips began to move. Jo continued her assault on him without mercy, using her lips, tongue, cheeks and even her teeth extremely lightly. Luke obviously couldn't hold back. He thrust deeper into her mouth as waves of pleasure washed over him causing his body to shudder. Suddenly, he let out a loud groan, followed by several shorter, softer ones, as his hips thrust up slightly with each moan. Jo felt the hot liquid hit the back of her throat and she squeezed the base with her fingers to prolong his pleasure. She enjoyed giving him pleasure as much as he loved giving it to her.

They lay silently in each other's arms for several minutes. There was no need for words. Eventually Luke got up and put some more wood on the fire and they ate some more food. The moon was up now and cast shadows on the sand from the overhanging trees and sparkled brightly on the water, like thousands of tiny diamonds.

For several more hours they stayed on the beach, talking, laughing, touching and making love. He played her several more songs and eventually, with some reluctance, they headed home and fell, exhausted, into bed. Luke would get the things from the beach in the morning.

"Luke, this has been the most beautiful, amazing night of my life, thank you so much," Jo whispered as they snuggled in bed. How she loved him with all her heart.

"You're very welcome, my beautiful Wildflower," he replied.

The next day was hectic with shopping for food and preparing salad, entrees and desserts. Luke wanted to buy them all already made but Jo insisted on making them. She enjoyed cooking and did it well. Luke rang his parents to tell them there was a party happening, not just them coming for tea, so his Mum insisted on bringing some food as well. Jo ensured she posted the letter to Jeff's mother while out shopping.

She found it hard to erase the smile from her face and constantly looked down at the ring on her left hand. It was a beautiful reminder that the previous night wasn't just a dream.

"I decided yesterday to make this party our engagement party," confessed Luke, catching her admiring her ring yet again.

"Ohhh," smiled Jo, "and what made you so sure I would accept?"

"Because you find me charming, handsome and irresistible," teased Luke. "But what really clinched it was when you didn't get up me for leaving the toilet seat up."

She threw a carrot, that she was about to grate, at him across the kitchen. He ducked suddenly, letting it hit the wall behind him.

"I'm going downstairs to set things up," he laughed. "It's not safe around here."

Jo shook her head and smiled to herself as she went back to her food preparations. When she was satisfied all was done, she rang her Mum to give her the good news. Her mother seemed a bit taken aback at first since they had barely known each other a month, but it didn't really surprise her. Next, Jo rang Meg, who was thrilled, especially after Jo asked her to be her maid of honour, which Meg happily accepted.

Guests began arriving around six thirty for the party. The sun was still up so some of the children happily splashed about in the pool. Luke enjoyed a few beers catching up with the rest of the band and crew. They all agreed that this tour had been the most successful and enjoyable one yet, but they were all happy to relax for the next couple of months. The last eighteen months had been full-on, with writing material for the latest album, recording, rehearsing and touring to promote it. A couple of the blokes teased Luke that he'd scored the best from the tour, referring to Jo. He happily agreed.

Luke's father offered to be the cook for the bar-be-que and once Jo, Kelly and Luke's mother brought down all the food he began. They spread the food out on a large table set up near the barbie.

After everyone had enjoyed a few drinks and eaten their meal, Luke stood up asking for everybody's attention as he had an announcement to make. He beckoned Jo over to his side and placed his arm affectionately around her shoulders as she put hers around his waist.

"You all know that I'm absolutely crazy about this pretty lady here," he began. There were a few whistles and laughs from the crowd. "Well, last night I asked her to marry me."

"And what did she say?" heckled Steve, good naturedly.

Luke and Jo looked at each other. It was hard to tell who had the biggest grin on their face.

"She said YES!" beamed Luke, suddenly swooping Jo up in his arms and swinging her around before planting a big kiss on her lips.

Everyone cheered and came forward to congratulate them, with some asking when was the big day.

"Soon," was all Luke would reply.

Everyone partied on as Luke brought out several bottles of champagne. David went home for his camera and shot lots of photos of the glowing couple. He found Jo to be very photogenic.

Gradually the guests started to leave, beginning with the ones with children, followed by Luke's parents. Luke put several of the single men, who had a bit too much to drink, up for the night. Kelly had gone home, having a busy work day coming up. David had stayed behind and as Luke was showing the stayers to their beds, Jo and David sat alone near the pool.

"Wow, Jo," said David. "Everything is happening so fast for you. Your head must be spinning."

"Mmm," agreed Jo, smiling. "These last few weeks have been incredible, except for...." She suddenly stopped herself, not wanting David, or anyone, to learn about the situation concerning Jeff.

"Except for what, Jo?" David urged.

Jo thought quickly. "Except for not being able to share tonight with my family and my best friend."

"Yeah, that's sad," consoled David. "You'll have to talk them into coming over, especially for the wedding."

"Oh, don't worry," enthused Jo. "They wouldn't miss that for the world!"

"It certainly makes us look slack in that department, doesn't it?" laughed David.

"Hey, we could make it a double wedding," suggested Jo.

David smiled and nodded, pondering the thought, then shook his head. "No, it's your special day. You two make the most of it. Kel and I will just plod along like we've always done. We're happy the way we are. A piece of paper won't change anything."

He poured Jo another bourbon and dry from the bar inside and they continued chatting until Luke came back downstairs. Jo found David to be friendly and easy to get along with that night, which made her wonder why she initially doubted him.

"They all tucked in?" Jo asked as Luke walked over and sat beside her after pouring himself a drink.

"Yep, snug as bugs in a rug," replied Luke. "Just hope no-one spews in the beds." He grimaced and Jo screwed up her face.

The three of them chatted a little while longer before David decided to call it a night. As soon as he disappeared in the direction of his house, Luke suggested a swim in the pool. Jo readily agreed and was out of her clothing, stark naked, before he was. They embraced and kissed before diving into the pool. Cuddles and touches soon led to each wanting more. Luke took her hand and helped her out of the pool. She knelt down on her hands and knees on the grass so Luke could enter her from behind, drawing forth a low moan from deep in her throat.

Little could they know, not far away in the darkness, a pair of eyes watched them intensely.

CHAPTER TEN

"So, Pete," Mo said, as they drove west along the Sturt Highway, "you haven't told me the real reason you wanted to get back to Perth in a hell of a hurry."

"Yes I did," Pete answered, looking up from the cigarette he was rolling. "I said I wanted to go back and see me family and mates."

"Yeah, yeah, I know you said that, but what's the REAL reason?" insisted Mo. "Runnin' from some-one?"

"Nuh," shrugged Pete. "I'm just sick of Sydney. Sick of all the shit that goes on AND I want to make it to my thirtieth birthday. There's no way I would if I stayed there any longer."

"Your THIRTIETH birthday!" shrieked Mo, reaching over and turning the radio down. "You look closer to FORTY to me."

"Thanks a lot Mo!" replied Pete indignantly, lighting his smoke and exhaling straight in her direction. "That's what I mean. I'll be dead soon if I don't make a clean break."

"So, what makes you think that Perth is going to be any different?"

Pete shrugged. "Dunno, but I have to find out." He almost added he hoped to catch up with an old friend – a very special friend, but thought better of confiding that much information to Mo, at this stage anyway.

"Where will you stay, with your Old's?" Mo asked.

"Hell no!" said Pete abruptly. "Me and the old man aint the best of friends. I'll stay with me sister, Debbie."

"What suburb is she in?"

"Subiaco," answered Pete. "It's fairly close to the city. Can you drop me off there? Where are you going?"

"I'm not staying in Perth," Mo replied, which made Pete frown. "I'm headin' up the coast further to Kalbarri. That's where my cousin lives. Not a bad little spot, right on the coast. Yeah, no probs, I'll drop ya at Debbies."

Suddenly Mo planted her foot to overtake a semi-trailer in front of them. She squealed as the adrenalin rushed through her veins, for just in front of them was a hill.

"ARE YOU CRAZY?" Pete shouted, holding on tightly to the door with one hand and the dash with the other.

The pink Holden swerved back on to the left side of the road just in front of the semi as a car appeared over the hill speeding toward them. The driver flashed his headlights and gave Mo the middle finger. Mo let out a loud "Yahoooooo."

Pete's heart nearly stopped. "Don't ever friggin' do that again, Mo!" He panted. "You scared the shit out of me! We could have both been killed."

"Yeah, but we weren't," laughed Mo. "For Christ's sake Pete, loosen up. We're only havin' a bit of fun."

"Like I just said, I'm thirty next birthday and I wanna live to see it." He took an extra deep drag on his smoke to try and settle his nerves.

"Hey!" cried Mo. "This reminds me of Thelma and Louise. Did'ja see that movie? Fantastic!"

"Wasn't bad," agreed Pete. "What? Are we supposed to be Thelma and Louise?" He laughed at the irony of those words.

"Why not? Well...... you may not exactly be Louise, but I sure as hell wouldn't mind being Thelma. Havin' Brad Pitt drool over my body. Yum!" She giggled in delight.

If only she knew, thought Pete to himself. *I wouldn't mind a bit of Brad Pitt, myself.*

"Well," ordered Pete, "just make sure our trip doesn't end the same way as theirs. There's some bloody big cliffs over where the Nullabor meets the sea. You just keep away from them!"

Mo laughed loud and full. "Don't worry, Petey Boy, I'll get you there in one piece." She turned the radio up loud again and sang along with it as they drove. Pete just rolled his eyes.

By sundown they'd reached a small town in central, southern New South Wales. They decided to check into the only pub they could see. It was a huge, old, two storey building with a veranda along the front on both levels. The paint was starting to peel and it was obvious it had seen better days, but she was majestic, proud and certainly would have thousands of yarns absorbed into her grand old walls. Mo stopped the car right out front of the pub. There were several other vehicles parked there as well, mainly dusty utes and four wheel drives.

"Ooh, might be some cowboys in town," said Mo, raising her eyebrows. "Could be interesting."

Pete looked at her and shook his head. Her orange hair was sticking out everywhere, her nails were painted black and her clothes were as colourful and mismatched as she and Pete were.

"They'll take one look at you and run the other way," grinned Pete.

Mo screwed up her face at him. "Yeah, well the women will do the same to you!"

Good! thought Pete to himself.

They got out of the car and looked around. The town appeared to have only one main street. Several shops, including a general store and a café were either side of the pub. A small group of children and a dog wandered aimlessly along the quiet street. One was kicking a battered football casually along in front of him.

"What a BORING place," groaned Mo, swiping several flies from her face.

As they walked into the public bar together everyone suddenly stopped what they were doing to stare at the two odd looking strangers. Old bushies ceased talking midway through a sentence, mouth still agape. Young ringers stopped their glass in mid-air as they were bringing it to their lips to drink. Even a blue heeler, lying under a table, sat upright for a better look. Mo and Pete froze and looked about the room. There were about fifteen men of various ages in the bar and several women. Lee Kernaghan's Planet Country belted out of the jukebox in the poolroom adjacent to the bar. Pete felt very uneasy and paranoid. Everyone, including the middle aged woman behind the bar, continued to stare at them.

"Well, whatcha's all starin' at?" demanded Mo loudly, but as pleasantly as she could. "We're just passin' through and we ARE earthlings! Well, I'm not too sure about this one though." She indicated Pete with her thumb. "I picked him up back along the road near a broken down spaceship."

Pete kicked her in the shin and gritted his teeth. His face was blushing red hot. How he wished the floor would open up and swallow him right now. Suddenly, everyone in the bar burst out laughing. Pete looked at Mo and frowned. "What the hell is goin' on?" he asked, bewildered.

"Come over and have a drink, Love," called one old timer, beckoning them with a wave of his arm.

He sat at the bar with two younger men. Mo thought they must be his sons. Boldly, she strolled over, feeling numerous eyes on her, but gradually the customers resumed what they had been doing just before Pete and Mo had walked in. Pete followed, feeling extremely uneasy. One of the younger men brought two bar stools over from an empty table near a window and placed them near theirs.

"The name's Hank," said the old man, extending his gnarled, weathered hand. His skin was leathery and brown, obviously from years of hard work in the sun. His welcoming smile showed several missing teeth and his nose was large and crooked.

"I'm Mo!" she stated, returning his handshake. "And this is Pete.......my brother."

Pete glared at her in disbelief which made her dig him hard, but discreetly in the ribs with her elbow. He shook Hank's welcoming hand then Hank introduced them to his two sons, Tony and Keith.

They were both around thirty and Mo realised they must work outdoors a lot too.

Tony, the older, larger one of the two was tall with brown, short, curly hair and a round baby face. Keith, was shorter with a crew cut so short it was hard to tell what his hair colour was. He had a moustache and goatee beard. They both had very tanned skin, but their upper face was white, obviously shaded by the hats they must constantly wear.

"You two look a bit out of sorts here," said Hank. "Where are yous from?"

Mo liked his friendly, direct manner. "Sydney!" she announced, "and we're going home to Perth." This was a new experience to Mo. She'd flown to Sydney when she'd first left Western Australia and had never spent much time in country towns.

Neither had Pete, for that matter. He ordered two schooners of beer when the bar attendant came to serve them. She gave him a suspicious look when she set the beers down in front of him and took the twenty dollar note he handed over. It didn't help his persistent paranoia at all.

They, well Mo mainly, chatted to Hank and his sons for an hour or so. Mo thought that Keith was a bit of "all right". Pete just quietly enjoyed his beers and only spoke occasionally. He decided that Mo talked enough for both of them anyway.

After several beers, he was feeling a little more relaxed. He booked and paid for two single rooms for the night then went to the car to get their bags and took them upstairs. While he was upstairs, several other locals had come over to chat to this odd looking, brash but friendly, young woman who had entered their local. Pete had a shower and came back downstairs to find Mo surrounded by men of various ages. The older ones seemed totally in awe of her, while the younger ones flirted non-stop. Pete shook his head and grinned to himself as he entered the bar. Mo certainly gained attention where ever she went and loved every minute of it. She eagerly accepted the drinks her admirers shouted for her.

"Mo, do you want something to eat?" asked Pete, tapping her on the shoulder.

"What? Oh, yeah, better I suppose," she answered, before going back to the joke she was telling.

Pete ordered two counter meals, steak and veg for himself and chicken and veg for Mo. Suddenly the small crowd around Mo broke out into raucous laughter. She had obviously delivered the punch line of her joke. Pete didn't feel like joining back in with Mo's group so he went out to the smokers area and rolled a smoke. A large, bearded man walked out from the pool room and asked Pete if he would like a game of pool, which Pete readily accepted. The other man set the balls up and had first break. It had been a while since Pete had played so he didn't fare too well in the first game.

Their meals were brought out before he started the second game so he and Mo sat at a table on the far side of the pool room to eat.

"Guess what?" giggled Mo as she began to eat. She was quite tiddly by now.

"What?" asked Pete, wondering what on earth she was going to come out with.

"Hank and the Boys have invited us out to their property tomorrow. They're doin' some brandin' and stuff with the cattle. I reckon it'll be wild! They said we can stay a few days."

"A few days!" exclaimed Pete, nearly choking on a piece of meat. "We're supposed to be going to Perth!"

"Yeah, I know," nodded Mo, dropping a pile of peas off her fork straight into her lap. "Woops," she giggled, picking them up one by one and popping them into her mouth. "There's heaps of time, Mate. S'long as we get there by Christmas."

Pete sighed deeply. He really didn't want to hang around here, but it WAS Mo's car so he didn't have much say in the matter.

"So," Mo continued, "if ya don't like it you'll havta hitch."

Pete thought briefly about that idea but then decided to stick with Mo. She could be a pain in the bum at times, but deep down he couldn't help liking her...... in a sisterly way. "I'll come to their place with you," said Pete. "But only for a day or two most. Someone has to keep you out of trouble..... sister dear." They both laughed and finished their meal.

The bearded man was sitting at the bar, waiting for another game of pool. He never offered his name to Pete and Pete didn't bother either. What was the point? They were only passing through.

Mo returned to Hank, Tony and Keith. Most other patrons had left the bar. Two men and one woman sat up the far end while several others dined at smaller tables, both in the bar and out on the veranda.

Always inquisitive, Mo wanted to know more about their cattle property. Hank was proud to fill her in. It was twenty-five thousand acres and they ran about three thousand head of cattle when the season was good. It was quite small is size compared to others in the district. Hank's wife, they boy's mother, had died several years earlier and, as neither son was married, the three of them ran the property together. Locals jokingly referred to it as "Bachelors Hill".

The men attempted to give Mo directions on how to get to the property, but as they were all pretty sloshed by now, the directions made little sense to anyone. After several arguments between the three about a left turn, or was it right? Two gates to open or three? Keith offered to drive back into town the next morning and let them follow him back out. It was situated twenty kilometres from town, along a corrugated, dusty road. However, nobody told Mo just what sort of road it was. The three men then left, saying they would see her and Pete tomorrow.

Mo watched Pete and the bearded man play pool. He didn't speak much and when he did it was short and abrupt. Pete had easily won the second game so the other man suggested they play for twenty dollars. After that win, Pete was feeling quietly confident so he readily agreed. He ordered another beer for Mo and a scotch and coke for himself. He'd had enough beer for one night.

The next game did not go so well. Pete accidently sunk the black while he still had one other ball left to sink. There went his twenty dollars.

"Double or nothin'" Pete declared to his opponent. The man just smiled, nodded and racked the balls up again. During the next game, the other man white washed Pete completely. Pete was left with seven balls on the table while his challenger sunk his one after the other and then the black. Pete realised he had been set up. This bloke was a hustler, but due to his size, Pete was not going to argue with him. No way! He reluctantly handed the money over to him and told Mo he was going to bed. He was totally pissed off! How could he let himself be sucked in like that? The other bloke purposely let him win one, or maybe he would have let him win the next one too, just to build his confidence up enough to go double or nothing. He fell for it hook, line and sinker!

Pete downed the last of his drink, ordered two cans of scotch and coke to take away and headed up to his room.

Mo wasn't far behind. "So, what's ya problem?" she called after him while staggering up the old, creaky, wooden staircase to the guest rooms.

"Nothin'!" snapped Pete. "I'm going to bed and you should too. You don't want to miss the Wild West Show tomorrow."

"Geez, you can be a cranky little shit, Pete!" Mo announced as she reached her bedroom door Pete had to direct her to. She put the key in, turned it and went to turn the door knob, but her hand slipped off as it turned and she lost her balance. The door flew open as her body weight fell against it and she went sprawling, face first, on to the floor of her room.

Pete's door was opposite hers and he was standing at his, about to fire an insult back at her when she fell. Suddenly he couldn't be angry at her anymore. He laughed so hard the tears were streaming down his cheeks. Mo was still face down on the floor. Her body shuddered as she laughed, squealed and snorted at the same time. Pete laughed even harder at her laughing. Luckily, she had shorts on instead of a skirt, or it probably would have ended up around her neck! That was a sight Pete was glad he didn't have to see.

Suddenly a man appeared in the hallway. "What's going on out here? Some people are trying to sleep!" He was not happy.

"Sorry Mate," Pete said, once he'd composed himself. "My fr.....
SISTER just fell over. You should have seen it!" He started giggling
again.

"Just quit the noise or I'll call the manager up." The man stormed
back into his room mumbling to himself and closed his door.

Pete helped Mo up and on to her bed. She couldn't stop laughing but
within seconds of her head hitting the pillow she was out like a light.
Pete breathed a sigh of relief, went to his own room and drank his cans
then fell asleep.

Just after sunrise the next morning, there was a knock on their doors
that signalled the breakfast trays had arrived. They'd ordered and paid
for them the night before. By the time they both dragged themselves out
of the beds, opened the doors and saw the trays of greasy bacon, eggs,
sausages and toast awaiting them, they had no desire to eat.

Pete picked up his tray and took it into Mo's room. "Dunno about
you, but I can't stomach this right now," he groaned shaking his head.

Mo yawned, rubbed her eyes and held her head in her hands. "Ohhh,
my head," she moaned, then searched in her bag for a headache tablet.
She swallowed two with the bitter orange juice that was on her tray.

Pete ate one piece of cold toast and drank his lukewarm coffee while
Mo had a shower. She felt a bit better after it and was able to force
down the egg and toast, even though it was cold by then. Pete showered
before they packed up and went downstairs to wait at the car for Keith.

The early morning sun hit and hurt their eyes as they reached the
car. Pete's mouth was unbearably dry and tasted shockingly bitter. He
needed something cold and wet.

"Want something to drink?" he asked Mo as he headed in the
direction of the café, relieved to find it open so early in the morning.

"Yes please," groaned Mo. She was sitting in the driver's seat, with
her head back on the top of the seat and her eyes closed, feeling the
painful pounding that hadn't yet abated, in her temples. "Straight
mineral water or lemonade."

Pete returned with a large bottle each of coke and lemonade which he handed to Mo. She unscrewed the cap and drank it down thirstily, while Pete did the same with the coke.

"You'll rot ya gut drinkin' that shit," stated Mo, screwing up her face.

"Too bad," replied Pete. "At the moment it feels like it's already rotten."

Just then a Toyota land cruiser drove along the street and pulled up beside them. Keith got out of the vehicle and walked over to Mo's side.

"Ready to go?" he asked cheerfully. "How are you feeling this morning?"

"We've been better," replied Mo, glancing over at Pete. "Yep, we're ready."

Keith got into his ute and started it up. Mo and Pete followed him along the street but before they'd even lost sight of the township, they hit a dirt road. Mo had to slow right down, not only because it was rough, but the choking dust generated form Keith's vehicle nearly blinded them. They couldn't even see his car in front of them.

"Shit!" Mo shrieked as she tried to dodge one large pot hole only to run smack bang into another. The car bounced so hard that Pete's head hit the roof. This didn't help the pain he already had there.

"FUCK!" he shouted angrily. "Slow down will ya!"

"Don't tell me how to drive!" she spat back.

Soon they came to a stretch of bad corrugation. Mo had never driven on anything like it before. The car was bouncing about over the road then began to fishtail. She immediately slowed to a crawl and just thumped slowly over every annoying bump. "This is worse than riding a trotting horse bareback."

Pete was attempting to roll a smoke. The bumpy road was making it impossible, so before long he gave up in disgust, putting the wad of tobacco back into the packet and picking up all the loose bits that had scattered over his lap from the vibrations. Suddenly, Mo skidded the car

147

to an unexpected stop on the side of the road, sending up even more dust. She jumped out quickly, slamming the door behind her.

"What's the matter?" frowned Pete. He turned to see Mo bent over at the back of the car and could see her body heaving as her breakfast dislodged itself and let fly. Pete grinned and suddenly realised that this was a good time to finally roll that smoke.

A few minutes later, amidst much moaning and groaning, Mo staggered back to the driver's seat and took a few sips of lemonade.

"Why did you let me drink so much last night?" She glared at Pete who just shook his head and rolled his eyes. Starting the car again, she drove on silently. Keith was waiting on the side of the road a kilometre or so ahead. When they caught up with him, he turned off the road and down a narrow track. An old, rusty drum was nailed to a tree, about shoulder height, where they turned off. The three men's initials were on it, followed by the surname, "Barton" and the name, "Valerie Downs". Mo assumed it must be their letter box. This track they were now on was rough, but at least it wasn't corrugated like the road.

"What the hell have you got us into Mo?" moaned Pete. "You don't know where he is leading us. He might take us into the middle of nowhere and chop us up into little pieces."

Mo looked at him and shook her head. "Don't be so paranoid. He's not gunna do that. We're just goin' to have a bit of fun. Have you ever been on a cattle station?"

"No, never! It doesn't interest me at all. I just want to get to Perth."

"If you don't stop whinging I won't let you get out of the car once we get there," she threatened, in a motherly way.

Pete just looked at her, then remembered her fall the previous night and burst out laughing. Once he could get the words out to remind her, she followed suit.

The laughter eased the tension and very soon some buildings came into view. They pulled up beside a large, old, lowset house with a veranda around it and several tall, leafy trees adjoining it. A huge shed sat behind the house and a few hundred metres further away, were more sheds and an extensive set of cattle yards, containing several hundred head of bellowing cattle of various colours. Most of the land on the property was cleared and almost flat. Mo was in awe of the view as she got out of the car and gazed about her into the far distance. Two brown, kelpie cross dogs came bounding over to the car, their tails wagging. Mo bent and patted them both.

Even Pete was impressed. He hadn't known what to expect but it definitely wasn't this. The grass in the paddocks was lush and green from recent rain and everything looked neat and tidy. Several large jacaranda trees next to the yards were blooming with their distinctive purple flowers, which created an almost mirror reflection on the ground beneath them caused from the flowers that had fallen. As hardened as Pete was to life, this scene almost took his breath away and he suddenly thought of his Mum and how much she would love to see it.

Hank and Tony came out of the house to greet them and Hank immediately offered them some smoko. Mo accepted but Pete only wanted a cup of good, strong coffee. Tony showed them the quarters out the back where they would stay in while there. It was a two room hut with four beds for extra stockmen to sleep when they needed to hire extra hands. Mo liked it and the beds looked comfortable. The rooms were clean but needed a paint job.

After smoko, Mo changed from her jeans into shorts, but Pete kept his on and they all headed for the stockyards to work. The morning was heating up as they walked over and Pete was beginning to regret it with every step. His head still ached a little and his stomach didn't feel so good. Mo was a little more enthusiastic, but due to her hangover, not her usual colourful self.

The cattle in the yards were from one of the numerous paddocks the property was divided into. The calves had to be branded, vaccinated and the bullies (male calves) castrated. The men had separated them from their mothers the afternoon before. The cows were in a small holding paddock on one side of the yards, while the calves were in the yards. Therefore, with around two hundred cows bellowing for their calves and the same number of calves answering back, the noise was quite deafening. Of course, the men were used to it, but the city slickers shook their heads and grimaced.

The branding irons were red hot in the gas furnace. Tony took Pete with him into the yard of calves to help herd each one up the long, narrow crush and into the head bail, as it was needed. The calves ranged from three to six months old. The older ones were bigger and, as Pete found out in a very painful way, had strong hind legs that gave a nasty kick. Clouds of choking dust that mingled with the smell of fresh cow poop, were swirled up as Pete and Tony brought a number of unwilling calves into the small V-shaped forcing yard, ready to send one up to Hank, who was to catch it in the headlock, where it would be held still for its ordeal.

Pete had been hoping they would have done it like in the old western movies – lassoing each calf and holding it down on the ground, but when he saw the sheer number of calves and the size of some of them, he was glad they didn't. The first kick to his bony shin was bad enough, but it wasn't to be the last for the day.

Mo watched in amazement and horror as the calf was caught in the headlock. Keith quickly opened the gate as Tony leaned his weight upon the side of the calf, holding its tail out the way, and keeping it still against the fence. Keith grabbed the branding irons from the blue flame and pressed them on to the calf's tender rump. An orange flame sprung to life as it singed some of the hair around the brand, and the calf bawled out long and hard while the smell from the burnt hair sickened Pete a little more. If the calf was a bull, Keith then grabbed the bucket with the antiseptic water, cloth and very sharp, small knife and did the castrating. Pete's eyes watered and he involuntarily crossed his legs, as he watched the swift removal of its testicles, which were placed in a clean bucket for use later. Meanwhile, Hank ear tagged and vaccinated each one. The whole process was over in about two minutes before another was brought in. By lunch time they were half way through the mob.

The Barton men and their visitors went back to the house for corned beef and tomato sandwiches along with lots of cold water. After lunch they were straight back into it. Pete had had more than enough, but he didn't want to look like a wimp in front of the other blokes. Mo had also had enough, but since she insisted on them coming here she felt that she had better keep her mouth shut.

By late afternoon the last of the calves had gone through. Pete was exhausted, sunburnt, dirty and the front of his jeans was splattered with smelly calf poop. He wanted a shower and bed.

Mo wasn't so badly off, as she had kept out of most of the action.

The calves were all reunited with their mothers and left in the holding paddock until early morning when the men would drive them, by motorbike, several kilometres to their paddock. They had water from a windmill and plenty of grass where they would spend the night.

"So, what's on the agenda for tomorrow?" Mo asked as they walked wearily back to the house.

"Well," began Hank, "tomorrow we've got to drive this mob back, fix a windmill in their paddock, do a few miles of fence, fix the truck up and wrestle some wild pigs that keep mucking up the waterholes. When are you two headin' off?"

"Tomorrow morning!" Mo and Pete both stated in unison. Everyone laughed.

The guests both had a shower then joined the Barton men on the cool, breezy veranda for a coldie or two. They all enjoyed the chat and a few laughs before Keith went to fire up the nearby barbie. Pretty soon steaks were sizzling and the aroma whetted the appetites of all. Mo helped Hank get some bread, sauce and salads from in the kitchen and put on the veranda table. Along with a prime piece of rump Keith also placed some other little cooked tidbits on Pete and Mo's plates, which they eagerly sampled.

"Mmm," said Pete, between mouthfuls. "What is this? It tastes pretty good." He reached for a second one.

"Mountain Oysters, Mate," enthused Keith, eating one whole. "Or in our case, Prairie Oysters. Get it in ya!"

"Oh My GOD!" exclaimed Mo as her eyes widened in absolute horror. She turned and spat hers on the ground then continued coughing and gagging.

"What?" frowned Pete, with no idea of what he was eating.

"You remember the knackers we cut out of the bull calves?" laughed Hank, happily biting into a huge one.

"BULL SHIIIIIT! No way!" spluttered Pete, spitting it out in all directions.

"NO, BULLS NUTS!" Hank and his sons roared with laughter.

Pete took a swig of his beer, swished his mouth, spat that out for good measure and downed the rest of the can to try and take his mind off it. "You coulda told us!" he snapped.

The laughter was infectious and pretty soon Mo couldn't help herself either. She did agree with Pete in that it was pretty mean trick to play on them, albeit a harmless one. "I'll just stick to steak thanks," she laughed.

Pete ate his steak and salad in relative silence then stated he was buggered and headed off to bed. His body ached all over and he was asleep pretty much before his head even hit the pillow.

Hank retired soon after and Mo, Tony and Keith remained on the veranda having more beers. Mo hoped for some time alone with Keith and was secretly pleased when Tony stood up and announced he was hitting the sack.

Keith sensed that Mo was attracted to him and, although he didn't feel physically attracted to her, he liked her personality and wasn't about to turn an opportunity down. There were not too many single women in the area.

They went to the quarters and had a shower there. Mo was sure nothing would wake Pete up. After the shower, she led Keith to her bed, as her body developed goose bumps in anticipation. She hadn't had a man in a long time. Just as she grabbed a condom out of her bag, Keith snatched it off her and placed it on himself before he had even touched her. She was expecting to do that after some foreplay. He pushed her down on to the bed and lay on top of her, kissing her sloppily, pushing his tongue toward the back of her throat. She nearly gagged. His hand poked and prodded between her legs for several seconds before he entered her roughly.

He moved down and sucked her breasts hungrily while thrusting in and out. After only thirty seconds he groaned and lay still, on her body. She couldn't believe it! She pushed him off her stomach and on to the bed beside her. He got up and walked into the bathroom. She heard the toilet flush and he walked back out fully clothed.

"That was great Mo, see you in the morning." He squeezed her nipple once before turning and disappearing out the door.

She lay there, frustrated and exasperated. "You bastard!" she cursed to herself. "You lousy, selfish, inconsiderate, slack, using, BASTARD!" This time much louder, picking up her boot and hurling it at the door he'd just walked through. Pretty soon tiredness won out over anger and she fell into a deep sleep.

The next morning, Tony and Keith had already left with the cattle when Mo and Pete got out of bed. Mo was pleased. She wasn't keen to face Keith this morning. After they showered and packed their gear, they sat down to a huge breakfast of cereal and mince on toast, that Hank had prepared. The steaming savoury mince smelt delicious and they both had a large helping.

Every muscle in Pete's body seemed to ache. He wasn't used to such full-on physical work. He had to sit down at the table very gingerly.

After breakfast they thanked Hank for his hospitality and got on their way. Mo groaned at the thought of that horrible, rough road again.

"So, did you get a bit last night?" Pete asked with a grin as they drove along the track to the main road.

"What?" snapped Mo. She was still pissed off about it.

"With Keith. I knew you were on to him."

At first Mo was going to keep it from Pete, but then thought, *What the hell.*

"Well, I thought I was goin' to, but the slack prick was a three thrust screamer! Talk about Wham, Bam, Thankyou Ma'am! Only I didn't even get the thankyou!" she shrieked. "It didn't do a single thing for me at all. Hell, it hardly even touched the sides! It's a wonder he doesn't need tweezers and a magnifying glass to find it in the mornings when he wants a leak!" She hit the steering wheel hard with one hand in sheer frustration.

Pete began to laugh.

"Get fucked Pete!" she growled at him.

"Just wish I could," he replied, still laughing.

Mo looked over at him and suddenly began to see him in a new light. *Why bother looking elsewhere when I have a man right here beside me?*

CHAPTER ELEVEN

Later on that day, after they had been driving back on the highway for some time, the car began to pull to the left.

"Oh, what's wrong, Ol' Girl?" Mo shouted above the radio, before pulling over to the side of the road.

"Probably a flat tyre," stated Pete. They both got out to investigate.

"SHIT!" stated Mo in frustration, placing her hands on her hips and looking down at the rear, passenger side tyre, going flat and hissing loudly before their eyes and ears.

"Hope you've got a spare," said Pete, rolling a smoke.

"Think I'm stupid or somethin'? Of course I've got a spare!" Mo glared at him before opening the back up and taking out several bags of gear so she could get to the spare wheel in the wheel well. She dragged the dirty tyre out and dropped it on the ground. It didn't bounce.

"Uh oh," said Pete nervously, bending down to feel the tyre. "It's as flat as a tack, Mo."

"WHAT!" she screeched, bending down to check it herself. I don't believe it!" She kicked the tyre hard with her foot. Several cars whizzed by but nobody had bothered to stop yet.

"Didn't you check it before you left Sydney?" Pete asked in disbelief.

"Of course I.....No! I bloody forgot about gettin' the spare checked!" She jumped about on the spot, screaming and cursing herself for a minute or so. Pete just leaned on the car, smoking his smoke and grinned at her.

"Now what are we supposed to do?" He suddenly realised their predicament. Here they were, stuck out in the middle of nowhere, the last town being a long way back, with two flat tyres.

"Are you with the NRMA or anything like that?"

"Nope! I let it go only about six months ago." She took a few deep breaths to settle herself down. "I'm stuffed if I know what to do now. I s'pose we'll have to stop someone and see if they have a pump."

A car came toward them so Mo jumped out on to the road a little bit, waving her arms about. The driver swerved around her, the male passenger shouted abuse at her and the car just kept on going.

"Yeah, well up yours too, Mate!" she yelled at them, giving the finger. "What's their problem?"

"They probably didn't realise that we're in trouble," shrugged Pete.

"Well, we sure as hell would not have been havin' a picnic out here in the hot sun, in the middle of nowhere!" she spat back at him. "They should've seen the tyre on the ground."

Pete walked around to the driver's door, leant in through the open window and pulled the bonnet lever. He then opened the bonnet and propped it open.

"Whatd'ja do that for?" frowned Mo.

"Now, at least, anyone that comes along will see we are in trouble."

"You're not as silly as ya look, Pete," Mo grinned at him. He glared at her. "Just jokin'," she added quickly.

Just then a four wheel drive ute came along, slowed down and stopped. A middle aged couple got out.

"Trouble?" the man asked in a friendly tone.

Pete turned away and rolled his eyes at the silliness of the question. *No Mate, we often come out here into the middle of nowhere and just sit.*

"Yes," said Mo, gratefully. "We had a flat tyre and the spare is flat as well."

"Could be a bit of a problem," agreed the man.

"You're tellin' me!" stated Pete. "I don't s'pose you'd have a pump?"

"No, sorry," said the man's wife as he inspected both flat tyres.

"Mmm," mused the man as he straightened back up. "The only thing I can suggest is us taking the tyres into town and getting them fixed. We've got a few things to do, but we'll be back in a couple of hours."

"A couple of hours," Pete grumbled under his breath.

Even though the couple certainly seemed genuine, and she appreciated them stopping, Mo knew it wasn't wise to trust anyone these days. She also didn't like the idea of sitting out here until they came back. "We'll come in with you," she said. "We're gettin' a bit hungry anyway. How far to town?"

"About fifteen k's from here," answered the man. "Where are you headed?"

"Perth," replied Pete.

"Wow!" laughed the man. "You sure have a long way to go yet." He picked up the spare wheel and put it into the back of his ute.

Mo dug around in the back of her wagon for the jack and wheel spanner. Pete grimaced when he saw it, remembering how he'd hit the bloke who'd beaten him up. The one he'd used was a little different to this one, but he imagined they'd both sound the same hitting on someone's skull. He took it off Mo and loosened the wheel nuts a little before she placed the jack underneath. Pete wound the jack up and the heavy old Holden groaned as it began to lift off the ground. They took the wheel off and Pete rolled it over to the couple's ute. It strained his aching muscles even more as he hoisted it high up, over the tray and into the back of the ute, alongside the other one.

"I don't think I would be a very good idea to leave your car out here by itself," suggested the man, shaking his head. "I doubt it would still be here when we get back."

"I'll stay," offered Pete. He was so stiff, sore and tired from the previous day that he didn't have any desire to do anything physical and he thought it would be a good chance for a sleep.

"Ok," agreed Mo, getting her bag from the car. "Don't let anyone steal it! I'll bring you back some food."

"I won't!" declared Pete, then handed her a fifty dollar note. "Put this toward the tyres."

Mo was taken aback. Pete could really surprise her at times. He could be cranky and lazy one minute then funny and caring the next.

She was liking him more and more, but still had not let on yet. She was hoping he would make the first move. "Gee, thanks Pete," she smiled then climbed into the cabin of the ute, after the wife had seated herself in the middle. She gave a big wave as they drove off.

Pete watched them disappear over the horizon and sighed before sitting back in the front seat. He remembered the marijuana that he had in the bottom of his bag and leant over the seat to find it. He didn't smoke it around Mo as she didn't like it.

At times, he just couldn't figure her out. She could be so wild and loved a drink but didn't like smoking a little joint or drinking anything with a lot of caffeine in it. As he rolled himself a joint he wondered if, underneath that loud exterior, she was just an ordinary girl. If not, he couldn't imagine a man that would be suited to her.

He smoked the joint and felt instantly relaxed. The hot sun was beating down, straight through the windscreen, so he couldn't lay on the front seat for a sleep. He looked into the back. Mo had so much gear that she had to lay the back seat down to fit everything in. Pete wondered what on earth could be in all those bags when he'd only brought one. Deciding that he didn't feel like shifting all the stuff to fit in, he still wasn't sure what to do.

Looking about him he noticed several small trees not far from the road. They were quite scarce in the area. The bit of shade under those trees looked extremely inviting, so he grabbed a travelling rug from the back and headed over to it. Spreading the rug out, he lay down and was soon fast asleep.

A large ant crawled over the rug and onto his shirt. It darted this way and that and was soon crawling up his neck and onto his face. He mumbled in his slumber and brought his hand up to brush the tickling sensation away. However, the ant was persistent and continued on its journey, reaching his partly open lips. In his sleep, Pete licked his parched lips and closed his mouth.

Suddenly, he sat upright, letting out a yell and spitting onto the ground. The ant had bitten his tongue. He stood up and cursed loudly. A movement out the corner of his eye caught his attention and he turned toward the car.

Two men were there. One was sitting in his seat looking into the glove box and the other was leaning in the back door going through the gear in the back. They both looked over at Pete when they heard him cursing. Obviously, they weren't aware that he was there.

"HEY!" shouted Pete, walking quickly over to them. "What the hell do youse think you're doin?"

The one in the back only seemed about fifteen and nervously looked at the other one as Pete strode over.

"We're just having a look," said the older one arrogantly.

"Well, get out of there and PISS OFF!" Pete demanded, noticing an old ute parked on the opposite side of the road.

"Who's going to make me?" the one in the front asserted, standing up. "You?" He roared with laughter.

Pete gulped. Even though he only looked about twenty, he towered over Pete in height and had shoulders nearly as wide as Pete was tall! AND a menacing scowl on his face, to boot. Then the younger one stood up next to him. He was nearly as big! Pete's palms began to sweat.

"What do you want?" he sighed, knowing it was no use trying to fight them off and he didn't feel like another beating.

Suddenly, he spotted the wheel spanner lying on the ground beside the jack. He quickly dived down, but the younger one was too fast and put his huge foot on it just as Pete was about to grab it. Pete slowly stood back up and faced them, his heart racing.

"Give us your money," demanded the older one, leaning over Pete threateningly.

"Haven't got any," Pete lied desperately. "My girlfriend has got a lift into town to get the tyres fixed and took it all with her....... She's pregnant," Pete added in a pitiful attempt to get them to back off.

"Bullshit!" said the older one before nodding to the other lad, who quickly grabbed Pete from behind by the elbows and held his arms back.

Pete struggled and kicked out, hitting the older one in the stomach. He heard a grunt then felt the man's fist drive hard into his stomach. He doubled over in pain as the air dispelled from his lungs in a gush. *Not again,* he thought to himself, a second before the man's fist came up and slammed into his face. Everything went black.

Pete heard crows calling out their mournful sound and the flies were crawling over his face as he slowly came to. He lay, flat on his back, staring up at the sky, trying to remember what had happened. His face throbbed as he brought his hand up to it. Touching the skin around his eye and cheek made him grimace in pain. Slowly, it all came back to him - the two young men demanding his money.

HIS MONEY! He stood up quickly, but shakily and checked all of his pockets. It was all gone! Shaking his head in anger and disbelief, he cursed the thieves. Thankfully, the car was still there. He staggered over to it and was annoyed to find everything in the back strewn about and in one big mess. They'd obviously gone through the whole lot.

He tried to ascertain how long he'd been passed out for, going by the sun, but he couldn't tell for sure, maybe half an hour. Then he remembered the grass and pills. After a frantic and fruitless search, he realised they were gone too.

"Fuck!" He punched the side of the car in anger and felt like sitting down and crying, but he knew that wouldn't do any good. After all the trouble he went to, to get the money and now it was gone, and they still had a LONG way to go. He was so glad he'd given Mo the money for the tyres. Suddenly he remembered something and a hopeful smile spread on his face.

He opened his door and reached down to where the vinyl lining meets the door skin, put the tips of his fingers in the small gap and pulled. The lining came away a little, just enough for him to squeeze his small hand through. Breathing a huge sigh of relief, he took out a small roll of fifty dollar notes. He'd hidden it there just as they were leaving Sydney, in case he was unlucky enough to be attacked and robbed again.

Although he didn't really expect it to happen, he realised now that it can, at anytime and anywhere. *WOW,* he thought to himself, *SO glad I thought of that.*

Just in case they came back, he put the money back inside the door skin for now and attempted to tidy up the mess his assailants left. He hadn't got much done when Mo and the helpful couple returned.

She got out and walked over to her car, throwing her bag on the front seat. Pete was still scratching around in the back, trying to stuff things back in their rightful bags.

"What are you doin', Pete?" Mo frowned, looking at him through the open back. Then she noticed his swollen eye. "What the hell happened?"

"Some bastards came along and rolled me," answered Pete angrily. "They went through everything."

"Shit! What did they take?"

"Just me money as far as I can see." He never mentioned the drugs. "But I'm not sure about the back here. I was out cold for a while."

The man brought the tyres over to the back of the car. Mo told him what had happened so he put the tyre on while Mo and Pete tidied up things in the back. They put the spare tyre into the wheel well, thanked the man and his wife very much and each drove off in opposite directions.

Mo passed the sandwiches and the bottle of coke she'd bought in town, to Pete and he got stuck into them.

"So, what happened while I was away?" Mo demanded.

Pete told her everything, except about being stoned and asleep. He said that he'd been sitting in the front seat when they pulled up.

Mo was angry, but relieved that Pete wasn't hurt worse and that nothing of hers seemed to have been stolen. She laughed when Pete told her about his hidden stash of money and that it was still safe.

"This has really put a hole in our bread, Pete," she warned. "We are gunna have to be careful from now on."

"I know!" He didn't have to be reminded.

They drove on until they spotted a sign for a caravan park ahead. No more hotel accommodation. From now on it was the cheapest they could find. It was already after dark when they arrived at the park, so they booked a van, showered and walked to the adjacent servo for a burger before going to bed.

Early next morning, Mo filled the car up at the servo, bought a cheap bag of oranges from a stand near the door and they hit the road again. By this time they were almost to the South Australian border. They had originally planned to go into Adelaide for one night and a look around, but they could not afford that now. By mid-morning they had crossed the border and stopped in Renmark for an early lunch. While they were eating, Mo studied the map for the shortest route to the Eyre Highway and Ceduna, which wasn't far from the beginning of the Nullabor Plain. She marked in blue pen the best way to go and instructed Pete to keep an eye on it so they stayed on the correct roads. They filled the car and continued on their journey.

"We haven't had much luck on this trip so far, have we?" mused Pete as they cruised along.

"Nope!" agreed Mo. "Hope nothin' else goes wrong."

"It won't......... it can only get better from here," nodded Pete.

They drove all day, only stopping for toilet breaks. Just on dusk they pulled into a servo for some petrol and food. A pub was next door and Pete couldn't resist going in and buying several bottles of cheap wine. Even though Mo complained about wasting the money, she realised she felt like a drink as well, so went in for a few tallies of beer, before they drove on a bit more.

When Mo had decided she'd had enough driving for the day, they found another road leading off the highway. Pete didn't have a license, so he couldn't relieve her of any driving. After travelling along the off road for a kilometre or two, they found a small clearing and pulled the car over, as far from the road as possible. The area was very isolated and they hoped that no-one would come along and bother them as they slept in the car. It was the cheapest and not such a bad option.

Mo rearranged the back, so she could put the back seat back up, although some bags had to go on the floor. Pete took the torch and gathered some wood to make a fire.

Pretty soon, the fire was raging, music was blaring from the car's ancient cassette player and they both had a bottle in their hand.

"Let's drink to what has been a lousy trip so far," laughed Mo, touching her beer bottle against Pete's wine bottle.

They sat in front of the fire chatting and laughing. Mo's first bottle was empty before Pete's and she had another opened immediately. It wasn't long before she was giggling incessantly and every now and then would touch Pete on the leg or arm when she wanted to stress a point. Pete ignored it at first and went on to his second bottle. Mo inched closer to him which made him a little uncomfortable, even though he was a bit drunk by now.

By the time she was half way through her third bottle, she'd plucked up enough Dutch Courage. "Pete….. we're pretty good mates, hey?"

"Mmm," agreed Pete, draining his second bottle. "Of course we are. You're a bit loud sometimes, but you're all right."

"Well, you're a bit grumpy at times," slurred Mo, "but I like you."

"Yeah, I like you too, Mo," said Pete, failing to get the drift of her conversation. He took another swig from his bottle and threw some more wood on the fire.

"No," Mo said, shaking her head and moving so that she was sitting directly in front of him. She leaned forward, almost overbalancing and had to put her hand down on the ground to steady herself. "I mean, I REALLY like you!

"Yeah," laughed Pete. "I REALLY like you too, Mo."

"No, no, no." She waved her finger around in front of his face and giggled. "I really LIKE you. You know……." She gazed into his eyes with a hopeful look. She could almost see two of him, but that didn't matter.

Pete stared at her for a few moments while her words sunk in.

He shook his head to try and make it seem clearer. Gradually it dawned on him what she was getting at. This was totally unexpected and he was too shocked to reply.

"So……. Why don't we make the most of this romantic spot?" she suggested, seductively rubbing her hands up his thighs.

"Mo! I….." he was bewildered as her wandering hands reached the fly of his jeans and fumbled around trying to undo it. He moved across the ground quickly to escape her clutches.

She had been sitting on her haunches and fell forward to the ground when he moved. "Wha'sa matter Pete," she asked dejectedly, sitting back up. "I thought you liked me."

"I do, but……"

"But what?" she implored, getting to her feet and staggering the several steps to Pete. He tried to stand and move away, but she was too quick for him. Mo grabbed him around the shoulders, planted a big kiss on his lips and rubbed herself against him.

He gave her no response and tried to push her away, but she was strong and held on tight.

"C'mon, Pete," she giggled. "Make love to me."

"Mo, you're too pissed," stated Pete, looking for an excuse that wouldn't hurt her feelings, or shock her too much. "And so am I for that matter."

"No, I'm not." She let go of his shoulders and stood in front of him, swaying a little. "And you'll be right." She reached for his crotch.

Pete had decided that his had gone far enough. Before her hand could grab him he was off like a shot, running blindly into the darkness, as fast as his skinny legs could carry him.

"PETE, COME BACK!" Mo called, staggering after him. "I don't wanna hurt ya. I just wanna root! Is that so bad?"

"Shit!" cursed Pete as he tripped and fell over. He could still hear Mo coming after him. He wished, right now, that he had been straight with her from the start, but he just never expected she'd get the hots for him. Picking himself back up, he continued to run from Mo. Suddenly a large figure loomed in front of him. It appeared to be moving. *Oh no, she's caught up with me!* Something scratched him down the side of his face and he felt a heavy, painful hit to the thigh. "There's no need to get violent!" he shouted. Trying to push her away, he copped another hit, this time to his hip. *She must have a BLOODY big stick in her hand,* he thought as he turned to run the other way. *This is bullshit!* His heart raced as he imagined her going crazy, foaming at the mouth, and all because he'd rejected her advances. Before he'd got far, he felt an extra hard thump to his back and flew forward through the air. In one split second his mind sped over dozens of thoughts. *Why does she want to kill me, when we have come this far? What will she do with my body? Hell, I will GIVE her what she wants if she is this desperate!* He heard himself scream as he hit the dusty ground with a THUD.

"Pete, wake up. Pete!" Pete slowly opened his eyes. It was daylight. Shit! Where was he? He could just make out Mo's blurry face leaning over him. He blinked several times to clear his vision. Gradually the events of last night came back to him. Letting out a blood curdling yell, he tried to get away from Mo. After she tried to kill him last night, he was NOT giving her another chance at it this morning. *But why didn't she finish the job last night?* He groaned as his back hurt too much to move fast or far.

"What the hell happened to you last night?'' She began to laugh. "I thought you had run away. You look like you have gone a few rounds with Mike Tyson."

Pete felt like he had too. He continued to stare at her in disbelief. "What the fuck did you hit me for?" he demanded bitterly.

"Hit you! I never hit you. I just wanted to have some fun!"

Pete sat up groggily. Mo offered to help him but he pushed her away. He could see the car about eighty metres away, through scattered trees. Every part of his body ached. Putting his hand up to his face, he was alarmed to find half dried blood on it, mixed with dirt. "You call this FUN? You nearly friggin' killed me last night with that big stick!"

"What the hell are you talkin' about?" retorted Mo. "I never hit you with a stick. When you pissed off into the bushes I only followed you a little way and then gave up. I went back to the car and fell asleep in the front seat. I only just got out. If somebody hit you, it sure as hell wasn't me." She stormed off back to the car.

Pete slowly stood up and looked at the ground around him. There were some marks in the dirt but he could only see his own footprints, apart from Mo's. "Well SOMETHING hit me," he grimaced. A movement over to his right caught his eye and he looked hard to see a small mob of red kangaroos disappear into the thicker bush. He looked back to the ground and not far from where he stood were fresh kangaroo droppings. Suddenly it dawned on him what had attacked him.

"MO," he called, painfully jogging after her. "I'm sorry I blamed you. It was a bloody big red kangaroo!" Mo was packing things back into the car when Pete reached her. "Did you hear me Mo? I said it was a kangaroo that attacked me. I'm sorry for gettin' up you."

She ignored him as she folded the blanket up and put it in the car before picking up their empty bottles and placing them into a plastic bag for disposal in a bin later.

"Mo," he pleaded.

Angry as hell, she suddenly turned to him. He stood before her, looking sore and sorry for himself. Several big scratches ran down one side of his face, one eye was bruised and swollen from yesterday's beating and he was dirty from head to toe. She couldn't control herself and burst into loud shrills of laughter. She was laughing and snorting so hard, she bent over at the waist and as she stood back up, the tears ran freely down her cheeks. Staggering backwards she hit the side of the car, luckily, as she felt like literally rolling on the ground laughing.

"It's not THAT funny," scolded Pete. He was in a lot of pain, but gradually he began to see the funny side of it all and started to laugh too. "At least, HE didn't steal me money!"

They roared with laughter for several minutes before composing themselves and getting into the car. They drove back out on to the highway heading west and stopped at the next servo to fill the car, have a shower and some breakfast. Neither was feeling the best, but they ate a meal and continued the journey.

After driving some time with the music blaring and not talking, Mo decided it was time to confront Pete. She turned the volume down and saw no sense in beating around the bush. "Why didn't you want me last night, Pete? Surely I'm not THAT bad."

She caught Pete by surprise. He was hoping she would have forgotten about trying to seduce him.

"Well?" she insisted.

"Um…" he shrugged. "I just didn't feel like it."

"Bull! No bloke EVER doesn't feel like it. You're not one of these that can't get it up after a few drinks are ya?"

"No!" snapped Pete. "Of course I can!"

Mo couldn't help feeling a little hurt. "If you think I'm ugly, just tell me."

Pete felt bad and decided it was time to tell her the truth. He hoped that she wouldn't boot him out of the car in the middle of nowhere. "It's not that, it's……"

"Go on," pried Mo.

"Look, I don't want to shock ya, Mo, but I don't really like women - any woman." He held his breath, waiting for her response. "Don't get me wrong, they're good to have as mates, but I just don't get off on them."

"Ohhhhh," said Mo after several moments, totally exasperated. "You mean you're a….."

"Gay," Pete cut in. He didn't like a lot of the slang words used for it. "Yeah, Mo, I am. Sorry."

She was quite stunned at first, but thought back to little things he'd said and done and it added up. It was still a surprise to her though. Intrigued to find out more about it, she urged Pete to open up and was pleased when he seemed happy to.

Pete was so relieved she took it well. It was a huge weight off his shoulders. He didn't mind talking about it, even when it came to how much his father hated him for it, but when she pried into his sex life with previous boyfriends he drew the line. Some things were personal.

Another night of sleeping in the car and by late the next morning had reached the Nullabor Plain. Mo refuelled before the expansive stretch of road, with nothing much to look at along the way. They tried playing "I spy" but had to give up after two goes each as there wasn't anything else to choose.

By late afternoon they'd reached the Nullabor Roadhouse. Mo had had enough driving and decided that they needed to sleep in a bit more comfort tonight so booked them into the caravan park beside the roadhouse. A welcomed shower, a hot meal and a few beers later found them sitting and laughing in their van. Pete admitted to Mo that he would miss her once the trip was over. They decided that no matter what happened or where either one went, they would always stay in touch.

Mo was exhausted and soon fell asleep, but because Pete had slept along the way that day, he found it harder. He lay his battered and sore body down on the narrow bed. With the injuries from the kangaroo, the kicks from the calves on Valerie Downs and the sore jaw and stomach from the roadside beating, he found it least painful to lay on one side. Eventually sleep found him.

Next morning, the long, straight road was, once again, their only friend.

"This is SO boring," complained Mo. "No wonder it is called the NullaBORE."

"I spy?" Pete asked in a little voice.

Mo just glared at him and rolled her eyes. Next thing, she started singing Baa Baa Black Sheep at the top of her voice. Pete grimaced, shrugged then joined in. They sang their way through all the nursery rhymes then made up their own versions of them. The time passed quickly.

At lunchtime they stopped to eat food they bought earlier, on the cliffs overlooking the Great Australian Bight. It was a breathtaking view and Mo was convinced she saw whales swimming along, some distance out, but Pete couldn't see anything.

That night they slept in the car for the last time. Pete's money had nearly run out and he was glad they were nearly to Perth. He hoped that his sister, Debbie, could put him up for a while. He began to wish he had rung her from Sydney to tell her he was coming. *Shit, what if she didn't even live at the same address anymore.* That was something he would have to face when, and if, the time came. He tossed and turned in the back seat while Mo snored softly in the front.

Next morning, they woke early for the final leg of their journey. Both were excited as they showered and ate a quick breaky at the servo. With the fuel tank full, water and tyres checked they headed off.

Today was the big day. Pete was excited but also as nervous as hell. He hadn't been back to Perth in over four years and he couldn't help wondering how much it and the people he knew, may have changed.

They passed through the mining towns of Kalgoorlie and Boulder and headed straight to Perth. In a couple of hours they were passing though grain and sheep country and lots of smaller towns. By late afternoon they'd reached Perth's outer suburbs.

Pete gave Mo directions to Subiaco and Debbie's house. They pulled up at her front gate a little while before dark. Pete was both nervous and excited, so he had to take several deep breaths before getting out of the car. Mo told him she would wait in the car for a little while. Opening the gate with sweaty hands, Pete then walked along the pathway to the low set of front steps. The house was small with a bull nose veranda. The small front yard contained a shady tree on either side of the pathway. Several plants and deck chairs adorned the veranda.

Pete knocked loudly on the door and waited. Soon it was opened by a little girl, no more than five years old.

"Who are you?" she asked Pete shyly.

Pete couldn't believe his eyes, could this be little Kate, who was only a baby when he left. "Kate?"

"Yes," she answered quietly.

Next thing, the door opened wider. "Katie, who is...." Debbie's mouth dropped open and her eyes nearly popped out of her head. "Peter!"

"G'day, Big Sis," he grinned.

"You little shit! How come you haven't written?" she demanded angrily then moved toward him.

Pete thought she was going to hit him but instead she grabbed him in her strong arms and hugged him tightly, laughing and crying at the same time. Debbie's nine year old daughter, Sarah, had come to the door by now too.

"Girls, this is Uncle Peter. Remember him?" Sarah nodded but Kate shook her head and frowned. "I hope you'll be staying for a while."

"I'd love to," replied a relieved Pete. "That's if you've got a spare bed. It's been a long hard road."

"Looks like it has been a bit of a painful one for you too," said Debbie, scanning his face. She was a nurse so she tended to notice injuries on people no matter how serious or minute they were.

"You have no idea!" laughed Pete, " I'll tell you all about it later, but first, is it okay for me mate to stay here tonight too. She has to drive up to Kalbarri tomorrow."

Debbie was surprised. "SHE? Of course she can."

"She's just a mate, Deb. Nothin's changed there." Pete went back to the car to get his bag and tell Mo to come in.

Pete introduced the two women. Mo liked Debbie instantly. She was a little larger built than Mo, with thin legs. Her hair was short and brown, her face rounded and full. The only resemblance to Pete, that Mo could see, was the fair skin.

Debbie welcomed them in and showed them to the room they would have to share, containing two single beds. After sleeping in caravans and the car most nights, these beds looked like the most comfortable beds in the world to Mo and Pete.

As she had already cooked tea for her and the girls, Debbie took some chops out of the freezer and placed them in the microwave to thaw quickly. Pete asked her about John, her husband, but she had to inform him that they had divorced six months earlier.

After welcome showers, Pete and Mo sat down to a home cooked meal of chops, vegetables and gravy. Over the dinner table, Pete was able to get to know his nieces all over again.

Once they were tucked up in bed, Mo offered to do the washing up so Pete and Debbie could have some time alone.

"Does anyone else know you're here?" Debbie asked. "You know, Mum would love to see you."

"No, no-one else knows. Yeah, I wouldn't mind seeing Mum, but I bet the Old Man still hates me guts."

"He hasn't mentioned you in ages, maybe he's cooled down a bit by now. Do you want to ring them?" She gestured to the phone on the wall, not far from where they sat.

"NO!" stated Pete quickly. "But if you don't mind, there is someone back in Sydney I would like to ring, just to let them know I got here okay. I had been staying with them, and I know they will be a bit worried."

"Go for it," relied Debbie, happy that he had some friends.

"I'd just like to sleep for a couple of days and get over these injuries. Then I'll think about seeing Mum and Dad. I hope you're right about him, but somehow....... I doubt it," he added sadly.

CHAPTER TWELVE

A week after their surprise engagement party and Jo was still floating on cloud nine. They'd spent most of the week discussing ideal dates, times and locations for their wedding. Luke wanted it to be as soon as possible and Jo wasn't about to argue. She loved Luke so much she would have happily married him the very next day after the party. They finally decided on a Boxing Day wedding. It would be more convenient with her family coming over for Christmas. When Luke had asked her where she would like to get married, she didn't hesitate in telling him that she had always fantasised about having a beach wedding. So it was settled – they would be married on the beach, at their special little cove, at sunset on Boxing Day. That gave them about a month to get organised.

Jo's parents booked to fly over a few days before Christmas and her brothers were due on Christmas Eve. Jo bought Meg a deep, sky-blue, calf length, off-the-shoulder dress to wear as her maid of honour. As it was a beach wedding it wasn't too flamboyant. Jo texted the pictures to Meg and she loved the look of it. Jo thought it would accentuate Meg's dark hair and fair skin.

Meg was initially embarrassed to accept Luke's offer of paying her and Darcy's fares over, but realised she didn't have much choice, especially when Jo informed Meg that she was NOT getting married without her there.

They discussed the importance of keeping it quiet. It was only going to be a small wedding with family and a few close friends of Luke's. He didn't want the media getting wind of it and swarming around, ruining their privacy. The drummer in the band had been married the previous year and had a fairly large affair. There were quite a few big names from Australia's music industry present and, of course, the photographers and reporters were there in droves. People were pushed and shoved about, insults were flung back and forth and the bride ended up in tears. Luke definitely did not want that happening to Jo.

Jo also preferred it be kept from Jeff's family. As much as she wanted to shout it to the world that she was marrying Luke Summers, she knew it would be best to keep it quiet a bit longer. In the near future she would get her Mum to put a notice in the local Sunshine Coast newspaper, but without a date.

There had been no new developments in the past week, regarding Jeff's suicide. Jo was sure his mother would have received the letter by now. She couldn't help wondering what her reaction to the letter was, and was almost tempted to call, but realised it was best not to. She had said everything she wanted to say in the letter. If they didn't believe her by now, that was their problem.

Meg had given the police her statement about the day she walked into the flat to find Jeff beating Jo. Jo's mother had not heard any more about it on the news so, maybe, it was finally over and Jo could put it behind her to concentrate on the new, exciting life ahead.

They would have the reception at their place around the pool and entertainment area. Luke refused to tell her where he was taking her for their honeymoon, except to say it was beautiful and hot and she wouldn't need many clothes.

"Babe, remember how you commented one day that the tank on my bike looked a bit bare?" said Luke, over breakfast one morning.

"Yeah," replied Jo.

"Well, I'm taking it into an airbrush artist I know, today and he's going to put a picture on it."

"Oh, that's sounds great," enthused Jo, sipping a fresh orange juice she had just extracted. "What will it be of?"

"You'll see." Luke smiled then bit into his toast, with no intention of telling her.

Jo knew it has hopeless trying to pry anything out of him. He was an expert at keeping her in suspense and surprising her. As much as it frustrated her at times, she knew he loved doing it and she was always guaranteed a big surprise that was well worth the wait. Immediately after breakfast he kissed her goodbye and rushed off.

"Luke!" she called after him as he went down the stairs. He stopped and turned back toward her. "How are you getting back home after dropping the bike off?"

"Don't worry, that's all under control."

He gave her that knowing smile and wink that sent her heart racing. She shook her head, laughed and waved him off before tackling the washing up and other housework.

She put on a Stonefish CD, turned it up loud and sang happily as she worked. The days were getting hotter so she wore only her bikini top and a pair of shorts. Suddenly, as she vacuumed the lounge area, she felt a presence in the room. She looked up and jumped with fright to find David standing at the top of the staircase. Even though the front gate was kept locked, there was a smaller gate between Luke and David's places for their private use.

"David!" Jo gasped. "You gave me a fright!" She switched the vac off and turned the music down.

"Sorry Jo, I didn't mean to. I knocked a few times and yelled out, but you didn't hear me."

"I'm sorry too. I like my music loud, especially when I am doing the housework."

"Is Luke here?" enquired David.

"No, he's taken the bike in to get the petrol tank airbrushed. It's a wonder you didn't hear him go. It wasn't long ago." She frowned.

"Must have been when I was in the shower. I just wanted to see him about something before I went to work, but I'll catch up with him later."

"No worries," replied Jo cheerfully. "I'll tell him."

David started to leave, then stopped and turned back toward her. "So, how's things with you? You must be excited about the wedding."

"I sure am. I can't wait!" she beamed.

"You and Luke make a great pair," smiled David, nodding. "I'm really happy for my little brother and you too. Jo, I know you've got two brothers back home, but if you ever need to talk to someone in a brotherly way, I hope you think of me. I'm starting to think of you as another sister, especially with mine so far away. Hey, that's something we've got in common, isn't it?"

"Yeah, I never really thought about it like that before." She was touched by his caring attitude. "Thanks David, I really appreciate that. So, can I give my new brother a hug?"

David walked eagerly over to her. Just as Jo went to hug him, he moved his face to hers and kissed her softly on the lips. "Welcome to the family, Jo." He smiled warmly, and squeezed her hand. "See you later. Have a good day." Then he disappeared as suddenly as he had appeared.

Okaaay, what was that all about? She felt a little bewildered and unnerved by his kiss. She couldn't shake a niggling feeling that there was more to his visit. *Surely a noisy Harley could still be heard above a running shower?* What the heck! Life was too good at the moment to worry about trivial stuff. She shrugged it off, turned the music back up and continued the vacuuming.

A while later, Jo was out the back pegging the last of the washing on the line, when she heard a car drive into the front yard. Puzzled, she put the basket back in the laundry and walked out to the front door. Her frowned deepened even further when she saw Luke get out of a sleek, little white sports car. He had a grin from ear to ear and carried a set of keys in his hand.

Shaking her head, she walked over and rubbed the smooth, shiny bonnet. "Nice car. Whose is it?"

"Yours! That is, if you like it."

Jo stopped and stared at him, mouth agape. "What?" she managed to gasp after a few seconds. "Mine?"

"Yep!" declared Luke with a huge smile. "All yours. I just bought it."

Jo couldn't stop her tears as she laughed and cried at the same time. "I LOVE it, and I LOVE you!" She hugged and kissed him before jumping into the driver's seat.

"I thought you would, and I thought it was time we got a more comfortable car than using the four wheel drive or the bike all the time. Let's go for a spin, Pretty Lady." He handed her the keys then jumped into the passenger seat.

Jo drove slowly until they'd got out of the yard and Luke had closed the gate with the remote. She smiled cheekily at him, revved the engine a few times then took off down the road. They cruised up and down the beach roads, along the city freeways and up into Kings Park which overlooks the city and Swan River. Luke suggested they hire a tandem bicycle and go for a ride, but Jo was more interested in the car. They bought some lunch and ate it under a shady tree, before continuing driving.

Once they did get back home, there were more wedding plans to take care of. Jo rang around and found a celebrant available on Boxing Day. Another thing ticked off the list. Next was finding caterers. They wanted to have mainly sea food and chicken with lots of delicious salads, desserts and entrees. Drinks would be endless and Luke made a mental note to check his bar and restock what was needed, including plenty of champagne. His mother had volunteered to make and ice the cake.

The main thing left for Jo by now, was finding the perfect dress. She knew a long flowing gown would not be very practical on the beach, but she felt she still had time to get something beautiful.

"What are you going to wear?" Jo asked Luke, as they sat at the table making arrangements.

"Don't know," frowned Luke. "I hadn't really thought about that yet. What do you reckon? I'm NOT wearing a monkey suit." Suddenly, he gasped. "Shit, I haven't asked David to be my best man yet. He probably thinks I have gone and asked someone else. I'd better go and see him. He should be home from work by now." He got up, quickly kissed Jo and almost ran down the stairs and out the door.

Jo went back to her list and came to "Flowers". She definitely wanted West Australian Wildflowers . As far as the entertainment went, she knew that Luke would happily organise that. He knew just about everyone in Perth with anything to do with music. Even though David was an amateur photographer, she knew they would have to still hire a professional if he was going to be in the bridal party. Her mind automatically went back to his kiss that morning. She tried to shrug it off, but it made her feel uneasy. *Surely, he didn't MEAN to actually kiss me.*

Back to the list. Rings - she knew they would both go in and choose them. Cars - wouldn't be necessary as they were only going over the road. In the past, she had often daydreamed of arriving at her wedding in a horse and cart, but this wedding, this man, THIS LIFE, was far beyond any of her wildest dreams and expectations. Some days she would still shake her head and wonder if she was going to wake up and find that it had all just been a dream.

She would have loved to invite Graham and some other friends from Queensland, but it just wouldn't be wise or practical. She would e-mail or text some pictures later on after the wedding. If she explained the circumstances she was sure they would understand. Just then Luke came bounding back up the stairs, smiling broadly.

"Well," Jo smiled expectantly. "What did David say?"

"He's rapt to do it, and so am I."

"Had he thought you had overlooked him?"

"No, I don't think so," replied Luke, shaking his head and sitting back down at the table after getting a beer for the two of them.

"Is that why he came over this morning?"

Luke was surprised as he took his first mouthful of beer. "What?" he frowned. "He never said anything about coming over this morning. What time?"

"Just after you left," replied Jo, equally as puzzled. "He said he had to see you about something. Didn't he tell you?"

Luke shook his head with a blank look on his face. "What did he say?"

"Nothing much," shrugged Jo. "He just wanted to see you and then we chatted for a few minutes about the wedding and things. Then he said he was happy for us and that I was almost like a sister to him." She thought it best not to mention the kiss.

"That was nice of him," replied Luke. "He thinks a lot of you. Poor bloke, that's probably what he did come over for and didn't want to admit it to me. He must have thought I was going to ask someone else. I won't mention anything about his visit in case it embarrasses him."

They worked on the plans some more. Luke knew someone who could do the video recording. He rang him and was pleased to be told that they could have a two man team to record from different angles simultaneously. Talking about video cameras made Luke remember to drag his out of the cupboard. He hadn't used it in months and had a great idea that would make their wedding video a bit different, but as usual, he kept his bride-to-be in suspense about his intention.

He knew what he wanted in the way of music for both the service and reception, and yet again, Jo had to wait and see. Phone calls to several florists enquiring after Wildflowers for the day were successful. It was all coming together perfectly.

A trip to a jewellery store was planned for one day soon. Jo rang Kelly and asked her if she would like to come with her to shop for a suitable wedding dress, when Kelly had her next day off. She was pleased to accept Jo's invitation. Jo had felt bad for not asking her to be in the bridal party, but she couldn't see any sense in having more than one attendant. She was relieved when Kelly assured her that she understood and was not offended.

Later that night, just as Jo was drifting off to sleep in Luke's arms following a luscious lovemaking session, she remembered it was his birthday in a few days. Hell! With everything else going on, she had completely forgotten. After racking her brain for a while, she finally came up with something special for him. For once SHE would be the one providing the surprise.

The next morning after they had been for a jog along the beach and played a few games of tennis, they decided to head into the city. It didn't take long to find the perfect matching wedding bands. Afterwards, while Luke was browsing around a music shop, Jo told him she was going into the dress shop next door, but rushed back to the jewellers to order his present. She showed the jeweller a rough sketch of what she wanted and was ecstatic to hear that it could be done AND be ready the following afternoon. She was sure he would love it. She still had quite a bit of money saved of her own so she didn't worry about the cost. He was worth every cent and then some.

That night they asked Kelly and David over to discuss some of the plans. They both seemed a little quiet and did not stay at Luke's for long. Jo had taken Kelly into the bedroom to show her some dresses and talk about what sort of dress she'd like for her wedding.

"They didn't seem like their usual selves tonight," said Luke after David and Kelly had left. "Did Kel say anything to you when you two were in the bedroom?"

"She just mentioned that they'd had a bit of an argument," shrugged Jo. "She didn't seem too worried about it."

"Hmm, hope they are ok," said Luke. "I'm so blinded by our happiness, I can't see anything else."

"I'm sure things are ok over there." Jo got out some chicken and salad for their tea, which was followed by some games of pool before bed.

"Luke, I just had a horrible thought," said Jo, as they walked hand in hand to the bedroom. "What if it's raining on our wedding day?"

"It won't," declared Luke.

"Oh yeah, and how can you be so sure?"

"Because it hardly ever rains here in summer time, we get most of our rain in winter, so stop worrying." With that, he picked her up and playfully threw her on to their bed before lying gently on top of her and kissing her softly on the lips.

"Does it rain much where we are going on our honeymoon?" she pried, hoping he would make a slip.

He looked up briefly from kissing her neck and smiled. "Nice try,Kiddo!"

Jo rolled her eyes, then sighed ecstatically as his eager lips and tongue found her breast.

The next morning Jo couldn't work out how she was going to slip into the city to pick up his present without him becoming suspicious. She purposely hadn't mentioned his birthday, hoping he would think she had forgotten amidst all the wedding plans. She nearly had! But this time SHE would be in charge of the surprise.

Luke was mowing the lawn as Jo was about to go out and tell him that she was going out to have lunch with Kelly to discuss the wedding dress. She had decided that that would be her excuse. As she was walking down the stairs, she heard Luke's phone ringing from the entertainment room. *He must have left it there by mistake,* she thought, picking it up. It was the airbrush artist ringing to inform Luke that the job was done and the bike could be picked up that afternoon. This created the perfect opportunity for Jo. She could drop Luke off to get his bike and she could go on to the jewellers to pick his present up. She knew her way around Perth by now.

Luke was happy that the bike would be ready so soon and hoped the picture turned out as well as he had envisioned. Once he'd finished the mowing, he dived into the pool for a refreshing swim, before they headed off into the city together.

Jo dropped Luke off at the artist's workshop and headed to the city, her head buzzing with excitement. She picked up his present and was glad to see it was perfect. Luke would love it, that she was sure of. Next stops were a lingerie shop, delicatessen and then an alternative shop for oils and incense. There was incense at home but she wanted a particular one – aphrodesia.

As she drove home she wondered how she was going to wait until tomorrow night to give Luke his surprise. Then she realised how he just loved making her wait for something, so he could too.

Driving into their yard, she wasn't surprised to see that Luke had beaten her home. He was standing near the open garage door, the bike was beside him, covered with a sheet. The huge grin on his face let her know he was pleased with the result. Her curiosity was boiling over. She drove straight into the garage and stuffed her purchases into her bag before getting out of the car. Lucky her bag was a fair size!

Luke walked over and kissed her. "What took you so long? I've been waiting ages for you."

"Oh, you have not!" she laughed. "I just wanted to go back to a couple of shops and have another look at the dresses."

"Find anything you like yet?" asked Luke, totally unaware she was keeping anything from him.

Oh, I certainly DID find something I like and you will like it too, she smiled to herself. "No, not yet."

He took her by the hand and led her over to where the bike stood. "Are you ready for this?" he asked excitedly.

"Yes," she laughed, dying to see what was on the fuel tank.

Luke leant down and took hold of the edge of the sheet that was almost on the ground. He looked up at Jo once more and smiled as he lifted the sheet slowly off the bike.

Jo looked at the top of the petrol tank and frowned. There was a face on it. A female face! She moved in for a closer look and gasped when she realised it was HER face. She was stunned. There, right before her eyes, was an airbrushed picture that was almost as clear as a photo. In it, her hair was hanging loose and wavy, her eyes sparkled and she had a warm smile on her face.

"Like it?" Luke asked nervously.

She took a deep breath as the tears came to her eyes. The artwork was sensational. She had never seen anything like it. The artist had captured her every detail perfectly. "I love it Luke," she whispered, choking back the huge lump that had suddenly formed in her throat. The picture showed her head and downwards to her bare shoulders. "Wildflower" was written beneath it. Jo slowly reached over and ran her fingers lightly over the smooth picture. She was totally mesmerised by it. "How.....how did he.....?"

"How did he get it so perfectly like you?"

Jo nodded, still touching the paintwork.

"I took in a few photos of you, good close up ones," Luke replied. "He did it off those. He's brilliant. Did you see the sides of the tank as well?"

Jo looked at both sides of the tank and shook her head in amazement. On one side was a beach with a perfect set of waves rolling in and the sun setting behind it. On the other side was the moon glistening on the ocean, with a perfect set of waves again. "It's so beautiful. The colours are fantastic!"

"I thought you might like it," smiled Luke. "Want to go for a spin?"

"I'd love to," beamed Jo. "I'll just race up and put some jeans on." When she got upstairs she put the stuff from the deli in the fridge and hid the other things away in the bedroom. She couldn't help smiling to herself in wicked anticipation of what she had planned for Luke the following night. Quickly, she changed into jeans and leather jacket before walking happily downstairs.

Luke was waiting for her with his leathers on. He started up the Harley and Jo jumped on behind, holding on to his waist. They rode through the open gate, Luke slowed to close it with the remote before they roared off down the road.

Jo loved riding on the back of Luke's bike, whether it was the exhilaration and freedom of moving so fast with the wind around her, or the closeness of Luke's strong body to hers. She held him tightly, but affectionately and pressed her chest into his back. He was HER man and together on the bike, they were as one.

The next morning, Luke's birthday, Jo pretended to still be asleep when he got up to go for a jog. He lightly tried to wake her, but she mumbled something about still being tired. Detecting a sigh of disappointment from him, she had to stifle a smile, move her head groggily to bury her face into the pillow. When he sighed again, louder, she had to bite into the pillow to stop herself from laughing. Once she was sure he had left the house she jumped out of bed. "Your turn today, Mr Summers," she sang to herself, looking out the window and seeing him jogging over the road toward the beach.

Quickly she made the bed with the black satin sheets she bought the day before and sprayed a little perfume on them. She wished she'd had more time to wash and iron them, but *what the heck!* Next she showered and wrapped herself in her favourite blue and white sarong. Luke loved seeing her in it.

Breakfast was next on the agenda. She hurried downstairs to the entertainment room and grabbed one of the leftover bottles of champagne from the engagement party. After placing it in an ice bucket and surrounding it with ice cubes she took it and two glasses out to a table by the pool.

Back up the stairs, singing as she went and continuously checking for Luke's return, Jo took out a serving platter from a kitchen cupboard. She cut up a small chicken and placed it on the tray, then surrounded it with fruit, cheeses and nuts before taking it to the table by the pool also. It was a perfect sunny day. *OH NO, the present!* She'd almost forget, so raced back up to get it wrapped and the card written in. She had just sat back down at the pool side table and placed the present in the centre of the table when she heard him open the gate. She was excited and nervous and hoped she hadn't gone a bit overboard.

Luke came back from his jog all red and sweaty. Coming into the yard, he didn't notice her sitting at the small table.

Normally, she would have waited until he'd showered, but not today. She ran over to him and threw herself into his arms. He nearly lost his footing and fell. "Happy birthday my gorgeous, sweet, sexy, honey of a fiancé." She kissed him long and passionately.

"W-OW!" exclaimed Luke, taken completely by surprise. He could see Jo was bursting with excitement and happiness. She grabbed him by the hand and led him over to the table by the pool. "You sly little thing," he laughed. "Here was I thinking you were too tired and had forgotten all about my birthday

"It was SO hard this morning, not to laugh when you were trying to wake me up. And forget your thirtieth? No way Jose." She popped the champagne, poured a glass and handed it to him, then poured herself one.

Luke couldn't wipe the smile off his face as he sipped the champers. This beautiful woman never ceased to amaze him. Right at the moment, his heart felt it could burst with love for her.

"Hang on a minute," said Jo, placing her glass on the table and racing upstairs to get the video camera. In no time she was back, and filmed Luke in all his sweatiness, sipping his champagne and pulling silly faces.

"I need a swim," he declared, taking his shirt, shoes and socks off before diving in. "Aren't you going to join me, Jo?" he asked when he surfaced.

She filmed a bit more then dropped her sarong to the ground and joined him. He wanted to kiss and caress her in the pool but she urged him to wait and got out. He soon followed and they dried themselves off before sitting at the table where Jo handed him the present.

He took another sip of champagne before opening the card then the present. Inside was a small gold pendant along with a gold chain. The three centimetre long pendant was a surfboard. Engraved on the top side of it, in extremely delicate detail, was a guitar and a Harley Davidson. Luke looked at in in awe before turning it over. He was amazed that it even had a slightly curved nose and three little fins up the other end. The only thing missing was the leg rope. Also on the back, were the words, LOVE YOU, JO.

Now it's my turn, thought Jo. "Well......... do you like it?"

"It's.......incredible, Jo," he smiled, shaking his head. "So, that's where you went yesterday afternoon?"

"Yep, among other places." She got up and placed the chain around Luke's bare neck.

It dawned on Luke that she must have some other surprises for him, but didn't let on to her. "You know, Jo, this pendant symbolises everything I love the most – surfing, playing music, my bike and especially you."

"Well, I hope I am top of your list!" she frowned before grinning.

"The very top," assured Luke, leaning over to kiss her. "Thankyou very much for this present and this little surprise this morning."

"This is nothing compared to what else I have in store for you today, and tonight," she added seductively.

"Mmm, sounds interesting. I can't wait."

Jo uncovered the food on the table so they could eat. Luke was hungry after his run, but Jo ate very little. After breakfast they went for a surf together. Just as they arrived back home, his mother rang to wish him Happy Birthday, then Casey called. A long and playful shower was enjoyed by them both before Jo took him to his favourite restaurant in the city for lunch. It was cosy for a while but several fans spotted him and wanted to chat and get pictures with their phones. He was happy to oblige them but wanted to leave as soon as they finished lunch.

Next, she took him to Kings Park for the tandem bike ride he enjoyed so much. They rode around the large park and found a quiet, shady spot to sit and relax. Luke dozed off with his head on Jo's lap. She couldn't take her eyes off his face as she caressed it lightly while he slept. He looked so peaceful and contented.

It was mid-afternoon when they returned home. Jo challenged him to a best- of- three in tennis, pool and darts. She won the pool game, he won the tennis and darts.

After a shower and five minutes sitting down, David and Kelly arrived with a present for Luke. It was a large framed photo of him and Jo, taken at the engagement party, just after they'd made the big announcement. They both loved it, especially since they had not gotten around to getting any pictures enlarged yet.

"Could you take a few pictures of us now please, David?" Jo asked, getting their camera.

"Yeah, no worries." He took shots of them standing and sitting together, then some of Jo sitting on Luke's lap.

Jo then wanted photos of the two brothers together and also some of Kelly and David together. They all shared a few laughs and some beers, before Kelly suggested to David they go home. Jo had told her very quietly that she had plans for her and Luke that night.

She placed a whole barramundi in the oven, wrapped in foil with herbs and garlic.

Even though it was summer, Jo wanted to light a fire in the fire place. Luke happily went along with it and brought up wood he kept downstairs in the garage. Before long, a flickering orange flame danced over the kindling. Then it began to smoke, so Jo moved the pieces about with the poker, until it settled again. Soon she was able to place some larger pieces on the flames.

Very soon the fish was done to perfection. Jo put on an Eagles CD, one of Luke's favourites, and they sat on the veranda feasting on baked fish and salad while sipping wine.

After their meal, Jo spread a thick doona on the floor in front of the fireplace and covered it with a sheet. She went to the bedroom to get the massage oil and lit several of the new sticks of incense and placed them around the lounge room, followed by numerous lit candles. After turning all the lights off in the house, she led Luke over to the doona. Asking him to take all his clothes off and lay face down on it, she disappeared into their bedroom.

When she returned several minutes later, wearing her robe, Luke had done as she asked. After putting a relaxation CD on the stereo, she knelt down beside him and poured some oil on to his back. She massaged every part of his back and neck, before moving down his arms, legs and feet.

Luke was in pure heaven. Jo had strong hands and she used them expertly to relax his muscles.

Once she was satisfied she had done enough on his back, she asked him to roll over so she could do his front. She smiled at how quick and eagerly he did so. Before she began massaging, she stood up and slowly untied her satin robe while gazing intently into his eyes. The robe dropped to the floor as Luke's eyes widened. Under it, she wore a sheer lace, cupped bra, laced, high cut undies, suspenders and heels, all in black. Her hair hung loose over her shoulders and she smiled at Luke, awaiting his response.

"Beautiful," was all he could manage to say, but his head was swimming with desire and anticipation. She knelt beside him again and poured some oil on to her hands then began to gently massage his chest. He couldn't help reaching out to touch her, but she pushed his hand back down by his side, telling him that, at this moment, HE was on the receiving end. He could handle that! Smiling blissfully, he couldn't take his eyes of her as she worked her hands over his smooth, muscular chest and stomach. The stunning sight of scantily clad Jo, the alluring smell of the incense, combined with the heat of the fire and her massage quickly sent the blood rushing to his loins.

As Jo's warm hands moved back up his thighs she watched his manhood stand tall, proud and ready. She poured lots of oil on to her hands and slowly started at the base of it, and, using both hands, moved up to the tip then slowly, but firmly, back down to the base. She heard an involuntary moan escape Luke's lips. Jo kept up her hand work, sometimes just tickling the top with light, feathery touches of her fingertips. Luke's hips began to move as the sound of his breathing deepened. Gradually, her hands moved faster as his moaning increased. Suddenly, his hips bucked and he let out a deep, guttural groan as he came in her warm hands.

"Happy Birthday," she smiled at Luke, as she gently squeezed the last drop from him.

"Wow! ThankYOU." While he was regaining his breathing, Jo got up and changed the music tempo. She put on Foreigners "Hot Blooded" and began to dance to the heavy, raunchy beat. Luke sat up to watch her, in total awe of her actions. She'd never put on a strip tease for him before. She bumped and grinded her way seductively around the space in the lounge room, never taking her eyes off him for one moment. He watched her run her hands up her thighs, over her stomach, then cup her breasts. *You are one stunning woman,* he thought, as he smiled appreciatively.

Slowly, she unclipped her bra at the front and wiggled her shoulders so it fell to the floor. Continuing to dance, she lightly touched her erect nipples with her fingertips, before sliding her hands steadily downwards. Suddenly, turning her back to Luke, she raised her hands high and dropped her head back so her blonde hair cascaded down her back.

Shaking her head from side to side several times, she turned to face him, standing only two metres away. As she teasingly licked her lips, she hooked her thumbs under the sides of her knickers and slowly slid them down her firm legs, throwing them to the side and keeping the suspenders on.

Jo walked over to Luke and knelt in front of him. After watching her erotic striptease he was as horny as hell! Without saying a word, he grabbed her around the waist and laid her on her back. He had to have her right now! She wrapped her legs around his back as he drove in deep.

Time was inconsequential as they made love in front of the fire to their heart and body's desires. Finally, they made it to the bedroom. Luke got yet another surprise to find the satin sheets. They were cool and smooth on his bare skin. He would find out in the morning just how slippery they can be when making love.

"This is the best birthday I have ever had. I will have to think long and hard to top this for yours. I love you so much, Babe," he whispered tenderly to her as they were drifting off to sleep.

"I love you too, and it was totally my pleasure," Jo replied.

The following day, Jo was in the bathroom when she happened to notice her tampon box in one of the drawers and frowned as something dawned on her. Her period was late. She had never been late before.

Then she remembered she'd forgotten a few pills that month. That wasn't like her either, but with everything that had happened, including worrying about the situation with Jeff, she'd simply forgotten to take them. She put her hand on her stomach. Was it just her imagination, or did she actually feel a little different than usual? Her intuition told her she was pregnant. She didn't know what to think. What would Luke say? They hadn't talked much about kids yet.

Nervously, she walked out to the lounge room where Luke was about to put on a CD.

"Luke," she said quietly, "I think I'm pregnant."

Luke glared at her, eyes wide and mouth agape. The CD case fell from his hands.

CHAPTER THIRTEEN

Pete crawled out of bed and dawdled to the bathroom to wash his face. As he did so, he looked into the mirror and was pleased to see the bruises and scratches had almost healed. He'd been at Debbie's for four days. Mo had stayed two nights before heading several hundred kilometres up the coast to Kalbarri. She was originally only going to stay at Debbie's for one night, but was still tired after their long, sometimes uncomfortable, trip and didn't feel up to the extra drive yet. Debbie certainly didn't mind her staying another night. She had got along well with Mo, even though they were totally opposite in personalities. Kate and Sarah had thought she was funny and were sad when she said goodbye to them.

"So, what are you going to do today, Pete?" Debbie asked as he walked into the kitchen for breakfast.

"Well, I suppose I should go and see Mum and the Old Man," sighed Pete, uneasily. "I can't put it off any longer. Thanks for not telling them I was back, Deb."

"I didn't like doing it. Mum misses you a lot," said Debbie, passing him a piece of toast fresh from the toaster. "But I knew how strongly you felt about it."

Pete buttered his toast and made himself a coffee. "I'll go to Centrelink and let them know I'm here now and I suppose they will send me to one of the employment agencies. If I'm gunna stay here a while I want to be able to give you some board," he said between mouthfuls of toast.

"Well, you can stay as long as you like, you know that. The girls love having their Uncle Pete here."

"Yeah," laughed Pete, "they're great. Where are they?"

"School," replied Debbie. "Do you want me to ring Mum and make sure she's going to be home today? She plays bowls a couple of days a week."

Pete thought for a moment. "Mmm, that's a good idea, but don't tell her," he added hastily.

Debbie rang their mother then gave Pete the good news that she would be home all day and their father would be out all morning. Debbie had told her that SHE was coming around to see her, but she would drop Pete off and go.

After breakfast Pete helped with the washing up and a little other housework before they drove over to their parent's house. It was three suburbs away and Pete was nervous but excited, during the twenty minute trip.

"It still looks the same," he said, when they pulled up in front of his old home.

"Yep, and it's still the same inside too. Come on, I'll come in for a minute." It was obvious to Deb he was nervous and she wanted to see the look on their mother's face when she saw Pete. She suggested he hide around the corner of the low-set weatherboard home.

Pete noticed the flowerbeds still looked so neat and flourishing, as he walked around the corner of the house. He heard Debbie knock on the front door and call out to their Mum. The door creaked a little as it opened then he heard his mother's voice. Just the sound of it brought a tear to his eye. He felt like a little kid again. How he wished he could just be a little kid again and have her cuddle him in her loving arms. *I wish you didn't hate me so much, Dad.*

"I've got a surprise for you, Mum," smiled Debbie, after they'd greeted each other.

"What is it, Love?" asked her tiny, grey haired mother.

Pete emerged from around the corner of the house and slowly walked toward his mother standing on the small veranda. "G'day Mum," he grinned nervously, before bounding up the four steps.

"Peter!" she cried. Tears welled in her eyes as she embraced her only son lovingly.

Pete couldn't hold his back either. They laughed, cried and hugged for several minutes.

Even Debbie had to wipe a tear from her own eyes at witnessing this happy reunion. "Well, I might get going now. Pete, will you be right to get home later?"

"No worries, Deb, I'll get a bus. Thanks for bringing me over."

Debbie farewelled her overjoyed mother and left.

"Come inside, Love," urged Pete's mother, taking him by the hand and leading him in through the front door.

The house was small but homely. Paintings and pictures adorned the walls. There were lots of photos about of Debbie and her family, but Pete noticed there were none of him, not even from his childhood. It stabbed at his heart but didn't really surprise him. He followed his mother into the kitchen and sat down at the small table.

"Would you like a cuppa, Love?" she asked, filling the electric kettle with water.

"Yeah, that'd be good, Mum. Coffee thanks." Pete looked about the familiar kitchen. It brought back hundreds of memories in only a second or two. "So when is Dad supposed to be back?"

"Not for a couple of hours yet," answered his mother. "Can you stay until then?"

Pete looked at her incredulously. "Are you kiddin' Mum? After the way he got into me last time. No way!"

His mother couldn't hide her disappointment. "But I don't think he'll go mad this time. It's been four years Pete. He never gets angry about you anymore." She made the coffee for him and a cup of tea for herself, before sitting opposite him at the table. "Would you like something to eat?"

Pete shook his head. He was much too nervous to eat. "But does he ever talk about me anymore?"

His mother hesitated. "No, not much," she replied sadly. "But I am sure that once he sees you, all that hostility will disappear. After all Peter, you're his only son."

They sat chatting over a second cuppa, which found Pete beginning to relax. His mother wanted to hear all about Sydney and what he'd been doing. He tried to paint as rosy a picture as he could without exaggerating too much. Sparing her some unpleasant details, he told a few little white lies. She'd have been too shocked and upset if she knew some of the things he'd done. He told her he'd had a job with a delivery driver, which was true, even though he only lasted two weeks because he came to work one day stoned. He asked his mother about her bowling and other interests. He was pleased she was still involved in the local craft group. The topic grew to Perth itself and if it had changed much in four years. But he was really anxious to find out about an old mate.

"Remember Luke Summers, Mum," asked Pete. "We went to school together and used to hang around a bit together after we left school. He's been here before."

"Yes," smiled his mother. "I do. He sure has done well hasn't he? I hear their songs on the radio sometimes."

"I'd like to go and catch up with him. Do you know if he still lives in that big house near the beach?"

"I ran into his mother, Rose, out shopping a few months back. I hadn't seen her in ages. We had a cuppa and chatted. It was so lovely. She said that the band were still on tour but would be home soon. He's probably back by now. Yes, she mentioned that he still lived in the same place."

"Well, I can't just rock up there. He's probably got armed guards at the gate," said Pete. "He might not be home either. I don't reckon his phone number would be listed. Hey, I know! Could you ring his mother and get Luke's number for me? Then I can ring him." Pete was getting excited at the prospect of seeing his old mate, but the smile suddenly disappeared from his face. "What if he doesn't want to know me now that he is in the big time?"

"I don't think Luke would be like that. He was always such a lovely boy, well mannered and polite. His mother told me he is still the same. I'll ring her now." She found Rose and Ted's number in her little personal phone book, by the phone in the lounge room, and dialled the number. A minute or so of small talk was followed by the reason she was ringing. She wrote down a number, thanked Rose very much and hung up. "Well, he's home from the tour. Rose said he brought a girlfriend back from Queensland and that she's a lovely girl. They're getting married soon." She returned to the kitchen and handed Pete Luke's number.

Pete felt an involuntary pang of jealousy, but knew it was stupid. His mind began to swim with memories............

He and Luke had been good mates since school. Luke had saved Pete's neck a few times in school yard scuffles and they just stuck together. Pete's feelings for Luke grew stronger over the years. He looked up to Luke and not just because he was taller, Luke was his hero. Eventually, in their late teens, Pete had plucked up enough courage to tell Luke just how he felt about him.

Luke was shocked. He'd had no idea of Pete's homosexuality. Never having had a man come on to him before, Luke didn't know how to handle it so just found it easier to avoid Pete. This saddened Pete immensely, as he had thought that they were good enough mates to discuss or get over it.

About twelve months after that revelation, they had come face to face at a party. They'd both had a few drinks so were more relaxed. He told Pete then in no uncertain terms that he only liked women and that they could still be mates, but JUST mates. Pete accepted that and they had a few drinks and laughs together. The previous tension had disappeared, and it was like old times again. Occasionally, Pete would jokingly tease Luke about being good looking or wanting his body and Luke would laugh and ignore it. Pete laughed on the outside, but deep down in his soul, he kept a secret hope that one day Luke might just change his mind because Pete loved him.

They remained mates but saw less and less of each other as Luke became more involved with Stonefish. The bands popularity soared which meant Luke was away on tours a lot or stuck in the recording studio. Pete had seen him briefly, a few months before he moved to Sydney. He just hoped he wouldn't be too busy to see him now.

"Thanks for doing that, Mum," said Pete, looking at the number written on the paper and realising that this was all that stood between him and seeing Luke again. "I lost my phone, can I use yours to ring him now?"

"Yes Love, of course you can. You know where the phone is."

Pete got up and walked into the lounge where the landline was situated on a small table between the two single lounge chairs. He was nervous and his palms began to sweat. Sitting down on one of the chairs, he took a deep breath and dialled the number. After several rings it was picked up.

"Hello, Luke speaking."

Pete was momentarily lost for words, until Luke had repeated himself. "Um.... Hello Luke."

"Who is it?" asked Luke, not recognising the voice and thinking it may be a fan or a crank call.

"It's me, Pete! Pete Wilson." Pete's heart was racing as he heard nothing but silence for several seconds.

"Pete!" exclaimed Luke. "How the hell are ya, Mate! WHERE are you?"

Pete felt so relieved. "I'm back here in Perth. At Mum's at the moment but I'm staying at Debbie's."

"Long time no see," enthused Luke. "How's your parents and Deb?"

"All good, but I haven't seen the Old Man yet."

"Oh, so you two still at loggerheads then?"

"I suppose so," sighed Pete. "He was ready to kill me last time I saw him, so I reckon it's just best to stay out of his way."

"Definitely," agreed Luke. "Hey why don't you come over later this afternoon. We are just heading out for a while to organise wedding stuff. Bring some clothes and stay a day or two."

Pete was thrilled. "Thanks Mate, that'd be great. Yeah, I heard you were getting hitched. She must be pretty special."

"She sure is! You'll meet her later. I'll catch you then."

"Yeah, see ya then." Pete smiled broadly as he hung up the phone, but the smile swiftly disappeared when he turned to see his father standing in the doorway, glaring at him. "Um.... G'day Dad." His stomach began to churn and his mouth suddenly went dry.

"What the hell are you doing back here?" demanded his father angrily. "You've got a nerve showing your ugly face in this house."

"Jim, he just got back from Sydney and came around to see us," stated Pete's mother calmly. "Please don't fight anymore. He's your SON!"

"I might have fathered him, but I don't want to know him. I don't want any poofters in my family! Now, GET OUT and don't ever set foot in this house again!"

Pete felt the tears well in his eyes and knew there was no point arguing with him. He was a large man with big strong arms and an extremely stubborn streak. He knew that nothing he could say would make his father change his mind.

Anything out of the norm was totally unacceptable to him. He believed that all homosexuals, drug addicts and 'misfits of society' as he called them, should be rounded up and shot. He was not interested in taking the time to find out how any of them got themselves into their situations. He didn't care that most of them didn't want to be that way, but often, due to circumstances beyond their control, they found themselves in a living nightmare.

"Jim, please....., " Pete's Mother begged.

"NO ALICE! He knew years ago he wasn't welcome here. I meant it then and I mean it now! And you're not to have anything to do with him either."

Pete saw his mother begin to cry. He walked over to her and patted her shoulder. He desperately wanted to hug her, but dared not. "I'd better go, Mum. Sorry for comin'." Giving his father a last look of contempt, he walked out of the house.

"And don't you ever come back upsetting your mother like that, YOU LITTLE QUEER!" his father shouted after him, threateningly.

Pete slammed the front gate shut behind him. He cursed his father as he walked along and he cursed the fact that he was gay. Hell! It wasn't like he woke up one morning and decided he wanted to be gay. He'd never known any other feelings. Girls had never appealed to him, even during the testosterone rampant teenage years. Through peer pressure, he'd dated a girl for several weeks but when it came to sex it was a total disaster. He eventually accepted what he was. It took a little longer for his Mother and Debbie to accept, but they did, even though not thrilled about it. He just wished other people could, especially his bigoted father.

He needed a drink after that upsetting confrontation, but was eager to get to Centrelink, so jumped on the next bus going into the city. After sorting some things out regarding his unemployment, he hit the nearest pub. Luckily he still had some of his money left. He almost downed his first beer in one go, before rolling a smoke. Once the acrid smoke filled his lungs he felt a little more relaxed. *A joint would go down well now,* he thought to himself, but he had none. Then he remembered he was going to see Luke this afternoon. With his mood greatly lifted, he had one more beer then headed home to Debbie's. She wasn't home when he arrived so he had a sleep while awaiting her return.

Later, when Debbie arrived home with the girls from school, Pete was sitting on the veranda with a coffee in one hand and a smoke in the other. Sarah and Kate happily greeted him before heading to the kitchen to fill their rumbling tummies.

"So, how did it go?" asked Debbie, sitting on a chair next to Pete's after she'd given the girls their smoko and made herself a coffee.

"Total disaster," grumbled Pete, staring at the ground.

"Why?" frowned Debbie. "Mum was thrilled to bits to see you."

"Yeah, SHE was! But then Dad came in and the shit really hit the fan. I don't know, Deb," sighed Pete. "Why does he have to be so bloody pig-headed?"

"Some people are just like that, I suppose," sympathised Debbie. "Did Mum get upset?"

"Of course she did! We were having a good time until he came in and he had the nerve to blame ME for upsetting her." He shook his head in anger and disbelief. "Then he ordered me out and told me never to set foot in the house again. It was more of a threat, actually."

"Don't worry," smiled Debbie, "I'll get Mum over here sometimes. You'll still be able to see her."

"Just s'long as HE doesn't come! There was one good thing that happened today though, apart from seeing Mum that is." He took Deb's nod and smile as an indication to continue. "I rang me old mate, Luke. Remember him?"

"Luke Summers? Of course I do. You two used to be good mates. He's done so well for himself now. I haven't seen him in years."

"Me neither, but he's invited me around to his place this afternoon for a couple of days. Would you mind taking me over there?"

"No worries," replied Deb. "I'd love to see him again. Hey, remember that time you and him were working on that old car at my place and you had to push it up and down the street to get it going. I don't know what the neighbours must have thought."

They both laughed at the memory and chatted about other things Luke and Pete had got up to. Both were keen to catch up with him, so as soon as the girls had changed out of their uniforms they all jumped into the car and headed to Luke's house.

Luke opened the gate with the remote as soon as he heard the buzzer. He was standing outside the front door, when they drove into the yard in Debbie's white camry sedan. The car had barely stopped when Pete jumped out.

"G'day, Pete," Luke grinned as he walked over to embrace his old friend. "Geez Mate, you haven't changed."

"Neither have you," laughed Pete. "Still as handsome as ever. Ouch!" Luke had playfully punched him in the shoulder.

"Hi Stranger," smiled Deb, as she got out the car.

"Deb! Good to see you." He gave her a hug. "Are these your girls? I remember Sarah, but I don't know the little one."

"Yep, that's little Kate." She introduced the girls and they said a shy hello.

Just then, Jo came outside. Luke introduced them and suggested they go and sit in the shaded area by the pool. After he brought out some cold beers, Jo and Debbie went upstairs to prepare some nibbles, followed closely by Sarah and Kate.

"Cheers," said Pete, tapping his stubby on Luke's.

"So! You're back in Perth! For good?" asked Luke after he'd taken a drink. "How did you get back?"

"Dunno how long I'll stay. Probably for good. Ha!" laughed Pete. "The trip back was pretty wild. I got a lift with this crazy chick, all the way from Sydney. Geez, you should meet her, Luke," Pete grinned, shaking his head.

"Well, where is she now?"

"She's gone up to Kalbarri for a while, but if she comes back I'll make sure you meet her."

"You sound pretty keen on her. Does that mean.......?"

"What? Nah, sorry to tell ya, nothin's changed there!"

"So I still can't turn my back on you?" joked Luke.

"No Mate, wouldn't be wise," laughed Pete. They chatted a while longer until the ladies came back with two trays of nibblies.

Sarah and Kate wanted to go for a swim, but hadn't brought their togs with them. After much nagging, Debbie let them go in in their undies. They happily jumped in amidst much giggling and splashing.

Debbie and Jo only had a lemonade each. Pete told Jo and Luke about the trip over which created plenty of laughs. Debbie and Pete wanted to know all about the tour and how Luke and Jo met. In no time it was getting dark, so Luke asked Deb to stay for a meal. He brought down some meat they'd bought earlier and fired up the barbie, while Jo and Deb whipped up a couple of salads.

Luke couldn't help noticing Jo fussing over the kids, especially little Kate. It made him smile. When she had told him that she thought she was pregnant, it had taken him a few moments to compose himself.

Once it had actually sunk in he was thrilled. Even though they had not discussed when they would actually like to have kids, he couldn't see why there was no time like the present. She had bought a home test kit that showed positive, but she hadn't actually gone to the Doctor to have it confirmed yet. They were both on cloud nine!

"So, when's the big day?" enquired Pete, biting into his steak.

"The twenty sixth, Boxing Day!" said Jo. She wondered if Luke would like to invite them.

"I hope you can both come," announced Luke. He'd been thinking of inviting them and hoped that Jo wouldn't mind.

Debbie was slightly taken aback as she looked from Luke to Jo. "Are you sure?"

Jo nodded enthusiastically, glad Luke had asked them. She liked both of them and knew that Luke and Pete had been mates for a long time.

"There is one condition, though," said Luke seriously.

"What's that?" frowned Pete.

"You can't tell anyone! It's top secret. We don't want any uninvited guests here. The service is going to be on the beach over the road, at sunset and the after party is here. It's only going to be a small wedding."

"Where's the honeymoon?" enquired Debbie.

"Good question," cut in Jo. "I've tried and tried to get it out of him but he won't budge an inch."

Luke smiled smugly then leaned over and kissed her. "AND.... Guess what else? We are going to have a baby," he sang as he patted Jo's stomach.

"Geez, that was quick!" laughed Pete.

"Well, it wasn't really planned that way," responded Jo, "but if that is the way it is meant to be then we're happy. I can't wait to have a little girl to dress up in pretty clothes teach her all the girly things."

Luke rolled his eyes and smiled. "And I can't wait to have a little boy to take surfing and to take for rides on the back of the bike AND to carry the guitar for me." He copped a playful slap on the arm from Jo.

Pete asked about David and Casey. He was surprised that David was still with Kelly and that they lived next door.

"They've been together a long time now," said Pete. "Any kids?"

"No, none yet," replied Luke. "Maybe we could give them some pointers." Everyone laughed.

They chatted on some more about the wedding and their respective families. Debbie then decided it was time to get the girls home to bed. She thanked Jo and Luke for their hospitality, saying what a great time it had been and drove off, after telling Pete she would see him in a couple of days.

Jo soon left Pete and Luke and headed up to bed. Luke suggested they go into the bar where he mixed a scotch and coke for Pete and a bourbon and dry for himself.

"I suppose David still hates me guts," said Pete after taking several sips.

"Oh, I don't know. He hasn't mentioned you in years. I wouldn't worry too much about it."

"I'm not worried," replied Pete, "but it just pisses me off a bit when I've never done nothin' to him. He's just never liked me, right from when we were kids."

"Yeah, but you know David, he can get in some funny moods at times and that hasn't changed," shrugged Luke. "So, tell me, how did you survive all this time in Sydney?"

"Ha!" laughed Pete. "I almost didn't. I was broke most of the time. I had to pull a few jobs. I'm not proud of that." His voice lowered.

"What?....... Oh I thought you said you had to pull a few Johns."

Pete was silent for a few moments. "Yeah...... well, I had to do that too, sometimes."

"Oh shit, Pete," said Luke, stunned.

Pete went on to tell him about the beating in the alley and others before that. He talked about the Drop-In Centre and how he got his money back from the man who'd beaten him. Pete had always found Luke easy to talk to and he held nothing back. Most of what he talked about he didn't want to say in front of Jo and Debbie. He spoke about the visit to his parent's house and how much it had upset him.

It was after midnight when Luke showed Pete to his room. Luke went to his bedroom, tripped over a shoe on the floor and fell on to the bed beside Jo. The noise and movement awoke her.

"You're here at last," she mumbled, looking at the bedside clock.

"Sorry Honey, we were so busy talking that the time just flew by." He let out a heavy sigh as he lay flat on his back.

"What's wrong?" asked Jo, placing her hand on his still-clothed chest.

"Poor ol' Pete. He's had a pretty rough time. You don't mind him staying here for a bit do you, Babe?" He took hold of her hand.

"No, of course not. Although, I must admit, when I first met him I didn't quite know what to think of him, but he kind of grows on you."

"Yeah," laughed Luke. "That he does. He's not a bad person, he's just lost control of his life somewhere along the line. Him and David don't get along though."

"Oh, why's that?"

"I really don't know. David's always hated him. He's going to crack up when he knows he's here, that I DO know."

The following afternoon, Luke and Pete had gone for a ride on the Harley, so Jo had taken Kelly's offer up of going shopping for a wedding dress. Jo finally found what she was looking for in tiny shop specialising in Asian and Indian clothes. It was an off-white colour with sleeves to the elbow, a vee neckline and buttons down the front. A belt would go around the waist and the skirt was calf-length and full. White flowers were embroidered on the front and back from the waist up. The hem of both the dress and the sleeves had off-white lace around them. Jo just loved it and so did Kelly.

Next were the shoes. After much searching she found a pair of off-white crocheted sandals, perfect for the beach. She also bought a blue pair for Meg. Then she found a set of matching pearl earrings and necklace to complete the outfit. She was excited and satisfied. A hairdresser would come to the house on the day to do her and Meg's hair and make-up.

They decided a cuppa was needed after all that shopping so found a table in a cosy street café.

"Did I tell you that David is thinking about getting back into music?" said Kelly, once they were relaxed at the table.

"No," replied Jo. "Sounds great though. I would love to see him and Luke on stage together."

"He doesn't want Luke to know, for some reason, so don't say anything, please," Kelly almost begged.

Jo thought that was a bit strange. "Ok, no worries. I wonder if he is worried about not making the grade?"

"Could be the reason. I guess, if no-one knows, especially Luke, he doesn't end up looking silly if that happens," replied Kelly. "But, he's certainly determined! He's renovating the wine cellar to make it into a sound proof room where he can practise. I just let him go for it, if that's what he really wants. He just seems a bit distracted lately even though he assures me everything is ok."

"Who knows?" shrugged Jo, taking a sip from her cup.

It was late afternoon when they arrived back at Jo's house. Luke and Pete still hadn't got home. Kelly helped Jo take the bags upstairs as they had also stopped for some groceries.

They'd only been inside a few minutes when David walked up the stairs. "G'day girls, busy day?"

"Hi Hon," replied Kelly, handing a bag of groceries over to Jo in the kitchen. "Yeah, you could say that."

Jo smiled and waved.

As Kelly picked up another bag off the table to pass to Jo, she noticed a pregnancy and childbirth book lying there. "Are you getting clucky already, Jo?" she laughed, picking the book up.

Jo stopped what she was doing. "Well, actually Kel...... I'm pregnant already."

David's eyes widened.

"When did you find out?" asked Kelly, surprised.

"Well, I've only done a home test so far and it was positive, but I'm going to the Doctor tomorrow for confirmation."

"That's happened fast," laughed David. "Congratulations! I bet Luke is pleased. So where is the proud father-to-be? I'll have to get him a cigar."

"He's over the moon. We both are, even though it wasn't planned. Him and Pete went for a ride on the bike and haven't come back yet."

"Pete?" frowned David. "Pete who?"

"An old mate of his from way back. I don't think Luke has mentioned his last name."

"Is he a scrawny little weasel of a thing?" asked David, shaking his head.

"Well..... yeah, I suppose he is." Jo wished she hadn't mentioned him.

"When did HE get back in town? He should've been dead by now!"

"A few days ago, I think. I'm not sure when he actually got back to Perth," shrugged Jo. "He's all right. He's polite and helps wash up and stuff. He actually makes me laugh."

"Did you know he's a poofter?" said David, more as a statement than a question.

Jo was slightly taken aback. "No, I didn't."

"So what if he is anyway. As long as he's not hurting anyone, he can be whatever he wants to be," said Kelly, still flicking through the book.

"That would be typical of your hippy ideas, Kelly!" he retorted angrily.

Kelly rolled her eyes and kept on reading.

Jo felt the tension in the air and it made her a bit nervous. "David," she said calmly, "it doesn't bother me that he's gay. Each to his own. I really don't mind having him around and Luke's happy to catch up on old times with him."

"Old times!" exclaimed David. "Did you know that those 'old times' were when Pete used to chase after Luke all the time trying to..... well I don't think I have to spell it out to you, Jo. He's not the type of person you want hanging around, especially now that you have a baby coming."

Jo looked at him for several seconds before she burst out laughing, followed by Kelly.

"It's NOT funny!"

"I'm sorry Dave, but I'm just trying to imagine little Pete chasing Luke around."

"I'm only trying to warn you, Jo," said David, indignantly. "I'd better go. Are you coming Kelly?"

"In a while," grinned Kelly.

"Fine!" David snapped and walked off down the stairs.

Jo looked at Kelly with her eyebrows raised. "Some-one's not happy....."

"Oh, don't worry about him, Jo. He's been like this on and off for weeks now. He's starting to give me the shits a bit."

Just then Luke and Pete rode into the garage before coming upstairs. Luke kissed Jo and greeted Kelly. "I just saw David going through the gate. He didn't look too happy, is anything wrong?"

"I mentioned that Pete was here and he got a bit worked up," said Jo. "I wish I hadn't said anything."

"I knew this would happen," sighed Pete. He wasn't too sure how Kelly felt about him, so he didn't say anything to her.

"Don't worry about him, Pete," smiled Kelly. "It's good to see you again." She noticed the look of relief on his face.

"I'd better go and see him," said Luke. "Be back soon."

Luke called out to David as he knocked on his open door.

"Luke!" said David. "I guess I should have been expecting you. Where's your little offsider?"

"If you mean Pete, he's at home. I wish you wouldn't get so wound up over him, Dave. He's never done anything to you."

"I can't stand him! Never have and never will. I hope he's not coming to the wedding."

"Yes actually, he is," said Luke. "But he's only too happy to keep out of your way. He's not interested in hassling anyone and he doesn't need to be hassled either."

David shook his head. "You were gullible to him back at school and he's still got you sucked in. What is it about the little weed, Luke? Don't tell me he's finally winning you over."

Luke took a deep breath and gritted his teeth. He could feel the shackles rising on the back of his neck. "I'll pretend I didn't hear that, David!" he said through clenched teeth. "Please," Luke begged, more calmly, "for mine and Jo's sake, especially Jo's, don't cause a scene at the wedding."

David suddenly relaxed. "Okay, I'll just ignore him then."

"Thanks Mate," said Luke. "I'd better go now. See you later."

"Yeah," replied David, following Luke to the door. "See ya." With contempt in his blazing eyes, he watched Luke head into the darkness toward his place.

CHAPTER FOURTEEN

The wedding day finally arrived. Jo's family, along with Meg, had made it safely to Perth and Casey had flown in from Adelaide. Jo had picked up her family and Meg from the airport. Meg's partner, Darcy, couldn't make it.

It was a very emotional reunion. Jo missed her family immensely, but was ecstatically happy with her life in Perth with Luke, and would never go back to Queensland, unless of course, Luke went with her. Everything had been organised down to the last detail and best of all, the weather had remained superb for an outdoor wedding. Jo's pregnancy had been confirmed and everyone was tickled pink by the news, especially Luke's parents. Jo's parents had been a little shocked at first, preferring they would have waited a bit longer, but, considering it was unplanned they accepted it well.

Pete had been back and forth to Luke's place since he initially stayed and, luckily, he and David had managed to avoid each other. Debbie had lent Pete some money to buy some new clothes for the wedding and she'd arranged for her girls to spend the night of the wedding at their father's place.

Christmas day had been a big one, with Jo's family and Meg. Luke's family had also been there for the day, including grandparents, aunts, uncles and cousins. He normally didn't see much of them but thought it would be nice for them to get to know Jo and vice versa. It was an extremely hot day, so everyone spent the day in or around the pool and under the shady trees.

Jo had realised that it would be impractical to try and stick to the old tradition of not letting the groom see the bride before the wedding, considering everyone being there and the service not being until late in the afternoon. She had kept her outfit hidden from Luke though. Not normally superstitious, she just didn't want to push her luck too far even though she didn't think anything could ruin their blissful life.

Luke and David dressed at David's place while Meg, Jo and her family got dressed at her house. The place was organised chaos most of the day. Luckily, the hairdresser arrived on time. She had no idea who the groom even was, as she didn't see him.

Finally, just before sunset, Meg, Jo and her father were ready to walk across the road, down to the cove at the beach. Jo hadn't been down there all day, so she had no idea what type of setting to expect. She knew that everyone else would be down there waiting.

"Well, Jo Love, this is it!" beamed her father proudly, holding his elbow out for her to take hold of. "Let's get you married."

Jo turned to Meg and smiled broadly. The two friends embraced quickly before the three headed down the stairs and past the caterers scurrying about. The delicious aromas they were creating almost made Jo's mouth water, except she was too nervous to even think about food yet.

Both ladies had their hair pulled back in a French plait. Jo had baby's breath flowers entwined in hers and Meg had blue lace through hers to match her dress. The sinking sun cast it's golden rays on the whispering ocean as the trio walked across the road to the sand track.

Jo hadn't been this nervous since she first met Luke, but these were different nerves. Back then, she'd been uncertain of his intentions and the future. Now, as she was about to marry the man of her dreams, she was bursting with exhilaration. Having her family and best friend here, as well as the new life she was carrying, made the day even more special.

As they came to the end of the track through the dunes, just before the beach, Jo stopped and gasped at the scene before her. The guests were all seated on white chairs arranged in two semi-circles in front of a small table, covered with a white lace tablecloth. Dozens of blue and white helium balloons were bunched together in small lots and tied to pegs in the sand. Small flowers were fastened along the balloon strings. Another table over to one side held several large bunches of wildflowers and also several bottles of champagne chilling in ice buckets. Beside these was a tray of glasses.

The marriage celebrant stood behind the small table, holding a book in his hand. Several papers lay on the table before him, as well as two white candles in blue holders.

Luke and David stood together, beside the small table. Each was wearing blue jeans, white joggers and a white, short sleeved shirt under a black vest. Of course Luke was wearing the special birthday necklace – he never took it off. Luke sucked in his breath and smiled when he looked up and saw Jo approaching. He thought she looked stunning and even heard David whisper a quiet "wow".

Jo couldn't help giving her handsome husband-to-be a little wave. She thought they both looked great in what they were wearing.

Being so mesmerised by Jo approaching, Luke almost forgot what he had to do. Prompted by a dig in the ribs from David he suddenly came back to reality. He grabbed his acoustic guitar from where it was leaning beside the table and began to strum.

As Jo approached slowly, on the arm of her Dad, Tom and behind Meg, she recognised the music. It was her special song that Luke had written, "Wildflower". She stopped for a moment, choking back a tear as Luke started to sing. She had no idea he would be singing it.

The photographer and two video cameramen were busy capturing everything on film. Jo and Luke didn't want a single moment missed. The three men were all known to Luke and he trusted them not to allow any photos or footage to leak out to newspapers or magazines.

Jo stood and watched as Luke sang her special song. She noticed he seemed to sing it with even more depth and feeling than the night he proposed. Glancing about the guests, she noticed several wiping a tear from their eyes, especially the two mothers. Suddenly a face in the crowd caught her attention, causing her to gasp, bringing her hand to her mouth. It was Graham, her former boss from Blazes hotel, seated next to his wife, Emma. He smiled happily with teary eyes and gave her a wave.

She had no inkling he would be here. It must have been yet another of Luke's amazing surprises.

Slowly, as Luke was finishing the song, she walked toward him. Her smile beamed so much that her cheeks ached but she couldn't take her eyes from his. A single red rose was her only bouquet while Meg carried a small bunch of colourful flowers. Jo's heart was almost bursting with excitement, love and pride as Luke finished the song and placed the guitar back down by the table.

Several of his fellow Stonefish members clapped and cheered. This prompted all the guests to follow suit. Luke laughed and took a little bow. Jo just looked at everyone and wiped a small tear that had escaped her eye.

When the crowd had quietened down, the celebrant began to speak. It was only a short, but touching ceremony. He welcomed everyone, spoke briefly about the meaning of marriage and read a small verse from the bible, at Jo's request. He acknowledged Tom as giving the bride away, before Tom took his seat next to his wife, Liz.

Next it was time for the vows. They had decided to write their own.

Jo held his hands as she spoke first – "Luke, I chose to be your wife, not only because I love and cherish you, but also because you make me laugh and allow me to share my innermost feelings. You also shower me with precious gifts of love, trust, kindness, fun and lots of surprises." She glanced at Graham who smiled and nodded. "You are my soul mate, Luke and best friend. Each and every day with you is filled with exciting new surprises and experiences. The days ahead will get even better as we journey through life together. I love you Luke Summers, with everything in my being."

Then it was Luke's turn. Looking deep into her blue eyes, he began – "Jo, from the very first moment I saw you, I sensed we would someday be here like this. Your beautiful smile and sparkling eyes light up a room and make my heart do cartwheels. In the short time we have been together I have never felt so contented, relaxed and happy. I love your boundless energy, your enthusiasm, your ...." He hesitated for a moment, almost saying 'body' but thought better of it. "Cheeky sense of humour and your gorgeous face." He reached up with his right hand to stroke it softly. "Our life together will be filled with fun, excitement and ......," turning to the guests, he placed his hand on Jo's stomach, "Nappies!" Everyone laughed. He turned back to Jo. "I love you, Wildflower." Tears had formed in his eyes and Jo reached up to lovingly wipe them away with her thumbs.

They both wanted to kiss each other desperately right then, but waited. The rings were exchanged and finally, the celebrant announced them husband and wife. At last! Luke took Jo in his arms and kissed her long and passionately. Everyone stood up, cheered some more then moved over to congratulate the ecstatic couple as the helium balloons were let go. After lots of hugs, kisses and handshakes the celebrant reminded them that they had yet to sign the register.

The bridal party surrounded the small table and signed the papers and certificate. While they were doing that, Steve, the lead singer of Stonefish, picked up Luke's guitar and began to play some slow, relaxing music.

Meg was in total awe being surrounded by the band members. The whole thing still seemed like a dream to her.

When everything was signed and dozens of photos had been taken, David popped several champagne corks, filled glasses and handed them around. Everyone toasted Luke and Jo, both grinning from ear to ear, just as the sun disappeared over the watery horizon. They'd used it as a backdrop for lots of photos. Everyone, especially those from the east coast, were enthralled by the beauty and magic of an ocean sunset.

Jo only took a few sips of her champagne and after everyone had finished theirs, or topped them up again, they all headed back to the house for the informal reception. The food and drinks were all ready and waiting, courtesy of the caterers.

When they reached the gate, Luke and Jo let everyone else enter before them. The guests all wandered over to the pool area. Once the newly-weds had come through the gate and Luke ensured it was locked, he picked Jo up in his arms and carried her over to the reception area. This brought woops of delight from the small crowd.

"Well, Mrs Summers, are you having a good day?" Luke asked her affectionately as they approached the cheering crowd.

"The best ever." She kissed him tenderly as she held her arms around his neck.

"Come on you two," scolded Steve good naturedly. "There's plenty of time for that later." He handed Luke a beer.

Jo sat down at a table beside Meg for a moment. "How are you holding up, Jo?" Meg asked.

"Great!" replied Jo. "I was worried I might have got sick, but I haven't had any morning sickness yet."

"Good. The ceremony was beautiful and it looks great here too," smiled Meg, looking around. The tables around the pool area were covered in blue and white tablecloths and bunches of wildflowers were everywhere. The bridal party's table had an extra large bouquet of flowers on it and two candles. Balloons were also strung up around the area.

Jo stood up and headed over to Graham. "This is such a surprise! I had no idea you were coming. It's not that I didn't want to invite you, but with everything that happened before we left...."

"Hey Jo, my best worker." The two embraced. "I know what happened. It was shocking all right. When Luke contacted me and asked if I could make it over, I was surprised. Happy for you of course. Bet you're glad you disobeyed your boss that night a few months ago hey?"

Jo just smiled and rolled her eyes. "You bet!" Just then, Luke came over. "How on earth did you pull this one off without me suspecting a thing?" she enquired, shaking her head. "It was the LAST thing I expected."

"Persistence and determination. The workhorse didn't want to drag himself away from his job at first, but I talked him into it," replied Luke.

"Well I'm glad you did!" laughed Jo.

Pete had gone into the downstairs toilet and was just coming out as David reached the door, about to go in.

"Well, well, look what the cat dragged in," remarked David.

"Look David," sighed Pete, "I don't want any hassles. I don't know what your problem is, Mate."

"Don't EVER call me MATE! I'll NEVER be YOUR mate!"

Pete just shook his head and went to walk away.

"I know what you're up to Wilson," David called after him. "And I'll be watching you."

Debbie couldn't stay at the reception long as she was on night duty, so at around nine thirty her and Pete said a reluctant farewell to the bride and groom and left. Pete knew he could have stayed but also knew that once Luke and Jo left, David would most likely hassle him.

Luke had organised a three piece band and they had been playing softer, background music since everyone had come over from the beach, but once the meal was over, they upped the tempo and volume a bit to get the guests on to their feet. After a few beers, several of the blokes from Stonefish couldn't resist joining in with the band, who certainly didn't mind. End result was everyone having fun.

The wedding cake was brought to the centre of the gathering, on a small table and Jo and Luke were called over to it. Luke had given the band a CD, instructing them which song from it he wanted played for the bridal waltz. While they cut the cake, Steve played 'Best of My Love' by The Eagles, on Luke's guitar. After the cake was cut, and before Steve had finished, fireworks exploded in the sky.

"Not again," laughed Jo, turning skyward.

Everyone turned their attention upwards as thousands of brilliantly coloured sparks noisily filled the sky. Many "oohs and ahhs" could be heard from the guests. When the dazzling spectacle was over, Bryan Adams' 'Everything I do' began to play. Luke led Jo over to a clear area near the band and held her closely as they slow danced

"Happy?" whispered Luke.

"The happiest I have ever been," she replied, holding him closer.

Soon David and Meg followed suit, then the parents and some of the other guests. Kelly danced with one of the blokes from Stonefish that was without a partner. David didn't even notice she was with another man as he was too busy watching Jo and Luke dance.

A little after midnight, Luke announced that it was time for him and Jo to leave for their motel. It was a room in a beach resort not too far from their place. As they were walking out confetti and rice suddenly seemed to appear from nowhere and rain down on them, tossed from eager hands.

Jo gasped as they reached her car in the garage. Some-one had got to it and painted all sorts of signs and pictures over it with a huge "JUST MARRIED" written along each side. Toilet paper was wrapped around it and tied in bows. Several tin cans were tied near the back axle, but the culprits had cleverly hidden these from view. The newly-weds didn't know they were there until they began driving along the road and the cans bounced noisily along behind them. Jo drove, and all they could do was laugh.

They reached their designated honeymoon suite, without being pulled over, much to Jo's surprise. Highlights of the room included a large spa bath, king-size water bed and lights that could be dimmed. A bottle of champagne was chilling on the table along-side two crystal flukes. Once again Luke carried Jo over the threshold and placed her on the bed, where they made love quickly but passionately. More to release all the built up excitement and passion throughout the day and night, than anything else. Luke then filled the spa, while Jo poured some champagne, a full glass for Luke and just a small amount for her. The next hour was spent relaxing in the spa and finally unwinding.

The following day, Jo and Luke arrived back at their house just before lunch. They were amazed to see the area around the pool was spotless. It was hard to believe that there had been a party there the previous night. Jo's brother's, Chris and Jon, cheekily admitted that they were responsible for the car and offered to clean it. Luke had removed the cans before they left the resort. Meg informed them that everyone continued partying for an hour or so after they had left and what a great night it had been.

Lunch consisted of wedding leftovers, and the afternoon was spent giving Meg and Jo's family a guided tour of Perth. They had to use both cars but the guests could understand why Jo had fallen in love with The City and its surrounds. Everyone was exhausted that night. The past few days had been extremely hectic, but thoroughly enjoyable.

The next morning Jo took her parents and Meg shopping in the city before driving them to the airport. Luke took Chris and Jon surfing and would meet the others at the airport later.

It was a farewell filled with mixed emotions, with Liz promising to come back just before her grandchild was due and stay a while. Meg stated she would come over when her holidays were due. With one arm around Luke, Jo waved them off, in between wiping the odd tear from her eyes.

Mr and Mrs Summers enjoyed a lazy afternoon, although Jo was still trying to find out exactly where they were heading the next day for the honeymoon. David and Kelly came over for a while and had a couple of 'post-wedding' drinks.

"So, how does it feel, Jo?" asked David as they sat down on the veranda.

"It feels fantastic," grinned Jo, looking at Luke.

"Dave, thanks for not worrying about Pete at the wedding," said Luke. "He was just there to have a good time and he left early."

"No worries. I'll never be friends with him, Luke, but I won't cause a scene anywhere. I never spoke to him at all at the wedding or went near him."

Kelly looked at David and frowned to herself. She'd spotted them having words just outside the toilet and wondered why he would lie about it, but thought it best to let sleeping dogs lie.

David agreed to keep an eye on the place for them while they were on their honeymoon, so Luke gave him a key, after which, Kelly and David left.

Jo found it hard to sleep, still wondering where they were going and hoping that she had packed everything she would need. It didn't help her one bit when Luke would say, 'If you need something we'll just buy it there.'

Luke's father turned up early the next morning to take them to the airport. He was like an older version of his son's and just as tall. Once they were at the airport, Luke couldn't hide it any longer as it was displayed on several monitors, with the corresponding time and also above their boarding gate. Jo was thrilled. She'd heard that Broome was beautiful

They arrived at their destination just after lunch, as the plane had several other stops en route. Grabbing a waiting taxi, they went straight to their luxury private suite at the Cable Beach Club resort, situated in lush, tropical gardens right beside Cable Beach. As Jo was feeling tired and a bit nauseous they stayed in their suite for a while. She didn't know if it was from her pregnancy or the flight up the coast.

By late afternoon she was feeling a little better so they went for a walk around the resort then over to the beach. The tide was right out and the sun was sinking low as they hit the sand. Jo gazed in awe at the sunset. Was it her imagination or was this one even more beautiful than the ones she was used to. It seemed almost pink and the water looked silver.

They walked toward the water, but because the tides in the area have a rise and fall of about twelve metres, they had a fair distance to go. When they were about half way there they had to stop and give way to a camel train, loaded with people, plodding along.

"What do you reckon about trying that tomorrow, Babe?" suggested Luke, as he waved back to some of the riders who'd waved to them.

Jo was a little hesitant. "I don't know. It doesn't look very comfortable, but...... I'll try anything once."

Luke smiled and took her hand as they continued walking toward the water's edge. There were quite a few other people on the beach as well, some swimming, some were playing games while others were just sitting or standing and watching the magnificent sunset.

"How are you feeling now?" asked Luke as they walked hand in hand back to the resort, once the sun had set.

"A lot better!" laughed Jo. "Must have just been the flight up."

"I hope so. We've got heaps of things to do here. Tomorrow, when we come down to the beach we'll go to a more secluded part up the beach a bit."

"Sounds good," enthused Jo, but she couldn't work out why he smiled in an odd way when he said it. She shrugged it off and playfully jumped on his back so he could piggy-back her back to their suite.

They dined in one of the restaurants at the resort and had an early night – it had been a big week and they were exhausted.

The following morning, Luke woke early to go for a jog along the beach. He didn't want to disturb Jo as she was sleeping so soundly. Besides that, he wanted her to take it a bit easier now that she was pregnant. *Pregnant! Wow!* He still couldn't quite believe it! *I'm actually going to be a dad!* He watched her for several moments while she slept. How he adored this woman so much. Slowly, he leant down and tenderly kissed her cheek. She stirred a little, than lay still again. He tiptoed out of the room and went for his jog.

When he got back Jo was in the shower so he decided to join her. He saw the look of surprise on her face when he appeared naked in the shower doorway and she welcomed him in with open arms. "Morning Gorgeous." He wrapped his arms around her waist and kissed her passionately.

"Wow, that was some good morning kiss!" she exclaimed when he'd let her lips go.

"It gets better too." He began to kiss and nibble her neck and chest. As his lips moved to her breast, she let out a little moan. He loved to hear her responses to his love making. "Lu-u-uke." The moan got louder and he smiled to himself as he continued his exquisite journey over her body.

Suddenly she pushed him back hard against the shower wall by the shoulders and ran out of the shower cubicle. He almost lost his balance and by the time he'd recovered it, Jo was bent over the toilet, dry retching into the bowl. His arousal suddenly diminished. He placed his hand on her back. "Are you okay, Babe?"

"No," she groaned, standing up and wiping the tears from her eyes. "I feel lousy." She rinsed her mouth out under the tap and swallowed a few mouthfuls of water before cleaning her teeth. "I can't seem to get rid of this horrible taste in my mouth." Screwing her face up, she began wiping herself with a towel.

Luke finished his shower, got dressed and found Jo lying back on the bed, her face pale. "Do you think you should try to eat something?"

"I really don't feel like it but I suppose I should," she sighed. "Just some toast will do."

Luke ordered some breakfast to be delivered to their suite and Jo managed to eat only one piece of dry toast. She couldn't bear to watch him tuck into pancakes and omelette or she would be sick again, so he ate his out on the balcony.

She soon started feeling a little better and decided a swim might make her feel even better still. They dress in togs, grabbed hats, sunscreen, sunnies and towels and headed to the beach. Luke directed her up the beach a little. They chatted as they strolled along, with Jo being oblivious to anyone around her.

"Here will do," stated Luke, stopping and spreading his towel on the sand.

Jo placed hers beside his, sat down and gazed around her. Suddenly she gasped. "Luke, that bloke over there hasn't got any clothes on!" She pointed to a middle aged man walking down toward the water, his body tanned from head to toe. Jo looked around her some more. She was stunned! There were about twenty-five people within a hundred metres or so and not one of them had a single stitch of clothing on. People of all ages, shapes and sizes, all naked, were sitting, lying or swimming with absolutely no inhibitions. Jo's mouth dropped open as the realisation dawned on her. This was a nudist beach! She turned to look up at Luke who was still standing. "LUKE!" she squealed, as he calmly removed his shorts before sitting down on his towel and flipping up the top on the sunscreen. "No wonder you had that strange look on your face yesterday when you mentioned coming to the beach today." She grinned and shook her head as she had another look around. It was some sight!

"You said you'd try anything once," he urged, rubbing sunscreen over his chest and stomach. "I dare you."

Hell, why not? She had been topless many times on beaches in Queensland and she knew that no-one would know her here. She took her bikinis off as Luke watched. "You'd better not perve too hard," she teased, "we don't want any embarrassing surprises popping up now do we?"

Luke laughed and shook his head. "Let's go for a swim." He jumped up and grabbed her hand to help her up.

Jo felt a little self-conscious as they walked to the water and was glad when they reached the waves. They both dived under and came up behind the breakers. The waves were quite small so they could swim or just tread water without being tossed about.

"Doesn't it feel a lot better than swimming with clothes on?" asked Luke, taking her into his arms.

"It sure does! Much better. It feels so natural and free." She put her arms around his neck and playfully kissed and nibbled his face. Pretty soon she felt him growing hard. Smiling cheekily, she let go of him and swam off in the opposite direction.

He was taken aback. "Where are you going? COME BACK!"

She pretended she couldn't hear him, ducked under several times and let the waves take her gently back to shore. She heard Luke call her again, but she just waved and smiled to him before walking to her towel and sitting down.

Eventually, Luke came out of the water and walked up to Jo. She was lying on her stomach with her eyes closed. Luke shook his wet hair over her back like a dog shakes itself. Jo jumped and turned to face him, squinting as the sun hit her eyes. "What did you leave me like that for?" He wasn't very happy. "I couldn't come out of the water with a hard-on!" He became even more annoyed when Jo began to laugh. "It's NOT funny, Jo. It's alright for you girls. No-one can see when you're feeling horny."

"Well, that'll teach you to bring me to a nudist beach without telling me first." She laughed harder.

As irate as he was, he couldn't stay mad at her and very soon began to laugh with her. "You wait, Mrs Summers, you'll get yours later."

"Is that a threat or a promise?" she teased.

"Oh, it's definitely a promise!" he replied with a wink.

It was a perfect day. The sun shone down brilliantly on the white sand and the crystal clear aqua water. Jo and Luke lazed on the beach for a couple of hours. Later in the morning they dawdled back to their suite for a shower, during which Luke faithfully kept his promise. Jo was tired afterwards and dozed a little before lunch. She was able to keep down some salad, then they ventured into Broome township for a look around. Luke had been there before, but Jo was amazed at the multi-cultural aspect of the town.

After visiting Chinatown they explored lots of little shops selling everything from local pearls to aboriginal art. They came across a place that offered motorbike tours of the town and grabbed the opportunity. While on the bikes they were shown the jetty's surrounded by the pearling luggers, the huge Japanese cemetery and many other spots of interest around the area.

Jo was exhausted when they made it back to the resort in the late afternoon. Along with postcards to send to family and friends they were also laden down with bags of souvenirs and presents. They ate in a different restaurant that night and went to bed early. Jo wasn't feeling too well.

The next morning they were dismayed to get up and find it cloudy with a threat of rain. Luke turned on the radio to try and hear a forecast. It was not good. A cyclone had formed overnight several hundred kilometres north of Broome and was heading southwards.

"Well!" stated Luke, switching off the radio. "There goes the rest of our honeymoon!" It was New Year's Eve and he had been planning to take Jo out somewhere special.

Jo was disappointed and a little nervous. "What should we do?"

"Well, I don't fancy staying here and getting blown away, so we'll have to go home. I'm sorry, Honey." He comforted her in his arms when he saw the look on her face. "But, I've got an idea, what if we hire a car and drive back? That way we can have a look at other places and as long as we've got a head start on the cyclone we should be right."

She didn't need convincing. "Yep, I like the idea."

Luke rang some car hire places and luckily there was one car for hire. Seems they weren't the only ones with the idea. Next he rang the airport to cancel their flights and then helped Jo pack up, before heading to reception to check out.

It was just beginning to rain as they headed southwards out of Broome. Jo looked back behind them.

"Don't worry, Babe," reassured Luke, rubbing her thigh. "We'll come back one day."

They drove all day and a little into the night until they reached Karratha, where they booked into a motel. Early next morning it was beginning to rain there as well, so they continued all day to Carnarvon and stayed in a motel again. While they were there, Luke rang ahead and booked two nights for them in Denham, knowing how much Jo would love that place.

They slept late at Carnarvan and were pleased to be told by the motel owner that the cyclone was now just a rain depression and heading inland in a south easterly direction, away from them. Jo was feeling sick again and could only eat a bit of toast for breakfast. They had a look around the town before driving the several hundred kilometres to Denham.

Jo was thrilled when she found out they were going to Monkey Mia, where the wild dolphins come to the water's edge to be fed and patted. She'd dreamed of coming here for years. The weather was sunny and beautiful with no forecast of rain for that area. Late in the afternoon, they went to the bay and sure enough, there were the dolphins.

"Aren't they just so beautiful," gushed Jo, as they went closer.

"Sure are!" agreed Luke.

There were lots of people about but the dolphins didn't seem to mind. Luke and Jo stayed until it was almost dark and then went back to their motel.

Next morning, just on sunrise, they visited the dolphins again before driving around some of the other beaches in the area. Jo collected lots of shells at Shell Beach and they had a picnic lunch at Little Lagoon. After lunch was kip time before returning to the dolphins one last time.

They slept late the next day before driving to Kalbarri. Many different wildflowers could be seen from the car. Spending two nights in Kalbarri gave them ample time to explore the rugged beauty of Kalbarri National Park, hire a row boat and row around the river and go up to the cliffs to check out the amazing views over the ocean.

The final leg of their journey back to Perth was more leisurely. Luke wanted Jo to see lots more wildflowers. She was amazed!   Acres and acres of brilliant colour, sometimes as far as the eye could see.

Just on dark they drove into their yard. While Jo was glad to be back, she was still a bit disappointed that their honeymoon was cut so short.

After taking the bags upstairs, Luke went next door to collect the spare key from David and let them know that he and Jo were back. Tea was baked beans on toast.

Later as they lay in each other's arms in their own comfy bed, Jo was sure she felt a tickle in her abdomen.

"Luke!" she gasped. "Feel that." She took his hand and placed it on her bare stomach.

"I can't feel anything," he said after several seconds.

"I'm sure I felt the baby move."

"Wouldn't it be a bit early yet? It's probably just wind!" he laughed.

"No," said Jo, "I reckon I felt her kicking her little legs around in there."

"Her? You mean HIM!" teased Luke.

"Could be both."

Luke's eyes suddenly widened.

CHAPTER FIFTEEN

Six months later and Jo's pregnancy was progressing well. She had suffered morning sickness on and off for about two months. Luke had done everything he could to help her and ease her suffering. They'd read countless books on pregnancy and childbirth and had been attending antenatal classes together. The weather was cold and wet by this time and Jo was happy to stay snuggled up in bed in the mornings. Their fireplace was certainly coming in handy.

Pete still came around now and then, and luckily he and David had managed to avoid each other. Debbie had lined him up a part time job with one of her friends, helping out in their landscaping and gardening business. He was trying to straighten his life out. While he still drank alcohol and smoked rollies, he no longer touched anything heavier. He was proud of himself and so was Debbie. He had not seen his father since the first homecoming visit, but his Mum had come around to Debbie's several times so as to spend some time with her son. He had exchanged a few phone calls with Mo, who had decided to stay in Kalbarri.

Kelly and David were still having their little squabbles but were still together.

Jo's mother had not heard anything more about Jeff's suicide at the airport, so Jo assumed it was finally all laid to rest. She hoped so anyway, as she had enough on her mind now with the impending birth. They turned the bedroom closest to theirs into a nursery and were both enjoying decorating it in all colours. Jo knew what sex the baby was, but was not telling Luke. That would be his biggest surprise of all. She almost did a few times, but held back at the last second.

The wedding photos and DVD had turned out superbly. They had a few favourites enlarged, framed and placed about the house. Jo was pleasantly surprised when they got the DVD back. Every moment was captured beautifully, but what really thrilled her was the 'extras' that Luke had put in. He had given them some extra footage of them together and they'd incorporated some of that into the wedding DVD. During the bridal waltz to, 'Everything I do', they'd added other little bits of Luke and Jo showing their obvious affection for each other. Jo absolutely loved it. That had been Luke's surprise that he'd promised her just before the wedding.

It was early one afternoon and Jo was resting, while Luke was downstairs working on some songs. The band still hadn't done much since the tour finished, except for the odd promotional appearance and helping out on a charity telethon. They'd gotten together several times at Steve's place to jam and muck around. Each one tossed a few ideas around for material for a new album, but nothing was official yet. Luke came into the bedroom with a look of concern on his face and his phone in his hand.

"What's up?" Jo asked, sitting up.

Luke sat down on the edge of the bed. "That was Col, our manager."

"Yeah...... you look worried."

"Remember how I said, when we were still on tour, that we didn't go to Asia because of some problems with the promoter there?"

"Yessss," frowned Jo, beginning to get the picture.

"Well, they've sorted things out and now they want us there. Apparently, the dates are already set."

Jo felt a surge of panic. "When? And how long for?" She didn't want Luke missing the birth.

"We fly over at the end of next week, for eight days. Don't worry Honey, we'll be back before Junior arrives." He smiled and patted her bulging stomach.

"I hope so," sighed Jo. "Do you really have to?"

"Yeah, I'm afraid so, Babe," nodded Luke, taking hold of her hand. "It was part of the tour deal. We promised them we'd do the shows once they sorted their problems out over there. I'll only be gone for eight days and I will ring you every day....... TWICE a day!" He lay down beside Jo to comfort her in his arms.

"I might ask Mum if she can come over early," said Jo. She hated the thought of Luke being so far away, especially with the birth getting closer, but she knew it was his career and he loved it. She would never stand in the way of his music.

Jo rang her mother that night and was happy that Liz cheerfully agreed to bring her plans forward. She would book her ticket for the day before Luke was due to fly out.

Jo was quiet during tea that night and Luke kept on apologising to her. After a while she was sick of hearing it and told him several times that she understood that he had to go. She also realised, that due to her pregnancy, her emotions were running on overdrive and she hoped they would settle down soon.

The next day the band had to get together to make some plans and begin some serious rehearsing. Then, every day until they were due to leave, Luke went to Steve's place for rehearsal in his studio. Sometimes Jo went to watch, which she enjoyed immensely, but some days she just felt too tired and heavy to do much. One morning they picked up Pete and Debbie on the way. They were tickled pink! Debbie hadn't seen them play together for years and Pete had almost made it to their last Sydney concert.

Jo's mother arrived, just as planned, the day before Luke left. She cooked them a special meal that night and went to bed early, feigning tiredness, but Jo knew she was disappearing so that she and Luke could have time alone before he had to leave the next morning.

They made love, gently and tenderly. After her orgasm, Jo was so overwhelmed that she cried. She held Luke tight all night, fighting sleep so that she could have more time to touch and hold him. The tears fell on her pillow as he slept peacefully beside her.

Jo wanted to make love again early the next morning and Luke didn't argue. She told him over and over how much she loved him. He kept reassuring her that he loved her too and that she had nothing to worry about. He'd be back in eight days and to look forward to their reunion. Jo smiled through her tears and nodded, but still couldn't shake the nervous feeling from the pit of her stomach. Luke packed his bags and ate a big breakfast before Jo drove him to the airport.

Everyone else was already there when they arrived. She noticed some of the other wives and girlfriends with their bags and it made her even sadder. They were obviously going with their men, but she knew that there was no way she could fly when she was so far along in her pregnancy. The others sympathised with her, but it didn't really help much.

Jo held tightly on to Luke's hand until the boarding call was made, then had to let him go. She'd held back as well as she could, but when he hugged her for the final time, a flood of tears soaked the top of his chest.

"I love you, Luke, so much," she sobbed. "Please don't ever forget that."

"I love you too, Honey," he whispered tenderly. "Don't YOU ever forget it either. I'll ring you when we get there."

"Please be careful over there."

He smiled and winked. "I will, and you look after yourself and our bub." He rubbed her stomach lightly and the baby kicked a little.

"Did you feel that?" asked Jo excitedly.

"I sure did! The little one's kicking up a storm in there."

"He probably wants to say goodbye to you too," said Jo, suddenly feeling sad again.

Luke raised his eyebrows. "Did you say HE?"

Jo had never referred to the baby as either sex before, but she suddenly felt compelled to tell Luke. "Yes," she confessed. "You're going to have a son."

"Wow!" exclaimed Luke, hugging her close to him again. "You've known all along, haven't you?"

Jo nodded. "I did want it to be a surprise for you on the day, but I just decided to tell you before you left."

"Well, it's a big surprise no matter WHEN I find out," laughed Luke.

"While you're overseas you might like to come up with a name for him," suggested Jo. "Nothing too way out, though."

"I'll think about it and let you know when I call you.......three times a day!"

"You'd better go now," Jo smiled sadly.

He smiled, kissed her passionately before heading through the boarding gate and on to the plane where the others were waiting. Jo rushed out of the terminal, wiping the tears from her eyes as she quickly walked through the car park to her car. She didn't want to see the plane take off into the sky.

She sat in her car for a few minutes to compose herself, wishing that her mother had come with so she could drive back. Jo wasn't really feeling up to it and the baby was moving a lot, making her feel very uncomfortable.

When she finally arrived back home, she fell into her mother's arms and sobbed. "I miss him so much already, Mum."

"Oh, my poor baby, of course you do," comforted Liz. "But he'll only be gone for eight days and you can talk to him on the phone a lot. Sweetie, you have to look after yourself and Bub while he's away. He won't be very happy if he gets back and you're sick."

"No, that's true. You're right and I'm just being silly." She had a glass of water and lay down on the lounge to rest.

The days went by very slowly for Jo, while Luke was away. As he promised he called every day, sometimes up to four times a day. She was thrilled to hear his voice but was always a little teary when she hung up. The tour was going well and they talked about baby names but had not come up with anything definite yet. Her mother was good company for her. Some days they went shopping or out to lunch, but Jo tired easily and liked to have a sleep through the day. She only had a few weeks to go now and would be glad when the pregnancy was over.

Pete and Debbie called around a couple of times to see how she was going. She liked their company and had them, and Deb's girls, stay for tea each time they came. Jo could tell Pete missed Luke too, probably more than he would let on.

Kelly popped over at least once a day, to say hello and have a chat. She was almost as excited about the baby as Jo was. David never came over while Luke was away and Jo wondered why. Jo asked Kelly, one day, how David was and she had just shrugged and said that he was all right. Sensing she wasn't happy with her relationship, Jo didn't want to pry too much so decided it was best to let it be and let Kelly talk about it if and when she was ready.

During the morning of the eighth day, Luke rang from Hong Kong to tell Jo that their plane would be landing in Perth at six PM that night. She was excited and couldn't wait for the day to pass.

Deciding to make a special 'Welcome Home' cake, she was busy in the kitchen with the radio on while her mother was pegging out some washing. A song played to which she happily sang along with. Suddenly, the song was abruptly cut short and a man's voice came on. "WE INTERRUPT THIS BROADCAST TO BRING YOU A NEWSFLASH. AN INDONESIAN AIRLINES PASSENGER JET BOUND FOR PERTH HAS CRASHED JUST AFTER TAKE-OFF FORM HONG KONG INTERNATIONAL AIRPORT. THE PLANE WAS DUE TO ARRIVE IN PERTH AT SIX PM. AT THE MOMENT AUTHORITIES ARE SEARCHING FOR ANY SIGNS OF SURVIVORS, BUT EARLY INDICATIONS POINT TO ALL LIVES BEING LOST. WE WILL KEEP YOU UPDATED AS MORE INFORMATION COMES TO HAND."

The tin of raw cake mixture that Jo was about to put in the oven crashed to the floor, splattering everywhere. "MUM!" she screamed. The room spun around her as she swayed to get her balance. Grabbing the edge of the sink, her heart pounded as her body shuddered with sobs. Suddenly she felt like throwing up so, with tears streaming down her face, she ran blindly to the toilet.

Her mother caught her in the hallway. "What's the matter?" she cried.

Without speaking, Jo pushed past her, shaking her head, and rushed to the toilet where she vomited uncontrollably into the bowl.

"Is it the baby?" asked Liz frantically, following her and placing her hands on Jo's back. She could feel Jo's body shaking.

Jo stood up and looked at her mother with red, watery eyes. "Luke's been killed!" she burst out, then falling forward into her mother's arms.

"What? How?" Liz helped her distraught daughter to her bed and lay her down as tears welled in her eyes too.

"The plane crashed....... Just after take-off," sobbed Jo. "I just heard it..... on the radio. Everyone was...... killed." She rolled to her side, buried her face into a pillow and cried hard. "Luke, Luke," she repeated over and over. Suddenly she let out a cry of pain and brought her knees up toward her stomach. Her pale face contorted as she sucked in her breath.

"Jo, Honey, are you in pain?" panicked her mother.

"YES!" screamed Jo. "Mum, call an ambulance!"

Liz grabbed the phone by the bed and dialled triple zero. She briefly described the situation and gave the address. After placing the phone back down, she ran to Jo's bathroom to get a wet washer to wipe Jo's face and a glass of water for her to drink.

Jo half sat up, took a small sip of water and slumped back down on the bed. She placed her hands protectively over her stomach and grimaced as Liz wiped her face.

"It can't be true," she mumbled. "Luke can't be dead. He CAN'T Mum!" She sat up, put her arms around her mother and burst into a fresh lot of tears.

Liz could feel Jo's baby moving jerkily as Jo's stomach pressed against her and she wished the ambulance would hurry up.

"Jo, are you SURE it was Luke's plane?" Liz asked as she moved Jo back a little from her by holding on to her slumped shoulders.

"Yes! It was leaving Hong Kong and......was due here at six PM, just like he.....told me.....this morning." She fell back into her mother's arms.

Just then they heard the ambulance siren wailing in the distance but getting louder. Liz lay Jo back on to the bed and raced for the remote to open the gate. The paramedics pulled up as close to the front door as possible before jumping out and coming upstairs. Liz hurried them up to Jo's bedroom.

Jo was standing up when they got there and said she'd walk down. They helped her to the ambulance as Liz grabbed her own handbag and the hospital bag that Jo had packed and repacked many times to pass the time while Luke was away.

Liz jumped into the back of the ambulance with her daughter and held her hand as they sped to the hospital. Jo's pain and discomfort increased as they neared their destination. By the time they'd arrived she had to be carried inside on a gurney. A doctor immediately came to her aide while her private doctor was called.

Jo was in agony, both physically and emotionally. Her doctor soon arrived and examined her while he learnt the facts surrounding her immediate situation. She couldn't feel the warm blood running slowly out of her and on to the sheet beneath. All she could feel was searing pain in her abdomen and the deepest, darkest pain in her heart from losing her adored husband.

Her doctor didn't want to add to her worry by telling her about the bleeding. "Jo," he said, leaning over her a little, ensuring she could hear him. "We're going to take you to surgery. The little fella's trying his hardest to get out, but your body isn't ready for it yet. We'll have to do a caesarean." Jo nodded weakly in return.

While Jo was wheeled toward theatre for prepping, her doctor spoke to Liz. "Her body has had a terrible shock. Her heart rate and blood pressure are both up sky high. We're going to have to take the baby. She's haemorrhaging slightly, but that's not unusual under these circumstances. The baby is traumatised so the quicker we can get it out the better."

"Will the baby be all right?" sobbed Liz. "And…..Jo. Will she…….." She couldn't get the words out.

"The baby should be fine, she only had a few weeks to go," assured the doctor. "I'm sure Jo will be too. She's strong and healthy and in the best hands here." He turned and headed quickly toward the operating theatre.

Liz frantically dug her phone out of her bag and called Jo's father, Tom, to tell him the terrible news. She wept uncontrollably as she spoke into the phone. She couldn't believe Luke was dead and now the possibility of losing Jo and the baby was too much to bear. Tom said he would be on the next available flight. Next Liz called David and Kelly's house. She didn't have their mobile numbers so could only leave a message on their answering machine. The following call was to Luke's parents. They had not heard the news of the crash so were distraught when they arrived at the hospital.

For what seemed like hours, they paced up and down in the waiting room sobbing and supporting each other at this sad and worrying time. Every time a nurse or any staff member came within their vicinity they would desperately ask them for some news. Later on they were joined by David and Kelly.

At last, the doctor appeared, looking exhausted. Everyone rushed over closer to him, questioning him with their bleary eyes.

"They're both fine." Those few words were met with heavy sighs of relief. "She had a little boy and he's perfect."

"What about Jo?" Liz asked anxiously. "When can we see her?"

"Well it was touch and go there for a while, but she's a super strong lady and she'll pull through. She lost quite a bit of blood and she's still heavily sedated. Not just yet for a while. I'll let you know when you can. You'll probably be able to see the baby before Jo."

David and Kelly decided to go home for a shower and tea. They'd come straight in once they'd got home from work. Liz and Luke's parents decided to remain at the hospital. They rang Casey to tell her the bad news and she made immediate plans to fly home. Luke's father still couldn't believe it about the plane crash so rang the airport only to have it confirmed. He was also told that Luke's name was on the passenger list. He was devastated. Just as he was telling the two ladies, Jo's father came rushing in.

"How's our little girl?" he sobbed, hugging his wife.

"She's okay and we have a grandson," smiled Liz amidst her tears. "But Luke's dead."

Tom shook Luke's father's hand and gave his mother a hug of sympathy. Everyone was crying.

Kelly rang the hospital and was told there was no change. She asked the nurse to tell the families that she would come up again in the morning. Her and David were too stunned by Luke's death to go out again.

Later that night the grandparents were allowed to see the baby through the large glass window of the nursery.

"He looks just like his Dad," sobbed Mrs Summers. She turned away and buried her face in her husband's chest as she cried.

"He's beautiful," whispered Liz.

They returned to the waiting area for news on Jo, to be told that they wouldn't be able to see her until morning, so they decided to leave. Luke's parents invited Liz and Tom over to their place. Tom and Liz would have rather been alone but they sensed that Ted and Rose didn't, after losing their son, so they went along with them. It was a long night. No-one felt like sleeping. Luke's parents were frustrated that they had not yet been given some official word that their son had been killed in a plane crash, but realised that they may not hear anything until the morning. Suddenly, the late night silence was broken by the sound of their phone ringing. Everyone looked at each other before Ted went to answer it.

Jo slowly tried to open her eyes. Strange thoughts and images were racing through her foggy brain. She didn't know whether she felt like laughing or crying. She could hear noises and voices but they all blended in together. *What is happening to me?* Feeling a surge of panic, she tried harder to open her eyes. Everything was blurry, her stomach hurt and she felt sick, but she could just make out Luke's face beside her bed. He was holding her hand up to his mouth as tears ran down his cheeks. The memory of the plane crash news came back to her, making her think she must be in heaven, or dreaming.

"Luke," she whispered hoarsely. Her mouth was dry and her throat sore from the tubes being in it. "Is it really you?" Tears ran out of the sides of her eyes as she tried in vain to sit up.

"Yeah Babe," he smiled. "It's me."

"B-but I thought ...... you were...... dead......plane crash."

"We got caught up and missed our flight, so we had to get the next one, but it went to Sydney first. I was trying to call you but there was no answer. We didn't know about the other one crashing until we got to Sydney. I rang David and he told me about it and how you and everyone thought I was dead, so he rang Mum and Dad late last night to tell them. I'm so sorry you went through all that, Jo, but hey," he smiled and winked. "As I have told you over and over you're stuck with me forever!" He leaned over and kissed her forehead then her trembling lips so gently.

"Our son's a little beauty," Luke continued with a big smile. "I've nursed him already."

"Is he..... all right?" Jo asked.

"He's perfect, just like you. I missed you like crazy."

"Same here," smiled Jo, reaching up to touch his face. "You look tired."

"I didn't sleep a wink, but don't worry about me, it's you that's in hospital!"

"We'd better come up with a name for him," said Jo. "Did you think of anything?"

"How does Benjamin Luke, sound?"

"Perfect," nodded Jo with a smile.

Just then her doctor came in. "Welcome back young lady," he smiled warmly. "You gave us all a bit of a scare yesterday, but not quite as bad as the fright YOU gave everyone, Luke!" He checked Jo over.

"Yeah, I know," smiled Luke, "you don't have to remind me."

The doctor talked to them both about Jo's condition and what exactly happened in the operating theatre. He also informed Jo that she would have to stay in hospital for up to a week. She didn't like that idea, but since her stomach felt like a ten tonne weight had been dropped on it, she knew she had no choice. As Ben was a little premature, the doctor also wanted to keep him in too, just for observation. Jo was relieved to know he would be with her and that she would be able to feed him while she was still in hospital.

Soon, one of the nurses brought the little bundle into them and handed him to Jo. Luke had helped her sit up a little and propped another pillow behind her head. Jo gasped as she saw her baby for the first time and began to cry.

"What's wrong?" asked Luke, worried.

"He's so beautiful, but I always thought we'd have a normal birth, with you beside me, holding my hand. Then they'd place the baby on my stomach and I'd be able to touch his soft skin, and hold him," Jo sobbed.

"Yeah, but it's all good, Honey," Luke reassured her, stroking her forehead. "Everything's all right and that's the important thing. I promise that, next time, I definitely WON'T go anywhere!" He saw the look of relief flood Jo's face.

Later that morning the four grandparents came in to see her. Liz cried tears of joy as she hugged Jo and Luke as well. Luke's Mum nearly collapsed as she hugged him in relief. Even though they had got the good news the previous night, it was still an emotional reunion, for all concerned. Despite Jo's pain and discomfort, she was the happiest she had ever been in her life right at that moment.

During her stay in hospital, Jo grew stronger every day. Luke was at her bedside from early morning until late at night. Jo's father returned to Queensland but Liz stayed on and visited her daughter every day. Luke's parents came up nearly every day and Kelly visited when she could. David didn't visit, saying that hospitals made him feel sick. Casey had flown over anyway, even once she knew that Luke was fine. She wanted to see her little nephew, but could only stay overnight.

Luke had rung Debbie and her and Pete had visited several times through the week. Jo's mother had rung Meg and she had sent a large bouquet of flowers to add to the numerous bunches adorning Jo's private room. Luke had ensured there were plenty of wildflowers among them too. The band members and their partners had also visited Jo throughout the week, all fully aware and grateful of how lucky they were to still be alive, after missing their designated flight.

After several days, when he was given the all clear, she was allowed to have Ben in the room with her, but she wasn't to lift him too much, due to the surgery incision still healing. She lay on her bed, with his little, plastic hospital cot as close to her as possible so she could stroke and pat him gently. Her heart swelled with love and pride as she would watch him sleep, never tiring of being amazed by the wonderful miracles of life and circumstance.

Finally, on the seventh morning after giving birth, she was informed she could go home that day. She and Luke were thrilled. Liz had stayed at Jo's and made last minute tidy ups and cooked up some meals that could just be heated as needed. She'd gone shopping the day before, expecting the release day to be imminent, and stocked up the fridge and pantry. She remembered, from when she gave birth, that as a new mother, the last thing you really feel like doing is going out shopping. Of course, as the excited Grandma, she also bought more baby gifts, even though she could see by the nursery that Jo already had more than enough clothes, toys and the like, for Ben.

Jo and Luke drove into their yard late morning, to see Liz at the front door, eagerly awaiting their arrival, with a huge smile on her face. Luke helped Jo out before taking the baby capsule out, while Liz carried Jo's bag and some flowers upstairs.

Even though she was relieved to be home, walking into the kitchen she was hit hard by the memory of the newsflash over the radio. She shuddered and felt a little overwhelmed. *The cake!* She felt disappointed that she hadn't baked it. *Don't be silly,* she scolded herself, turning to hug Luke after he put the capsule down gently on the dining room table.

"It's ok, Babe, everything is good. You have nothing to be worried or frightened about."

Jo smiled and walked over to have yet another look at their precious son, sleeping so soundly in the capsule.

"Isn't he gorgeous?" murmured Jo, as Luke came up behind her and placed his arms around her shoulders. "Everything's just so perfect."

"You bet," assured Luke. "And it always will be!"

CHAPTER SIXTEEN

For the next three months following the birth, life was wonderful, but hectic for Jo. Her mother had returned to Queensland, her camera loaded with photos, a week after Jo came home from hospital. Meg had rung or e-mailed Jo several times and she was thrilled to see all the pics Jo regularly texted or put on Facebook. Jo had also sent pictures to Graham and several of her other old friends.

Luke's mother, and often his father, came over every second day to help her with the housework. That was her excuse anyway, but Jo knew very well that they just came over to fuss over their adorable grandson. Luke was doing most of the housework and cooking.

Kelly came over after work most afternoons. She couldn't help feeling a little clucky herself. David took lots of photos of them all. Along with what Jo took nearly every day, she had miles of taped footage and thousands of photos.

She had recovered well from the surgery and had no more medical problems. Feeding Ben herself, she welcomed these times to strengthen the bond between mother and son. Luke sometimes felt a bit left out during these sessions so Jo would let him hold Ben while he suckled on her breast. He was totally in awe and would stare, mesmerised, at his son as he guzzled the warm milk. Luke soon became an expert at changing nappies, not even minding the poopy ones.

Jo was putting Ben down to sleep one afternoon when the phone rang. Luke was outside cleaning the pool as the weather was beginning to warm up nicely. Jo answered the phone to find Debbie on the other end.

"How's things, Deb?"

"Well, I'm fine and the girls are good, but I'm a bit concerned about Pete. He's not there by any chance hey? He got a new phone recently but isn't answering it."

"No, we haven't seen him for a few weeks now. Luke was wondering about him last night. Is something wrong?" asked Jo.

"No, I don't think so. I just haven't seen him in days and it's not like him to stay away without letting me know. He was saying a couple of weeks ago that he hadn't been feeling too good," replied Debbie. "If you see or hear from him, can you get him to ring me please."

"Sure will!"

"Thanks Mate. Oh, and give that gorgeous boy of yours a kiss for me ……. The LITTLE one!" Deb laughed.

"I think I can manage that," laughed Jo, "See you later."

As soon as she hung up the phone she went outside to tell Luke of the call.

"Hmm, that's strange," he frowned. "I wonder what the little bugger's up to?"

He called Deb later that night and the next morning but she still had not heard from him. She gave Luke Pete's mobile number and he tried that as well, but still no luck. Debbie wanted to call the police but Luke assured her that he may have just slipped back into his old ways and to give him another day or two yet.

Later that day, Pete turned up at Luke's gate. Opening the gate, Luke got a shock when he saw him. Pete was dirty, unshaven and looked as though he hadn't slept in days.

"What the hell happened to you?" demanded Luke, closing the gate again.

Pete shook his head grimly. "Oh Man, you wouldn't believe what's happened. Can I have a shower?"

Nodding, Luke urged him in the door and Pete went straight to the downstairs shower. Running up the steps two at a time, he told Jo and asked her to call Deb and let her know he was here. Then he rummaged around in his wardrobe and drawers for some clean clothes for Pete. They would be too big for him but at least they would smell better than the ones he'd turned up in.

Pete came out of the shower in Luke's tee shirt and shorts. Luke couldn't help laughing a bit but when he noticed Pete didn't do the same, he realised that something was seriously out of whack. "What's wrong, Pete," Luke asked, placing his hand on Pete's shoulder.

Pete looked from Luke to Jo then back to Luke. "Um.... Can we go for a walk somewhere. Over to the beach maybe."

Jo was a little hurt. She thought she and Pete were good friends now, but she knew that the friendship between he and Luke was stronger so she respected that.

"Yeah, Mate, whatever you like," replied Luke, beginning to feel a bit uneasy. He kissed Jo and followed Pete out the front door. As they walked across the yard, Luke turned back to Jo, who was standing at the door, shrugged his shoulders and shook his head. He saw the equally puzzled look on Jo's face as she waved to him.

Pete and Luke walked silently across the road and sat atop the highest sand dune, looking out across the blue ocean. Luke thought it would be best to let Pete speak when he was ready.

Taking a tailor made cigarette out of a pack in his shirt pocket, Pete lit it and dragged deeply. After a few moments his bottom lip began to tremble as he tried to speak. "I've......." He took a deep breath. "I've got AIDS!" he sobbed.

Luke was stunned and speechless! He just sat there, staring at Pete who had now buried his face in his hands and was openly crying, his thin body wracked by shudders.

"Are....are you s-sure?" Luke eventually stammered.

Pete nodded. "I had the test done a couple of weeks ago and got the results back the other day."

Luke inhaled a deep breath and looked up into the sky, unsure of what to say. "Did..... did they say how bad it is? If it's just HIV you know there are drugs that can stop it getting any worse."

Pete shook his head. "It's past that stage. It's AIDS! I'd been feeling crook for a while but I thought it was from too much drinkin' and smokin'.'"

"Does anyone else know?"

"No!" replied Pete, "and I don't want them to either. I know you'll need to tell Jo, but don't let her tell anyone else.......please. I've gotta get used to it meself before everyone else knows."

"How did you feel when they told you?" Luke realised that was a pretty silly question as soon as he asked it, but he just couldn't think of much to say right then.

"How do ya think? I didn't exactly jump for joy!" Pete angrily stubbed out the cigarette butt.

"I'm sorry, Mate," said Luke, patting Pete's shoulder. "I'm just trying to understand how you must be feeling."

"I feel..... empty......stunned.....scared. Fuck man! I'm scared!" He began to cry again. "Why me, Luke? I know I've done some bad things, but I never thought I'd end up dyin' like this." He wiped his eyes. "You know, Friday is me thirtieth birthday. Hell of a birthday present, aint it?"

Luke shook his head and wiped the tears from his own eyes. He just wished he knew what to say to Pete that might make him feel a little better. "Are you going to have some counselling?"

"What's the use?" shrugged Pete, staring straight out to sea. "I'm gunna die and nothin' anyone says can change that." He lit another cigarette and inhaled deeply.

"At least you could talk to others in the same situation and there must be something out now that can hold off the symptoms."

"You mean prolong the agony, no thanks. In the words of James Dean, 'Live fast, die young and have a good looking corpse.'" Luke just stared at him with raised eyebrows. "Well, all right," grinned Pete. "Skip the 'good looking' part. But seriously Luke, I'd rather have a good time with what I have left."

"I can understand that," nodded Luke. "I'd probably do the same."

Pete turned to Luke. "Have you ever had an AIDS test?"

"Yes, actually. They're not a lot of fun, especially waiting for the results."

"Have you ever thought about dying?"

"What? No, not a lot, except for when Jo had Ben and they thought I'd been killed in the plane crash. I tried to imagine what she was going through and then thought about it a bit. I got my will updated then."

"It's a bit of a blowout really isn't it?" asked Pete. "I mean, you spend your time searching for a good buzz. Smoke a few joints, drop some speed or whatever, but in the end nothin' is like the ultimate high..... goin' through that tunnel. I've been there a couple of times, you know. It's going to be interesting to finally see what's out the other end."

"I don't think anyone should be scared of dying," said Luke. "I believe in life after death..... or something like that. I'm not sure what, but I reckon there has to be more than just one life."

"I hope you're right, Mate! One thing's for sure, if I did get another chance I sure as hell wouldn't stuff that one up. Hey, whatever you do, DON'T tell David! He's the absolute last person I want to know. He'd probably laugh and say I deserved it. In a way I do, I suppose." He became solemn again.

"Nobody DESERVES it!" asserted Luke. "Now get that out of your mind."

The sun was settling low over the ocean when Pete said he should get back to Debbie's. They chatted a little while longer then Luke offered to take him back on his bike. Pete was pleased about that and felt a little better. Luke always made him feel better.

"What do you reckon about a party for your birthday?" asked Luke, as they walked across the road toward his house. He hoped it would cheer Pete up a bit.

Pete was surprised. "What...... here?"

"Yeah, why not?"

"Who'd come?"

"Well, Debbie..... and Steve and the Boys, and .... You must know a few other people by now. Anyone from where you work?" asked Luke.

"Nah, not really," replied Pete as they neared the house. "I'm not that crazy about the other two blokes. They're dickheads!" He laughed, causing Luke to as well.

"What's tickling you two?" asked Jo, from the top of the stairs as they walked up them.

"Pete was just talking about his work mates," grinned Luke, kissing her on the forehead. "Hey Babe, Friday is Pete's birthday. Would you mind if we had a little party for him? We'll have it outside so Ben's not disturbed too much."

"Yeah, sounds good. About time we had another party."

"Thanks Jo," smiled Pete, gratefully.

"Well, you tell Deb about it and I'll organise everything else. Come on Mate, I'll drop you home." He kissed Jo and said he'd be back soon.

When Luke arrived back, Jo had cooked their tea and was sitting at the table feeding Ben. He was a good baby. Ate and slept well without too much fuss. Luke served up the meal while Jo put Ben to bed. Once they were settled into their meal, Jo's curiosity got the better of her.

"What was wrong with Pete this afternoon?"

Luke wasn't sure what to say, even though he thought of nothing else riding back after dropping Pete off. He wished he didn't have to tell her, but knew it couldn't be avoided. "He got some bad news back from the doctor's."

"That doesn't sound good. What's wrong?"

"He's got..... he's HIV positive," replied Luke slowly.

"What!" Jo gasped, dropping her fork full of food.

"He found out a few days ago," said Luke sadly. "That's why he hasn't gone home. He's just trying to let it sink in."

Jo was just as stunned as Luke was. "What's he going to do?"

"Dunno," shrugged Luke. "He's not interested in counselling. He definitely doesn't want David knowing, so don't tell Kelly will you?"

"Well, I won't but that's a shame. She may have something that can help him. Does he know how he got it?"

"He didn't say, but he's been living a pretty rough life in Sydney and being gay….."

Jo pushed her plate aside and stared at the table in front of her. "I'm not really that hungry anymore."

"Are you still happy to have his party here on Friday?" asked Luke, hoping that, for Pete's sake, she hadn't changed her mind.

"Yes, of course. I'm not going to ban him from the house because of it. He will have to be a bit careful while he's here though. I do know that you have to do a bit more than just touch someone to catch it. Poor bloke. I bet he's feeling scared."

"He sure is," nodded Luke, "and as much as I've tried, I can't even begin to imagine what he must be going through. I think the party will cheer him up a bit though. That reminds me, I'll ring the boys and see what everyone's up to Friday night." He stood up and picked up his phone while Jo cleared off the table. After he had made several calls he helped her with the last of the washing up.

"Are you going to invite Kelly and David?" asked Jo, letting the water out of the sink.

"I don't know what to do about that situation," frowned Luke. "I just wish things were different there. I know Kelly would come and Pete would like her to, but he would prefer David stay away. I'll go and see them now," he sighed. "Hopefully, David will just choose not to come."

"Luke!" David exclaimed, finding him standing at their front door. "What can we do for you at this hour of the night."

Luke walked in. "I just came over to invite you and Kelly to a party on Friday night."

"Did I hear 'party'?" enthused Kelly, walking into the lounge room where David and Luke had just sat down.

"So, what's the occasion this time?" asked David.

"Well….." Luke hesitated. *Shit, I HATE talking to you about Pete!* "I know you won't be too keen, Dave, but it's a birthday party for Pete, just a small one."

"Ha! With the amount of friends he's got, it certainly wouldn't be a big one!" David sniggered.

Both Luke and Kelly shot him daggers. "Well, I'm going to go," stated Kelly. "Thanks Luke."

"You can," replied David. "Look, if it makes you happy, Luke, I'll come for a little while and I'll even be polite to him."

"Thanks, Dave," sighed Luke. "But you really don't have to come if you don't want to." *You REALLY don't!*

"No, I'll come and stay a bit."

Luke jumped up from the chair. "Righto! Eight o-clock. We'll have a few nibblies and fingerfood. See you then." He walked quickly back home to Jo.

Jo was about to have a shower when he walked inside. "Want to join me?" she smiled.

"Definitely!" He stripped off and stepped into the shower cubicle.

"We're pretty lucky, aren't we?" she asked as Luke began to rub soap over her chest and shoulders.

"We sure are," he murmured before kissing her hungrily on the lips. "I really need you right now, Jo!" He lifted her up and she slid down on his waiting hardness. "I've never been more grateful for you and Ben than I was this afternoon. I love you so much, Jo." If I wasn't for the running water, he knew Jo would have seen the tears in his eyes.

"At least we have the rest of our lives together," she smiled at him before clutching him harder to her and letting out a small moan.

CHAPTER SEVENTEEN

The afternoon of Pete's party Luke decided to do some maintenance on his bike. He heard the house phone ring and a few minutes later Jo came down the stairs.

"That was Debbie. She can't come to the party. Someone called in sick at the hospital and she's been called in to work."

"Oh, that's a shame," said Luke. "I hope Birthday Boy can get here. I might have to go and pick him up."

"No, she said that the lady that babysits for her will drive him over. She's giving her some extra money." She turned and went back upstairs when she heard Ben crying.

A few minutes later David walked into the garage. "What are you doing? Trouble?"

"Don't know yet," replied Luke. "It's just making a few strange noises lately. She's still running well though." They chatted a bit about the bike before Luke glanced at his watch. "Shit, I'd better leave this and go and get ready."

"Yeah, I think you'd better, Mate," laughed David, before walking back to his place to get ready as well.

Luke had one more check that the bar fridge downstairs was full and that the nibblies were ready on trays. When he was satisfied that no other preparations had to be done he headed for the shower.

Kelly was the first to arrive, soon followed by Steve and his wife. Not long afterwards the other members of the band and their partners arrived. They all sat out near the pool, enjoying the crisp, spring air. Ben had stayed awake a little longer than usual and once Luke had showed him off to everyone, Jo took him upstairs to bed. She came back soon after and placed the monitor on the table in front of her so she could hear if he woke up.

"I wonder where the guest of honour is?" said Luke, looking at his watch. It was now nine-thirty. Everyone shrugged and shook their heads.

Soon a car pulled up outside the front gate. Luke heard Pete shout as the car drove away. He opened the gate and closed it again once Pete was through. "Where have you been? The party started two hours ago."

"Sorry," mumbled Pete, walking unsteadily toward Luke. "I got side tracked."

Luke could see that Pete had already drunk a fair amount, but under the circumstances, he didn't really blame him. "It's all right, Mate, you're here now."

Everyone greeted Pete as he walked over to the pool side tables. They sang Happy Birthday and Jo brought out the cake that she'd made in the morning. She even had thirty candles on it.

"Wow!" said Pete, wiping a tear from his eye. "This is the best birthday I've ever had."

Steve had bought him a bottle of scotch as a present. Pete wasted no time in opening it and pouring himself a drink. Jo handed him a bottle of coke to top up the glass, but there was more scotch in it than coke. Just as Pete was taking his first mouth full he saw David coming across the yard toward him and grew tense.

"Happy birthday, Pete," smiled David, shaking his hand.

Pete felt stunned into speechlessness. David was actually being nice to him! He watched as David walked over to Kelly and got himself a beer before sitting next to her.

"I'm glad you're being friendly to him for a change," said Kelly.

"It's only for tonight, because it's his birthday. Don't get too excited."

Everyone partied on, singing along with Luke and Steve playing their guitars. Pete was pretty drunk by this time but he certainly looked happy. Suddenly, Steve began playing 'Knockin' on Heaven's Door' and Pete disappeared into the toilet. Luke soon noticed he was gone. When he did come back a bit later, Luke could see that his eyes were red. He went up to Pete and apologised for the choice of song, but Pete just shrugged it off, saying that he was all right. He poured himself another scotch and coke and joined in with the next song.

As some of the guests were about to leave, Jo heard Ben stir on the monitor, so she quickly said goodbye to them and turned to go upstairs.

"Jo, do you mind if I come with you?" asked David. "I haven't seen my little nephew for a while." He could see Kelly chatting to Pete over near the pool.

"Yeah, no worries," replied Jo, heading up to the nursery.

When she got there, Jo picked Ben up and began to undo her shirt buttons to suckle him. She noticed David turn away. "It's okay," she laughed. "I don't mind if you stay."

"Are you sure?"

"Of course. It's nothing to be embarrassed about." Ben attached himself to her nipple.

David watched in fascination as Ben suckled on Jo's breast. When he'd had enough, she held him up to her shoulder for several minutes to burp him, before changing him and returning him to his cot.

"That's amazing," said David, shaking his head. "You're amazing." Slowly, he reached over and stroked her cheek. He saw her turn her face away, but he gently turned it back toward him. "You're very beautiful, Jo. I've thought that from the first time I met you."

"David, I......" She felt very uncomfortable.

David slowly leaned in toward her face and was about to kiss her.

"What's going on here?" frowned Luke at the door. "I heard the voices on the monitor." He could only see the back of David's head but he could tell that his hand was raised.

David jumped a little. "I was just telling Jo, what a beautiful baby you have."

Jo was nervous so leant over to check that Ben was asleep. She didn't want the brothers to fight, but she was taken aback by David's show of affection toward her. The tension in the air was so thick she could have cut it with a knife. David excused himself and went back downstairs.

Luke knew he was lying and was annoyed, but couldn't be bothered arguing with him tonight. He took Jo's hand and led her into their bedroom. "What was HE doing when I turned up?"

"I-I'm not sure," stammered Jo. "I think he was going to kiss me. It took me by surprise."

"That bastard! He's doing it again!" fumed Luke. "I won't say anything tonight, but I'll go and have a talk to him tomorrow. I've had a gut full. I thought he was over all that shit years ago."

"What shit? What are you talking about, Luke?"

"His jealousy. I'll tell you all about it tomorrow." He took her in his arms and kissed her, but Jo could feel the tension still in his body.

When they went back downstairs a short time later, the other guests were ready to leave, including Kelly who had to work the following day. David left a while after Kelly, thanking Luke for the party before he headed off in the direction of the divider gate. Jo decided to leave Pete and Luke to it and went up to bed.

Luke and Pete moved to the bar in the entertainment room. Luke was still pissed off with David but he tried not to let it show. He didn't want to spoil Pete's birthday. Hell, he realised it might be the last one he has!

They were sitting on opposite sides of the bar chatting about the party when Pete suddenly touched Luke's hand. Luke was taken aback, but he didn't think Pete would try anything so he just left his hand there.

"You know what the best birthday present of all would be, Luke?"

Luke drew a deep sigh and hoped that Pete was not going to say what he expected him to. "No, what?" he asked, slowly moving his hand out of Pete's reach.

"Just let me love you. Just once before I die," he pleaded. "You don't have to do anything."

Luke was horrified when he realised that Pete was serious. "How can you even think such a thing? You know how I feel about that, I've told you over and over! And especially now!" Luke stood up, turned his back on Pete and placed his hands on his hips. He really didn't need this on top of having to deal with David coming on to Jo.

"Please Luke," begged Pete, with teary eyes. "I love you. I always have. It would mean so much to me."

"NO!" declared Luke through clenched teeth, turning to face Pete. "Never in a million years! You're my mate and that's all I can give you. I'm sorry you've got AIDS and I'll do everything I can to help and support you but I can't give you the one thing you want the most. Now, I think you'd better go upstairs to bed and we'll just forget this conversation ever happened."

Pete remained silent while Luke helped him up to his bed for the night. He felt sad, angry, embarrassed and thought it best to not say another word. He collapsed on the bed and was almost instantly asleep.

Luke could tell Jo was asleep so he went back downstairs, poured himself another drink and mulled over the nights events. He was annoyed with Pete, but still felt a bit sorry for him. David was another story though. There was no excuse for his behaviour and Luke would let him know the next day. He was too worked up to go to bed yet, so tidied up after the party. When he finally did go to bed, Jo woke up.

"Sorry it's so late, Honey," He took her in his arms and kissed her tenderly.

Jo sensed something was not quite right. "What's wrong Luke?"

He told her about Pete, without going into too much detail. He added that, although he felt sorry for him, Pete had no right to assume that Luke would be interested in having sex with him.

"I know how to make you relax," she purred, nibbling his chest before moving slowly down his body.

"You sure do, Babe," he sighed when she hit the bullseye.

Next morning, Luke got up early, saying he wanted to go for a ride on his bike. Jo could tell he was still a bit angry and agreed that a bike ride would help ease his tension. He went into the spare room to wake Pete and offer to take him back to Debbie's.

"Jo, come here!" Luke called.

She walked in and was shocked to find the bed roughly made and empty. They looked at each other and frowned, before checking the bathrooms and all around downstairs. Pete was nowhere to be found.

Luke was annoyed. "He probably feels bad about last night and hasn't got the guts to face me." He went into the garage to put his bike back together.

Jo heard Ben cry and went up to him. While upstairs she heard the bike start up so took Ben with her back down to wave Luke off. She could still see a troubled look on Luke's face as he put his helmet on.

Luke saw Jo and Ben standing there so took it back off to give them a hug and kiss. "I'll be right, Babe. I just need to clear my head. I love you." He smiled and winked before putting the helmet back on and roaring out the gate.

Watching her beloved husband head northwards along the coast, she hoped all would be okay, but she had a niggling, heavy feeling that everything was about to change.

CHAPTER EIGHTEEN

Hours passed and Luke had not returned home. Jo was beginning to get worried. She rang his mobile only to find it had been switched off. Not wanting to bother anyone else, she busied herself with housework and Ben, to pass the time, but it would not ease the feeling of dread in her stomach. By late afternoon, she called Debbie, to ask if Luke had gone there to see Pete. She had not seen or heard anything of him and mentioned that Pete come home in the early hours of the morning and was still in bed. Jo thought it best not to tell Debbie about Pete coming on to Luke.

With Ben in her arms, she walked through the semi darkness over to Kelly and David's to see if they had heard from Luke. David said he had not seen or heard from him and excused himself to go and have a shower. Jo tried Luke's mobile for the umpteenth time, still nothing.

"I just don't understand, Kell," panicked Jo. "It's not like him. Something must have happened to him."

"I agree, Jo, it's not like him." She gave her friend a comforting hug.

"I'll just go back home and wait some more. I might try his parents, but I don't want to worry them unnecessarily...... ohhhh, I just don't know what to do for the best." Jo's mind was in turmoil, full of "should I" or "shouldn't I" and generally fearing the worst.

On arriving back at her house, Jo decided to call the police. She knew she HAD to do something. They informed her that if he had not returned home by the morning they would begin a search. It still didn't ease her worry.

Early next morning, she called Rose and Ted to tell them about their son being missing. They were upset and came right over. Once they arrived Jo called the police back. Thirty minutes later a police car pulled up at her gateway. Four police officers alighted from the car, including two detectives. Jo immediately gave them a picture of Luke and one of his bike plus details of when he left and in what direction, saying he was a bit tired and upset, but omitting the sordid details as to why. She'd barely slept a wink, and could hardly think straight. The police told her they would organise a search by the police department as well as the local SES group.

After the police had left Jo decided it was time to call her Mum. The tears burst forth as she tried to speak.

Liz had to ask her to repeat herself several times before she understood the terrible situation Jo was in. She tried to assure her daughter that he would be fine.

Kelly came over early to stay with Jo. It was Sunday so work wasn't an issue. David arrived a little after Kelly.

"Any word yet?" he asked.

"No," sobbed Jo. "Nothing! What do you think might have happened to him?"

"Wish I knew. It's just not like him to up and leave you."

Jo was horrified. "He hasn't LEFT me! He must have had an accident, he was tired and upset." She glared at David, not saying anything about him coming on to her, out of respect for Kelly.

David quickly looked away from Jo. He didn't want Kelly knowing either but badly wanted to fix the situation between him and Jo. "Well, if it's anything I've said or done, I'm really sorry, Jo. I haven't exactly been very nice to him since Pete came along. Is there anything I can do for you now?"

"Yes, go and help look for your brother!" She didn't need to have any more hassles.

"I can do that," replied David and left.

Around lunch time a police car arrived back at Jo's. She had left the gate open since the morning, to provide easier access for the authorities. Jo ran down the stairs to greet them, hopeful of good news but fearful of bad. As soon as she saw the looks on the two officer's faces she knew it was bad.

"We have found something, Mrs Summers."

Jo gasped, fighting back new tears. "What?"

"About twenty k's north of here a Harley Davidson was found in the grass among the sand dunes, not far from the road. It appears to have run off the road at high speed. Would you come and identify it?"

"Y-yes, I will...... but what about Luke? Did you find him?"

"There is no sign of the rider at the moment. We've got all available personnel combing the area, including a boat and air search."

"Boat? Air?" Jo frowned, shaking her head. "Why?"

"The bike is not very far from the water. It is possible that the rider could have been hurt and wandered on to the beach and ended up in the water."

"Ok.... I'll just see if Rose can watch Ben." She raced upstairs and told Luke's parents what was happening, asking them if they could look after Ben while she went with the police.

"Of course, Love," assured Ted, patting her on the shoulder. "Don't worry about us here." He put one arm around his worried wife while wiping a tear from his eye with his other hand.

Jo's shaky palms were sweating and her stomach churned as she travelled in the back seat of the police car. *WHY? WHY? WHY? WHY did this happen?* Silently she cursed both Pete and David for causing so much upset. *Don't be silly, it's not Luke. Oh, God, what if it is?* The thought was unbearable. More tears stung her eyes and she had to use her shirt to wipe them as she had forgotten tissues in her haste to get to the scene.

When the car pulled up, the sight before her made her gasp. Along with several police and SES vehicles an ambulance sat waiting. She jumped out of the police car and ran to the ambulance, expecting to see Luke in there, about to be taken to hospital. It was empty. She turned toward the ocean and saw several people standing about in the dunes, looking down at something shiny in the long, spindly grass.

Taking a deep breath she followed the police officers who had driven her, over to the roped off area. Her legs were weak and shaky, and it all seemed like a dream, a horrible nightmare. *I have to wake up soon.* She shook her head to try and clear it.

Instantly she recognised the bike. It was impossible not to with the unique air brush paintings on the fuel tank. Many sets of eyes were on her, waiting for a response.

Jo's bottom lip quivered as she dropped to her knees beside the bike. Placing her hand on the side of the tank, she felt like she had suddenly been kicked in the stomach. Her heart raced as she tried to open her mouth to speak. Somewhere in the distance she heard a scream, a long, painful scream. "Noooooooooooooooo." Then she realised it was coming from her own throat. She jumped up and ran blindly through the dunes to the water's edge calling Luke's name as she went. The tears, combined with the strong ocean breeze, stung her eyes. Once on the beach, she ran one way, then turned and ran back the other, scanning the frothy waves for any sign of her beloved husband. Finding nothing, she slumped to the sand, and cried hard, her weary body shuddering as she gasped for breath.

"I think we have our answer," said one police officer to another.

Just as a female officer reached Jo to try and comfort her, there was a shout about thirty metres away along the beach. "I found something!"

Several police and SES members rushed over. Jo looked up, as the words sunk in. The female officer helped her to her feet and she walked slowly over to see what was found.

Several people were crouching down on the sand. When she arrived two of them moved aside. Lying on the sand was a mobile phone. Jo instantly picked it up. It was wet and damaged, but she knew immediately it was Luke's. She just nodded, still unable to speak, then brought the phone up to her chest and clutched it to her saddening heart.

"Over here!" Everyone turned in the direction of that voice. A man walked over holding something in his open hand. "This caught my eye in the sand."

Jo looked in his outstretched hand and saw, to her absolute horror, the necklace she gave Luke for his birthday. There was no mistaking the one-of-a-kind surfboard pendent with the pictures and message from Jo engraved into it. Shakily, she reached over and took it out of the man's hand. The chain was gone, but the pendent was fine. Tears ran freely down her cheek as she remembered the excitement of getting it made for him and the wonderful day and night they shared for his birthday. Again she just nodded, totally oblivious to several other hardened officers and volunteers wiping tears from their own eyes.

Another volunteer came running over to the small crowd. "I just found this. I don't know if it means anything." She held up a piece of freshly torn material.

One of the police officers took it from her and held it up to Jo. "This looks like it could be a piece of torn shirt. Does it look familiar?"

Jo frowned and looked at it closely. "Yes," she finally whispered.

"Can you remember what coloured shirt your husband was wearing when he left?"

Concentrating hard, she shook her head. "But he does have a shirt with that colour pattern on it. I..... I can't really remember if he had it on that morning or not. He had his leather jacket on.... and jeans."

Next thing a flock of seagulls began to screech louder and fly erratically just out behind the breakers. The search chopper came over in the direction.

"Shit, look at the size of that!" exclaimed one searcher, causing everyone to look out to sea.

Jo gasped loudly as she saw what everyone was looking at. A huge white pointer was thrashing about, grabbing at the school of fish that the seagulls obviously wanted also.

"Please take me home," sobbed Jo.

"Yes, certainly," said the female officer, realising that Jo had just learned of Luke's probable fate.

Arriving back at her house, Jo could hardly find the energy to get out of the car. Rose and Ted appeared at the front door, looking worried but hopeful.

"Would you like me to tell them?" asked the officer.

Jo just nodded in return, feeling numb. She watched the police officer get out of the car and walk over to Rose and Ted. It was like it was happening in slow motion. Watching the policewoman's mouth move, she then saw Rose slump against Ted, her mouth open against his chest, crying her eyes and heart out. Ted's both arms encircled his wife and he openly wept as the officer walked back to the car.

Kelly came downstairs and out the door, took one look at Rose and Ted and burst into tears, trying to hug both of them.

"Come on Jo," urged the officer softly, holding her hand out.

Jo took hold of it and got out of the car before walking slowly over the other three.

"It's not confirmed yet. We shouldn't jump to conclusions until his body is found." She numbly walked up the stairs to check on Ben, who was still sleeping. The second she laid eyes on one of the many enlarged photos about the house with Luke in, she burst into tears. Finding her phone, she called her mother. She really needed Mum right now. Liz told Jo they would be on the next available flight and that she would also tell Meg.

The time passed in a blur for Jo. A police car drove into the yard in the late afternoon containing two of the officers who had come early that morning. Again, Jo ran down to greet them, hoping for some positive news. One got something out of the back seat and walked slowly over to Jo, standing just outside the front door.

"Do you recognise this, Mrs Summers?"

Jo's heart sank to new depths. It was a helmet, Luke's helmet. She knew it so well. "It's his."

The officer turned it over and Jo shuddered to see a jagged piece torn out of it just near the strap. She knew it had to have been torn by a shark. "Where did you find it?" she sobbed.

"The chopper spotted it about twenty k's north of where the bike was, floating with the current. The rescue boat went and retrieved it. I'm afraid that…."

"You think he's been eaten by a shark, don't you?" she stated loudly, shaking her head. "It doesn't prove a thing! He's still out there, somewhere." The tears flowed again. "I just know it! PLEASE......., Don't give up on him yet, please." She clutched one of the officer's hands in hers.

"We won't, but it will be dark soon, and they will have to call it off until first light again. It's been nearly two days now Jo....."

"I don't care, he's a strong swimmer, maybe he got washed ashore further up or down the coast." Jo knew she may have been grasping at straws but was not giving up yet.

"The boats and choppers have gone right up and down the coast, at least one hundred k's each way. If he was on the beach, they would have found him, I'm sure. We will come back tomorrow. Do you have anyone with you?"

"Yes," replied Jo, "Luke's parents are here and Kelly."

Jo dragged her weary body and heavy heart up the stairs to tell them about the helmet. The police took it to get it examined to determine what did tear it. Another long, lonely night lay ahead for Jo. She received a call from Meg and it lifted her spirits slightly to talk to her best friend.

The next morning, Jo received a phone call to say the search was resuming, but was gently told not to hold out much hope. In her head she knew they were right, but her heart wouldn't give up. Mid-morning saw her worried family arrive from Queensland. Luke's parents had rung earlier to see if there was any news and told Jo that Casey was on her way over from Adelaide.

Kelly had gone to work, but David came over to see Jo around lunch time. "How are you holding up, Jo?"

Jo took one look in his face and for a split second saw Luke. She burst into tears and slumped against his chest and closed her eyes. It felt like Luke's arms about her. She held him tighter, hoping that, when she opened her eyes, it would be him.

"I'm sorry Jo," he whispered when she'd let go of his embrace. Scanning David's sad face, he looked so much like Luke it almost scared her. It was almost as if Luke's spirit had jumped into David's body. *Don't be silly, Luke's spirit is soaring high, free as a bird.*

Late that afternoon, three days since Luke had left, the familiar police car drove into the yard. The same two officers got out, both looking very sombre. Rose and Ted, along with Casey, had arrived. Everyone was together when they broke the devastating news.

Forensic tests had concluded that not only had the helmet been ripped by a shark but also the piece of clothing, once part of Luke's shirt, also contained small traces of blood.

"I'm afraid that there is no point continuing the search now. The boats and choppers covered new areas today as well as going back over the closer areas. The SES scoured further along the coast line, but nothing else has been found. I'm so sorry."

Jo ran to the nearest toilet and threw up violently. Everyone shed fresh tears, amidst head shaking and hugging.

That night, Liz made toast and eggs for all, but no-one felt much like eating. After Jo bathed and fed Ben she carried him over to Ted. "Would you like to hold him?"

"I'd love to," choked Ted, taking Ben gently from Jo. He smiled at his grandson as a tear rolled freely down his cheek.

When Jo lay Ben in his cot a little time later, she gently stroked his face. "How am I going to tell you, Little One?" Everything suddenly overwhelmed her. She went into her room and collapsed on the bed, clutching Luke's pillow to her and cried hard. Feeling like she was losing her breath, she suddenly felt very light headed. Sucking in air as she sobbed, she was slowly able to regain her breathing. Taking an extra deep breath, Jo rolled over on to her back and stared at the ceiling. She could still smell the scent of Luke's aftershave on his pillow. Suddenly she felt him beside her and reached over, only to find emptiness.

A large wedding photo of them on the wall caught her eye. In it they were both smiling happily. Jo stared at Luke's handsome face and gasped when he winked back at her. "Luke," she called softly, getting up and walking over to touch his face on the photo. *This is crazy.* Sadly, she lay back down on the bed.

Sometime later, she went back out to her guests. Everyone had gone to their own homes except her family, who, of course, were staying. Kelly had given her some herbal sedatives to take, which Jo eagerly swallowed. Anything to get some sleep. She knew that, in her dreams, she would be with Luke. At least no-one or nothing could ever take that away from her.

The next morning she awoke with a smile. She and Luke had been surfing then made love on the beach at sunset. It was so beautiful, but as her eyes focused and the hard, real memories came flooding back she began to cry into her pillow. The tears from her eyes felt painful enough, but it was nothing compared to the ones falling from her heart. They were like shards of glass, stabbing and shredding every devastated part of her exhausted body and sad, lonely soul. She didn't hear the soft knock on her bedroom door or the door open.

"Jo, Honey, I've brought you a cuppa and some toast," her mother said as she entered the room.

"I'm not hungry, Mum, thanks," replied Jo, wiping her eyes with a tissue.

"Love, you have to eat," stated her father following closely behind Liz. "How are you going to be able to feed Ben if you don't eat?"

Jo sat up suddenly. "Ben!"

"He's okay, we gave him some baby cereal and a little juice. He's as happy as Larry out there with Jon and Chris," assured Liz.

"Yeah, and I even changed him!" nodded Tom proudly.

Jo smiled at the thought of her Dad changing a nappy and reluctantly sat up so Liz could place the tray on her lap. Realising that she couldn't remember the last time she ate, the toast disappeared quickly, at least easing the need in her stomach.

Once she'd eaten and drank her tea, she managed a shower. She kept telling herself that there was a lot to do today. People to ring, things to organise. *Oh God, please give me the strength to get through this.* Discovering she had hardly any milk she made Ben up a bottle of formula which he didn't mind.

Liz took him outside for a walk in the pram while Jo made some calls. First on the list was Debbie and Pete.

"Hi Deb......it's me, Jo."

"Hi Mate, how's things? If you are ringing about that slack brother of mine. He hasn't left the house since he came back the other morning after the party. He doesn't seem too happy about something. Has Luke said anything? Maybe...."

"Deb," Jo cut in, "Luke's been....... Luke's dead!" She burst into tears again. Just whenever she thought she had no more left to cry, another lot would flow.

Silence for a few moments, then, "What?"

Jo took a deep breath and told her everything she knew, from when he left on the Saturday morning up until late the previous day when it had officially been confirmed that he was lost at sea.

"Ohh, Mate, can I do anything for you? I am so sorry," sobbed Deb, in shock.

"Can you tell Pete. I know he'll be devastated. And..... Deb..... just be my friend."

"You can count on that."

Jo felt so grateful. "Thanks Deb," she said quietly. "I will let you know when the memorial service will be."

When Jo finished the conversation with Deb, she jumped as her phone rang. Checking the number, her heart sank again.

"H-hello Steve."

"Jo, I just heard on the radio that Luke was killed! What the hell is going on?"

"I think you and the boys had better come over."

"We'll be right there."

Jo heard voices outside and looked out to see Casey and her parents had returned. She was glad. It comforted her to have Luke's family around at this time. Everyone came upstairs and greeted each other, but there were not many words to say. Casey asked Jo if there was any more news on Luke. Her hopeful look quickly faded when Jo sadly shook her head. Rose busied herself with some housework and it wasn't long before Jo heard the washing machine going. Ted asked Jo if she wanted to organise a memorial service. She wanted one, but didn't feel strong enough to do it herself so left it to Ted, adding that Steve would probably be happy to help.

After cups of coffee and tea had been drank, Jo carried Ben out on to the back veranda. She noticed Rose down near the clothes line, pegging out the washing. Watching sadly, she saw Rose pick up one of Luke's shirts and hold it to her cheek for a moment before pegging it on the line. The sight made her hug her son tighter, not understanding the pain of losing a child, and hoping she never would.

Steve and the rest of the band members turned up and Jo went down to greet them.

She sat with them at one of the poolside tables to tell them all terrible news. The strain and emotional pain were beginning to take its toll. Jo felt exhausted, and asked them upstairs to talk with Ted about a memorial service. Just as they were sitting down at the table to begin discussing plans, David walked in.

"What's going on?" he frowned.

"We're about to discuss a memorial service for Luke, sit down," said his Father, beckoning him to another empty chair.

"I'm not that good at that sort of thing. Whatever you want to do is ok with me. As long as Jo is happy with it." He looked at her sadly.

Again, Jo jumped when her phone rang. She frowned as she looked at the screen, not recognising the number. In her heart she hoped it was someone saying they'd found Luke, alive.

All eyes were on her as she spoke briefly, mainly giving one word answers, but always frowning. Finally she hung up.

She looked about at all the questioning faces. "That was the police. They've examined the bike and......" she drew a deep breath, "there were no skid marks at all. It seems that the brakes failed. There was no brake fluid in it at all and none on the sand where it crashed." She shook her head, bewildered how Luke could overlook such an important thing when he was working on it. Then she remembered how upset he was that morning and how quickly he put the parts back together.

Everyone was shocked and shook their heads as to how and why, but the plans for the memorial service continued. Agreements and phone calls were made and it was to be in a huge church at Scarborough Beach in two days time. Steve asked Jo to write an obituary and he would organise for it to be put in the newspaper. A dozen crumpled sheets of paper and just as many damp tissues later, she was satisfied with the result.

Early the next morning, a sound of a motor bike awoke Jo. She jumped out of bed and ran out on to the front veranda, expecting to see Luke ride in. But, no, it was someone else passing, along the road. Her aching heart sank yet again. Each phone call or every time she heard the gate buzzer she expected it to be Luke.

Later that afternoon a taxi pulled up at the front gate. Liz had gone out to open it. Jo went out, expecting to see Pete, not having heard from him since the party. She was surprised when Meg got out, carrying a small suit case with her. New tears flowed as she hugged her best friend. Once she'd got Meg settled in, the phone rang. It was Debbie wanting to know when the service was to be held. She also told Jo that Pete had taken the news very badly and she hadn't seen him since. Jo was worried about Pete, and asked Deb to tell him to please come to the service, if she sees or hears from him.

Jo had another restless night and so did Ben. She assumed he could sense something was wrong and was, by now, missing his Daddy. Meg slept on a mattress in Jo's room, which was a comfort to her.

The following day was the hardest. Jo didn't know what to wear and she cried more often than she did the day before. Finally she settled on a plain black dress and black shoes. After dressing Ben in a dark blue and white suit, she put little shoes and socks on him. Her Mum walked into her bedroom as she was about to come out.

"How are you holding up, Sweetie?"

Suddenly Jo felt a strange sensation wash over her and she sat back down on her bed. "Mum, I am sure I heard Luke calling me last night. It was like he's somewhere not too far away and hurt. He was asking me to help him."

Liz saw the look of desperate yearning in her daughter's eyes. "It would have just been a dream, Love. They can seem so real at times." She hugged both Jo and Ben close to her heart. "Are you ready to go?"

"Ready as I ever will be," she sighed sadly. She had wished she didn't have to take Ben, but there was no-one who could look after him, and on the other hand, she felt comforted having him with her, as he was part of Luke.

Lots of people were already gathering outside the church when they arrived. Jo, Ben and Meg went in her car, driven by her brother Chris. Jon and their parents drove in Luke's car.

Jo was shocked when several photographers took her photo as she carried Ben into the church. She tried to cover his face with her hand as Chris told the photographers where to go!

Walking in a daze up to the front seat of the church, it just seemed like a dream to Jo, another nightmare. She had Luke's parents, David, Kelly and Casey one side of her, while her parents sat on the other. "Stonefish" and crew sat at the front on the other side of the aisle, while Meg, Chris, Jon and Debbie sat on the pew behind Jo. Debbie told Jo she still hadn't seen or heard from Pete so had no idea if he was coming or not. She assured Jo he would if he could, if only for Jo's sake.

Knowing that Luke would never want morbid music played at his funeral, she'd arranged with Steve to have some of his favourite music playing in the background, starting with an Eagles CD.

She stared at the small table up at the front of the church, only metres from where she sat. On it was a large, framed photo of Luke, surrounded by flowers, including bouquets of wildflowers. Steve had arranged for a guitar shaped wreath, which sat beside the photo. *What the hell are we all doing here? Luke's not dead!* She felt the panic rising and began to stand up, wanting to run out the church. Liz grabbed Jo's arm and comforted her until her breathing slowed down a little and she was able to sit back down.

Slowly the church filled to capacity with lots of fans having to stand outside the front and side doors. Jo looked back behind her and was overwhelmed to realise that so many people thought so highly of Luke. Many people were openly crying and she even saw Molly Meldrum sitting a few rows back from her.

The minister walked slowly to the podium. He welcomed every-one, spoke briefly about why they were there and about life and death. When he had finished Steve stepped up to the podium and unfolded a piece of paper.

He fought back tears as he spoke about when he and Luke had started the band and the funny situations they had found themselves in at times. He also talked about their hard work to make it as far as they had and how Luke was largely responsible for that, through his sheer dedication and eagerness to try new things. Wiping the tears from his eyes, he mentioned Luke's devotion and love for his wife, Jo and baby son, Ben. He finished off by saying what a good mate he was and how he would be greatly missed by many people.

Jo's body trembled as she sobbed, listening to Steve speak.

Next, David got up and spoke fondly of Luke from their childhood. He talked about their little squabbles but added that they always made up and were mates as well as brothers. Wiping the tears from his eyes, he apologised that he couldn't say anymore and quickly sat down.

Just as the minister was about to invite anyone else who wished, to come up and speak, Jo stood up and walked toward the podium. She hadn't planned to speak, thinking that she wouldn't be able to, but suddenly had the urge, even though she had no idea what she was going to say.

She wiped her eyes, cleared her throat and began to speak. "I've only known Luke just over a year, but that year has been filled with more love, laughter and excitement than I've known in my entire lifetime. He was so gentle....... Sweet and caring." Again, she wiped the tears that were falling freely from her eyes, like they had a mind of their own. "He was always thinking up new ways to surprise me and when I'd try to get it out of him, he'd just wink..... and smile and say, 'You'll see'." Jo stopped and bowed her head for a moment, placing her hand over her eyes. "B-But I always knew I was in for a special treat. He was my best friend, my soul mate and I'm going to miss him more than words can describe."

She wanted to continue but couldn't. Turning to go back to her seat she stopped at the table containing the photo and flowers. Slowly she raised her hand to his face in the picture while looking deeply into his brown eyes. As she opened her mouth to speak, she collapsed into a heap on the floor. The crowd gasped and everyone in the front pews rushed forward to help her. Initially, she seemed unconscious, but soon opened her eyes. Her father and David helped her up and back to her seat.

After checking that Jo was okay, the minister asked if anyone else would like to speak. Casey spoke briefly of her beloved brother but had to cut it short. Col, the band's manager also spoke fondly of Luke and the privilege he felt at having known him. A "Stonefish" ballad played while a slide show of pictures played on the big screen, beginning with Luke as a small child, and ending with him holding his own baby. The minister then concluded the service.

Jo couldn't wait to get out of there and to the car. As she was heading out the side door, Debbie caught up with her. Giving Jo a hug, she apologised for Pete not showing up. Jo told her it was okay, thinking to herself that, giving Pete's condition, a funeral may have been too unbearable. Quite a few strangers came up to her and offered their sympathy. Eventually, they could all get in the cars and head home. A wake had been arranged at the house for friends and family.

After changing out of her funeral attire, Jo asked her Mum and also Rose if they would watch Ben as she had somewhere she needed to be.

"Are you going to be okay, Love?" asked Liz, realising that Jo was intending to drive.

"Yeah Mum, I'm fine." Jo grabbed her bag, keys and some flowers before heading to her car and driving out the gate where she then turned north. Listening to a Stonefish CD as she drove, she arrived at her destination in next to no time. Pulling up on the side of the road, she walked toward the rumbling ocean, carrying the flowers. It was a cloudy windy day and the ocean seemed angry. Sitting down on the highest sand dune, metres from where Luke's bike was found, she took a deep breath and looked out beyond the breakers.

"Luke, please watch over Ben and me. Help me to bring him up to be as wonderful, talented and caring as you are." She wiped away the tears. "I'll tell him all about his Daddy and play him all the Stonefish Cd's. I'll even teach him to surf, BUT..... I won't let him have a ...... motorbike. I know you loved your bike...... and I loved being on it with you, but...... I can't bare to lose him too. I'll show him all the DVD's we made and get a special one made of you just for him." The choppy waves crashing on the shore seemed to want to drown out her voice, to stop her from continuing. She wondered if they were trying to tell her to go away as they have Luke now! *That's crazy,* she thought to herself. Could she hear him calling her again? No, just a bird calling out as the noisy wind blew.

She got up and walked over to the beach. Throwing the bunch of flowers into the choppy waves, a fresh lot of tears flowed. "Goodbye, my Love..... I'll see you in Heaven. Wait for me at the gate."

She turned and trudged wearily back to her car. The drive home seemed to take ages as the finality of it all began to sink in. Her beloved husband was dead! Never coming back! What on earth will she do now? Fear and panic set in as she drove into her yard.

Luckily her mum came right over when she pulled up. Jo got out and fell into her Mother's comforting arms. "What am I going to do without him, Mum?" Her body shuddered as she cried long and hard.

Most of the guests didn't stay too long for the wake, realising it was too hard on Jo. Once everyone had left, Jo and Meg went to the bar in the entertainment room. Jo had put Ben to bed after a bottle as her milk was drying up.

"I need a drink, Meg! Like I've never needed one before."

Meg found the bottle of bourbon and some dry then poured them each one.

"This was Luke's favourite drink, you know," said Jo sadly.

"I know, you told me once," smiled Meg. "Here's to Luke." Meg raised her glass to Jo's before they took a mouthful.

Jo asked Meg about mutual friends back in Queensland and also if anything else had ever come up about Jeff's death. Meg informed her that lots of people were shocked and upset at Luke's death and, no, she had heard nothing more about Jeff.

"I wonder if his family will think that I deserved to lose Luke," mused Jo, sadly, as she poured herself another drink. "Maybe I did."

Meg noticed it was much stronger than the previous drink and she had not even finished hers yet. "Don't be silly, Jo. Of course you didn't!"

"I suppose Luke and I had more love and happiness in our short time together than a lot of people have in their whole lifetime. So, I'll be forever grateful for that. At least no-one can ever take our precious memories away from me."

"That's true," agreed Meg. "He will always be looking over you and Ben."

"You know, the two men I've loved the most have both died. I wonder if I'm jinxed or something."

"Now, you're really being silly, Jo."

"If the next man who loves me dies, then I'll know it's true. Hell, what am I saying! I can't imagine there being someone else. I don't ever want anyone else. I just want Luke back!" She rested her head atop her hands on the edge of the bar and cried. Her body shaking with grief. Meg walked around Jo's side of the bar to comfort her.

Just then her parents walked in the room. Liz encircled Jo in her arms and Tom hugged them both.

"Honey, we might call it a night, will you be all right?" asked Liz, desperately wanting to help her daughter overcome her grief and loss, but realising that only time could do that.

"Yeah Mum, Meg's here." Jo kissed her parents good night and watched them walk out the door. "They are just the best parents...." smiled Jo, as she poured herself another drink.

The next morning Jo didn't feel so well, but at least she'd had the best sleep since Luke had died. Everyone was drained so the day was spent lazing around the pool. That night, after tea Liz asked Jo if she would like any help to pack up any of Luke's clothes and things.

Jo was horrified. "No way, Mum!" she cried. "I'm not touching any of his stuff yet."

"I'm sorry, Honey, I just thought it may have been easier on you if you didn't have to do it yourself." She wished she hadn't brought the subject up.

"It's ok, Mum," Jo softened. "I'm no-where ready for that yet, and when I do, I'd would rather do it myself. But, thanks for offering."

The following day Meg, Jon and Chris flew back east. Liz stayed with Ben while Tom and Jo took them to the airport. It was a heartwrenching farewell and it was then that Jo decided to go back to Queensland with her parents for a while.

Liz was thrilled when Jo informed her of her decision once they got back from the airport.

"I don't know how long I'll stay, Mum, but I do know that I need to get out of this house for a while." Luckily, she was able to book tickets for the same flight, the next day.

Jo realised how much Rose and Ted would miss her and especially Ben so she spent the afternoon at their place so they could see more of him. Casey was still there as well. Naturally they were sad, but understood Jo's need to get away, and were happy when she assured them she would return.

After coming back home, she went over to tell David and Kelly of her decision and to ask them to keep an eye on things at her house. Kelly wasn't home from work yet.

"Come in," smiled David, beckoning her inside. "How are you holding up?"

Jo just shrugged and forced a smile, but the tears welled in her eyes.

"Come here," said David, taking her into his arms and holding her tightly. "Oh Jo," he whispered, stroking her tear stained cheek, after she'd let go of his embrace. "I just wish I could make you feel better."

"You do," assured Jo, amazed at how much more like Luke he seemed to be becoming.

"Would you like a drink or something?" David asked, still holding her gently by the shoulders.

"Yes, cold water would be nice."

He handed it to her just as Kelly walked in the door. She gave Jo a hug before putting her bag down and taking her shoes off.

Jo told them of her plans to go back to the Sunshine Coast for a while and gave them a key for her place. Kelly told her she would miss her lots but understood. Jo noticed David frown when she told him as if he hadn't expected it. Kelly excused herself to go to the toilet.

"Jo, are you sure that's a good idea? You may never come back!" David said.

Jo couldn't help noticing that he seemed almost panicked about it. "It's okay, Dave, I will be back, just don't know when."

"But I would've, I mean WE would have looked after you and Ben. It just won't be the same without you here."

"What won't be?" queried Jo, sensing he was holding something back.

"Everything!"

Jo frowned as he walked out of the room. She couldn't understand why he seemed so concerned, almost agitated about her decision.

Kelly walked back in and the two friends embraced a sad goodbye. David never came back to say goodbye to Jo.

As she walked back to her house she felt so empty and alone. She just didn't know where she belonged any more. It was impossible to tell yet, if she could continue living here without Luke, but she knew she couldn't take Ben away from his family. All she did know right then was that she had to go home with her family to sort herself out.

The next morning they called a taxi with a baby seat, to take them to the airport. It was pretty cramped with the three adults, Ben and the luggage. She'd also called Debbie to let her know she was going and to give her some contact numbers.

As they drove away from the house, Jo looked back at it and cried softly. She had so many beautiful memories of her time there with Luke. "STOP!" She suddenly called out. The car came to an abrupt halt.

"What's wrong, Jo, did you forget something?" asked Tom.

"It's Luke! I feel like I'm leaving him behind."

"Jo, Sweetie, he will be with you where-ever you are, ALL the time," reassured Liz, taking hold of her hand.

"I know," Jo sobbed. "Keep driving."

So many thoughts swirled in her head. She didn't even know if she was doing the right thing. Then she remembered David's reaction the previous night. That really puzzled her. What exactly did he mean, *everything?* Luke's words came back to her as well. He was going to tell her something about David the day he disappeared, but he never had the chance. She wondered what it was. Perhaps she would never know.

CHAPTER NINETEEN

A week later, Pete decided to go to Kalbarri to see Mo. He really missed her lately and it had been over a year since they had seen each other. A couple of times she had planned to come down to Perth, but each time something came up, like car trouble or no money, so she never made it, which disappointed him.

Mo had got herself a job in a café which she enjoyed more than the one in Sydney. Not being able to afford a house to rent and with limited room at her cousin's house she chose to live in the local caravan park. It was a small caravan, but comfortable and she had told Pete in her letters that he was welcome to come visit anytime. Mo missed him too although she had made several friends, there was no-one quite like Pete. She knew she could really be herself around him.

When Debbie finally saw him she was cranky that he did not go to Luke's memorial, but Pete assured her he WAS there, standing outside one of the doors. He just couldn't go inside and face Jo, it just hurt too much. He felt bad then, when Debbie had told him that Jo had gone back to Queensland. He wished he could have seen her, so instead, wrote her a letter which Debbie was happy to post for him.

After Debbie had dropped her girls off at school one morning, she drove Pete to the outskirts of Perth so he could hitch a ride north. Pete thanked her and kissed her goodbye. She waved to him standing with his solitary bag on the lonely road, as she turned the car around and drove off, back toward Perth.

Pete drew a deep sigh, turned around and began walking, pondering his life with every step. He felt so lost and lonely. His best mate was dead. He knew he would be soon as well, at least, now he felt a little less frightened by the prospect, believing that he would see Luke again. He felt bad that he still hadn't told Debbie about his condition, but he was careful at her place and he just didn't see the point in worrying her anymore. She would probably tell his Mum and then SHE would tell his father...... THAT was the last thing he wanted!

After about twenty vehicles had whizzed past without so much as slowing down, Pete was thrilled to see a semi pull over in front of him. He ran toward it.

"Where are you headin', Mate?" asked the large, bearded driver. Unfortunately, he reminded Pete of the man who'd licked him in pool in New South Wales while they were on their way to Perth.

"KALBARRI!" shouted Pete, above the rumble of the idling engine.

"You're in luck, so am I. Jump in!"

Pete couldn't believe something finally was going his way. The bloke seemed all right and he could take Pete all the way. He scrambled up into the high cabin and threw his bag at his feet. The truck roared and moved off.

"What's ya name?" asked the driver.

"Pete!"

"How 'bout that, so's mine! Big Pete! How do you do, Little Pete?" He extended his left hand to Pete.

Pete shook the large, outstretched hand. "Pretty good….. Pete!" They both laughed.

Driving on, they laughed and chatted along the way about anything and everything. After stopping for a quick lunch at Dongara, they arrived in KALBARRI later in the afternoon. Big Pete dropped Little Pete off at the caravan pack, bade him farewell and good luck before continuing on to the local shopping centre to unload. Pete waved to him and then walked to the park office to ask for directions to Mo's van. He hoped and prayed she'd be there as he hadn't told her he was coming.

The lady in the office eyed him suspiciously before giving him directions to Mo's van. "Are you booking in?"

"Dunno yet. I'll let you know later." He turned and walked off in the direction she'd shown him.

He saw the bright pink holden before he found her van and the familiar sight of it made him smile. After knocking on the caravan door several times, he was dismayed when there was no answer. Suddenly he heard a shrill scream behind him.

"PETE!" Mo yelled, running up behind him and giving him a hug that nearly winded him. "How the hell are ya? I didn't know you were comin' up."

"Hey Mo," he laughed, hugging her back. "Yeah, I just decided to come. Hope you don't mind."

"Of course not, Dude. Come in!"

He followed her inside the van. It had a double bed up one end and a table that could be converted to a bed at the other. It was small, but looked bigger on the inside than out. For some reason, it surprised him that it was tidy.

"Let's go and get some beer," Mo suggested. "This calls for a celebration."

"Good idea," agreed Pete. He didn't feel like he had anything to celebrate but he sure could go a beer. Although he got on well with Mo, he wasn't sure yet if he would tell her about his medical situation. He realised that she had the right to know, especially if he was planning to stay a while.

They drove to the pub and got a carton of stubbies. Mo only had a small fridge in the van, but she knew they would drink lots of them before they got warm.

"So, are ya stayin' a while?" Mo asked, on the way back.

"If you'll let me," grinned a hopeful Pete.

"Of course I will," shrieked Mo, "But you'd better go up to the office and pay. They're pretty snoopy around here and I don't wanna get kicked out."

When they pulled up at the van, Pete went straight up to the office and paid for a week. That was all the money he had on him and he didn't have much more in the bank.

"So, whatcha been up to?" Mo asked when they'd sat down at the table and cracked their first beers.

Pete told her about the part time gardening job he'd had and talked about Debbie and her girls with love. He could see the disgust in Mo's eyes when he told her about the day he went to his parent's house.

Although he had briefly mentioned these things in his phonecalls, he hadn't gone into much detail.

He talked about the ride up to Kalbarri with Big Pete and then asked her what she'd been doing for the past year. She showed him photos from her cousin's wedding and told how one of the guests had offered her a job in his café. She was happy to take it but didn't expect to still be there twelve months later. She told him a bit about Kalbarri and about the cliffs just out of town.

Pete was eager to see them. He felt there was something majestic and powerful about cliffs, especially when they overlook the ocean.

"Who's is that?" laughed Pete, pointing to an old push bike standing just outside the door of the van, under the awning.

"Mine!" snapped Mo indignantly. "What's wrong with it?"

"Nothin'," replied Pete, wondering why she was getting so defensive. "It's great!"

"Well, it's a hell of a lot cheaper than driving the holden, especially when you don't have to go far."

Pete nodded in agreement while opening two more beers.

"So, have you got your license yet, ya woose?" laughed Mo.

Pete just looked at her, grinned and shook his head before taking a swig of his stubby.

After several beers each, Mo took a cold chook, some bread and salad out the fridge and made them both a sandwich. She noticed that Pete went unusually quiet while he was eating. Right from when he arrived she sensed that there was something else troubling him. Now was as good a time as any to enquire.

"Pete, you look pretty unhappy. I can see it in your face. You know that you and me can talk about anything, right?"

Pete looked at her as the tears welled in his eyes. After opening another beer and lighting a cigarette, he began telling her all about Luke, starting from when they were kids. He didn't leave out a single detail, feeling the need to let it all come out. He appreciated that Mo didn't even frown when he mentioned the times he'd come on to Luke and despite that, how they'd remained friends. Pete talked about Jo and how highly he thought of her, and also mentioned little Ben. Wiping the tears from his eyes, he then spoke about the birthday party Luke had put on for him.

Finally, he talked about Luke's death, the memorial service and how he just couldn't bring himself to enter the church. He confessed to Mo that he just didn't feel like living anymore. What was the point? He had no money or job, his father hated him and forbade his mother to see him. His best friend was dead and Jo had gone back to Queensland. Whether she returned or not was anybody's guess.

Mo cried as Pete poured his heart out to her. She'd never seen this side of him and guessed that he'd never seen her cry either. Right then she wished that she had have met Luke and Jo. She had heard of Luke, of course, because of the band, but she was surprised that Pete was such good friends with him, since he had never mentioned him on their trip over. Pete cried too and Mo offered him a hug of comfort, which he politely refused.

"Well, you've still got me.... And Debbie," smiled Mo, taking hold of his hand. "And don't you ever forget it."

The next day, Pete wandered around Kalbarri while Mo worked. Eventually, he sat under a tree by the river, laid down and dozed off. He wasn't feeling the best, and wondered if it was the beer or his condition. While he was asleep, he dreamt that he was telling Mo he had AIDS and she was so shocked and disgusted that she kicked him out of her van, telling him to never come near her again. He awoke with a headache and stressed about telling Mo. It was a hot day, so he took his jeans and shirt off and dived into the cool river. At least that made him feel a little better physically.

Just as he was getting dressed, Mo rode toward him on her pushie.

"Finished work?" asked Pete, when she stopped beside him.

"Yeah. Here, eat this." She handed him a ham and salad roll wrapped in plastic.

Pete shook his head. "Thanks, but I'm not hungry."

Mo shrugged. "Oh well, I'll just take it home and put it in the fridge for Ron."

"Who's Ron?" Pete frowned, thinking she must have a boyfriend or a dog maybe.

"You know, Later Ron," laughed Mo.

Pete shook his head and laughed as they headed back toward the caravan park.

Late in the afternoon, Mo took him for a drive up to the ochre cliffs that overlook the ocean.

"Wow, this is great!" enthused Pete as he got out of the car. The cliffs were quite jagged and Pete walked to the edge to watch the waves crashing on the rocks far below. He suddenly decided he would tell Mo here and now that he had AIDS. If she freaked out he would just throw himself over the edge. He had to get it out of his system. "Mo, I have to talk to you about something serious. Let's sit over here." They walked over to a grassy patch he'd pointed to and sat down.

"What's wrong, Pete? I thought you told me everything last night."

Pete lit a cigarette and stared at the setting sun for a moment before he spoke. This reminded him of when he broke the news to Luke, but he was much more concerned about Mo's reaction than what Luke's would be. He took a deep breath. "Mo, I'm gunna tell you something pretty bad, but I'm worried how you'll react. You might not wanna know me after I tell ya." He dragged deeply on the smoke, avoiding looking directly at her.

"Pete, I know you're no angel and I'm pretty broad minded. I don't think there's anything you could say that would shock me that much."

Pete raised his eyebrows and hoped she was right.

"Well, what is it?" urged Mo.

"I found out a few weeks ago that I've got ..... AIDS," he said quietly, wiping a tear from his eye.

Mo's mouth dropped open but no sound came out. She was shocked into speechlessness...... for once.

After a while, Pete looked at her and noticed her stunned expression. *This is it. She'll treat me like a leper now.* He looked over toward the cliff, his heart pounding.

"That's heavy, Man," said Mo eventually. "Are you sure? Maybe they made a mistake. Doctor's do sometimes you know." She fought back tears.

Pete shook his head sadly. "There's no mistake. I'm gunna die, Mo." He began to cry silently.

Mo put her hand out and was about to touch his shoulder when she suddenly pulled it back, unsure what to do.

Pete saw her pull her hand back, put his head in his hands and cried even harder.

"Ah, shit, I'm sorry." She leaned over to Pete and put both her arms around him. He rested his head on her shoulder and they cried together for several minutes. "So is this the real reason you were talking about suicide last night?" She wiped her eyes and let him go.

"Mainly," nodded Pete. "I just hate the thought of getting really sick and suffering toward the end. I'd rather go with a little bit of pride left, not that I deserve to have any at all."

"Bullshit! Don't you ever let me hear you talk like that again. You're not a bad person, Pete, you've just had some bad breaks. "

"So, what are you gunna do, Mo?" Pete asked anxiously.

"What do ya mean?" she frowned. "Do about what?"

"Me! You won't want me stayin' with you now."

"Of course you can still stay. Do ya think I would just turf you out? Hell Pete, I wouldn't do that to a mate. You'll have to be really careful, that's all. Especially if ya cut yourself..... and sex is definitely out of the question!" she added in pretend seriousness. She noticed that that brought a smile to his face. "That's better," said Mo, standing up. "Now, let's go and have a swim before it gets dark."

"I can't believe you took it so well," said Pete, shaking his head as he got to his feet. "I thought you'd really freak."

"Mate, you're not the first person to tell me they have AIDS," Mo said as they walked back to her car. "One of my best mates died from it a few years ago in Sydney and I know of a few others with HIV too. Don't worry, I know a lot about it."

The days dragged by for Pete. He developed a nagging cold that he just couldn't shake and had hardly any appetite. Depression had set in, and as much as he knew Mo was trying everything she could to cheer him up, nothing worked.

She'd borrowed some fishing lines from her cousin and encouraged Pete to use them while she was at work. He did so, but the time alone just made him think more about his illness and how much he missed Luke.

After giving it a lot of thought and feeling that there was no alternative he decided that the only thing to do was to join him, but he wouldn't tell Mo beforehand. He knew that she would only try to stop him and his mind was made up now. Mo had been great to him, even paying his way when his money ran out, but he couldn't bludge off her forever. He decided to write her a note to help her understand his decision.

It was raining the following day so Mo drove to work. Pete fought back the tears as he waved her off. *God, I hope you understand Mo.* As soon as she was out of sight he found a pen and paper and sat down at the table to write.

DEAR MO, I'M GOING AWAY TO EASE MY PAIN. PLEASE UNDERSTAND AND DON'T BE SAD OR PISSED OFF WITH ME. I'VE GIVEN IT LOTS OF THOUGHT AND IT'S WHAT I WANT. I'LL BE FREE OF PAIN, MONEY HASSLES, LONELINESS AND HOPEFULLY, I'LL BE IN THE SAME PLACE AS LUKE. YOU'VE BEEN GREAT AND I LOVE YOU HEAPS. CAN YOU PLEASE TELL DEBBIE AND TELL HER I LOVE HER, AND MUM TOO. IT'S A RELIEF ACTUALLY. SEE YA ON THE OTHER SIDE, PETE.

He left the note on the table and walked outside to Mo's push bike. The tears blurred his vision as he got on and began peddling out of the caravan park. He knew he was doing the right thing. The only thing!

When he arrived at the cliff top, he stood the bike up on its stand, walked over to the edge and looked out over the grey ocean. The rain had eased to a light mist. That, combined with low cloud, made the day dreary and sad enough to match Pete's mood and intentions. Were the clouds weeping for him too, he wondered. *Don't be an idiot, as if they'd care!* Staring down at the waves crashing angrily far below him, he began to think about Luke. Suddenly, memories of the party came back to haunt him. They were flashbacks that only lasted a nano second each, but they disturbed him greatly. It bothered him that they were confusing him so much. *What the hell do they mean?* The constant, thunderous crashing of the waves took his attention. They seemed to be calling to him.

Mo had worked a later shift that day and it was after dark when she returned home to her van. She thought it was odd to see no light on as she pulled up not far from the door. *Pete must be asleep,* she shrugged to herself. As she walked to the door she noticed the bike was gone. Now she was really puzzled. She knew he wouldn't be at the pub as he had no money.

"PETE!" she called out as she stepped inside the van and put a light on. No sign of him. She was about to drop her bag on the table when she saw the note.

"No!" she gasped in horror as she read it through. "You bloody idiot!" Slumping into the seat beside the table, she expelled a huge sigh and shook her head. The tears stung her eyes as she reread the note. Even though he had talked about suicide, she didn't really believe he would have gone through with it.

She didn't know what to do. Where had he gone? Then it suddenly dawned on her - the cliffs. Of course! She ran to her car and drove as quickly as she could the several kilometres up to the lookout area.

Crying and cursing him, she hoped that she would get to him in time, but then realised that there are lots of cliffs around Kalbarri. He could have gone to any of them.

As she approached the lookout she'd first brought him to, she saw her bike standing alone in the glare of her headlights. Skidding to a stop beside it, she jumped out of the car. "PETE!" she called frantically, running over toward the cliff top. There was no response, only the sound of the waves crashing far below. Mo raced back to her car, grabbed her torch that she always carried, ran back to the edge and tried to shine it down to the bottom. *Damn!* The batteries were too far gone to even see half way down properly. She called to him as loudly as she could several more times, then slumped to the ground and cried.

Eventually, she looked up and out at the dark sea. The car lights were still on and the beams were reaching the water several hundred metres out. She watched the shimmering surface, hoping in vain to see him bobbing about.

With a sigh of defeat, she realised there was nothing more she could do there, so she decided to go home and return the following morning. With a bit of a frustrated struggle, she loaded the bike into the back of the station wagon, cursing Pete as she did so, and drove home.

Sadly, she read the note over and over, hoping that he had found some peace. Knowing that sleep would not come easy, she decided to call Debbie and tell her the grim news.

"Hello Deb, it's Mo."

"Oh, g'day Mo. How are you? How's Pete?"

"Um..... things are not so good, Deb." *Shit! How am I going to tell her that her only brother has just killed himself.* "It's about Pete."

"What about him?"

"He's been pretty depressed lately. I've been tryin' to cheer him up as much as I can," said Mo, fighting back the tears.

Debbie laughed. "Well, if you can't nobody can!"

"I couldn't and he.... Has just.... While I was at work he....." She burst into tears.

"Mo, do you mean he..... took his own life?" asked Debbie in disbelief.

"Yes Deb," sobbed Mo. "He left a note and rode my pushie up to the top of some cliffs and jumped off. He said to tell you and your Mum that he loves you both and that you've gotta understand."

"Understand! How the hell am I supposed to understand?" cried Debbie. "I know he misses Luke a lot, but he really was starting to straighten his life out and things were going well for him. He had that job and a home here. He did start going off the rails again a few weeks before Luke died but I thought he'd snap out of it but once Luke died, it was like part of Pete did too."

"Deb, he just didn't want to live anymore. Not just because of Luke..... but also because he had...... he was very sick Deb. He didn't have much longer anyway. I'm so sorry." Mo cried some more.

"What on earth do you mean Mo? What was wrong with him? I know he didn't look that great lately, but he's always been pale and skinny."

Mo was reluctant to tell her, but knew she had to. "He had AIDS Deb. He didn't want anyone else to know. He didn't want to worry you and he said that he had been really careful at your place. Luke was the only person he told before he told me."

Debbie was silent for a little while. "H-how long had he known for?"

"He found out not long before his thirtieth birthday. I remember on the trip over he said that he wanted to reach thirty."

"Well, I guess that does explain a few things," sighed Debbie. "Like why he disappeared that time and why he wouldn't go inside at Luke's service. The little bugger! He could have told me. He must have been so scared." She began to cry.

"Can you please tell your Mum, but not the part about having AIDS. Can you also tell Jo Summers too. I think Pete would want her to know. I'll go back up there in the morning for a look, maybe he's just hurt somewhere."

"Okay, thanks Mo. I've lost Jo's number but I'll call Luke's brother, David, and ask him for it. They would be in touch with her."

"I'll stay in touch," promised Mo. "Bye Deb."

Mo turned her phone off and put it on the table, dropped her head into her hands and cried long and hard. When she felt there were no more tears to cry she trudged wearily to the shower block, hoping a long hot shower might help her to sleep.

No such luck. She had a restless and sleepless night, finally dozing off just before dawn. Luckily she didn't have to work the next day.

At around eleven AM the next morning she was awakened by a loud knocking on her door.

"All right, all right, I'm comin'!" she shouted crankily.

It was her boss, asking her if she could work a couple of hours over lunch time as one of the others had just called in sick. Mo was reluctant, but her boss was desperate, so she agreed.

Realising that she didn't have time to go back out searching for Pete, she dawdled to the shower block with a heavy heart. After her shower she thought about ringing the police, but decided she'd wait until after she had been back up there after work.

The time at work dragged and she was relieved to finally knock off at two thirty. She hadn't been very nice to the customers but couldn't help it. Her boss took her aside at one point, to find out why she wasn't being her usual jovial self so Mo explained about Pete. Her boss apologised and told her to go home there and then, but Mo said she'd stay a bit longer and promised to try and smile.

As she rode her bike into the park and was approaching her van she saw somebody sitting on her step. She frowned. It was Pete! She jumped off her bike in mid-flight, squealing out and grabbing him in a bear hug as the bike crashed into the side of her car, before falling on its side.

"Ya little shit! Ya really scared me!" she shrieked, laughing and crying at the same time.

"I'm sorry Mo. I was goin' to go through with it, but I changed me mind at the last second."

"But I was up there last night, looking for you. I called and called. What the hell happened?"

"I went for a walk and then I got lost and it got dark, so I laid down and went to sleep and found me way back this morning. Geez, I'm hungry!"

"So am I!" stated Mo, realising she hadn't eaten since the previous day. "But you should ring Debbie. I called her last night and told her that...... that you'd taken your own life and she was really upset."

"No! I don't want to ring her yet. Do you know if she was going to tell Jo?"

"Well, she said that she'd lost Jo's mobile and would ring David and get it from him or ask them to tell her." Mo frowned. "But why don't you want to tell them that you're okay?"

"It's even better if David thinks I'm dead too," said Pete, as they went into the van and got stuff out of the fridge to eat. "Just let everyone think I'm dead for a while."

"What the hell's goin' on, Pete?"

"I want to get my revenge on someone!" he stated angrily. "It will be easier if I'm supposed to be dead."

"You've lost me," said Mo, shaking her head.

"Just before I was about to jump over the cliff, I started to remember things from the night of the party. Things that I had totally forgotten. Me and Luke had had a bit of a fight and I'd crashed out in his spare room, but I woke up later and felt bad about it so I decided to get out of there. I walked down the steps being really quiet so's not to wake anyone. They've got inside stairs and to one side of them is the garage. When I got to the bottom of the steps and was headin' to the door, I heard a noise in the garage. I was in darkness, but there was a torch on in the garage and I peeked in."

"What did you see?"

"I saw someone doing something to Luke's bike."

"Who?" frowned Mo.

"David!" spat Pete angrily.

CHAPTER TWENTY

Jo had spent her time in Queensland at her parents place, attempting to come to terms with Luke's death. Her heart ached heavily and she cried often. If it wasn't for little Ben she didn't know if she would have been able to go on. He was now smiling a lot and Jo noticed the dimples, just like Daddy's, were forming in his cheeks already. Luke's birthday had been the hardest day of all and it was on that day she decided that it was time to return to Perth. As it almost Christmas, she planned to stay with her parents for Christmas day and fly back to Perth early the next morning. It would have been their first wedding anniversary and Jo had an overwhelming need to be at her and Luke's place for it.

She'd spent quite a bit of time with Meg and had seen Graham. He was pleased to see her, but his heart ached for what she was going through. He knew right from the very start just how much she adored Luke.

Although she was tempted to go to Jeff's grave for some sort of closure there, she decided against it and also against visiting his family. She mainly stayed at her parent's home, as facing lots of people, anywhere, was daunting for her. Luke's death was still mentioned by radio Dj's and other media, so it was hard for her to avoid the constant reminders.

Kelly had rung twice, not long after Jo had left Perth, to see how she was coping. Jo had also rung David and Kelly's house several times to see how everything was. David had rung her once and when Jo has asked to speak to Kelly, she was told that Kelly wasn't there and he didn't know where she was. Jo had thought this was quite odd.

Jo had also kept in contact with Luke's parents as well. They missed her and Ben immensely.

Early in the morning of the twenty-sixth of December, Liz and Tom drove Jo and Ben to Brisbane airport. Even after so long, she didn't feel comfortable going to Maroochydore airport after what Jeff had done.

She said a very tearful farewell to her parents and boarded the plane, hoping she was doing the right thing and would be able to cope once she got back to Perth. She loved Luke's family almost as much as her own and knew they would do everything they could to help and support her. Jo appreciated that, but she also knew that being around them would remind her more of Luke and make her feel even more sad and lonely.

The trip was a long one and Ben slept most of the way in her arms. She couldn't take her eyes off her precious baby and talked to him even when he was asleep.

Tears came easily to Jo's eyes when she saw Luke's parents waiting for them at Perth airport. Rose rushed over, hugged Jo and then took Ben from her, while Jo hugged Ted.

"Welcome back, Jo," smiled Ted with tears in his eyes. "We've missed you. Both of you!" He took Ben off Rose and cuddled him. Ben didn't know what all the fuss was about.

"How's Kelly and David?" asked Jo as they walked to the car.

Ted and Rose looked at each other before Rose spoke. "When is the last time you talked to either of them, Jo?" she asked hesitantly.

"Last week. David rang me. What's going on? He sounded a bit strange when I asked about Kelly. She's all right isn't she?"

"Yeah, she's fine," replied Ted. "Well, last time we saw her she was. They've split up."

"What!" Jo gasped. "When?"

"A couple of weeks ago now," sighed Rose, shaking her head. "I don't know what happened. David's not saying much. Perhaps he'll talk to you about it, Jo. He thinks a lot of you, you know. I get the feeling he feels like he needs to look after you now that...... Luke's not here." She wiped her eyes.

"Yeah, we do seem to get on pretty good," nodded Jo. "Maybe he'll confide in me, but Kelly and I are good mates too. I hope she's ok."

They drove up the coast road toward the house. Jo was growing nervous. How was she going to feel being back there without Luke after weeks away?

"I came over yesterday and put some fresh food in your fridge and made sure everything was clean for you and Ben," said Rose as they pulled into the gateway.

"Thanks Rose," smiled Jo sadly. It reminded her of the first day Luke had brought her home. How exciting that had been.

Ted opened the gate using the remote control that they keep, drove through and closed it again. Jo looked up at the house in front of them. She half expected to see Luke walking out the door with a big smile on his face. How she wished that could be true.

Ted and Rose carried her gear upstairs while Jo walked slowly around the yard with Ben. She wasn't sure she was ready for this yet. Walking over to the pool fence she was surprised to see how clean it was, the way Luke kept it. She stood quietly by the pool fence, looking at the small tables and the barbecue. Suddenly, all the laughter and noise from their pool parties became loud and clear again. She could hear Luke making the announcement at their engagement party. She heard their wedding song and felt Luke's strong arms around her as they slowly danced. Closing her eyes, Jo hugged Ben to her and swayed gently.

"Jo," said Rose, touching her on the arm.

Jo jumped and turned around. "Sorry, I was miles away." She wiped a tear from her eye. "What's up?"

"Do you want us to stay for a while, or would you rather be alone. We could take Ben home for a few hours if you like," suggested Rose.

"No! I mean.... Thanks, but I need to keep him with me."

"That's okay Love," smiled Rose, sadly. "I understand."

Jo walked over to the car with her free arm around her mother-in-law. *Poor Rose. She probably wants Ben with her for the same reason I do.* "Actually, Rose, if you want to take Ben for the afternoon, it's okay."

Rose's face lit up. "Thankyou Jo." She took Ben in her arms and kissed his soft, warm head, which made him giggle. "Oh, I love the sound of a baby laughing." She kissed and tickled him a little, which made him giggle harder. "I have food and formula at home for him. I thought you may want some time alone when you got back."

"Thankyou again, Rose," Jo smiled, before she kissed Ben's forehead.

Rose took him to Ted who strapped him into the baby seat in their car. "Thank's Jo," smiled Ted, taking hold of her hand. "This means a lot to Rose.... And me. We've really missed this little fellow."

Jo smiled and nodded.

"We'll bring him back before dark, unless you want to come over and stay the night with us," said Rose.

"No," replied Jo. "Thanks, but I'd rather stay here tonight. It's our wedding anniversary," she added sadly.

Rose and Ted knew that but they didn't want to bring it up for fear of upsetting her too much.

Jo waved them off and watched them drive though the gate. When she could no longer hear their car driving along, she slowly turned toward the house. Taking a deep breath, she walked through the front door.

She looked into the garage. Her and Luke's cars were sitting there side by side. Even they looked lonely. As she turned to go into the entertainment room she glanced up the stairs. They looked twice as high and steep as they used to. She wondered if she would be able to climb them.

Stepping into the large room, photo's of Luke and of both of them stared down at her from the walls. She shuddered, suddenly feeling very cold. As she looked closely at one of the band on stage she could distinctly hear them playing and singing. Luke's hand seemed to move on his guitar. Then she looked at the one of him on his bike. It used to be her favourite. He looked so carefree and happy on it, but she couldn't bear to see the bike. Reaching up, she took the large mounted photo off the wall and placed it under the bar. "I'm sorry Honey. I've got to do this. I know you'll understand."

A large wedding photo caught her eye next. They were standing on the beach, with the setting sun behind them. It was a beautiful photo, one of Jo's favourites of the wedding. She slowly ran her fingers over it. "Oh Luke." The tears ran freely down her cheeks. "I miss you so much." It became too much for her and she sank to the floor and cried.

Eventually, when she felt there were no more tears left, she was able to get up on shaky legs and walk up the steps. Needing the handrail for support as she dragged her resisting body to the top.

Everything was the same as when she left, only neater. More photos on the walls watched her. Walking into the kitchen she remembered some of the more elaborate meals they cooked up together. Luke loved cooking, as she did. She'd give anything to just be able to sit down to baked beans on toast with him now.

As she left the kitchen to walk down the hallway she looked over at the fireplace and remembered the night of his birthday and her brazen striptease for him. She smiled through her tears at the wonderful memory.

Her heart was aching right up to her throat as she entered their bedroom. Jo stared at the bed, remembering the exciting, passionate nights they'd shared there. She turned and went into the ensuite for a shower, hoping it may make her feel a little better.

After dressing, she walked back into the bedroom and gasped when she looked at Luke's bedside table. The photo of her, that has always been there, was now gone. She looked over to her side and was relieved to see the one of him still there, smiling back at her. Jo searched around on the floor and in the drawers beneath, but the photo was nowhere to be found. Thinking she must have put it somewhere after Luke's death, she shrugged it off and went back out to the lounge room.

Some DVD's in the cabinet caught her eye. Shakily, she took their wedding disc out and put it in the player. Picking up the remote control, she sat apprehensively back in the large, soft lounge chair and flicked it on.

She sat mesmerised through it, fiddling with the hem of her shorts. When it was time to share the vows, Jo couldn't help reciting them over again along with the DVD. Everyone was beaming so happily that day, especially her and Luke. Little could they have known that their perfect world was soon to be so cruelly shattered. Jo watched as they cut the cake and kissed, but when the bridal waltz began and the other home footage started showing, it became too painful and she was forced to switch it off. She lay down on the lounge chair, buried her face in a cushion and cried long and hard. Her body shook as the sobs wracked her violently. Eventually, she cried herself into a restless sleep.

"Jo, wake up." Luke was calling her! She forced her eyes open. Her vision was blurred but she saw him leaning over her.

"Luke?" she gasped.

"No Jo, it's me, David."

Jo rubbed her eyes and sat up to see David crouching beside the lounge.

"You must have been dreaming. You were twitching and sobbing. Are you ok?" he asked.

Jo just stared at him for a few moments. His hair was a bit longer which made him look so much more like Luke.

"I…. I think so. I'm glad to see you, Dave," she said, reaching over to hug him. "I miss Luke so much," she sobbed on his shoulder.

"I know, Sweetie, so do I," he replied, holding her tightly to him.

"David, is it true about you and Kelly breaking up?" Jo frowned after she'd let go of his embrace.

"Yeah, I'm afraid so," nodded David, sitting on the lounge beside her. "Did Mum and Dad tell you?"

"Yes, but only when I asked how you both were. But why? I thought you two would have lasted forever."

"I used to think that too," said David, sadly, "but we just weren't getting along very well anymore, so we decided that we'd both be happier if we didn't live together anymore. We still get on okay, but it's definitely over NOW."

Jo wondered why he emphasised the word "now", but couldn't be bothered questioning him. They chatted a while about Jo's flight over and about Christmas. Both agreed it was their worst one ever. David asked about Ben and was pleased to hear that she'd let his parents have him for the afternoon.

"Jo, I have some other news for you that you probably won't like..... at first, anyway."

"Oh no, what?" sighed Jo, wondering what else could go wrong.

"It's about Pete. You know, Pete Wilson."

"What about him? Is he ok?" frowned Jo.

"No, he committed suicide."

"What! When?" Jo felt a fresh lot of tears coming.

"Up at Kalbarri, apparently, a week or so ago. His sister, Debbie, rang me because she'd lost your number. She asked me to let you know, but I thought it would be better to tell you in person, rather than over the phone."

"Poor Pete," sobbed Jo, shaking her head.

David took a deep breath before continuing. "There's more Jo and it gets ugly, but you have the right to know the truth."

Jo was getting nervous. "What?"

"The night of Pete's party, I'd left to go home and later I remembered that I wanted to ask Luke something, so I came back. I got to the door downstairs and I heard Luke and Pete having an argument. Did Luke tell you about it?"

"He was a bit annoyed with Pete when he came to bed, but he didn't say much," replied Jo, almost adding that he was also annoyed with David that night, but decided she'd bring that up another time. She was too anxious to hear what else he had to say.

"Well, Pete was coming on strong to Luke, really strong. You know what I mean?"

Jo nodded.

David continued. "Luke was telling him off and Pete turned really nasty."

"Wh-what happened then?" asked Jo.

David hesitated a moment, choking back a tear. "He threatened Luke."

Jo gasped, not liking the sound of this. "How?"

"He.... He told Luke that he'd be sorry and that he'd make him pay for all the years of rejections. He really sounded like he meant it Jo. I saw the vicious look in his eyes."

Jo was horrified. "You don't think that he....."

"Caused the accident? Yes, I do, Jo!"

"But they'd been mates most of their life. Pete loved Luke!" cried Jo.

"Exactly!" said David angrily. "It's what they call a crime of passion. If HE couldn't have Luke, then nobody else could either. So the little bastard killed him and made it look like an accident." He put his hands over his eyes for a moment.

"But, I just don't think Pete would do something like that," stated Jo, standing up and walking over to a window. "He didn't seem to have a mean bone in his body."

David followed her and placed his hand on her shoulder. "I've known him a long time, Jo. Believe me, he's done some terrible things to people. He should have been in jail."

"Why didn't you say or do something then, David?" Jo demanded. "Luke might still be alive!" She began to cry.

"I wanted to, but I couldn't prove anything and I couldn't find Pete anywhere afterwards. I didn't think he would have been capable of rigging the bike to crash. Hell, it never even occurred to me that he'd try and do something that would KILL Luke! I thought he'd just go away and never come back. I hoped so anyway." He began to sob. "I should have just ran into that room, grabbed him and taken him out to the pool and thrown him in to drown. God, how I wish now I would have!"

"Don't torment yourself, Dave," consoled Jo, giving him a hug. "We can't bring Luke back."

"But it all adds up, Jo. Why did he disappear from here before morning, and why didn't he go to the service? He didn't have the guts, that's why. He probably had some grand delusion of them being together in death. I hope that, wherever they are, Luke is giving him hell."

Jo was silent for several minutes, trying to absorb everything David was telling her. "It does make sense, doesn't it!" she said bitterly. "To think, I let him into my home and became his friend. The little lying.... Bastard. He killed Luke! My husband! I knew Luke wouldn't have been that careless with the bike. If Pete was still alive I would kill him myself." New tears flowed, more from anger than sadness.

"Jo, I hate to say this, but remember I DID try to warn you about having him around," he said, holding her by the shoulders in front of him.

"That's right, you did. I just wish I would have listened to you. Oh well, he'll be rotting in hell by now."

Just then the phone rang. It was Rose telling her they would be bringing Ben home soon. Jo thanked her and hung up.

"David there's something you didn't know about Pete."

David groaned. "What other surprises has he in store for us?"

"He had AIDS, or so he said. Maybe that was a lie too."

David was shocked. "When did he tell you that?"

"A few days before the party. That's the main reason Luke put on the party for him, to cheer him up. He was really scared and depressed, Luke said."

"I'm not surprised. All the more likely it is that he would do something crazy. The shock of finding out would have affected his mind.... And he had nothing to lose anyway, the dirty little poofter. At least he can't hurt you or Ben anymore." He held her in his arms for a moment. "Jo, there's something else I want to tell you."

Jo hoped for something good for a change. "What's that?"

"Kelly and I couldn't have kids," he said sadly. "We've been trying for years."

They had sat back down on the lounge. "Oh Dave, I'm sorry, I had no idea. Kelly never told me that." Jo briefly thought that was a bit odd, considering how close her and Kelly had become.

"So, I wanted to ask you, no, tell you, that I'm going to be here to look after you and Ben. It's the least I can do for Luke now." He took hold of her hand and looked into her eyes.

"I…. um….David, this is a surprise, but I don't know what I'm going to do yet." She let go of his hand, got up and went to the kitchen for a drink of water. This was totally unexpected. *Or was it?* She shook her head. Sometimes David really confused her. It certainly had been a day for surprises ….. or shocks.

"You don't mean that you might leave Perth, do you?" he panicked, walking after her into the kitchen.

"I really don't know," replied Jo, pouring another glass of water and handing it to him. "It might just be too painful and sad for me to stay here."

"I can understand that, but I'll tell you something else that I wasn't going to," said David, leaning against the kitchen bench as Jo sat down at the table. "I had a dream the other night about Luke. He was telling me to look after you and Ben for him. It seemed so real, Jo, I'm sure he really was telling me."

Jo shook her head and fought back the tears. This was all becoming too much for her on her first day back. "David," she began, looking down at her hands folded on the table in front of her. "I care a lot about you and we've always got on well. It would be easy to …… lean on you for love and support, but I would only be fooling myself and using you….. as a substitute for Luke, because you are naturally the next closest person to him. It would be just too convenient for us to be anything more than friends, besides I'm nowhere near ready to replace Luke yet. Far from it!" Tears burned her eyes. "I'm sorry."

David sat down on a chair beside Jo. "No, I'm sorry Jo. I didn't mean to pressure you or upset you. That's the last thing I would do. I don't mean for us to live together or anything like that. I just want us to be good friends and I want you to know that I will always be here for you….. always."

"Thanks," she smiled. "I appreciate that."

Just then a car drove into the yard. From habit, she jumped up and went to the lounge window to look out, even though she knew it would be Rose and Ted returning with Ben.

"Your Mum and Dad are here. I'm just going into the bathroom to wash my face," said Jo, heading down the hallway. She always tried to not let Ben see her upset and she was sure her eyes would be red now.

As she walked into her bedroom to go through to the ensuite, she stopped and gasped. Her photo was sitting back on Luke's bedside table.

CHAPTER TWENTY ONE

David walked down the internal steps to his wine cellar cum sound proof music studio. His heart was pounding as he reached up and took the silver key from a high ledge above the door. A smaller key jingled alongside it on the key ring. Sliding the key into the lock he was both excited and apprehensive. Some things were going his way, others, like Jo's uncertainty about staying in Perth, needed some more work. He was confident he could win her over though. *There's no choice in the matter, she is mine!*

He opened the door to total darkness, so flicked on the light. There was no movement coming from the mattress at the far end of the room. *No you don't! You are not dying on me now, the fun has only just begun.* Walking across the room to the mattress, he was relieved to hear a moan.

"How are you going? It's such a beautiful sunny day outside," he said sarcastically.

Brown eyes looked up at him, full of pain and a thousand questions. The parched lips moved to speak. "What are doing to me, Dave? What the hell is going on?"

"Oh, there's a lot going on, but nothing you need to worry about. You won't be around much longer anyway, now. Everyone already thinks you're dead," he grinned.

"How long have I been here for? And Why?"

David tossed an apple he'd brought down, which was accepted by the one free hand. The other was handcuffed to the wall. "Because I like to torment people who've given me a hard time, and treated me like SHIT!" He emphasised the last word angrily. "You've been here a while now, most of the time I've kept you unconscious."

"For Christ's sake, David, I'm your brother! How do you think Mum and Dad would feel if they knew you had me chained up here like some deranged animal?"

David's anger grew. "Leave them out of this! You've had this coming for a long time, Luke. It has always been Luke this, Luke that, Luke was always the best, the favourite. Nothing was too good for Lukey boy!"

Luke scoffed. "That's crap! You have a good life. You get treated the same as me by Mum and Dad."

"No.... no, no, I DON'T! It has always been YOU! You had the big break into music, I slaved my guts out for years playing in my band, but were we that lucky, oh no, of course not! YOU got to travel, to live the easy life and YOU always got the best girls! The prettiest ones always flocked to YOU! Remember Sally Benson in high school? Well she agreed to go out with me, BUT as soon as she saw you, I was forgotten."

Luke frowned, trying to remember what or who he was talking about. His head hurt, and the other aches and pains were gradually easing, but not the one in his heart and the fear and confusion coursing through every vein in his body. The last thing he remembered was riding on his bike, feeling angry at Pete and David. When he came to a curve he had tried to put his brakes on to slow down a little, but nothing happened. He recalled flashes of flying through the air and hitting the sand with a thud. Next thing he knew, he woke up on a mattress, with one wrist handcuffed to the wall, and a bucket beside him. The searing pain in his left leg and his inability to move it, had told him it was broken. His shoulder and ribs were also very sore. He scratched at the whiskers on his normally bare chin and shook his head. "I don't remember, but whatever I have done to you, I'm sorry, okay." He reached for the opened plastic bottle of water beside the mattress and took a large drink. "I'd just like to know how the hell you got me here and WHERE I am."

"It was all a lot easier than I thought it would be. I got this room ready for you, it's amazing what you can buy off the net these days," David nodded toward the handcuffs. "Actually, I did plan to play music again, down here, where no-one could hear me, especially you, but then

I came up with the idea of putting YOU down here. It just all fell into place from there. You and Pete had a blue at his party and once you had all gone to bed, I decided that your bike needed a little bit of MY kind of maintenance." He sat down on a chair, several metres from the mattress which Luke was lying on. Casually, he rested one foot on the other knee, placed his hands behind his head and leaned back to get more comfortable. "See, I know you so well Luke, that I knew you were pissed off with me and Pete and I knew you'd go for a ride the next morning."

"What if Jo had have come with me? You could have killed her," Luke interrupted, with tears of frustration and anger welling in his eyes.

David froze for a second. He hadn't thought of that. He became agitated. "Well, it didn't happen did it? So don't even THINK about that possibility. She's fine! Anyway, I jumped in my car and followed you that morning and actually saw you go off the road." He grinned sadistically at the memory. "Geez, that was a sight. I pulled up and went over to you, expecting to find you dead. But you were still alive. I wanted to just throw you in the ocean, but I thought this would be more fun."

Luke fell back flat on the mattress and stared at the ceiling, wiping a tear from his eye. He couldn't even tolerate looking at this brother, or the monster he had obviously become. "Jo" he moaned quietly to himself.

"Are you listening to me? Of course not!" David jumped up from the chair, and quickly sunk to his knees near the mattress while grabbing Luke by the scruff of the shirt and pulling him up toward him. "You better fucking listen, Luke! And DON'T even bother mentioning Jo's name again! You're DEAD to her! She has moved on..... with ME!" Angrily, he dropped Luke back on the mattress, letting go of his dirty, ripped shirt.

Luke groaned from the pain shooting through his ribs and shoulder as David pushed him back. Pain so bad, it left him oblivious to the smell of his unwashed body, hair and clothes. Fortunately, David had installed air conditioning which Luke was grateful for. He desperately hoped he wouldn't add the misery by turning it off. He knew David was delusional about Jo. *She would NEVER fall for him and his charms..... Please Jo, NO.*

"As I was saying, Golden Boy, I carried you to my car and dumped you in the back seat. No one came by and saw me. Then I realised I had better make it look like you went into the drink, so I pulled the chain off your neck, ripped a bit off your shirt, grabbed your phone and your helmet and threw them all into the ocean, with gloves on, of course. Lucky, there was a bit of blood on the helmet from the scrapes on your face. That must have attracted the sharks to it, so when it was found there was a big bite taken out of it. How lucky was that, hey?" laughed David, sitting back on the chair. "Your pendent, phone and bit of shirt were all found too and identified by Jo. You're dead Mate!" He laughed again.

"You'll never get away with this, you know," said Luke, shaking his head.

"Ah, but I HAVE got away with it. Case is closed! The bike was at fault. Everyone thinks you're dead. Jo has been back a few days now. I've been over with her most of that time."

"What do you mean, 'back'? Where did she go?" frowned Luke, aching to see and hold his beautiful wife.

"She went back to Queensland with her family for a while after your memorial service. Ha! You should have seen my act at it. I got up and talked about what great mates we were, but had to cut it off when I pretended to break down and cry. It was so convincing."

"Where's Kelly?" asked Luke. "She'll find out I'm here and get me out."

"Not a chance, Mate, she's gone! We split up and she moved out. It's just me here now in this big house and beautiful Jo next door, all alone, sad and lonely."

"Stay away from her, and Ben, please," begged Luke, realising he was in no position to get angry at his captor.

"Too late," David smiled smugly. "I've spent the past two nights with her, ALL night. God, she's beautiful. We made love for hours, she wore me out."

"LIAR!" shouted Luke angrily. "She WOULDN'T!"

"Really? Well, how about this. I have kissed that cute little heart shaped mole on her left bum cheek and those perky boobs, hmmm, they taste so nice. He whole body tastes so sweet, you know what I mean."

"NO!" Luke let out an angry, frustrated growl while trying to yank the handcuff chain out of the wall. He pulled and pulled with his free hand, but it would not budge, and only succeeded in increasing his pain, both physically and emotionally. He knew Jo had a heart shaped mole on her left buttock but he just couldn't understand how David would know, *unless*...... *NO!* He just couldn't bear the thought of it.

"Settle down, Lukey," patronised David. "You are only hurting yourself more. No need to get so upset. You best forget all about Jo. You see, she has confessed to me that she only came to Perth to get away from her Ex-boyfriend. Yep, she told me all about it, what happened at the airport and what he did to her. You were just her ticket out of there." David's mind briefly flicked to all the hours of research he did on Jo, after some little thing Meg had said at the wedding, which got his mind wondering and led him to discover all about Jeff. "Oh, I nearly forgot, she asked me last night if I would like to adopt Ben. Of course I said yes. He's already calling me Da Da."

Luke gritted his teeth and fought back the tears. "You bastard!"

"Sticks and stones, Luke, sticks and stones," David said sarcastically while shaking his head. "Hey, you want to hear the latest on your little poofter mate, Pete?"

"What about him? He'll see through you and warn Jo."

David laughed. "Not likely. He's dead. I mean fair dinkum DEAD! He couldn't live without you anymore, oh my hearts bleeds for him, NOT! What a load of shit. But seriously, it's true. He went up the coast somewhere and jumped off a cliff. How ironic. He thought you died in the ocean, so he jumped into it. Oh, Jo was sad at first, but then when I told her that it was HIM that rigged your bike, you know, a crime of passion – if he couldn't have you then no-one could. Anyway, she got angry and is now glad the little prick is dead. SO.... As far as Jo and I are concerned you two are together in heaven or somewhere and her and I are together here in real life. It all worked out for the best, hey? Geez, I'm good! There is absolutely no-one that knows what I have done." He stood up, puffing out his chest. "The power, Mate! I feel like a God! Jo worships the ground I walk on now. Even early this morning, she begged me to make love to her again and again. She can't get enough of me. She told me it was the best sex she'd ever had. Ha! You're not the big stud you thought you were, Luke."

The anger was boiling over within Luke, and it took every ounce of restraint he had not to let it show. He knew it was what David wanted to see and gloat over. Deep down he HAD to believe that Jo wouldn't be with David. "Ok Dave, whatever you reckon. You've won. Now what are you going to do with me?"

"Hmmm, not sure yet. I'm really enjoying this whole thing. I'll keep you here a bit longer yet before I decide. I will keep you updated on Jo's and my blossoming love affair. Maybe, I'll film little Ben with my phone and show you too. That would be fun. You would like to see him, wouldn't you?"

Of course Luke felt he wanted to see Ben, desperately, but was sick of playing into David's hands. But then if he didn't, David might kill him sooner. His mind was in turmoil. "Yes," he answered, trying to remain calm. "I would like to see my son."

"Hey, I almost forgot what I want to show you. Be back in a minute." David ran out the door.

Luke could see the open door and prayed something would give at that moment. He scanned the area around the mattress for anything that might cut the chain. Nothing. *Damn!* He pulled at the chain, the cuffs and also where it went into the wall. Not a chance! He could see the keys still in the door lock and guessed the smaller key would be for the handcuffs. It was pointless. He was too far away from it. He shouted out for help, as loudly as he could, in the vain hope another person may be upstairs and could hear him. All it did was make his throat sore. The tears of hopelessness, despair and frustration flowed and he didn't bother trying to stop them. It was no use.

"Quit the yelling," said David, coming back into the room with some newspapers in his hands. "No-one can hear you. Give it up!" He was angry again. "Here!" He threw the papers down beside Luke. "Read about your death and what everyone had to say about it. You made the papers big time. Looks like the band won't be going on without you." He turned to go toward the door again. "I'm out of here, going to go and see that gorgeous wife of yours for some horny fun." He locked the door behind him, leaving Luke lying on the mattress, fuming.

"Come on Jo, please get my vibes..... I'm here..... alive," he mumbled in desperation. Trying to get his mind of David with Jo, he picked up the newspaper to see his picture on the front page above the article about his disappearance and subsequent death in the ocean. "NOOOOO," he cried out long and hard.

CHAPTER TWENTY TWO

Pete had desperately wanted to get back to Perth as soon as he realised what David had done. He had no money at all and Mo's boss had begged her to stay a bit longer while the holiday rush was on. She agreed, only if Pete could get some work there too. So Pete begrudgingly accepted the dishwashing job. Mo was granted leave from the second of January, so they had a bit of time to get some money together.

At Pete's request, Mo had rung Debbie to tell her that the police had searched for his body and all they found was his tee shirt washed up on the rocks. She hated lying to Debbie, but Pete made it sound like an integral part of his plan, so she couldn't refuse.

Debbie sadly accepted Pete's death and informed Mo that their parents and Jo Summers had been told. She assumed that a police report and death certificate would come in time. Given Pete's circumstances and his wishes, she didn't push the matter.

Finally, after the waiting had dragged painfully by for Pete, they were on their way back to Perth. He was determined to bring David down. Nothing else mattered.

"Have you worked out just exactly what you're goin' to do yet, Pete?" Mo asked, as they drove into the outskirts of Perth early in the afternoon. She'd barely gotten a word out of him all the way.

"No," replied Pete, deep in thought. "I'll explain everything to Deb and she will be able to help us come up with something. I really want to talk to Jo too."

They arrived at Debbie's house and luckily, her car was in the carport. Pete and Mo walked to the front door and knocked. Pete was nervous. Deb would get the shock of her life when she saw him.

Debbie opened the door and let out a gasp, then her face drained of colour. "Pete?" she whispered, not believing her eyes.

"Yeah Sis," he beamed. "It really is me! I didn't really commit suicide, well I was going to, but I just went away for a while to think about some things."

She hugged him tightly to her and cried tears of relief. "Don't you EVER do that to me again, you hear! How long have you known that he was still alive, Mo?"

Mo's eyes widened, "Um...."

"She's known for a while Deb, but I made her keep it a secret," cut in Pete. "Look, there's something pretty heavy goin'on. I only just remembered it recently. It'll freak ya right out! Come inside and I'll tell ya. Where's the girls?" Pete asked as they walked into the kitchen.

"They're over at John's for a week while he's on holidays. They miss him a lot. So, what's this all about and what's so important that you had to fake your own death. Sounds like something out of a soap opera," she laughed as she put the kettle on.

"Well, I didn't set out to fake it, it was going to happen," he stated, then noticed the shocked look on his sister's face. He continued on, telling her everything he remembered seeing as he was leaving Luke's place the night of his birthday party. "So, David DEFINITELY thinks I'm dead?"

"As far as I know. I rang him after Mo told me and he said that he would tell Jo," said Debbie shaking her head. "The bastard! How could anyone do that to their own brother?" Anger flashed in her eyes amidst some tears.

"Because he wants Jo for himself, that's why!" Pete replied angrily. "I've noticed things at times when he was around Jo. I could see the look in his eyes and hear it in his voice. He's probably planned it all along and was just waitin' for the right chance. You know, he's always hated Luke, deep down. I can remember him saying once, when we were kids, that he wished Luke was dead. I've always hated HIM for that!"

Debbie just sat there for a few moments in stunned silence. She didn't know David very well but had always found him to be pleasant and just couldn't imagine him doing something so horrible. Then she gasped as she remembered something. "I saw Kelly at her clinic a couple of weeks ago and she told me that her and David had split up."

Pete felt panic rising. "Do you know if Jo is still in Queensland? I hope to hell for her sake she is. If he gets to her while she's so down, he'll slime his way into her life, like a snake."

"I really don't know," replied Debbie. "I was in touch with her when she first went back over, but then lost her address and the number she gave me and I haven't heard anything from or about her. I can't remember what her maiden name was to find her parents number again either." She shrugged her shoulders in defeat.

"Well, what about Kelly?" urged Pete anxiously. "She'd probably know. It would be good if we can get her to come over here. Can you ring her at work, Deb, and ask her please."

Debbie quickly found the number for the clinic and dialled. In next to no time she was speaking to Kelly and asked her if she could come by after work. After giving her the address she hung up. "She'll be here in about an hour."

Pete and Mo were relieved, but at the same time, they were all worried.

"Pete, are you ABSOLUTELY sure, without any possible doubt, that you saw David at the bike that night?" asked Debbie.

"Yes!" assured Pete. "I just want to kill the mongrel!"

They passed the time waiting for Kelly by discussing possible ways of bringing David down. In no time, her car was pulling up behind the pink holden. Debbie went out to show her in to the kitchen where they were sitting.

Kelly got the shock of her life when she walked in and saw Pete sitting there. "I-I thought you were dead!" she exclaimed. "But it's good to see that you're not," she laughed as she gave him a quick hug. "David told me the last time I spoke to him."

Pete introduced her to Mo and the two women shook hands.

"So, what's going on?" frowned Kelly. "You sounded pretty worried on the phone, Deb."

"Where do I start?" said Pete, more to himself than anyone else. "Do you know where Jo is, Kelly?"

Kelly nodded. "Yes, she's back here in Perth. She came back last week. Why?"

"Oh no," sighed Pete. "Have you seen her?"

"No, not yet," answered Kelly, still frowning. "I've rung her once but Ben was crying so we didn't talk for long and I went around to get the last of my stuff from David's the other day, but Jo wasn't home. We've been really busy at work over Christmas and New Year, so I haven't had a chance to catch up with her properly yet. What's going on?"

Pete took a deep breath as he felt his heart pounding. "I don't know how to tell ya this, Kel, so I'll just come right out with it. It'll shock ya. David did something to Luke's bike to make it crash. He wanted him dead!"

Kelly's jaw dropped for a moment before she spoke. "That is the most ridiculous thing I've ever heard, Pete!" she said angrily. "David wouldn't do anything to...." She stopped suddenly in midsentence. "How do you know?" she asked quietly, while taking the cup of tea that Mo had made for her. "Thanks Mo."

"I saw him! The night of the party. I was leavin' because me and Luke had a bit of a blue and I'd crashed out upstairs for a while. When I was about to go out the front door I heard a noise in the garage and looked in to see David crouching down at Luke's bike. He didn't see me though."

"But why has it taken you so long to say anything?" frowned Kelly, fighting back the tears.

"I had forgotten about it 'til I was about to jump off a cliff at Kalbarri and then we couldn't get down here any sooner. So I let everyone still think I was dead, especially David, so we could work out what to do and get Jo away from him."

Kelly was silent for a minute, deep in thought. "It all fits together now," she said eventually. "David wants Jo, doesn't he?"

"I reckon so!" said Pete angrily, while Mo and Debbie nodded in agreement.

"You know, when I think back to when Jo first got here, I realise that that's when David started acting differently and our hassles began. Oh, I don't blame Jo," she hastily added. "A blind man could see how much she adored Luke, but she is beautiful and David would have noticed that. He did always seem to be jealous of Luke, no matter what Luke did or had, although he never came right out and said it. But to KILL him?" She shuddered as her face paled. "When I rang Jo last week, she said that David had been over and that he'd been a good support to her. You know, we were planning to have a baby, but as soon as Jo announced her pregnancy, David suddenly decided that he didn't want kids and made me go back on the pill. He must have been planning this for ages. He would have decided that he'd rather be a father to Jo's baby than mine!" She began to cry. "I just can't believe he could be so twisted." Suddenly she gasped. "We have to get her away from him!"

"We know," replied Pete. "That's what we're tryin' to figure out how to do and make the fuckin' animal pay for what he's done. I bet he's feelin' pretty smug with himself right now."

"Pete, is there any doubt about what you saw that night?" asked Kelly. "You were pretty out of it."

"I know," replied Pete, regretfully, "but I'd had a sleep and wasn't too bad by the time I left. Yeah, I'm sure."

"Well, I think we should try and get Jo over here..... right now," suggested Debbie. "The sooner we get her away from him the better. In her vulnerable state, he could suck her right in."

"Yes, he certainly can be charming when he wants to," said Kelly, bitterly. "Do you want me to ring her?"

"Maybe Deb should," suggested Pete. "We don't want her getting suspicious of anything yet. If you ring her Kel, she might say something to David."

Debbie dialled Jo's home phone and waited. "Not home," she said, hanging up.

"Try Luke's parents," suggested Kelly. "She goes there a fair bit." She told Deb the number she knew off by heart.

Rose answered the phone and Debbie chatted to her for a minute before asking if Jo was there. She was and Rose put her on.

"Jo, it's me Deb"

"Deb! It's good to hear from you. How are you?..... I heard about Pete."

Debbie thought it was a bit out of character for Jo not to have offered her sympathy, but then she shrugged it off, realising that Jo would still be mourning Luke. "I'm okay. I'm sorry I never contacted you again over in Queensland, but I lost your number. I think the piece of paper must have got mixed up with Sarah's homework or something. Sorry to ring you there, Jo, but I need to see you as soon as possible. Any chance you could come over here right away?"

"Probably not, we are just about to have tea and Ben is a bit grizzly. He's cutting teeth. What about first thing in the morning? Actually, yes I want to see you about something too. Something serious."

"That would be good, Jo. It's pretty important. So is about eight o'clock okay for you?"

"Yep, that'll be fine, see you then."

Debbie frowned as she hung up the phone. "She didn't sound like herself at all. She said she wanted to see me about something too. Something serious."

"I wonder what that can be," puzzled Kelly.

A worried look spread over Debbie's face. "I don't know. She'll be here around eight so we'll find out then. Can you be here, Kelly?"

"I sure will! I want to get her away from that mongrel just as much as you all do."

"It was strange," said Debbie shaking her head. "Jo didn't sound the slightest bit sorry or upset when she mentioned that'd she'd heard about Pete dying."

"Well, I s'pose he's filled her head with a lot of bullshit about me," snarled Pete. "But I'll make the bastard sorry..... if it's the last thing I ever do!"

CHAPTER TWENTY THREE

The next morning Jo was nervous as she drove to Debbie's house. Although she knew that Deb would have loved to see Ben, she thought it best to drop him off at Rose and Ted's house in case there was conflict once she'd informed Debbie of what Pete had done to Luke's bike. There was every chance Deb would defend her brother, that was natural, but there was just too much evidence pointing to Pete having caused Luke's accident and his subsequent death. Jo knew she just HAD to convince Deb of that and she really wasn't looking forward to it.

David had spent a fair amount of time with her in the week since she'd returned to Perth. She appreciated his company and support. He was the one person who could really understand her loss and they often cried on each other's shoulder.

On New Years Eve, he had taken her out to a restaurant and then to a night club, but she'd wanted to come home early, not feeling comfortable out in crowds, especially without Luke by her side. Driving back to Rose and Ted's that night to pick Ben up, Jo had remembered the previous New Year's Eve. Her and Luke were on their honeymoon and were driving back from Broome to escape the impending cyclone.

She had rung Steve several days after arriving back in Perth. He was still upset over Luke's death. The band had no idea what they would do with Luke gone. None of them really felt like continuing but Steve told her that they had enough songs for a new album, including 'Wildflower', and then they'd decide their future.

As Jo pulled up in front of Debbie's house she wondered whose the pink holden was. Nervously, she took several deep breaths before getting out of her car and walking to the front door. Just as she was about to knock, Debbie appeared at the door.

"Hi Jo, it's good to see you."

"Hi Deb, you too."

The two women embraced before Deb beckoned Jo inside and into the lounge room. She heard noises coming from the kitchen and assumed it must be the owner of the car outside.

"How are you holding up, Mate?" Deb asked sadly, as they sat down on the lounge.

"Oh…. Okay, I suppose," sighed Jo. "David's been a rock for me. He's really helped me come to terms with things." Her mind was in a jumble, wondering how she was going to broach the subject of Pete. "Um…. Deb, I've got something to tell you ….. it's about Pete….. he…."

"I want to talk to you about him too Jo….. and David," Debbie cut in. "It's not very good news I'm afraid."

Jo wondered if Debbie had somehow found out what Pete had done. "What? Is it about the cause of Luke's accident?"

"Well…. yes," replied Debbie, surprised. She wondered if David had felt guilty and confessed to Jo what he'd done.

"You don't seem that upset about it, Deb," frowned Jo.

"Of course I am! It was a hell of a shock. I don't know what would have been going through his mind when he rigged Luke's bike to crash," said Debbie, shaking her head.

"I don't know either," agreed Jo sadly. "I never thought Pete would do something so terrible. Luke was supposed to be his best friend." She wiped a tear from her eye.

"Pete!" exclaimed Debbie. "You think PETE rigged the bike?"

"Yes…. Isn't that what you're talking about? David said…"

"David!" spat Debbie angrily, "is the one who did it, NOT PETE!"

Jo frowned and was about to speak up in defence of David when Pete walked into the room. Her jaw dropped as she felt the colour drain from her face, quickly replaced by heated, angry red. "PETE!" she screamed, jumping up and lunging at him like a leopard attacks its prey. "You killed Luke didn't you? You were supposed to be his FRIEND! I could kill YOU!" The tears streamed down her face as she punched into Pete.

"JO, NO!" shouted Pete, grabbing her by the wrists. He'd never seen such intense hatred in her eyes before. "It wasn't ME! David rigged the bike because he wants YOU."

"THAT'S BULL" cried Jo, kicking into Pete's legs.

Debbie got up and grabbed Jo from behind just as Mo walked into the room.

"Jo, it IS true," said Debbie. "Sit down and we'll tell you some shocking home truths." She was a little angry at Jo for flying into Pete, physically and verbally, but she realised that David must have done a good job brainwashing her.

Jo reluctantly sat down on the lounge. "This had better be good!" she sniffed.

"This is Mo, a friend of Pete's," said Debbie, pointing to Mo standing over near the door.

Jo just nodded in her direction, not in the mood for idle chat. Just then Kelly walked in the front door.

"Kelly!" exclaimed Jo, jumping up and hugging her. "They're trying to tell me that David rigged Luke's bike to make him fall off."

"I think it's true, Jo," said Kelly sadly. "He's not the person you think he is OR that I thought he was either, for that matter."

Jo was bewildered. "I don't understand any of this." She began to cry. "Pete, you're supposed to be DEAD!" She sunk back down into the lounge chair. "Will someone please tell me what the hell is going on?"

"Jo," Pete began, "when I was in Kalbarri, I was so depressed that Luke was gone and ..... about other things too, that I wanted to end it all by jumping off a cliff. I was staying with Mo." He indicated toward her. "She's the one I got a lift over from Sydney with. Anyway, just as I was about to do it, I started to remember things from the night of my party. Jo, I SAW David at Luke's bike when I was leaving your house. He didn't see me though."

"You were so pissed, Pete, how could you remember anything from that night?" Jo snapped.

Pete shrugged. "It came back to me. I guess my subconscious was kickin' in or something like that. I left your place that night because I knew Luke was angry with me and I was embarrassed after puttin' the hard word on him. I managed to climb the fence and hitched back to Debbie's."

"Why didn't you come to Luke's memorial service? I was really disappointed that you didn't."

"I WAS there!" replied Pete. "I was standin' outside one of the side doors. I was too sad to come in. I saw you walkin' to your car and Deb catching up with you. I wanted to come over too, but…. I just couldn't." He wiped tears from his eyes. "I went to Kalbarri soon after that. I'm sorry I never came to see you, but I knew your family was there with you."

"But I still can't believe that David would want Luke dead. His own brother! He's been really upset over his death too. NO!" Jo quickly shook her head. "He wouldn't do that to Luke, or to me!"

"It's because of you that he did it, Jo," said Kelly calmly, as she sat down beside her.

"What?" frowned Jo, growing more confused.

Kelly took hold of Jo's hand. "Jo, David was smitten with you right from the start. Oh don't worry, I don't blame you. He just had to have you. He's always been jealous of Luke, always wanting what Luke has got. He wanted us to stop trying for a baby as soon as you said you were pregnant."

Jo shook her head. "But he told me that you couldn't have kids. He's said you have been trying for years."

Kelly felt her anger at David growing rapidly. "That's a lie! I'd only been off the pill for six months and I'd had a miscarriage five years ago."

Jo was stunned. "B-but he's been so good to me." She began to sob. "He wouldn't do anything to hurt me."

Pete could feel the hatred burning inside him. "No, he probably wouldn't hurt YOU, but he didn't think twice about killing his own brother so the path was clear to have you. I don't trust him, Jo, if he knows you know he could very well hurt you. I reckon he'd believe that if he couldn't have you than no-one else could either!"

"He said that about you and Luke, Pete," said Jo.

Kelly shook her head in utter disbelief at how far he had stooped. "Then he had to get rid of me. Jo it wasn't my idea to split up. I wanted to stay with him, but he just got so moody and we were fighting all the time over little things. He tried to blame me, but now I realise that he wanted me to get sick of him and leave so he wouldn't look so bad."

Jo sat on the lounge chair absolutely stunned – rendered speechless by all these shocking revelations. It was tragic enough that she'd lost Luke, then to discover that Pete, who was supposed to be their friend, caused his death. NOW she finds out that he's ALIVE and claiming David, Luke's own brother and some-one who she trusted and leaned on for support, actually caused the accident. She still may not have been so convinced if only Debbie was backing his claims up, but KELLY was agreeing to everything, as well as adding her own fuel to the rapidly intensifying fire. *Could all this possibly be true? Could David really have wanted Luke dead because he wanted me for himself?*

Her mind wandered back. She remembered the first time she met David and how he'd looked at her and touched her hand when he shook it. Then there were the many times he would come to their house claiming to want to see Luke when he would have known he wasn't home. And the kiss the morning he surprised her doing the housework, also another attempt at a kiss that fateful night in the nursery when Luke walked in. Luke was going to tell her something about David when he died. That must have been it. *It all MUST be true!* Jo suddenly gasped. "The photo... it must have been him!" She looked around at the others, wide eyed.

"What photo?" frowned Pete, sitting down on the other side of Jo, to where Kelly was sitting.

"When I got back from Queensland, I walked into our bedroom and noticed that a photo of me that always sat on Luke's bedside table was gone. I looked for it, but it had completely disappeared. I wasn't that worried about it and soon fell asleep on the lounge. David was there when I woke up and we talked for a while. Then I went into our bathroom and saw that the photo was back on Luke's side, where it should be. He must have had it while I was away and thought that I wouldn't notice if he put it back while I was asleep. The mongrel! How bloody stupid does he think I am!" Jo bowed her head and placed her hand over her eyes.

"Jo, speaking of photo's, there's something else I have to tell you.... And show you," said Kelly, nervously.

Jo wondered how much more she could take. "W-what?"

"The other day when I went back to the house to get the last of my stuff, I found some photo's hidden away in a box at the bottom of the wardrobe. David must have taken them. They're of you and Luke ..... making love near the pool one night."

Jo's heart sank and she felt the colour, once again, drain from her face as Kelly took the photo out of her bag.

"I took one out, hoping to get the chance to tell you, but I didn't know exactly what I was going to do, until today that is. I'm sorry Jo." She handed the photo to Jo.

Sighing deeply, Jo stared at the picture. It was her and Luke all right, taken the night of their engagement party. David was the last one to leave and he did have his camera with him, having taken lots of photos at the party. He must have been sitting over in the darkness, watching them. Jo was repulsed! "Where's the toilet?" she asked frantically as the contents of her stomach churned. Debbie grabbed her by the hand and quickly led her in the right direction.

"WOW!" exclaimed Mo, shaking her head. "That prick needs his balls cut out!"

Kelly felt disgust. "It sickens me to think that he was probably getting off while he was watching them, and how many times he would have looked at the photos."

"So, what do we do now?" shrugged Mo, finally sitting down on one of the single lounges. She'd been a bit bewildered by everything she'd heard and felt sorry for Jo.

"Get the bastard!" stated Pete, eyes blazing.

"We'd better see what Jo wants to do," said Kelly.

Jo walked back into the room, her eyes and face red. "There's something I don't understand with that photo, Kelly. How come we didn't see any flashes?"

"You don't need a flash with that camera if there is enough light behind the subject and you zoom right up."

"And the pervin' sleaze certainly zoomed right up!" spat Pete, picking up the photo from where Jo had dropped it on the floor, and looking at it briefly before handing it back to her. The heart shaped mole could be clearly seen.

"I don't want to look at it anymore," sobbed Jo, tearing it into lots of little pieces. Debbie took them from her and threw them into the fireplace.

"Kel, there's something else that I'm almost afraid to ask you."

"Go ahead, Jo," urged Kelly.

"The times that you and….. HIM had a key to our place, did he go over there much?"

"Lots of times, I'm afraid. When you were on your honeymoon he always seemed to have a good reason, but while you were in Queensland he wouldn't even tell me he was going over there. He would just disappear and later on, if it was night, I'd see a light on, of if it was daytime, I'd see him coming back from your direction."

Jo shuddered at the thought of what he could have been doing in her home all those times and wondered if he'd taken anything else. "Have you found anything else of mine?"

"No," Kelly shook her head, placing her hand on Jo's shoulder in comfort.

Suddenly Jo stood up. "I want to confront him!" She began pacing the floor. "I want to hear the killer confess," she stated through clenched teeth and fists.

"I think you should go to the police," said Debbie. "He might hurt you, Jo."

"I agree," nodded Kelly. "It wouldn't be safe for you to just confront him. You never know what he's likely to do now. He's obviously lost it completely."

"Well, I wanna come face to face with him!" declared Pete. "I wanna see the shock on his face when he sees that I'm alive AND when I tell him I know what he did! I don't care what he does to me. If bringin' him down is the last thing I ever see, I'll die happy."

"We're going to have to wait until he comes home from work this afternoon anyway," said Kelly.

"No way!" said Jo adamantly. "I'm not waiting all day. I'll call his mobile and ask him to meet me at home. He'll come running like a little puppy. Argh! He makes me sick!" Her mind was made up and nobody was going to stop her getting the truth out of David. She took her phone out of her bag and walked out on to the veranda.

Debbie sighed heavily as she looked at Mo then Kelly. "I don't like this. She can't go and see him alone."

"She won't be alone!" stated Pete. "I'm goin' with her."

"Well, I'm going to the police," said Kelly. "Will you come with me, Mo?"

"You bet!" enthused Mo, jumping to her feet.

"Well, I'll stay here and wait for any news," said Debbie. "There's not much I can do anyway."

Jo rushed back into the lounge room. "Okay, he said he'd be home in about an hour. Pete will you come with me?"

"Sure will! You didn't say anything to make him suss didja?"

She shook her head. "No, I was careful. I just told him I wasn't feeling well."

"Mo and I will go to the police. We'll tell them to get there just after he does, if we can," said Kelly. "Jo, please be careful and try to keep him there until we get there. He's not getting away with this."

"Oh, it won't be hard keeping him there.... IF Pete and I can control our anger....." She rolled her eyes, knowing that it would be difficult.

"A tape recorder would come in handy," suggested Mo.

"Great idea, but I haven't got one of those little ones," said Jo, disappointedly.

"Bummer. Sarah's ipod would have been great, but she has it with her. Hang on, I think there is one of those older style little ones here somewhere," said Debbie, rushing into one of the bedrooms. In no time she was back out holding it in her hand. "Yes!"

"Check the batteries," said Pete anxiously. He was raring to get to David.

Debbie found another tape for the machine and turned it on. Nothing. She quickly went into the kitchen, opened the bottom drawer and took out some new batteries and inserted them. It worked like a charm. Everyone breathed a sigh of relief.

"Great, thanks Deb," said Jo, taking it from Debbie and putting it in her bag. "Let's go, Pete!" She grabbed him by the hand and headed out the door.

Kelly shook her head nervously. "I have a bad feeling about this. I can't help thinking it's all going to blow up in our faces. Come on Mo." The two women walked hastily out the door, leaving Debbie there alone to worry.

CHAPTER TWENTY FOUR

Mo and Kelly drove as fast as they legally could to the nearest police station. A young, female officer came over to help them when they arrived at the front counter.

She immediately noticed the worried looks on their faces. "What's wrong, Ladies?"

"We want to report a murder, well it was supposed to be an accident, but we know now that someone caused the accident and who it was," stated Kelly.

"Yeah," added Mo. "Our mate, Pete, who committed suicide, got the blame by this other bloke, who really did it and Pete's now told us what he saw David, that's the other bloke, do the night of the party."

"Hang on, slow down," said the confused officer. "You're not making much sense! If 'Pete' committed suicide, how could he have told you about 'David'?"

"Well, he didn't end up doin' it. He got lost for the night," continued Mo. "Anyway, David still thinks Pete's dead and Pete's gone over there with Jo to confront him and get him to confess."

"You'll have to send someone over there," urged Kelly. "David is dangerous. There's no telling what he might do to those two, although he probably wouldn't hurt Jo."

"Who's Jo?" asked the officer, wondering about the validity of this wild story coming from a hippie and a punk with orange hair and black fingernails.

"Jo is Luke's wife," said Mo. "He's the dead one."

The policewoman shook her head. "But I thought you said Pete was dead, but not really."

"No!" emphasised Kelly. "Luke was killed off his motor bike weeks ago, and David, who's his brother, caused the accident."

"But why would his brother want him dead?" frowned the officer.

320

Kelly gritted her teeth in frustration. "Because he wanted Jo for himself!"

"Well, who are you?"

"My name is Kelly Houston. I'm David's ex-partner."

"An' I'm Mo! I'm Pete's mate."

"So, Ms Houston, you're angry with your ex-boyfriend, is that it?"

"Yeah, you could say that!" replied Kelly in disgust. "He kicked me out, told lots of lies, to both Jo and me AND he killed his own brother, who I happened to be good friends with."

"Was there something going on between you and his brother?"

Kelly rolled her eyes. "NO! Nothing was going on between Luke and I. My boyfriend was in love with HIS wife, so he got rid of Luke so he could have Jo."

The officer couldn't make any sense of it all. "So, was his wife on with your boyfriend too?"

"NO!" shouted Kelly furiously. "She was devastated when Luke died."

"Well what's Pete got to do with it?"

"Pete was Luke's mate and he loved him too. He's gay," Mo said, suddenly wishing she hadn't.

"So, was Luke gay?"

"No!" said Mo angrily. "Pete was. Luke was full on hetro."

"Look," said Kelly, trying to stay calm, "the bottom line is that Jo has just found out that David killed her husband and she and Pete have gone to confront him. He's crazy and is likely to do anything, especially if he can kill his own brother."

Another uniformed officer walked over to where the three ladies were talking. He was an elderly, greying man with a red, puffy face and a large stomach. "What's going on here? I could hear you all from way over there."

"Sarge, these two ladies claim that they know that an accident wasn't really an accident and that the dead man's brother caused it because he was in love with his wife."

"Well, I'm in love with my wife too, but that doesn't make me want to kill my brother," he answered, almost laughing.

Kelly and Mo looked at each other in sheer frustration.

"You know," Kelly stated through clenched teeth, "while we are here trying to get through to you two, somebody could be getting killed!"

"What is the name of the deceased?" asked the sergeant.

"Luke Summers," answered Kelly. "He was a member of Stonefish." *That's an Aussie rock band you geriatric twit!*

The female officer's eyes widened in obvious recognition.

"Yes, I remember that happening," said the sergeant seriously. "There were some suspicious circumstances surrounding his accident but we couldn't pinpoint anything. I think you'd better come in and sit down and tell me everything you know."

Mo and Kelly looked at each other in utter relief, before following the sergeant.

CHAPTER TWENTY FIVE

Jo could feel her body trembling as she heard David's car drive into her yard. Even though she had left the gate open, more for the police than him, she was furious that he seemed to feel so much at home at her place to just drive into her yard instead of going next door and walking over. She had put a jacket on to conceal the recorder. Switching it on, she sipped a glass of water then wiped her sweaty palms on her shorts as David came bounding up the stairs.

Pete was waiting in one of the bedrooms, shaking as well, but more from anger than fear. The showdown was finally here!

"Are you okay, Jo?" David asked, his voice full of concern. "You didn't sound too good over the phone. Where's Ben?"

"He's at your parents," replied Jo, not able to look him in the eye.

"What's wrong?" he asked tenderly, putting his hand on her shoulder. She pulled away abruptly and began to cry. "Hey," he whispered to soothe her, placing his arms about her shoulders.

As hard as she tried, Jo just couldn't hold her anger in. "Don't touch me!" She flung his arms away with her hands. "You murderer!"

"What are you talking about, Jo?" he frowned innocently.

She was livid. "You frigging know, David! YOU rigged Luke's bike, didn't you?"

"Jo, how could you think that? I thought we agreed that Pete had to have done it." He was becoming agitated.

"WELL, PETE DIDN'T DO IT!" she yelled at him through her tears. "I know that much is true."

"And how do you know that? The little punk is dead!" shot David angrily.

Pete walked silently into the lounge room. "That's what YOU think, David."

David spun around and felt the blood drain from his face.

"Don't worry, I'm not a ghost," snarled Pete, walking closer to David, who remained speechless. "I saw you at Luke's bike when I was leavin' the party, but you didn't see me."

David shook his head. "That's crazy. You're just saying that because Luke wouldn't let you have your dirty way with him! You did it thinking that you had nothing else to live for, since you got AIDS."

Pete looked at Jo questioningly.

"I'm sorry Pete," she lamented. "I told him when I thought…."

"It doesn't matter now, Jo," he consoled her. "All that matters is that David gets what he deserves."

"What about the photo, David?" Jo demanded. "The one of me beside our bed."

David shrugged. "What about it?"

"You took it while I was away, didn't you?" fired Jo. "And the night of our engagement party, you took photos of Luke and me making love by the pool." She noticed the incredulous look on his face. "DON'T try to deny it. Kelly showed me one of many that she found in a box at the bottom of a wardrobe. That's sick! How could you do it? I thought you CARED about me. I thought you were my FRIEND! I trusted and confided in you." She leant on the back of a chair, feeling short of breath, hung her head and cried.

"DON'T try to deny it any longer, David. It won't get you anywhere," shouted Pete.

David knew he was beat, for the moment anyway. "All right! So I DID rig the fucking bike. And you want to know how?"

Stunned, Jo looked up at him through tired, teary eyes. *FINALLY, some honesty!*

"I drained all the brake fluid out so they'd fail, hopefully at high speed. And they did." He was proud of his achievement. "Luke deserved it!" he added angrily.

Jo noticed his face suddenly change. He looked like some deranged monster from a horror movie.

"How can you say that?" she sobbed. "What did he ever do to you?"

"Ha! You thought he was just perfect didn't you? Well, he sure had you fooled. Underneath that smooth charm he was a selfish, arrogant bastard. Always had to HAVE and BE the best and he didn't care who he hurt in the process."

"STOP IT!" screamed Jo. "I'm sick of you bagging people who aren't here to defend themselves. Luke was nothing like that so just cut the shit, David. I've had enough!"

"How the hell didja think you'd get away with it?" asked Pete. "And then to think that you could just live happily ever after with his wife. You're sick!"

"Well, I would've got away with it if you hadn't shown your scrawny little face back here. You should be DEAD, Wilson!"

"I HATE YOU!" shouted Jo, lunging at him and then punching him in the mouth. David grabbed her by the arms and threw her down on the lounge.

"DON'T you hurt Jo!" Pete shouted as he too lunged at David, but he wasn't quick enough. David grabbed the fire poker from the fire place just behind him, raised it quickly and brought it down hard and fast on Pete's skull. There was a loud, sharp CRACK as Pete grunted and fell to the floor, spraying spittle with the expelled gush of breath. Warm, crimson blood slowly oozed out of the wound on to the cream coloured, plush carpet. Pete was silent.

"PETE!" screamed Jo, rushing over to his side. She was relieved to see that he was still breathing.

"You bastard!" she shot at David, "this will be your second murder!" Picking up a heavy ornament from the coffee table she hurled it with all her strength. He ducked and it smashed against the wall behind him. "Kelly and Mo have gone to the police and they'll be here any second. You're going to rot in hell, David, where you belong."

"I haven't killed ANYBODY, and there's NO WAY I'm going to jail!"

"LIAR! Just how do you think you're getting out of it now?" Jo yelled at him defiantly.

"Because I'm leaving...... and you're coming with me." He quickly grabbed her around the elbows from behind. Jo struggled and kicked back toward his groin. It was bringing back memories of Jeff's attack. She hit him in the knee and he grunted, letting go of her right arm. Immediately, she swung it around and clawed his face with her fingernails, drawing blood.

"OUCH! You shouldn't have done that, Jo!" he threatened, bringing his free hand up to his face. She used this momentary lapse of concentration on his part, to bring her right knee up into his groin. He let go of her for an instant. While he was preoccupied, she pulled the cassette recorder out of her pocket and dropped it on the lounge, still turned on. Jo made a dash for the stairs, but he was too fast and grabbed her again.

"Not so fast, Jo." He held her securely this time and hurried her down the steps. She knew he was too strong for her.

"David, please," she sobbed. "Where are you taking me?"

"You'll see," he stated, heading out the front door. "It wasn't supposed to be like this Jo, you've ruined everything now, you know." He half dragged her to the driver's side door, pushed her up to the side of the car and leant against her. Holding her with his body he was able to momentarily let go with one hand to open the door.

Jo screamed and struggled some more, but to no avail. She looked at the gate, wondering where the hell the police were. David got his door open and roughly shoved her in, still holding one of her wrists.

"And don't even THINK of getting out the other side, or I WILL kill you!"

She looked in his eyes and knew he meant it. "I won't," she whispered, trembling with fear.

David started the car up and roared out the gate. Jo thought the police or Kelly and Mo would come along from the direction of the city and recognise this car but, to her absolute horror, he went in the opposite direction.

CHAPTER TWENTY SIX

Kelly and Mo skidded to a stop in Jo's front yard, right behind the police car. They all raced inside and up the steps.

"THEY'RE GONE!" shouted Mo, as she and Kelly quickly looked about the house. "Pete!" she cried, spotting him lying near the fireplace. She ran to him and checked his pulse. He was alive – just. A large red stain lay on the carpet near his head.

"Oh no!" Kelly quickly took out her phone, intending to call an ambulance. Immediately, one of the policemen told her one was already on its way as injuries were anticipated.

"David must have done this to Pete," stated Mo, looking at the fire poker lying not far from Pete. "He must have taken Jo too."

"We'd better search the whole house and yard thoroughly," said one officer just as a second police unit rushed into the yard.

Mo helped the police search, but kept rushing back to Pete, checking he was still alive and giving him encouragement. Kelly went over to David's to see if he was there, but as soon as she could see his car was not there, she ran back to Jo's house.

"David must have her in his car," said Kelly frantically, as she noticed that Jo's was still in the garage.

"Can you give us a description of it?" asked one of the officers, taking out a notebook and pencil. "Also of the two people in question."

Kelly described the vehicle and gave them the plate number. Just as she was about to describe them, a wedding group photo on the wall caught her eye. "This is them!" she stated, pointing out Jo and David.

One of the policemen radioed back to the station reporting a probable abduction describing the car and the occupants. After he finished his call, he turned to Kelly. "All the stations will be alerted and there will be roadblocks set up. Do you have any idea where he may have taken her?"

"No," answered Kelly, tearfully. "Hang on, his family own a holiday house down at Margaret River. He could have headed down there."

"We'll alert the Margaret River police."

Suddenly an ambulance came screaming into the yard. Mo raced down the stairs and out the front door.

"HE'S UP HERE," she shouted to them. "HURRY!" She ran back up the steps.

The paramedics rushed up the stairs carrying a stretcher. Kelly pointed over to Pete.

While they were placing Pete on the stretcher, Kelly spotted the tape recorder. "The tape!" She picked it up and handed it to the policeman. They had told them at the station that Jo had taken the tape recorder with her.

"I'm goin' with Pete!" declared Mo with tears in her eyes, as the paramedics were about to take him downstairs to the waiting ambulance.

"Don't you want to hear the tape?" asked Kelly, pointing to it in the officer's hand.

Mo was torn. She did, but she also wanted to be with Pete.

"We'll go to the hospital as soon as we've listened to it," reassured Kelly.

"Okay," replied Mo reluctantly.

As the paramedics left with Pete, the officer rewound and turned on the tape. They all sat in stunned silence as they heard David's confession loud and clear. Mo and Kelly both grimaced and fought back tears when they heard the sickening crack of a poker against skull.

As soon as the tape was over, Kelly and Mo rushed to Royal Perth Hospital.

"God, I hope Jo's all right," sobbed Kelly.

"So do I," replied Mo. "And I hope we get to the hospital on time."

CHAPTER TWENTY SEVEN

"David, this is crazy!" cried Jo as they sped along a road she didn't recognise.

"Well, it didn't have to be like this, Jo. I love you. I have right from the start. We could have had a good life together, you, me and Ben..... and the other kids we'd have."

"But, you KILLED my husband. Your brother! And all this time you've been watching me, haven't you? Just waiting for the right opportunity to attack, like a wolf stalking its prey! You even got up at his memorial service and spoke of him, just to make me think how great you were."

"I didn't actually kill him, Jo. It was the bike that killed him, or the bank he went over or whatever. I didn't touch him!" stressed David.

"I told you when I got back from Queensland that there would never be anything between us."

"You would have changed your mind. You would have grown to love me," he replied, trying to convince himself as well. "You still can."

"Never!" she spat back at him.

He pulled over into a service station. Jo hopes of an escape soared.

"Don't you try a thing," he warned, piercing her with his murderous eyes. "Come with me." Taking hold of her hand he practically dragged her out the driver's side door after him.

He kept her close to him as he opened the petrol cap and filled the tank. Jo looked around, desperately hoping to catch somebody's attention.

"Turn back this way!" he snarled quietly at her while squeezing her wrist hard.

Jo whimpered in pain, fear and frustration.

"And when we go inside to pay for this, if you make one sound or movement out of line, I'll strangle you there and then." After locking the petro cap he brought his hand slowly up to her throat. Jo held her breath. David squeezed her neck lightly before suddenly kissing her on the lips. "Let's go."

They walked inside to pay for the fuel. Jo hoped her face would reveal her fear, but there weren't many people about.

"Do you want anything else, Darl," asked David casually, as he handed over the cash for the petrol.

Jo just shook her head before taking a small step back a little from his side and frantically began to silently plead for help from the second attendant behind the counter. The tears ran down her cheeks. The attendant saw her and frowned. Obviously to Jo, he had no idea what she was trying to communicate.

Suddenly, David grabbed her wrist and squeezed it hard again. He took the change from the woman who served him and turned abruptly to leave, pulling Jo with him. "I warned you Jo!" he threatened through clenched teeth, dragging her to the car and pushing her into the front seat.

"I didn't do anything!" she protested.

"DON"T LIE!" he shouted at her. "There's a mirror up the back of the counter. I could see what you were doing, trying to get that blokes attention."

"Well, what else do you expect me to do?" she demanded. "Just sit back and let you drag me around the countryside. AND you're a fine one to talk about lying!"

David started the car and sped away from the service station. "You've really blown it now. I had a surprise planned for you back at my place. I was going to take you there once everything cooled down. You would have loved it. You would have been so happy.... BUT..... it's too late!"

Suddenly Jo thought of Ben and began to cry. What if she never saw him again? That thought was unbearable. "David, what about your parents.......and Casey? Just think how much this will upset them. And little Ben. You've killed his Daddy and now you're taking his Mummy away from him too!"

"Luke was always their favourite anyway," he shot back. "They wouldn't miss me if I wasn't around. Ha! They'd probably even be glad."

"No, they wouldn't," urged Jo. "They love you too. Casey told us in Adelaide when we first came over, how much she missed you."

"Yeah, well Casey's all right, but it's too late now."

"No, it's not," pleaded Jo. "Just turn around and go back. I won't press charges against you, I promise!"

"Do you think I'm stupid? You'd run to the cops as soon as my back was turned. Remember, I'm the one who killed your precious Luke."

Jo began to cry. She had to get away from this maniac anyway she could. Undoing her seatbelt with her right hand, she reached for the door handle with her left.

"WHAT THE HELL DO YOU THINK YOU ARE DOING?" David shouted, noticing her movement and reaching over to grab her.

"Let me go. I'm getting out!" cried Jo, trying to push his hand away.

"Like hell!"

During the struggle, the car had veered to the right hand side of the road. David didn't see the truck coming around the bend straight toward them.

Jo did. "LOOK OUT!" she screamed, automatically reaching for the steering wheel.

David grabbed the wheel and pulled the car back sharply to the left side of the road, but he was going too fast. The jerking of the wheel caused it to swerve off the road, roll down an embankment and explode into a massive fireball.

CHAPTER TWENTY EIGHT

Pete slowly opened his eyes to see Mo, Kelly and Debbie standing around his hospital bed. He could feel the heavy bandage around his aching head.

"Welcome back Little Brother," said Debbie. "You had us all worried for a while."

"I..... don't feel..... so good," whispered Pete, grimacing in pain. "I can't..... see real well...... either."

"You'll be okay, Mate," reassured Mo, fighting back the tears from her eyes. "When you get outa here, we'll have another crazy trip, hey?"

"There's only one place..... I'm goin'," replied Pete weakly.

"Pete, I've got a surprise for you," smiled Debbie through her tears. She walked out of the room and returned a moment later with their mother.

"Mum!" The tears flowed freely from Pete's eyes. Shakily, he lifted his hand up to the loving, trembling one she was offering him.

"Peter, my baby," sobbed Alice. She leaned down and kissed his hollow cheek.

"I'm so..... glad you....came, Mum. Dad?" He saw his mother cry harder and just shake her head. Pete closed his eyes for a moment, trying to cope with the physical and emotional pain. "Jo? Is she okay?"

"She's okay," answered Kelly. "David took her in his car and they had an accident. Jo was thrown out and she's only got a broken arm, some minor burns and a few scratches and bruises."

"David?"

"He was killed," replied Debbie.

"Good!" replied Pete in a hoarse whisper. "S'long's Jo's okay. That's all .....that.... matters now. Mo, I ..... want .....to ask you..... something."

"Anything!" nodded Mo, moving around to the other side of the bed and taking hold of his other hand.

"What's Mo..... short....for?" he asked, his voice becoming barely audible.

"It's Molly," she laughed, fighting back the tears that were beginning to burn her eyes. "But don't you dare tell anybody."

Pete smiled a little and shook his head slightly. "I.... just....thought of.....something."

"What's that?" asked Mo, holding his hand firmly and biting her trembling bottom lip.

"I made....It....to.....thirty." Then with a satisfied smile, Pete closed his eyes for the last time.

CHAPTER TWENTY NINE

Jo's face lit up and her heavy heart suddenly lightened when Ted and Rose brought little Ben into her hospital room. With tears in her eyes, Rose handed her grandson to his mother. He smiled as Jo hugged him to her, her own tears falling from her chin and rubbing off on the top of his head.

"I'm so sorry, Jo," said Rose, shaking her head. "I just don't know what to say. Debbie and Kelly told us everything. David was always a bit moody, but we never imagined he would have done something so terrible as to betray his own brother then KILL him." She cried harder and leaned into Ted's chest for support. He held her tightly with one arm while wiping his own tears away with the other hand.

Sadly, Jo noticed how much Rose and Ted had suddenly aged.

Kelly came into Jo's room. "How you doing?" she asked, sitting down and patting Jo's good arm, which was around Ben.

"Okay," shrugged Jo quietly.

"I called your Mum," Kelly said. "She'll be here tomorrow night."

"Good ol' Mum," smiled Jo through her tears. "Pete?"

Kelly shook her head sadly. "He didn't make it, but he asked about you and was really glad that you were okay."

"If it wasn't for him….." Jo shuddered at the thought. "He's a hero and he doesn't even know it. One thing is certain though."

"What?"

"He won't be in the same place as David. He'll be with Luke now," she smiled as fresh tears dripped on Ben's head. "They're probably just having a bourbon and dry, or a scotch and coke as in Pete's case. Then they'll go for a ride in Harley Heaven."

CHAPTER THIRTY

The next morning Jo was released from hospital. Luke's parents brought her home and stayed with her for a while until Ben went down for a sleep and she was comfortable for some 'alone' time.

Slowly, she wandered aimlessly around the house, feeling completely lost and unsure what to do. The events of the previous morning had left her totally shattered and she couldn't wait for her Mum to arrive that night. Suddenly, she heard Kelly calling her as she walked up the stairs.

"Oh, hi Kell."

"Hey Jo, are you okay?"

Jo sighed heavily. "I just don't know how I'm supposed to feel at the moment. I'm sore and tired and just so....I can't even think of a word to describe how I feel about what David did. It just makes me so sick. I can't even stand looking out over to his house without thinking about it."

"I can understand that," nodded Kelly. "I'm just about to go over there one last time to make sure there is nothing important to me still there. The house will be mine now, but there is no way I could ever live there again. I'm sorry Jo. I have decided the best thing would be to just get the house bulldozed and sell the block."

"It's okay, I understand. To be honest I don't think I can stay here either. It just doesn't feel right anymore. I just want to go home to Queensland. I know it'll upset Ted and Rose, but we can visit."

"I.... don't suppose you want to come over with me?" asked Kelly. "I don't know, maybe it could give you some sort of closure or something."

"No," said Jo, shaking her head adamantly. "Definitely not! Sorry. I think I might ring a real estate and see if they want to come and have a look at this place. Oh, I don't know. Maybe I'll wait until Mum comes and get her advice."

"Okay, well I'll pop back over when I'm finished and stay a while, if you want me to." She gave Jo a comforting hug before going down the stairs.

Half an hour later, after Jo had spoken to her Mum on the phone, she walked out onto the back veranda to water the pot plants. A movement at the gate connecting the two house yards caught her eye. In a split second she assumed it was Kelly returning, but it was not Kelly.

A tall, dirty man with unkempt hair and whiskers was standing just inside her yard. Jo frowned and shook her head. It looked like David, but couldn't be, he was dead! Was it his ghost coming back for her? Her heart raced as she became frightened. Next thing Kelly came through the gate and held the man's arm for support as he began to limp toward the house. A chill shot up her spine and out to her fingertips and a hundred crazy thoughts sped through her head as she hurried inside, down the steps and out the back door. *What is going on?*

She looked at Kelly's huge smile. "What....who?"

Kelly's tears were rolling down her cheeks as she beamed at Jo. "Look who I found locked up down in the cellar."

Jo walked a little closer and saw tears in the man's brown eyes. Eyes that looked worn down and tired, but they bore into her soul. Her heart jumped. Then the cracked, dry lips parted in a smile. She knew that smile anywhere. *But, it's not possible! It just couldn't be! She had to be dreaming!* She gasped and flung her good hand to her mouth as her jaw dropped open letting out a loud sob. "Luke..... is it really you?" She was shaking and felt like she would faint. Everything seemed to be spinning.

"Yeah, Babe," he whispered in a sob. "It's me."

With her knees threatening to buckle under her, she slowly walked the several steps to him. Her heart felt like it was about to explode out of her chest as she reached up and touched his dirty face. He was skinnier than before and the clothes just hung on him. She hadn't even noticed the smell.

"Jo, he told me that David took him back there after the accident and kept him there to torment him about you. He'd told Luke that you and him were 'together'. I assured him it wasn't true, just another of his sick, twisted ideas," said Kelly, shaking her head.

Suddenly, Jo fell against her adored husband's chest, wrapping her free arm around his back as he held her tightly with his arms. Weeks of consistent grief, sadness, fear and confusion all poured out of each of them as they cried long and hard. When neither had any tears left they slowly pulled apart a little. Luke leant down and kissed Jo tenderly on the lips. There was no doubt. This was her Luke.

"Are you hurt bad?" asked Jo between uncontrollable sobs. "What did that bastard do to you?" She had a million questions to ask, trying to get her head around it all.

"He didn't hurt me physically, Jo. Mentally and emotionally it was torture and he loved every minute." Luke shook his head in disbelief. "I never thought he'd go that far. Kelly said he killed Pete. Poor little Mate, I'm going to miss the little bugger. I just hope he knows how grateful we are for what he done."

Jo and Kelly helped Luke into the house and up the stairs. "He had me convinced that Pete had rigged the bike," Jo said as they slowly reached the top. "But then Pete came back, after we all thought he'd died and told us what he remembered from the party."

"I tried to tell him everything that has happened, as I was getting him out," laughed Kelly.

"I need a drink, then a long hot shower," stated Luke. Jo quickly got him a drink of water, then helped him to the shower, but not before he looked in on his cherished son, still sleeping soundly.

"I'll head back over there now, Jo," called Kelly.

"Hang on, Kel," called Jo, running back out to the lounge. "Tell me how you found him. I just can't believe it!" She was crying and laughing at the same time.

"Well, I just suddenly decided to go down and see what he had in that room. GOD! I never expected in a million years that I would find

Luke! The key was in the door - David obviously didn't count on me ever going back there, but I still had an old extra key I got cut years ago- so I just went into the cellar and flicked on the light." She widened her eyes while shaking her head. "I didn't recognise him at first, but he knew me of course. He had to tell me who he was. The poor bloke, to think all this time, he was just right there."

"I knew it!" declared Jo. "I often felt he was close by me."

Luke called from the shower. "Ok, Kel, see you later and thank you SO MUCH!" Jo hugged Kelly long and hard in sheer gratitude.

After his shower and shave, she helped him dress in clean clothes as much as she could with one arm in plaster. "You need to go to the hospital."

"Soon," he assured her, limping to the bedroom and lying down on the bed. "Come here, I just want to hold you. This will be better than any medication."

Jo lay down and snuggled into his arms then leaned up on her good elbow just to look at him. "I just can't believe it. You are here." She began to cry again. "It has been so horrible believing I'd lost you and trying to cope with it."

"How many times do I have to tell you, Babe, you are stuck with me forever!" He smiled and those irresistible dimples stood out, as they do.

"I think we should phone a few people," urged Jo.

"Later. I just want some time with you," he smiled, pushing her back down on her back. "Things will get crazy once word gets out, let's just have this time together now. I love you so much, Mrs Summers."

"And I love you too, Mr Summers." Her whole body ached in delicious anticipation as his yearning lips moved down her neck while his fingers undone the buttons on her blouse.

EPILOGUE

After Jo and Luke had enjoyed their loving and emotional reunion, she called his parents and asked them to please come straight over, not telling them why. Rose nearly had a heart attack when she saw Luke, but was fine. Their reunion with their son was filled with tears and laughter.

His parents drove him to hospital where he was treated for his crash injuries, including surgery on his broken leg that had mended crooked. Jo's Mum arrived a little later and was overjoyed with the news. She and Jo went straight up to the hospital where Luke would stay for several days.

Jo also contacted Meg, Debbie, Graham and Steve, the lead singer of Stonefish. He and the other members wasted no time in getting up to the hospital to see Luke, all happy and eager to get back into their music.

Next day it was all over the papers, TV and the net.

Once Luke was well enough, he, Jo and Ben, returned to Broome to complete their honeymoon that had been cut short. The weather was perfect and they found the peace and tranquillity that had been cruelly taken from them for weeks and weeks.

Three weeks after returning from Broome, they were deliriously happy to discover Jo was pregnant. They decided to stay in the home they loved so much. Nine months later they welcomed their beautiful daughter into the world.

Stonefish released a new album that went straight to number one.

Kelly had David's house demolished and soon after, the block was bought by a couple with a young family. They became good friends with Jo and Luke and once they'd built a new home they set about landscaping the yard. That all but took away any horrific reminders of David's house and "dungeon."

Kelly remained close to Jo and Luke but soon met and married a wonderful man and they immediately began trying for a baby, the first of two that they would have.

Mo stayed on at Debbie's until after Pete's funeral, which, unfortunately, his father did not attend. She also spent some time getting to know Jo and Luke. Once Pete's ashes were available, she took some of them up to Kalbarri to scatter into the ocean wind above the cliffs. She stayed on in Kalbarri, where she too, met a man with lots in common with her and happily settled down. Occasionally, she would remember her and Pete's crazy trip to Perth and have a chuckle to herself.

ABOUT THE AUTHOR

Julie McCullough lives with her husband and two children on a small farm at Rosedale, Qld, Australia, where she breeds rare chooks as well as organically producing much of their fruit, veg, meat and dairy products. After having short stories and non-fiction articles published she now publishes her debut novel, "Of Wolves And Wildflowers".

Julie can be contacted through www.juliemcculloughnovels.com.au